Beyond the Will of God

Also by David Biddle

TRYING TO CARE: A STORY COLLECTION

Go to: amazon.com/author/davidbiddle
for more work by this author.

Beyond the Will of God

A Jill Simpson Mystery

DAVID BIDDLE

FLAT BRANCH PRESS

This story is a work of fiction. Names, characters, places, and incidents are mostly a product of the author's imagination. Where real people's names are used, their thoughts, words, and actions are entirely made up. In addition, this work does not condone the use of illegal drugs of any kind for recreational purposes. Please note that improper use of drugs can be harmful and even lethal.

None of this story is real. That's why they call it fiction. This work is intended to entertain, to provoke thoughts about important issues, and to open the reader's minds.

FLAT BRANCH PRESS

ISBN: 0615655408
ISBN-13:978-0615655406

DEDICATION

For Johnnie and Steve, brother riders on the storm—gone to the great gig in the sky far too soon.

CONTENTS

And they also threw this in my face, they said,
Anyway, you know good and well
It would be beyond the will of God
And the grace of a king.

Jimi Hendrix, "1983…(A Merman I Should Turn to Be)"

PROLOGUE

Journal Entry 1320: Cecil Miller

I found it on a number of bootleg recordings first, but there are a few examples of it on studio works as well – all from groups who understand what is possible. On the live recordings, you hear it best. There's a certain moment where something happens with the music and everything comes together. You have to know what to listen for, though, or you won't experience it.

I have a bootleg copy of The Allman Brothers' famous Fillmore East concerts. Unlike the album they eventually produced, my bootleg is completely unedited. Nothing has been cut out or re-engineered or overdubbed. In my bootleg you can hear the moment when the band comes together, when the whole auditorium comes together. It's extraordinary. About a minute after the long drum solo there is a part of "Mountain Jam" where Duane Allman and Dickey Betts are trading licks and the band is building to a crescendo when something just happens. You are vaulted out of your own thoughts and taken away for a moment. It's just for a moment – at least I think it is - but it's one of the most beautiful feelings I've ever experienced.

I interviewed a woman who had been at that concert in New York City. March 13, 1971. Second show. She's dead now. She said she began to feel something about halfway through "Mountain Jam"; that her sense of self was disappearing and that the music was taking over. The feeling began to grow in intensity as the drum solo came to an end. She says it was hard to remember what happened exactly, but as the song – which is over thirty minutes long – moved forward and Berry Oakley moved into what has to be one the greatest R&B bass solos of all time, it felt as if everyone in the Fillmore was psychologically linked. It was hypnotic, she said. The bass kept driving harder and harder. Then, quietly at first, Dickey and Duane come back in, tossing the main theme back and forth between them. The counterpoint of the two guitars, the play and rhythm of bass and drums and the murmuring sonic envelope of the organ just sweep everyone in the room away. And then it happens. It is subtle. She said the guitars sounded like they were playing questions to the audience – deep, sad, important questions. Then Duane moved off on his own to give the answers. He plays a slide lick over and over for at least eight bars and the whole time you're waiting for him to figure out where to go with it, but what he's doing is gathering you in with him; he's calling to you, "I don't have the answer yet." But something is building. And then it's there, just at the 24-minute mark. Duane goes way up the neck with his slide and hits 56 notes – I've counted them - and at note 51 you feel yourself slipping into a different frame of mind. It's like you're vaulted into another dimension of your soul. Everything is in harmony. Everything is beautiful. You are, dare I say, for that brief moment, One with the universe.

I found it again on a bootleg of the Grateful Dead doing "Playing in the Band" at the Oakland Coliseum in 1979. The recording is dreadful. It was made in the middle of the audience. The concert itself was lively and energetic and that comes through on the tape regardless of quality, but you also hear crowd noise during the sets. In particular, there is a most annoying girl who was close to the taper and every measure and a half or so she lets loose with a high-pitched, shrieking yodel lasting anywhere from two to ten seconds. It is more than a little distracting. So you have to work very hard to pay attention to the music. That may be a blessing in disguise though, because the same kind of Allman Moment occurs in the middle of an extended Garcia solo – and since you have to work harder at listening, you hear it very clearly – right near the 11:30 mark in the song. Again, the guitars and audience reaction come together and you feel this shift in your emotions, almost like you were there, like something has just clicked into place – that moment, from the past, has been waiting for you to come back to it. I've listened to that tape over one thousand times and the same feeling hits me every time.

I've experienced the same moment in person several times as well. During a weekend jazz festival I attended one summer, the headliner on Saturday night was a group I'd never heard of before: The Chicago Art Ensemble, fronted by Lester

Bowie on trumpet. In just under four hours they played three songs – three very long, incomprehensible songs. For the most part, the nine-piece combo was confusing, dissonant, out of synch, interminable, and loud. They were playing Chaos to us and it was having, on me anyway, a profoundly negative impact. But near the end of the last song something happened. Out of nowhere the whole group came together. There was a very short pause and I could feel something shift inside me. The musicians all looked to Lester Bowie and he took two steps forward and then launched into a lyrical, thought-melting trumpet solo. It was like the classical virtuoso trumpeter Sergei Nakariakov on acid playing Bach. I didn't know what was happening for maybe three minutes. And then just like that, the group pulled away and dove back into agonizing chaos. They ended the concert blasting the final stanzas of Ornette Coleman's "Race Face" and I left wondering if the Art Ensemble knew something we didn't.

A similar thing happened the next night with Sun Ra and His Universal Arkestra. Sun Ra was the buzz act for the whole festival. He had just come out of retirement. It was a decade before his death. I had never heard a note of his music in my life.

We were prepared for something strange when we saw that the Arkestra was made up of some 37 musicians. From my sixth-row seat, I could tell that several of the Chicago Art Ensemble's percussionists were playing as well.

Sun Ra and his bandmates also went dancing with chaos. If I hadn't been somewhat initiated the night prior, I probably would have left. This time a strong sense of vertigo took hold of me before the end of the first song. Two hours later, as they finished the second composition, I was seasick. But several minutes into the third piece it happened again. I felt it coming several minutes earlier. Even more importantly, I heard the sound this time, as if someone was whispering to me, and then a very low-decibel popping noise. At that point a small, cream-colored African guy with a goatee and bright silver hair took a few steps forward, raised a golden soprano sax to the audience, and began to play what to this day is one of the most moving and profound instrumental solos I have ever heard. It was otherworldly. Each note sparkled and glistened with a thousand different emotions. He played it for several minutes, and there is no question that everyone in the room was feeling his music as one mind. When he was done, he bowed and smiled and stepped back into the horde of musicians. I never saw him again for the rest of the evening.

Perhaps the most famous example of this phenomenon was executed by The Doors in the original, analog version of their studio-recorded "Riders on the

Storm." This finally gave it all away to me. Morrison goes through his throaty lyrics, never failing to send us into a dream world (you can hear a time-delayed whisper echo in the background which is the last thing Morrison ever recorded), and as he finishes the second verse, the Fender Rhodes piano, soft cymbals, and guitar begin to converse, preparing for the extended jam that makes the song one of the quintessential soundtracks of life. There is a clear and unmistakable popping sound, like a bottle being uncorked, as the musicians move off into their groove. You feel time shifting gears just before the haunting guitar and electric piano take off down the road together. Whenever I listen to it, I feel the top of my head open up. My thoughts become inexplicably rearranged.

You can't find the same thing on the digitized and remastered CD version of the album. They took the popping sound out. Now there is just a very subtle silence between the chord progressions. Maybe after Morrison died they figured they didn't want to give away the secret anymore. But it's still there on my old vinyl record. You have to listen carefully, but it's there. This is why I've been doing these experiments for so many years. I want to understand. I need to understand. I need to bring this out so that everyone realizes what is going on, what we've been dealing with, and how hard it is to live normally once you know what is possible. There's something very important with music and how it relates to the magic of the mind that we've forgotten.

Part I
Finding the Dead

Something is happening, but you don't know what it is, do you Mr. Jones?
-Bob Dylan

CHAPTER 1

It is 10:30 on a hot June night and Frank Harris has been following gravel roads for over half an hour. With the humidity, the air is lit to a near fog and filled with flying creatures churning in the sudden promise of his rental's high beams.

Just a quick side trip before he would check into his motel – that's what he'd thought anyway. Although he comes from Philadelphia and has spent most of his life on the East Coast, the Missouri River has special significance to him. In fact, it is the only thing he's looked forward to about this trip to the middle of the country.

Growing up in the suburbs of Philadelphia, Harris read stories of Daniel Boone, Lewis and Clark, and Jesse James traveling through the frontier and moving west along the Missouri. He also read biographies of Mark Twain and his many escapades as a youth on the tributaries to this river. The Missouri is the little sibling of the Mississippi. It is a ribbon of water winding through America's middle, arriving on the eastern side of its namesake state at Twain's Big Muddy just outside of St. Louis in St. Charles. Even though Twain would always be associated with the more famous Mississippi, he also wrote of the Missouri. Harris had been intrigued by the descriptions of the landscape surrounding this lesser body of flowing water. Twain had written of the Mississippi as the "gentle sister." The Missouri, on the other hand, he described as a "savage river…descending from its mad career through a vast unknown of barbarism, pouring its turbid floods in the bosom of its gentle sister." The chaos and violence appealed to Harris.

Traveling in his rental car across this rich bottomland, tunneling into the black summer darkness and wondering what exactly he thinks he might find in this lack of light, Harris listens to the local rock station. It is the twenty-first century and they are still playing '70s tunes here: old Joe Walsh, Eagles, electric Neil Young, and Nitty Gritty Dirt Band.

After a while, the Allman Brothers' *Hot 'Lanta* comes on, beginning with Gregg's organ intro and the slow build of Berry's bass along the twin percussion machine of Butch Trucks and Jaimoe Johanson. Then, finally, the storied dueling guitars of Dickey and Duane: the opening reverse almost dissonant, blues run of Dickey's, and the melodic, background riff-to-chord-to-riff of Duane using his muffled slide. And all the while the rat-a-tat percussion of Butch and Jaimoe keeping time and moving the best blues ever played forward down the countless roads of their listeners. For more than forty years every time Harris hears The Allman Brothers Band it is like he's never heard them before. *Hot 'Lanta*: the arpeggio runs, the notes gaining in tempo all the time, faster, and so too the rental car Frank is driving. He hears the gravel crunching under the music even in the air-conditioning, until, finally, the quick drum solo, the rhythm of his mind driving down a road in the darkness, understanding there is, somewhere, probably a river to the right, watching the parched ivory, stone-festooned road pour into existence and the smoke-hot air, the slowing band playing as one, the pounding timpani, the pause, and the full crescendo ending – kettle drums pounding out some inexplicable message, perhaps a reminder that not everything is as clear as he wants to think it is.

Harris's memory seeks the next song on the album – *Whipping Post* – but the female announcer comes on instead saying, *"That was the Allman Brothers, recorded live at the Fillmore East in New York in 1971. It's 10:57, hot and sticky – as usual. I'm Sara Hartwood and this is KFRU radio. The news will be coming up right after these announcements. I've got some vintage*

Woodstock cuts you haven't heard in years and then we'll dip into Eric Clapton and Cream. It's all coming up on the other side of the hour."

He passes a car parked in the woods, noting three silhouettes and a foggy windshield which makes him think of marijuana smoke and quiet conversation.

He'd stopped smoking pot when he graduated from college. Alcohol was more effective. Done in the proper dose, it actually turned off the mind and gave him snatches of time where his thoughts could almost stop and he simply had to react to the world as it came at him.

"At the top of the hour, officials continue to prepare for what Chief of Administration Robert Wilson of the Columbia Police Department terms – in a serious tone of authority – and I quote, 'any eventuality.' With the huge influx of visitors to the region and an invasion of the international media all looking for Elvis, hotels and motels throughout central Missouri have actually turned on the NO on their vacancy signs. Booneville and Rocheport-area motor lodges are full for the first time in history. Columbia is about like it would be if both Nebraska and Kansas came to play football against the Tigers on the same weekend.

"We don't know what to make of it. Wilson and the CPD certainly have their hands full. Personally, I'm getting a little intrigued. This summer marks something like the 38th year since The King died. Maybe the 39th, I don't know. The latest rumor has it that Elvis was actually at Altamont. And I've got the tape to prove it. Maybe I'll play it for you all after midnight. Right now we gotta take a break and earn our keep. Don't go away. Classic rock comes back in 90 seconds."

Harris turns the radio off, glad that his boss, Aaron Treestat, has pulled strings and booked him a room in a motor lodge. The tone in the DJ's voice is interesting, he thinks. No question, there is a strong sense of mockery already at play here. How can anyone in media believe something so cliché and fantastic? And what does it say about the country when Elvis sightings have taken on the same significance as miraculous healing statues of the Virgin Mary or paintings of Jesus that bleed tears? Still, if the announcer is playing to listeners with such a tone, it's likely that those in other parts of the country – readers of his own publication – will pay attention long enough for him to do his work. Harris's job as a tabloid journalist is to use unknowns and half-truths as hooks. In one way it is the lowest form of writing imaginable. Readers don't care how he reports things, they just want to be titillated a bit – a nice vacation from their mundane, waiting-for-something-big lives. But in another way, Harris feels that his writing is almost poetry because he takes the fantastic and bizarre, the virtually impossible, and makes it real, makes it, in fact, simple and obvious: devil worshipping actors; starlets on eating binges because their famous husbands are having affairs with the equally famous neighbor's seventeen-year-old *au pair*; a TV comedian's love child turning up years later as a closing pitcher for the losing team in the World Series; love letters from JFK unearthed after the death of a mob mistress. It is Harris's job to make the improbable not only believable but downright commonplace.

Several more cars hulk together at the edge of the umbra of his headlights. Half a mile later, he notes that the shadow of trees on the right side of the road has given way to a gaping blackness. He knows without doubt that he is driving close to the water. He stops, turns off the lights, and gets out.

Three things make the darkness seem alive: the electronic pulse of insects everywhere; the deep sound of water rolling by with unlimited power; and, finally, the heavy scent of that water in the stale, windless air – the smell of centuries and decay, the smell of life carried forth forever by gravity and natural purpose, the smell of traveling sediment, catfish, floating human debris, pesticide runoff, and diesel slicks. In the darkness it all comes to him as a faint taste in the back of the throat, the flavor of emptiness and heat and the river – sweet and wholesome, like bread, but tangy and with a slight aftertaste of sulfur and ammonia.

His vision hovers above the moving water, seeking its dull, inevitable flow. He hears the scree and click of cicadas, grasshoppers, crickets, and locusts. Lighting a cigarette and thinking about the bottle of scotch in his luggage, he feels the first drops of sweat trickle down his back. He wonders if he still has what it takes to concoct a story like this. He is out of his element, wandering in the night gloom of river bottom country, feeling that the Missouri River is a cosmic animal moving into worlds he can only guess at. In the darkness, especially, the river is everything he's imagined it would be.

*

The bar is crowded, full of loud women and men drinking Miller and Pabst Blue Ribbon by the time the boy comes in through the fire exit in the back. Stein's is not a place where people dance, but Elvis Presley's "That's All Right" blasts through the room anyway, fracturing talk into loud exclamations that startle the boy. He sees the two men he is looking for, Jimmy Harper and Dean Belkin, sipping beer in a corner of the room. The boy half crouches as he makes his way around the back of the pool tables to where they sit. Jimmy jumps when the boy tugs at his shirtsleeve. It isn't advisable to touch people after ten o'clock at Stein's – even Jimmy Harper.

"Well now, you made it after all," says Jimmy.

The boy nods. His black jacket and pants are of a very old cut, something from the '40s perhaps. He wears a stiff, wide-brimmed straw hat. His shirt is made of heavy white linen. He is an Amish child.

"You ready, Deano?" Jimmy asks his drinking buddy as he stands. Dean drains his Miller and picks up a brown paper sack clinking with bottles. He rises from their table and looks around the room as casually as he can.

Satisfied that no one is paying attention to them, Jimmy says: "These all of 'em?"

"Yup," says Dean. "Let's get out of here."

In the alley a slight chill meets them. It is June, but the evening has grown cool from a long, hard thunderstorm late that afternoon. Jimmy rolls down the sleeves of his denim shirt. Wearing only jeans and a brown T-shirt, Dean rubs his arms. "Should I go get my sweatshirt?"

"No time," says Jimmy. "This kid is clearly on a mission."

The boy pulls his coat tightly across his chest and heads up the alley toward the street, carefully avoiding the lights shimmering against wet trashcans and grease-stained alley pavement. Without a word, all three walk along the wall of the building, moving in and out of the shadows. There is a sound ahead, low murmuring, and from behind a double Dumpster emerge three young men, none older than Dean or Jimmy. All three wear the same clothes as the boy. Two have thin, curly black beards and no moustaches. They are not wearing their traditional Amish hats. The other, younger perhaps, is clean-faced and wears his hat back on his head. There is something very different about him, almost intoxicating. It is partly in the way he propels himself, as if he is wading through knee-high water. The upper body, especially around the shoulders, does not move. The back remains straight and true. He creates motion from the waist down striding into the shadows. His eyes show that he seems to understand their thoughts. He makes Jimmy and Dean feel that this secret meeting they are about to have is under control. This is the one Buzzer had told Jimmy about. All three brothers look at Dean's sack expectantly, then walk ahead without a word.

Exchanging somewhat bewildered glances, Jimmy and Dean follow the boy who leads them fifteen yards behind the others. Still, no one says anything. All they can hear is the tinkling of Dean's bottles and the occasional cloth-ripping sound of pickups driving down wet streets.

They follow for perhaps twenty minutes, staying in the shadows as much as possible. Fayette is a small town. Most of the homes are already dark, save for the occasional purple glow of a living room TV. The houses are simple structures, rectangular in shape, with two large windows in front and a door in between. Yards are barely delineated and flow into each other. Lawns are strewn with rusting metal objects – old steel-framed lawn chairs, dented buckets, tractor parts, and pickup bed canopies. Many of the lots have also become resting grounds for automobile skeletons, ancient tractors, and farm equipment. Piles of lumber and brush have formed in random spots, along with stacks of rotting fence posts and heaps of gravel and soil. There are no sidewalks. The group makes their way along the edge of the road on the shoulder bordered by a culvert brimming with rainwater.

After another quarter mile they come to a bend in the road and turn off into a sizeable field occupied by hunched piles of hay. They walk in single file as the crescent moon moves out of smoky clouds, dimly lighting the field. Dean has always wondered about this field. The walk is warming him.

Coming to the top of a long ridge, they can see the lights of Fayette at the bottom and a truck weaving along Route H. They go over the crest and continue walking down the other side. Jimmy grumbles something that Dean can only guess at. This wasn't part of the bargain. They respected the need not to be seen, but they hadn't planned on a walk through muddy fields all night long. There is still a chance it could rain again.

The three in the lead move faster once they have crossed a small creek. The moon shifts to a dull, smudgy orange sliver, partially obscured again by clouds. Dean figures they're going around the town, heading north toward the Hungry Mother Wildlife Refuge. They are definitely walking, he thinks, through fields he has never explored in his nine years working for Buzzer.

At the top of a rise, the three in the lead stop next to a large hay pile and one of the brothers carefully rustles up the hay with his hands.

"Hmmm. Not here," he says.

"Look again," says the non-bearded brother, who pushes his hat up again to expose his soft forehead as he moves closer to help.

"Here!" calls the first triumphantly. He pulls two large dark objects from the pile near where the others have been watching.

All six crowd around in a circle, exchanging shy, somewhat embarrassed glances. The beardless brother takes the hats and hands them to Dean who in turn carefully hands him the parcel he has been carrying. The boy fades into the darkness.

"Top one's for you; other is for him," says the second brother, pointing to Jimmy.

They try on their hats.

"It fits me perfectly!" says Jimmy.

"Ah, mine too!" says Dean. "Buzzer was right. You boys make the best hats in the Midwest." He slaps the second brother on the back.

The hat makers are busy opening their bottles of Wild Turkey. Once uncorked, though, the three of them seem to hesitate at the idea of taking a drink.

"Shit, I'll take a pull on that Turkey," says Dean. "Show you how it's done." The one closest to him hands over the bottle gratefully.

Jimmy can see that Dean is helping break the ice with their new friends, but he doesn't feel like being sociable. "Deaner. Jesus, man, we gotta get out of here. It's a good forty minutes back to the truck and it's gonna rain sure enough."

Ignoring his friend's warning, Dean sucks hard on the bottle and feels the hot bourbon ignite in his chest.

"You better go slow on this till you get the hang," he splutters. "They don't call it the Hurtin' Bird for nothing."

"Hey, wait a minute. Where are *your* hats?" he asks, looking at their new friends.

"Home," says the younger one. "Only way to get the ones for you out of the house was for my brothers to wear them."

Dean hands the bottle to Jimmy, smiling conspiratorially at the beardless Amish brother.

*

They are half drunk and walking in silence back toward the road. At first it is like a slight whisper coming off the wind. The sound begins to grow after a few seconds, swirling, moving in and out of the sonics created by moving air. Dean rotates his head slowly from side to side.

"You hear that?"

"Yep."

"What the fuck is it?"

"Don't know," says Jimmy. "Thought it was the wind blowing across my ears, but it stays with you no matter which way you turn your head."

He looks back at his friend in the dark, listening, his mouth open, twisting his eyes into a questioning squint, slowing his gait.

"Yeah, and I feel weird, like there's something going on, too..." Dean says.

Jimmy is silent for a few moments, then replies, "Same here."

They continue to listen. After a few minutes the noise dies down. The wind hisses through the trees, back to normal.

"'S why I like drinking at Stein's, Deanie. None of this weird shit ever happens in bars...'cept down in Columbia maybe, but..."

"Shhh, here it comes."

They stop walking. Standing in the darkness, the sound comes to them, clearly and distinctly now. It's electric guitar music. But how? Where? And the sensations the two feel are eerie, as if they're standing naked in the middle of a circle of people; they are horny, they can communicate through their thoughts.

"It's coming in with the wind," Dean finally comments.

"Yeah. Man, I feel really weird."

They continue to listen. There is no melody, it isn't rock and roll, or blues, or jazz. Occasionally, a note is bent or what sounds like a whammy bar hugged, a pitch sustained, a power chord strummed to end a long phrase. But there is no pattern. The whole thing is dissonant, the notes so fluid it's almost as if the sounds are sliding into the air instead of being plucked.

"Where is that coming from?" asks Jimmy.

Dean shakes his head. "There's a mess of pastureland around here with no roads connecting things. Fancher owns the property more than likely, but I don't know. Maybe it's just a party." Dean is working hard to keep his mind on the situation, but memories are trying to find their way into his awareness. *Why couldn't she have stayed?*

"Where the hell is that coming from?" asks Jimmy again. "We need to check this out."

"Thought you wanted to go home," Dean says.

"I doubt it's coming due with the wind," responds Jimmy, "but if we start following the wind back to its source maybe we can home in on the music when we need to shift."

They walk into the wind. Random half-thoughts come unbidden to each of them – punch lines to jokes, obsessive impulses, vague concepts, unfamiliar emotions. Neither man is willing to comment on what he is feeling. Both wonder if the other is experiencing the same thing. Electronic notes whirl through the air in an ebb and flow with gusts of wind. They walk for a quarter of an hour across a slow-rising field of waist-high grass and weeds, cross a gully into a stand of trees, and then the sound dies with a plaintive, mumbled, electric guitar "Thank you," sliding up one string, punctuating the "you" with a single, dulling note on the next string down.

They wait for several minutes. Dean lights a cigarette.

"Wind better not change or we're lost, Jimmy."

"No, we aren't. We just gotta keep the moon to our left, is all."

"I hope you're right."

"I am."

"Man, this is weird," says Dean.

"Yeah."

"What do you think?"

"Don't know."

"UFO?"

Jimmy snorts and looks up at the trees.

"Deano, why can't this just be a situation where someone's playing an electric guitar in the woods?"

"Well, it could be, except...well, I don't know, Jimmy. Did you have any weird thoughts coming up here? I mean, that didn't make any sense? You know, sort of meandering around, sort of half yours but not really?"

Jimmy waits to answer, still listening: "I don't know, man."

They are silent after this, waiting for the music to pick up again. The wind is beginning to blow harder. "Jimmy, I don't feel very drunk here. Fact, I feel rather close to sober, 'cept for that weird shit drifting through my mind."

Jimmy sighs, shaking his head. "We could just kind of make an educated guess which way to go after it."

"I think we ought to head home," says Dean.

"Fuck that, man! We just spent twenty minutes tracking this thing. Right before it died it sounded like it was coming from that direction." He points through the trees. "Let's just head that way for a few minutes," he continues. "See where we end up. We probably walked about a mile or so. I bet we find some kind of road before long, and then we might know where we are anyway."

"What time is it?" asks Dean.

"Probably around 1:00 or so. I'm tired too, man, so we won't go much further. Promise. Okay?"

They start off in the direction Jimmy pointed and come to a steep, almost cliff-like rise. Climbing to the top, they are surprised to see a lone, dull light in the valley below.

"That's probably it, Jimmy." Dean whispers. "Think it's a campfire?"

"You know, this layout all of a sudden seems familiar," Jimmy says. "I think I've been near here before, actually. This is definitely another one of those pieces of Fancher's land. We cleared a bit of these woods out for him maybe six years ago. Pretty close to the bluffs right here. Maybe a half a mile at most. There's no road in, though. Never could figure out what that old fucker had us doing. Used to be part of one of those secret military installations. You know, those old missile silos everyone talks about? Wanna go see if we can find one?"

Dean doesn't answer at first. He lets the memories take over. Fancher's name has reminded him of McKenna. She left her father years before. But she'd also left Dean. McKenna Joombs Fancher. She'd changed her name to McKenna Joombs and was touring the country with a band. She'd sent several postcards. In the last one, maybe two years back, she'd said she was never coming home again.

Jimmy tries to look at his friend in the muddy darkness. "Sorry, Dean, I didn't mean to bring her up."

They both stare into the valley without saying anything, lost in their respective thoughts of McKenna Joombs. They'd both loved her, but she had only loved Dean.

They hear a series of loud, echoing, cracks, like gunshots or a quick set of lightning reports.

"Thunder?" asks Jimmy.

Dean is still brooding. Finally, he says, "Don't know. Didn't see any lightning. Rifle, maybe? Could be some idiot hunting."

Gradually, the sound of rain comes toward them. And as the drops begin to fall harder, the light they're watching slowly fades. They find themselves staring into a dull blackness where the glow had been.

Jimmy moves under some trees to watch for the light and listen for the weird guitar. Nothing comes. They have no answer. It's getting very wet. Dean, still lost in thought, finally moves under the trees, too.

When they make it to the truck, the rain has stopped and the streets of Fayette are deserted. It is nearing 2:30 a.m. They are soaked through. Neon Busch sign is the only light inside Stein's.

*

Journal Entry 345: Cecil Miller

The sticky clock tells me I've just turned 30. It is midnight and outside I hear the wash of cars funneling down the Drive far below my apartment in the cold Chicago night. My life has changed forever. I have finished in one sitting Jim Schnabel's book, Remote Viewers: The Secret History of America's Psychic Spies. *All of the mental games I thought my mind was playing on me when I was younger were not games. Schnabel's book is proof. It has to be!*

In the book he describes the work of what was a secret group of special espionage labs that were started in the early '60s at Stanford Research Institute mostly on contract to the CIA and managed by a guy named Hal Puthoff. Work expanded to the Army's Intelligence and Security Command (INSCOM) under a number of commanders and various code names including Gondola Wish and Grill Flame.

What came to be known as psi research (short for psychical research) had been brewing for some time. Schnabel documents what for centuries had been studied by pre-scientists and early scientists. Phenomena such as clairvoyance, hypnosis, psychokinesis, mesmeric trance, magnetic sleep, artificial somnambulism, shamanistic healing, and, of course, my specialty, psychedelic dream journeys, had all been known to intellectuals and academics for eons. Psi is just a way to bring all of this together.

Remote Viewing (RV), as it became known, seems to have come about as a way of harnessing psychic power to perform cheap, low-risk espionage. Rather than sending spies out into the field to gather intelligence and sneak around, Puthoff and people at INSCOM screened military and related personnel for certain experiential histories and trained them to perform remote viewing operations.

One very strange thing about the book is that Schnabel never tries to figure out these switching systems. To transcend space and time the way he has described it, even on the imperfect level that he writes of, is to go far beyond science. What is the mechanism making things happen here? Does everyone have this ability? Is one of the goals of society to actively set up rules of order and reason that end up limiting the relevance or even the validity of this Psi world? If all of this is true, if even one of his stories is true, then science and religion are both in the balance, and what we think of as Reality is so limiting and so fractured from truth as to be virtually meaningless.

It is for this reason that I write here in my journal tonight. On my 30th birthday I have decided to discontinue my studies in cultural anthropology and join the field of parapsychology. There is a secret to all of these notions. There must be! I will find it out and I will make it work for human beings.

CHAPTER 2

Felix Erdenheim is nearing his appointed drop site. He has been flying helicopters for more than twenty years. During the first decade of his career, he flew smuggling runs for the Consolidated American Reformers of Marijuana Laws. Erdenheim had smuggled dope. But most of the work was philanthropic in nature. CARML's top brass dealt only with oncology departments in need of cannabis to help alleviate patient suffering. This made it easy for Erdenheim to justify the risks he took. His father had suffered immensely before succumbing to bone cancer. Felix's father had been a chopper pilot in Vietnam and taught his son everything there was to know about flying and dealing with danger.

One by one, most of his CARML regulars were busted or they'd dropped out of sight. He had several close calls himself, but Erdenheim usually possessed a special sense when it came to trouble, something learned from his father. Now he flies different assignments, more or less on a freelance basis. He figures this work is illegal, too, but he doesn't know how. He figures there are others who make runs like his, but he has no idea who these guys are, how many there are, or even when they fly.

Drops are staged several times a month over a part of Missouri farmland close to a bend in the Missouri River. It's all pretty haphazard, and there doesn't seem to be a real schedule. He'll get a two-ring call in the middle of the night, then go to a random pay phone somewhere nearby to call in the special number they give him. The male voice on the other end will simply list a string of digits and a time.

He'll take off in the Black Whisper 1000 from a small airfield outside of St. Louis and fly northwest over Iowa, then on to Nebraska, then down south along the Missouri River to finally bank back eastward toward the lights of Columbia heading for his target several miles southeast of Fayette. Most of this is under cover of darkness, and all with the air-jet propulsion system specially designed for the Black Whisper.

The Whisper is a modified version of the old Black Hawk A-100 helicopter, fitted with an experimental jet turbine for the main rotary engine. The relative quiet of the turbine gives the helicopter its name. There are only five in the world. They were designed as special operations assault carriers after the initial success of the Black Hawk in Vietnam. The other four are owned by the Israeli Air Force.

The original prototype turbine was designed by Saddam Hussein's engineers after they witnessed the destruction caused by Desert Storm forces flying Apaches and Black Hawks. The Whisper, though, was manufactured by Norfolk Industries and Hovercraft on a research contract to the U.S. Army with help from several of Hussein's defecting engineers. But when the first five were completed, the Army no longer wanted anything to do with them. They were too expensive, and it was determined they weren't quiet enough for the investment. Only one was sold. The other four were given to Israel by the Clinton Administration in a secret trade for concessions on West Bank policy. Felix Erdenheim made the only purchase. His slightly used Black Whisper 1000 cost over $19 million. The money came from his unknown client. There is little question in Erdenheim's mind that his client is a heavy player – and he's pretty sure he doesn't want to know what they're up to.

The Whisper is used strictly for deliveries. Whoever hired him required that he disarm all the artillery the chopper carries and reprogram the radar system strictly for defensive maneuvers. Felix has never touched a gun in his life, so this doesn't bother him a bit.

The cargo changes from outing to outing – sometimes it's electronic equipment or cases of canned food, maybe diesel fuel or large quantities of aluminum piping; sometimes it's farm equipment, or a generator and laboratory utensils, or cartons of medical supplies, boxes of mason jars, or expensive fresh grapefruit and avocados.

From his father, Felix also learned to just do his job without asking questions. So when he's not making his runs, Felix tries not to think about what he does for a living. Clearly, something illegal is going on, but he has no idea what it is and he is happy enough in a state of well-paid ignorance.

Marijuana had been fairly easy. But this new situation is more lucrative. In three hours he will be home again eating an early lunch at Suzie's Cafe and talking to his stockbroker on the mobile. Life is good. The only tough part is actually pushing the cargo out the bomb bay hatches. There are two problems with this. The first is that he has to put the bird into the auto-hover mode so that he can move back to push the drop-cases through the hatches. And he has to do this without getting tangled up in the netting and the parachute lines. The second problem is that in order to make things happen quickly, he must open the hatches several miles west of the target, meaning that for maybe thirty to forty seconds the doors are open and the chopper's belly glows the same dull red as the night illumination in the cockpit. Generally, he still has momentum when he flicks the hover switch, so he is still coasting forward. This is dangerous if he's close to treetops or if there are crosswinds. The gyro system compensates only up to a certain point.

It is possible, too, that one of these nights someone on the ground will see or hear him. The extra sense that has kept him out of busts sometimes starts to surface when he flicks on the nightglow lighting, but it all happens so quickly that it never has a chance to affect his behavior. He doesn't like these vague and tentative pangs of fear. But for the $20,000 he makes working one long night every few weeks, he can take the risk.

*

Several miles east, Robert "Smokey" Hughes more feels the hum in the air than hears it. He knows what this sound means. It's the third time since late winter he has encountered the near silent helicopter, but he's never gotten a good look at it. Planting has gone bad this spring, what with the hard weather and all, and he has been forced to work late into the night on the few good days his tractor can handle the deep mud of the bottomland. He watches the sky while puffing on his pipe taking a break from fixing his disk harrow. It is nearing 4:30 a.m. At the first fluttering hum in the air he extinguishes the running lights of the vehicle and douses his droplight. Wrenches and screwdrivers rest in a row on the flat crossbeam of the disker. They begin to vibrate as the helicopter eases closer; their steel lies mute and dark in the thick night air.

It comes over Reed's Hill fast and low, like a dark mythic beast in the last lunge before a kill, an almost imperceptible low growling rage. In the darkness, for some reason, Smokey Hughes catches a momentary flash of red on the full underbody of the helicopter. Maybe it's a painted Day-Glo flag or a new kind of infrared scope, he can't tell. The thing seems as big as a semitruck but shaped aerodynamically with lines so perfect and true, the sheer mastery of design shoots a chill through him. He has never seen anything like this, and it scares the shit out of him.

This is government, he is sure of it. The militia is finally under surveillance. Trouble is coming. He'd known it would happen, and now, here they were – black, silent, probably armed, and ready for battle. It's time to call Sumter and tell him. Sumter would know what to do. He always did.

CHAPTER 3

Jill Simpson gets the call at 3:40 in the morning. Thirty minutes later she turns her vehicle onto a gravel road running behind the Forum Shopping Center. She's had less than two hours of sleep. The usual shriek of insects is strangely absent. She parks between two patrol cars, both empty but with their engines still running. There is no wind and the night has grown hot again after a post-midnight rain. She turns both cars off and pockets the keys.

Wading through weeds and undergrowth lining the road, she locates where the barbwire has been removed and steps across. Low murmurs and bright flashes like lightning tell her where her men are before she gets to The Dip. At the rim she finds three uniformed officers milling about the site, combing the ground for evidence. She watches them quietly for a few seconds. At least they finally have the method down. Two of them work the ground in straight lines, the third is taking pictures. They are being moderately careful.

"Fuckin' Simpson takes her time!"

She expects this. It is Hughes. The other two, Baines and Heimer, don't respond to him. Everyone is used to Hughes and his attitude. He'd been like that since at least aged fourteen when she'd first met him at the Pancake House. They'd both worked the graveyard shift then – her as a bus girl, him in the back as a dishwasher.

"Been watching you for about five minutes, Hughes," she says quietly down into The Dip. All three flashlights train on her face at once. Heimer chuckles softly and returns his light to the ground. Hughes keeps his on her face. Baines goes back to taking pictures.

"I don't know which of you was driving," she continues, "but, Hughes, take these keys and don't lose 'em." She tosses the handful of keys at him and drops down into The Dip.

Jill hides a smile. Hughes knows better than to say what he's thinking. He is obliged to mumble curses to himself in order to regain his dignity. She ignores him. He is an asshole, she reminds herself, but he's also a tough motherfucker, and he has come through for her several times in touchy situations.

"Hey, Sarge," says Heimer as Hughes goes back to his job.

"Is this a kid?" she asks, squatting to get a closer look. "Huh! Not much blood here." The heavy white shirt has absorbed a small amount of blood into a crusty palm-sized stain. "There should have been a direct hit and something more bloody than this. Weird."

She rolls the body over and is pleased to find no exit wound. An easily located slug will speed the investigation and allow them time to focus on other clues.

"I take it the call really was anonymous and there are no witnesses?" The three men concur by their silence.

"God, I haven't been here in a while," she says nostalgically as she flashes her light around the area. Heimer's smile tightens just a notch as he looks to see if Hughes and Baines are listening. It doesn't really matter.

"I've never been here before in my life," he says in mock innocence only she can understand.

The Dip is a depression in this sloping pasture that served for several decades as a perfect place for young people to do illicit things. When they were teenagers, Jill and Heimer had come here often to smoke cigarettes and drink wine after he got his driver's license. The summer before she ran away from home they spent many Saturday nights smoking pot and talking late, high on MDA or Black Beauties or whatever was popular. She winced as she remembered nights smoking PCP. Last year she'd stopped a kid high on the stuff from tearing his eyes out.

Jill and Tom Heimer had been friends for most of high school - until she ran away from home. One night they each took a full hit of blotter acid and had been through the peak of the trip and were on the downside, *attached*, as they called it, questioning life and why things were the way they were. It was the old "Nothing Matters" talk, and it had led finally to her statement that she was running away and would either figure out how to get a job as a cop or would work her way through law school by waiting tables.

Nothing mattered. Why should she stay at home with her family when her parents were so strict and controlled her every move? Why should she finish up the year? Why was it so hard to make things work in life?

It happened then. They were attached so it really didn't take much by way of courage on his part. He leaned over and tentatively kissed her. She still remembered it, thirty-one years later. At first it didn't seem right. They were friends. But half an hour later that had changed. Maybe it was the drugs, maybe it was them, maybe it was just the way sex was supposed to be, but it was the first time she'd ever let go and been able to enjoy herself. They did it twice more before it was time to leave. It had been unprotected but she only worried about that the next morning. What she thought of mostly as they lay together in the warm darkness, smoking Lark cigarettes and stroking the exposed parts of each other's bodies, was the kissing part. She'd kissed enough guys who'd had their hands all over her before. Even those she let put their hands down her pants hadn't done the same thing to her. There was definitely something about kissing when two genitals were locked together that could complete the experience. It was this kissing that led to her orgasms each time. She couldn't get enough of him when he was inside her. She went crazy. Her tongue shot all around his mouth. She licked and sucked as deep into him as she could, like tasting the greatest secret the world had ever known.

But it wasn't Tom, whom she understood she would never love, it was life; it was what had eluded her always until that moment. It was pure, physical pleasure never conceived as a possibility until the moment he leaned over her. It was the loss of self to the joining with someone else. It was the finding of an absolute center that she had never known could exist – pure, total self-absorption. It was the consumption of another being and then the letting go of everything in raw, abandoned orgasm with the feel of hot liquid and swollen glands, and then lying under the stars looking into dark blue infinity afterwards.

"Word is, Jill," begins Heimer, keeping the light on the ground, "a call came in a bit after three about a disturbance, and that Limerick Lane was the place to look."

"And it was anonymous?"

"You see anyone waiting to be interviewed?" says Hughes.

Heimer continues: "I told dispatch to put the tape of the call on your desk. No one could tell me whether it was a man or a woman, but I'd say it was probably the fucker who did this himself."

"Or herself maybe. Don't jump to any conclusions, okay Tom? You know what I think about that. Now, what else?"

"Well, you can see we got a kid here. Maybe he's what, nineteen or twenty? He's Amish, I think. Least in dress. He smells like booze, though – a lot of it. And whoever did this maybe had it all planned out. Probably at thirty-feet, or so. One shot in the chest. Bull's-eye."

Jill bends over the body to look at the wound again more carefully. Standing, she pulls surgical gloves out of her breast pocket and puts them on. She clips the big light to her belt, pulls out her penlight, and places it in her mouth. Rolling the body over, she carefully inserts her index finger through the shirt into the wound.

"No ID, of course," says Hughes over his shoulder. "Fuckin' Mennonites."

"He's Amish, man!" responds Baines.

"How come he doesn't have one of those funky beards, then?" asks Hughes.

Baines sighs and says, "They don't all have beards. Besides, look at him. He's not much more than a kid."

"Well, I don't guess I'm an expert the way you are, Officer Baines."

"Whatever," Baines replies quickly. "He wasn't carrying much of anything. We got no idea who he is, where he's from, whether he was shot here, you name it."

"He probably wasn't shot here," says Simpson.

"How do you know?" asks Heimer. Hughes and Baines look up from the ground.

"I'm not positive, but the bullet entry isn't angled much at all. That kind of trajectory doesn't make full sense for this terrain. Look, there's nothing but slope here."

Simpson clears her throat. "I'm not committing anything to paper or even formal theory until I've had some decent sleep. And stop what you're doing right now. Clearly, we're looking in the wrong place. If he was shot up on the hill or anywhere else, then we need to wait till daylight to look for footprints, pieces of clothing, whatever. And something's bothering me...."

She thinks for a moment. Her subordinates watch her. The sound of crackling gravel from across the field indicates the paramedics have arrived.

"Okay, Jonesy will be here in a minute," she finally says. "Baines, you and Hughes go to the road and help them bring the stretcher and equipment, and take a few more pictures before you move the body. I want us walking through here now as little as possible."

She waits for them to leave. Heimer turns to her, his body language more intimate now, more a respectful friend.

He says: "He was dumped here, then. Is that it?"

Jill hates the way supposition from singular facts leaves her unable to get a clear picture of anything. "Or maybe there was another gunner on the other side, maybe he wasn't drunk, maybe the shooter was on the ground here, maybe...." She stops. "Maybe we better wait for the pictures and for Jonesy to play coroner. Gotta run ballistics too, even without the weapon."

"I agree," Heimer says. "Something about the angle of the body just doesn't seem right—" He's about to tell her more when Jonesy and his sons arrive. The boys are excited. They've been working with their dad for nearly two years and this is their first real homicide.

The look in the Jones boys' eyes is the look that anyone in the town would have exhibited, Jill thinks: morbid fascination. It makes her angry for a brief moment. Death is so unreal to most people, she thinks. To her, death is the most important thing about her job. It's why she chose police work over law. She doesn't deal with death much, but when she does, she realizes this is why police are needed more than anything else. Someone has to deal with atrocity. "It boils up our fluids as much as sex and food and music," she says quietly studying the body.

A chill comes quickly to her, then passes. She says, more to the body than even to herself: "My job is finding the dead and then helping everyone deal with the implications."

Jonesy is the only other person who understands this. He is usually the first on the scene. Sometimes he doesn't need his boys to carry victims. He knows she'll be along soon enough to help him with the stretcher. Usually it isn't a homicide, though. Usually they deal with car wrecks, sudden heart attacks, or drug overdoses. This time, though, it's murder.

The scene feels strange, but she'll think about it later – after a few more hours of sleep and breakfast at The Pancake House.

CHAPTER 4

"Sir, you've read the memo?" Loretta Josephson knows her boss, Major Tyle J. Sandover, isn't going to welcome the interruption.

"No, Josephson, I haven't read the memo yet. I'm still thinking." Sandover has been up half the night preparing his briefing to the subcommittee. The meeting, as usual, has been scheduled for 6:00 a.m. sharp - all the better to limit media awareness.

"Sir, the committee is waiting. They need your answer."

"God damn it, I know that. I'm just sick of this whole thing is all."

"I understand, sir. But they're waiting."

"Look Jo, I can't get through this. It's too damned ridiculous. Why are they doing this to me?"

She wants to give him an answer that makes sense, but can't. As far as she can tell, he's been demoted to the flaky cases and she with him. At one time they'd operated together coordinating domestic intelligence assessment efforts with the Bureau of Alcohol, Tobacco and Firearms. They had a staff of over thirty field agents and communications centers in San Diego, St. Louis, and just south of Philadelphia in New Castle, Delaware. Sandover should have made colonel and then finally general and gained assignment to the Joint Chiefs before the end of the first decade of the new century. It hadn't gone that way, though. Domestic espionage was illegal – especially when you got involved in spying on groups like the National Rifle Association and the NAACP. He'd made too many enemies on both sides of the fence. The word was out that they were going to nail him and the whole operation. He had a choice: come clean and fall on his sword, or figure out how to get out of the way. It wasn't pretty, but he'd figured it out. The only place he was untouchable was in Special Issues where the social scientists and the psycho-pharmacologists worked. They were usually assigned an advisory role to field units from the more public operations teams. There was no choice but to suggest the "lateral" assignment.

SI had been viewed by the national security community as the astrology of the covert world since at least the early 1960s. They'd been brought in to give background on cult leaders, militia groups, and sometimes political activists. Their job was more about research and less about spying, but that didn't hinder Sandover from carefully adjusting his unit's scope of service. He couldn't help it. He loved intelligence work. The group had grown slowly, expanding their usefulness over the years. Unfortunately, Sandover also put himself back in a situation where he needed to deliver.

As her boss adjusts his reading glasses to attempt a review of the memo once again, Loretta Josephson slips out the door and heads for the subcommittee's meeting room, hoping to stall them further while Sandover thought through how he was going to explain the funding request for this one. He reads the memo again:

MEMORANDUM

To: Major Tyle J. Sandover, Liaison – Deputy Director Special Issues Unit, CIA

From: Dr. Arthur Gold, Associate, Rand Corp.

Subject: General observations on Central Missouri phenomena

In our last NSC briefing, you asked that I provide documentation on the opinions I presented verbally. Your particular concern was the alarming situation in

Missouri where, beginning in the spring of this year, several thousand people have traveled due to a belief that the deceased entertainer, Elvis Presley, has been sighted within a 50-mile radius of Columbia. Your concern, and the concern of many in the NSC meeting, was the meaning behind such an irrational situation and whether there is any threat to the national security from this bizarre behavior. As I stated emphatically in the meeting, I do not believe it is possible to come to meaningful conclusions without firsthand observation. I am aware that Lieutenant-Colonel Danworth and Undersecretary Adams feel this whole thing to be a flash-in-the-pan situation that will dissipate by Christmas. But I am not so sure. If anything, I see more irrational behavior coming down the line with the media, not less.

Furthermore, there are basic IRS and Treasury issues surrounding the Baptist group connected to these Elvis sightings. As you know, we are also gathering information in the field on this organization's links to militia groups in the area. Additionally, if this religious organization demonstrates that it can significantly enhance its membership-base internationally by spawning insinuations about a deceased pop star, other organizations may follow suit.

In addition, we aren't sure whether there is a correlation or not, but we have been tracking a longtime representative of agricultural business interests in the region who bought up one of the Trident III missile silo fields decommissioned in 1973 near Whiteman Air Force Base. The field in question is identified under the nomenclature SF-19 and consists of nine hardened underground facilities connected by access tunnels and air ducts totaling some 3.5 miles in length. SF-19 sits beneath nine farms located just east of the Missouri River. The gentleman in question is named Lucas Fancher. He has not been seen for more than three years – and has not paid taxes in over fifteen years (there is no evidence he has an income).

Most alarming is the fact that many of the Whiteman silo fields were part of a decommissioning contract issued to Millman Demolition Industries. As you will recall, Millman is the contractor who recently discovered irregularities in their record-keeping process dating back to the early 1970s and have advised that not all field inventories were adequately salvaged. We therefore do not know what equipment may still be in the possession of Mr. Fancher.

In summation, a significant number of questionable activities are underway in this region. We have little understanding of the parameters involved. I therefore wish to recommend that the committee utilize funding to further investigate the situation in Missouri. We should stay ahead of the curve here. If events continue to escalate, it is imperative for us to understand developments and to take appropriate action in order to control impacts. As we have discussed at length, NSC's job is about control.

It may well be that the whole thing dissipates into yet another simple fringe cult harping on some singular past event. But things could move the other way as well, drawing in more and more believers and followers. The real problem is that if escalation occurs beyond a certain point, or if there are connections between this farm representative, these militias, and the Baptist minister, there will be no way to predict outcomes. This is potentially a significant risk – especially in light of possible IRS difficulties, a covert armed militia organization, and nuclear security interests of the nation. We don't need another Ruby Ridge or Leonard Peltier massacre.

It is impossible to come up with meaningful data without an investment in direct observation. As always, I am willing to work with you and your staff to establish an action plan and to deploy the appropriate field resources. Please do not hesitate to contact me in the usual way.

Note as well that there has been little charge against our retainer for nearly five months and that the committee can therefore, if it chooses, use extensive resources to set up this project. I do have a field contact in place and also have an agent nearby who can easily be tasked. I am, as always, available for further consultation on these matters.
/AG:fyeo

*

The flight path home is as meandering as the one he took to fly over Fayette. Erdenheim goes southeast another several miles, then cuts north-to-northwest at Finger Lakes and tracks twenty-five miles up to the Moberly Airport where he puts down for coffee, biscuits and gravy, unloads a legitimate shipment of medical supplies, refuels and then heads back to St. Louis.

His work could, of course, have something to do with the militia groups he's heard are present in the area. Maybe he's dropping stuff for them to live on. Or maybe it is for a covert operation by some federal agency. He knows that in a few spots around the Midwest militia communities are all that is left inhabiting some of the smaller rural towns. Those families who have tried to stay on the land are either driven out by organized hostility or gradually assimilated into the militia's ranks. Ever since the voting fiasco of 2000, people all over rural America have been less than happy with their government.

Erdenheim contemplates all of this as he flies over the darkened landscape, watching the horizon for the glow of St. Louis. The gravy-covered Moberly biscuits have loosened his bowels. He lets himself consider where the gravy has come from and how old it is. They eat mostly swine and fowl down there now. Often gravy is made from the old ones found dead near the road or destroyed out of pity for their feebleness. Dog is possible, too, or even cat. At least Columbia is still on trucking routes. His thoughts turn then to Suzy Martino's curried carrot soup back home in St. Charles and whether it will go better with Chardonnay or Cabernet Sauvignon.

CHAPTER 5

In his motel room, Harris rests a glass of whiskey on his stomach. Insomnia is a hard thing to understand but it is a good reason to drink. He'd been a well-built, handsome man until nicotine, alcohol, and cynicism marred his face and made his shoulders sag. At 47, he has dark circles beneath his eyes and perpetual creases on his forehead and the corners of his mouth. His teeth and fingers are permanently stained from the habit of chain smoking whenever he is revved up by a project. He is a large man – nearly six feet, four – but softening. His once confident stride has degraded to a sort of limping shuffle which might make him appear vulnerable – save for one thing: his piercing, sky-blue eyes.

The empty Dewar's bottle stands on the bedside table amidst notes he's been making for his article, cigarette ashes, a Big Mac wrapper, a filled ashtray, and the TV remote control. He went to bed naked, but around 2:00 a.m. the starchy, plastic sensation of motel sheets started to make his skin prickle. He lies under the bedspread now, fully clothed, with the air-conditioner on high. The room is bathed in the smudgy blue of television light. It's now past three, and Harris knows he isn't going to get any sleep. He has turned the volume down on a talk show after filling his glass to the brim with the remaining scotch.

Treestat's assignment is to go into the middle of the country to interview a psychic passing herself off as some sort of angel or God knows what from the next world. Treestat seemed more affected by all the changes to the media business than nearly anyone Harris knew. It was all about hype and innuendo now. The blending of nightly news with shows like Entertainment Daily and Reality Nation had professionalized the paparazzi approach to the point of ridiculousness. So, here he was, out of Philly, staring into a last glass of scotch in the early hours of another hot day, assigned the job of interviewing some clairvoyant who claimed she had talked to none other than Elvis Fucking Presley himself.

Harris made a name for himself as the last person to interview Jerry Garcia, and had been out drinking with Jeff Buckley the night of his weird drowning in the Mississippi a couple of years later. It was just dumb luck that he had interviewed King Jones in Kansas City on the night the performer put a bullet into his own brain – or was it?

He guzzles the tepid whiskey fast now in four throat-stunning gulps, hoping to pummel his body with enough sedation to doze for at least a few hours before he needs to go to work distorting yet another sincere loony's story.

It's pretty good work, really. Not too demanding, if you can handle a keyboard and make deadlines. Harris and *Midnight's* other reporters usually concoct stories over lunch, or they might do a long-distance phone interview with a retired jeweler bragging he's seen a UFO, or a housewife addicted to large doses of diet pills claiming the government has bamboozled her out of a winning lottery ticket. After sightings of Princess Diana became commonplace, Treestat hired a full-time Photoshop specialist who is now the highest paid person in the office. If necessary, too, she will stage photos to go along with a story. It's easy. You just need money and people who will do whatever you say without asking questions. Sometimes, when Harris feels like he needs a trip, he might go out in the field to do an interview. But usually he works from his desk, surfing information networks, diddling around with Google, and uploading potential stories as often as possible.

The best thing is that their readers know it's all bullshit. But that's what they want. It's like All-Star Wrestling for the gossip-hungry. Occasionally a lawsuit comes their way, but usually that just sells more papers and more advertising space. All he wants to do now in this godforsaken town is get drunk and smoke cigarettes.

He has done the research. The Reverend Montgomery Sumter, minister of an obscure Baptist group called the Third Christian Witness Church, was at the heart of the Elvis situation, claiming he'd been in contact with The King for years. The Reverend had already presided over at least one revival meeting visited by someone who looked a lot like the pop star. And now he promised both the media and Elvis fans throughout the world another visit at the next meeting, and that this time, somehow, the visit would be far more momentous. Harris had run into enough of these guys over the years. Religion and politics were the venues for this breed, professions where results were less important than emotion and belief – and money.

The connection between Elvis and religion had always been something easy to exploit, Harris thought. But if this Sumter was simply trying to make money, this was certainly a bizarre way to do things. It was too public and too obviously a scam.

Monty Sumter's career began with a short-lived religious revival show on Columbia's Channel 17, which was canceled after two years. The show specialized in bringing local social oddities on air to talk about their paranoia and addictions, with young Monty launching into his "healing" routine just before the final commercial break. Monty's older brother Bud was the show's executive producer – as well as the station's owner.

Where possible, Monty's guests tried to help him too. If they were wheelchair-bound, they would launch themselves across the room into his arms; if they were afraid of heights, they would declare a new understanding of life and climb the station's scaffolding; if they were dyslexic, they would miraculously read the 487th page of *War & Peace* to the audience as if they were Alistair Cook. There was plenty of speaking in tongues and divine possession as well. And the J-School writers who critiqued the show in the local press worked hard to be fair and objective, but according to the articles Harris found, there was no evidence Monty had permanently healed anyone or had even just changed their lives. The show eventually fizzled, brotherly love notwithstanding.

Bud Sumter, Monty's big brother, showed up a good deal in the town's history beginning in the mid-'70s. He was the county sheriff for nearly three terms. The guy never got directly involved in politics after his law enforcement days, it seemed, and it was unclear where his money originally came from, but Harris stumbled across the name quite often in the news articles he downloaded.

To get a full fix on the guy, Harris ran a number of keyword searches using a special set of meta-base algorithms he had written. As usual, he managed to obtain a large portfolio of news items and articles, but found no real answers. What he found, though, was interesting enough. Bud Sumter had been elected sheriff three terms in a row – opposed by the diminutive Republican party only once, the first time - then strangely seemed to drop out of the picture for a while. The research showed that Sheriff Sumter had been implicated in a gambling operation. Harris knew such stories well. Sumter had ultimately resigned – in exchange for testimony perhaps, or simply as his sole punishment. Harris figured Sumter's source of money probably had been leftover contributions from campaign days. There was no smoking gun, of course, and around 1994 he resurfaced in the news as the buyer of the local ABC affiliate, Channel 17.

Bud and Monty Sumter were clearly the sources of the whole Elvis situation. Harris needed to be careful. He didn't want to blow what little cover the Sumter brothers had. If he worked it just right, the story would be good for at least another month.

Stubbing out a cigarette, he notes the dark nicotine stain on the filter. He pinches the middle and watches a tiny bead of liquid rise to the end of the cotton. He knows he's smoking too much already. Unless he thinks about it, he will take two drags for every one breath of air, almost in rhythmic sequence. And the drags are long and hard. This is usually a sign that he is either nervous or unhappy.

Since the previous morning, boarding the plane in Philadelphia, he has been anxious about something that he can't put his finger on. His thoughts race, but at the same time seem clearer than usual, even now as he lies on the bed half drunk, full of nicotine, sleepless for nearly twenty-four hours. The drone of the air-conditioner seems different. He listens to the whoosh of air spreading from the beige grates and the click and hum of the machinery pumping phase-shift fluid through its cycles. The vibrating drone of the compressor gives him the feeling that he is still on the jet flying over the flat, open farmland of Ohio, Indiana, and Illinois. He focuses on each sound made by the window unit. With his eyes closed and the mild nausea from near nicotine overdose, he feels himself surfing the current of dry, processed air rising into the room. It's a very subtle feeling, but he knows something different is about to happen. He is not sure whether this comes from being surrounded by the glittering floral walls of a Holiday Inn double, or whether he's just more aware than usual – thanks to the slate-wiping effect of advanced alcohol immersion. Perhaps his mind is simply fumbling around for meaning in its nether regions, tripping over some as yet unidentifiable, personal issue that he does not wish to acknowledge. All of which, he smiles, is why alcohol is such a good way to go.

No, thinks Harris, this assignment is going to be a Chinese water torture exercise, complete with chanting insects, hot parking lots, and a hotel swimming pool surrounded by lavender gravel.

It is nearing dawn and the liquor stores don't open until late morning. He figures he'll have breakfast at the restaurant down the road – The Pancake House – and try to get his thoughts moving in the right direction before he stops for more booze – maybe some beer, too. Then he'll head out for the scheduled interview, go to the Sumters' big Elvis revival meeting, and hopefully find time to check out the river in daylight. What a fucked up part of the world.

Part II
Waiting for Elvis

As the story found its twists and turns, as it made a labyrinth, as it moved with the momentum of a flood in a museum, strange creatures appeared: Elvis Christ, Elvis Nixon, Elvis Hitler, Elvis Mishima, Elvis as godhead, Elvis inhabiting the bodies of serial killers, of saints, fiends. Each was a joke of course; beneath each joke was bedrock, obsession, delight, fear.

- Greil Marcus, *Dead Elvis*, 1991

CHAPTER 6

Cecil Miller is a parapsychology graduate student at the University of Chicago and has been performing a psychotropic experiment on himself for more than a decade using the designer agent EGG-68. He knew full well that it was no longer possible to employ the scientific method. The drug had opened up too many new avenues of awareness. His memory seemed to operate on a random basis; his ability to solve simple problems was often intermittent at best. But he was a smart guy. He always had been. And his new psychedelic consciousness, which was more or less permanent, gave him strange intuitive abilities as well. Unfortunately, these psychic powers were rather sporadic and usually inconsequential, but he was up for the challenge.

Journal Entry 217: Cecil Miller

This rock and roll thing goes into the heart of us. It comes through by amplified energy that is in-synch, perfectly hooked into Time, primed by rhythm. It lodges in the cerebellum like a sticky clock.

I watched a documentary on Dead Heads last night. At the end there were snippets of Ken Kesey talking about the Dead and Acid Tests. He talked about how the Acid Test really was a Test. Some passed, some didn't. He didn't really give an explanation of what it meant to fail, but he gave an example of passing: A man came into a Test dressed in a business suit carrying an umbrella. He was given the "customary cup" and a few hours later Kesey says he saw the man watching his shadow and parading around with the umbrella over his shoulder saying: "The king turns left. The king turns right." He watches his shadow all the while and turns back and forth. He'd passed the Test, says Kesey.

Most likely the guy passed because he figured out that he is his own aesthetic, his own source of comedy, bodily experience, words, symbolism, and all other forms of energy and meaning rolled into one, making him both the center of the universe and the butt of all divine and philosophical jokes. The guy finally got the absurdity of life. He understood he was both nothing and everything. If you were one or the other but not both, that wouldn't be funny. But once you see that you are absolutely and completely insignificant and at the same time connected to everything, including God maybe even, then it becomes possible to laugh, to really laugh, to laugh that cosmic clowny laugh which is the laugh that puts you far beyond the world you lived in just the day before. It puts God in your pocket. It lets Him see Himself as little more than an extension of your own absurdity.

Perhaps then, a question comes: is it good or bad allowing God to realize His own absurdity?

Perhaps such an understanding is what God needs in order to be released from the seriousness of the world, the turmoil of being connected to us and to this confusion we call Life. It helps God laugh too, helps God laugh the big bellyaching, open-mouthed, tear-in-the-eye laugh that is always floating in the air if you're paying attention.

"Good morning you mother fuckers," says God. "I'm going to go off and read a book for a change and maybe take a dip in the Creek. I should be back by lunchtime. You ought to be okay on your own. If you're feeling murderous or lonely, just lie down in the sunlight over there and take a nap. I'll wake you with some lemonade, fresh cold cherries, and those little cheese and tomato sandwiches that you love."

Kesey also talks about why Dead Heads do what they do – did what they did. He is forthright, direct, and simple: "They're looking for magic."

And he gives evidence of it. He talks about what happens during a concert, how the Dead are playing and people are dancing and grooving but they're sort of dancing on their own, each of them, different rhythms, different little egos with separate notions of Time and Space; and everyone there is looking and waiting for this moment when you can feel it all come together. He says it's like a tiny shaft of light coming from a chink in the moment that opens into a whole new realm where everything becomes linked. The Grateful Dead is no longer playing music in their heads, they are playing what's in the air. He says people will wait four hours during a concert for that one moment when it all comes together and they are all linked.

He's not just making it up, either. I've been there. I remember that feeling, like a bottle is being opened up, almost the sound of tearing cloth. And the groove is there.

Why are we ignoring this? It might be the only way to save ourselves.

*

On his way to the University of Chicago campus every day, Cecil fantasizes about a world where music in malls and elevators is played by live bands (not that there would be bands playing in the open, but that the music piped into those public places would be performed by a live band in, say, the loading dock area or a back room in the lobby). He muses on this idea often. What a world it would be if that kind of thing happened.

And then it does.

The sounds are fluid and surreal. He feels as if he is walking through a movie. It's like nothing he's ever heard before. The chord progression is basic, maybe D-C-G, but the rhythm and tempo keep changing, and the tone moves from ominous to happy to bittersweet almost haphazardly. He follows the guitar mostly, and it creeps through blues and dissonant jazz and then to what amounts to speed punk, acid-hop, and finally rock. Each note from the piano sounds like an individual drop of rain, each chord a splash on an otherwise empty flat calm sea in the early morning.

He is walking through a mall at around 2:30 p.m. The lunch crowd is gone. Kids are still in school. The wide halls are nearly empty and echo with this music. He keeps walking, fearing that it will end, wondering if this is an auditory hallucination. The guitar seems to be turned down lower in volume than the other instruments and the drums just whisper out a cadence. The bass, piano, sax, trumpet, and synthesizer carry the weight of the sonic work. But the guitar makes the sound special. Careening through styles and riffs from numerous repertories, the guitar seems to whisper unspoken thoughts.

Cecil fears it will all end if he stops walking. So he keeps moving through the mall, the sensation that he is in a movie welling up inside him, making him feel as if he's being watched, as if he is a movie himself.

He wanders up through three levels. Each time he rides the escalator, the music drifts off into the open atrium air. He moves back down the three levels circling the atrium, covering the entire floor area of each level before heading down to the next. He has to keep moving.

On the ground floor he finds stairs marked for access to the sub-basement. With nowhere else to go, he hesitates for a moment, waiting for the music to end – which it doesn't – and then heads down. At the bottom is an unmarked red door. The quality of sound changes here as he opens the door. The music becomes more resonant and pure. Walking down an empty hall, he realizes the sound is getting louder and that it no longer comes from speakers. Turning a corner, he sees an open door marked "Machine Shop." In the anteroom he finds the band – seven in number. He stands at the doorway and watches. They are young - maybe in their early twenties. The guitarist is African with a goatee and dressed in a long silk dashiki and blue jeans. He wears a wide, silk headband. An unlit cigarette dangles from the side of his mouth as he rests his chin on his chest and plays his instrument, eyes closed.

The other six musicians are white. They watch the guitarist intently. After a few minutes the drummer notices Cecil in the doorway and nods slightly in recognition. The bassist and two horn players notice him as well. Finally, the pianist and the man sitting before a keyboard and a bank of computer screens also notice him. The guitarist keeps on playing with his eyes closed.

*

Every several weeks Cecil abstains from drugs for a few days to give his mind and body time to recover. It is a pattern he's been following for nearly ten years. The worst of it is that while he is capable of recording thoughts and images rolling through his mind when he is high, he's in no condition to stay fully caught up with the scientific literature coming out on new designer drugs and their effect on remote viewing. He sticks mostly with EGG-68. He knows this mindscape well enough and worries a bit anyway about muddling up his research with different psychoactive responses. He is, after all, expected to be systematic about his work – even if he can't really be scientific. So, he lets others play with the less predictable substances.

EGG-68 was concocted in a Danish lab in 1987. It is the only non-toxic overt tri-beta inhibitor ever developed. There are numerous electro-chemical roles that it plays in enhancing the molecular capacity for the mind to perceive differing energy systems. It is a highly refined, very unstable sugar that is derived from synthetic nicotine. The instability of the sugar ensures that it flows throughout the brain and the rest of the nervous system with uniform capacity. In the lab, prior to freeze drying, the substance is poured out on glass pans and looks like egg whites, except for a subtle tinge of hazy turquoise sheen. There are 74 forms of tri-beta inhibitor that have been experimented with over the years. All except the 68th version caused varying forms of neural and electro-muscular death in lab rodents. EGG-68 is used by a number of psychotropic research facilities throughout the world. Cecil Miller, however, is the only researcher performing experiments on himself.

His initial tests were scientific enough, mostly following early efforts of the original remote viewing researchers – except for his use of a newer hallucinogen. Ninety minutes after ingesting a carefully measured quantity of EGG-68, he would close his eyes and work through the mesmerizing kaleidoscope of shifting fluorescent shapes until concrete images began to flash before him and big chunks of foreign awareness and sensation would come hurtling through him. If he was careful with his breathing, it was sometimes possible for a whole scene to open up before him.

In the first studies, Cecil asked his advisor's secretary to write down the schedule for her daily errands and then place the list in a sealed envelope. He then asked her to leave the envelope locked in the security department's safe. On his first try he spent six hours floating in and out of her experiences. When finally he was able to write things down – it had been somewhat difficult – comparison of the list with his log was almost perfect. She was shocked to read his descriptions of people she had talked to and that he had recorded the exact amount of money she'd spent on groceries, department supplies, and gasoline.

From there the tasking became more elaborate. He tried using observers sometimes, but found that his thoughts got tangled up with theirs too easily.

The coordinate exercise developed by Ingo Swann at the Stanford Research Institute was a piece of cake. Miller astounded fellow students and several professors in the anthropology department by having them secretly write down mapping coordinates for some place well known to them. He would then go into his office and come out late in the afternoon with a written description of the place and sometimes even the name of the closest town if the position chosen had distinguishable architecture or geographic formations.

After nearly a year of this research, Miller began to question the need for experimentation. He gave himself over to playing with free-form connections and found himself mentally wandering through different parts of the world. The point of these exercises quickly moved from developing a new type of remote viewing, something he termed hyperviewing, to seeking an understanding of the mechanism that made this all possible.

Cecil was beginning to worry about himself, though. He knew that his quest to understand the EGG experience and how it related to remote viewing and other psychic phenomena had altered his mind and his life forever. He had few real friends, he heard tiny voices when he was straight, sometimes he had trouble sustaining an erection when he masturbated. And when he was drugged, he would sometimes be incapable of talking. Speechlessness was the main drawback to his technique.

Although controversial, classical remote viewing was still being funded quietly by the military. But Miller's technique, while more accurate than the basic tried-and-true methods developed by the Stanford Research Institute and the Army's INSCOM program, revolved around the ingestion of research substances that made the remote viewer practically a vegetable. Many who were aware of his work felt that since the method rendered him almost catatonic at times (at least in the early days before he'd learned to function with the drug's boundaries), it had very little merit as an applied intelligence gathering tool. The novelty of his discovery was soon forgotten. In its place his colleagues had moved to distance themselves. It was as if he had cut a path through his mind into a different level of awareness and was stuck there. Within an hour of taking his usual dose he would move through the uncomfortable emotions of paranoia and the useless rooms full of hallucinations into the EGG experience itself. He had learned to stay there sometimes for as long as a week without sleep by timing the ingestion of his doses and fasting, drinking herb teas and staying away from alcohol.

Journal Entry 1284: Cecil Miller

I have managed to convince the Stanley Society of the merits of my research for a multi-year research grant.

The Stanley Society is obscure enough and their research is essentially secret. But I have access to all the EGG-68 I need and a stipend for living expenses well into the next decade.

On top of my grant-funded research, I am also required by the Stanley Society to work occasionally on special assignments for several government agencies assessing the use of psychedelic drugs for intelligence-gathering purposes. This is very exciting. As a result, I have been instructed to travel to Columbia, Missouri, where a field agent on a special RV assignment will brief me.

Finally, I get the opportunity to put my talents to use!

Need to make sure I've got a thirty-day supply. Will transport in three glass vials marked as insulin.

I must note, however, that lately my trips have been somewhat disorienting. There is, of course, with EGG-68 the possibility of personality dissociation, even schizophrenia, and I must guard against that. Something strange is happening, though – I know that. I'm not sure what, but I don't have time to worry. I'm looking forward to this new test very much!

*

This is when things began to unravel for Cecil Miller. At first he thought he had just taken too much EGG. But halfway into a trip something snapped that he would never get back – not until he found his way to the source of his thoughts and uncovered what had popped into his mind and would not leave. All it had taken were the words, "Columbia, Missouri" and a 900-mg dose of EGG.

That night he packed his laptop, his drugs, and several changes of clothes, phoned his contact in the Stanley Society for instructions on who to meet, then left his apartment. It was a perfectly rational thing to do. He had stumbled on the discovery of a lifetime, and he had to see things through.

At 8:15 p.m. he boarded a bus bound west to Topeka making stops throughout Missouri. He figured he would never return to Chicago. Somewhere in central Missouri things were happening far away from the normal world that people lived in. This realization was both terrifying and fantastic. Someone was inside his mind talking to him.

CHAPTER 7

Jill Simpson sits in her living room listening to a mixed tape of Jeff Buckley songs drinking a decaffeinated Pepsi and smoking a cigarette. The couch has become a more comfortable sleeping place than her bed. She doesn't want to think about the murder case so she concentrates on the song that Buckley did with Patti Smith just before he died – "Beneath the Southern Cross." *"To be not here, but here, forsaken, equatorial bliss, walk through the callow mist, dressed in scraps, who walked the curve of the world...who grieves not anyone gone to greet lame the inspired sky."* Buckley only sings a small bit of backup, but to Jill it is one of the more haunting fragments of evidence that demonstrated Buckley understood the power of voice. Buckley had created in his short career - as short as Jimi Hendrix's - a handful of recordings in which song structure, melody, and the effect of vocalization had gone beyond what was sonically acceptable and expected. She'd had many a discussion with her son about that – so many years ago now. They'd listened to Buckley's pain and confusion, his shrieks and wails, the way he held onto notes and used his five-and-a-half-octave voice to thrust his entire soul into the listener's experience. It was uncanny. Only Hendrix and Elvis had been as gifted and magical. Her son had pointed out that the proof something was up with Buckley's talent came in reading his lyrics without listening to him. It was terrible to read Buckley's words. At times they were trite and derivative; he used fragments of literary allusion and what had to be throwaway lines from movies. At other times his poetry was disjointed and clunky. Reading his words, Jill felt as if he was struggling to appear profound and deep. And then she listened to him sing those same words and she was astounded by how he delivered himself into each syllable, managing, somehow, to transform what she knew was shit into powerful, moving emotional statements, vocalized emblems of promise and loss. Buckley was nothing short of a genius.

The tape shifts from Patti Smith to Buckley's perfect incantation on unattained love, "Lover, You Should Have Come Over," but thoughts of Elvis put her back into her detective's mindset. She knows that the murder isn't keeping her up. It's more the simple fact that a young man – a boy really – has died unnecessarily. She is too familiar with unnecessary death and too familiar with thoughts of young lives cut short. A palpable sorrow tries to enter her mind, but she fights it off by thinking through procedures for when she gets back to the office. She has to meet with executive staff and report on the crime scene and obtain permission to take on the assignment. There has been too much concern about appearances ever since the Elvis sightings began. There is also something else going on that she can't figure out. She can feel it in the air whenever she walks through the back halls where the executive offices are. It reminds her of the old days when she was just coming up. There had been a run of drug busts in the region that had stirred the backroom boys into a buzzing frenzy of whispers and abruptly ended conversations. Now it was back, but she had no idea what was going on this time.

*

Harris lies awake on the king-sized bed in his blue pastel room at 5:40 a.m. He's thinking about the extinction of silence. It is a matter of expectation really. Silence can only occur in our heads, but it's hard to get to now. There is too much going on in the world.

His glasses have slipped to the end of his nose. His swimming pool eyes are somewhat dazed and out of focus since he needs the glasses to see properly, and because he is still mildly drunk. A drone vibration from the window HVAC unit is all he hears, that and the persistent white noise whir of the squirrel-cage fan, the compressor hum, and the gentle slur of moving, dry, cool air flowing into the room.

Harris has only recently started drinking and smoking heavily. There had always been beer and cigars, but these days he maintains self-sedation with scotch or bourbon and simultaneously keeps his skin crawling with the souped-up nicotine of Marlboros. This pairing of stimulants is all he needs to maintain an edge for his projects and a general disgust for the world at large.

Divorce has a way of making even the most health-conscious male turn to self-destruction. For Harris, things were particularly tough. Vicki simply ejected from their life fourteen years ago. After three sleepless days of panic and badgering the cops, he got a call from her. She was in New Mexico. She'd had enough, she said, of his ridiculous job working for the Simmons Investigation Group and the risks he took hacking for them. She was tired of living with the clutter of machines and wires and dusty gadgets. He'd talked of going to law school or even starting a career as a journalist, but he'd continued to earn his living for more than ten years by putting the finishing touches on the demise of other people's lives for a glorified blackmail group masquerading as a detective agency. When was he going to get a real career? When was he going to stop with the childish games? She told him it embarrassed her to talk about him to old friends.

Harris had no idea when she had started making her plans, but for him the marriage began to end when he met Aaron Treestat's assistant, Janie. Strange, but he hadn't even been attracted to her at first – not really, not any more than he'd been attracted to other women. But *she* certainly was attracted to *him* – in a weird kind of way.

He had seen Janie off and on in the apartment building for a year. She seemed to work odd hours. Everyday at 11:20 in the morning he left his computers and modems and headed out of the apartment immersed in what was then an unexplained self-disgust. And there she would be almost every day standing in the lobby leafing through her mail, reading the paper, or just gazing out the window.

She was a bit short, with long, straight, ash-brown hair, bangs cut at eyebrow level. There was something unsettling about her, something about the eyes, the way she never seemed to look at him but was clearly aware he was near her. It was, he learned later, a function of being stared at all the time. He saw her at other moments of the day as well. On her way out one evening, dressed in jogging attire – a tight gray T-shirt and fluorescent orange shorts – she smiled at him and said hello. He liked the shape of her breasts. Turning to watch her walk out of the building, he noted her calves were muscular. She moved easily, like she had once been an athlete.

Several weeks later he was on his way down to the laundry room with a basket of white clothes thinking about how to track down his current assignment from Simmons, Reese Boysen, when she got on the elevator. Boysen had left his third wife in the lurch with two young kids and four other step-kids. He'd disappeared when it was discovered he owed local, state, and federal taxes of over three quarters of a million dollars for nearly six years' worth of cash business in the taxi industry. Boysen's wife was the client.

Janie was wearing a work-shirt buttoned to the neck, tucked into baggy black sweatpants. They were the only two on the elevator. Harris didn't say anything to her, mostly because he was considering various pseudonyms Boysen might use on the Internet and mentally ticking off server systems he knew could be accessed easily. But somewhere in the middle of his thoughts he realized she was staring at him and that the atmosphere in the elevator was thick with something he couldn't exactly put a finger on. He looked up as the door opened. She began to walk out, hesitated, reached into his basket of laundry and picked up a pair of his underpants. No one was in the lobby. She turned and looked at him, smiling, the pants dangling from her middle finger. It was not exactly a provocative moment. The pants were soiled with yellow and brown smudges in the appropriate places. If anything, it was embarrassing. She casually dropped the pants back into the basket. The door closed, and he went down to the laundry room with something new to think about.

After about fifteen minutes, once he had put the two loads in and started the washers, she came into the room. She looked him in the eyes. He felt numb from his waist down. There seemed no way to do anything except embarrass himself with a hasty departure.

But it didn't turn out that way. They were alone in the room. The washers were spraying hot water into the cotton fiber of his white clothing. She closed the laundry room door, slid the latch to the locked position, and walked up to him while unbuttoning her work-shirt. She wasn't wearing a bra. Her breasts, only partially exposed, held shadows unnaturally, her skin a dark, pearly translucence that made his neck twitch and caused a slight swelling, it seemed to him, at the back of his tongue. She didn't say a thing. He was helpless and felt his penis unfolding with desire. It wasn't a question of saying no. He thought of something he'd heard on TV: *"Women spend their whole lives looking for the right man to do it with; men spend their lives looking for any woman who will do it with them right then and right there."*

One hand went to a breast. The other he placed on her tummy and slid down under her sweatpants. She wasn't wearing underpants, either. She chuckled quietly, and then moaned softly against his chest. His fingers played a moment over the crinkled mass of her pubic hair, then moved to cup her full vulva. He heard her breathing stop. Parting her soft lips with his middle finger, he was surprised at how easily it slid inside and how warm and wet she already was. There wasn't much chance of his turning back. He brought the finger out, trailing it upward to find the flashpoint of her clitoris. It was tiny, but firm, and he imagined it under lights, smooth, pink-white, pulsing with the focus of all her nervous system.

Grabbing his head with both hands, she pulled his face toward her and more bit into his mouth than kissed, her tongue rolling against his inner cheeks and teeth, diving deep and pulling back in licking strokes of ravening, almost predatory hunger. Her taste was slightly acidic somehow and reminded him of roasted eggplant, but there was a sweetness under the tang, and that, mixed with the spicy aroma of what he would later learn was simply the way Ivory Soap interacted with her skin, suffused him with her sexual need. It was as if her desire were filling his mind through the wafting ghosts of her aroma and flavor. Her palms were dry and cool, and their contact with his half-grown beard and cheeks pulled him into another world, a world from which he would never return. He moved his hands now to her waist and stroked down over her hips, tucking inside the elastic of her sweatpants, and then out again.

"I want you to taste me," she said to him. "Do you want to eat me? My pussy wants you to do that. I want you to do that. I want your face sucking and licking me. I want you to make me come and tell me what I taste like."

She put her hand now between his thighs. "You're a bit hard, aren't you?" she murmured. "But are you hard enough? I want to sit on your face first and come all over you, but then I want to suck you hard enough so that we can…."

He started to laugh. His hands rolled down through her sweatpants around her butt cheeks, and he gently pulled her to him in a way that allowed him to pulse her weight against his right thigh. With even pressure, he rocked her up and down just slightly. She buried her face against his neck and let him stroke her body into his. He could hear a low moaning sound winding its way up through her throat.

Just as they began to find a good rhythm, she broke away from him and said, "Your wash will take thirty minutes. Let's go up to my apartment. I've got something I want to show you." He hadn't said a thing.

*

It was predictable. Harris didn't feel guilt really, just a sense of loneliness. He missed his wife Vicki's smells and the way she held onto him afterwards, rubbing her nails back and forth across his back, her legs wrapped around his waist, gently pulsing.

This was different. He still hadn't said anything to this woman. She rolled off him when they were through and lit a cigarette.

"I guess, I ought to tell you my name," he ventured.

"Mmm."

He waited, a bit stunned still at what had just happened. He thought how amazing it was that variation in sex and the new aesthetic of a strange woman could be so enjoyable. She'd been on top, of course, but still…she knew how to ride them both into the same point together. He'd enjoyed watching her at the end there, rocking and bucking on top of him, using her fingers, rubbing her swollen vulva with her eyes closed and her head thrown back, staring at the ceiling or into her own private vanishing point. Watching her so ecstatic was all it took for his own release, too. It had been a bit more enjoyable than he would have liked. This new naked body made him want to do it again.

"Frank Harris. Apartment 1245-C," he said, finally. The apartment number seemed appropriate.

"Janie Hawthorn," she replied, sticking out her hand to shake. "And, actually, I know all about you. You work for Simmons Investigation Group. You're a hacker of sorts."

"That's sort of it," he said, shaking the hand of this naked woman dangling a cigarette from her mouth.

"Mmm?"

"I usually end up stretching the legality of privacy issues. Doesn't feel quite right."

"For such little compensation, huh?"

"Yeah," he managed. "That, too."

"So, what's the big deal? For a married man you certainly know how to let a girl have her way with you. Why don't you just figure out how to use your skills for more money."

Harris couldn't say anything to that. He was wondering if he would be able to get hard again, that and whether she would tell him when it was time to leave.

"Your clothes will need to go into the dryer soon. You want to come back for more when you're done?" She rolled to her back and stabbed the cigarette out in the ashtray, yawned and stretched.

Reaching for his penis, she gently held it at the base with her fingertips and slid the condom off. She held the milk-colored sheath of latex in the air between her thumb and forefinger.

"It is in the smallest things," she mused, "that we find the best evidence of how simple and ludicrous we are. AIDs is such a phenomenal triumph of natural biology over the ultimate aspect of human consciousness: sex. How utterly humiliating it must be to have your desires dulled by such a small and hideous creature as this. This is like the skin of some generic hairless rodent. If I were a man, I would think this evidence of a feminine conspiracy. Before AIDs we had almost beaten God. Can you imagine how great life would be again if we could just figure out how to eradicate that fucking disease?"

She flipped the limp piece of latex skin across his chest into the wastebasket on the floor near the television stand.

"I work evenings myself mostly," she continued. "We could do this all day if you want. I knew it would be good. I also know your wife is a knockout. But I also know that she works long hours, doesn't she? You clearly don't get enough, 'cept maybe on weekend mornings if you're lucky. I'm not after an affair anyway. I just thought a good fuck would be a nice way to get acquainted."

He didn't know what to say. Ever since Vicki had started her work with Sherra Studios, he'd had to plan their evenings in advance in order to get her to bed before she would be too tired.

"How do you know so much about me?" he asked.

She sat up, leaned against a pillow, and stroked his chest. "It's my job. I work for *Midnight America*. The tabloid. I'm really only one of several assistants to the editor, but I'm trying to work my way into TV. This building isn't in Society Hill or anything, but occasionally interesting people move here. The landlord gets $200 a month to furnish us with new tenant lists. Judy Collins lives here sometimes, as well as Steven Farrah the environmental activist, and Art Carney's daughter. Then there's the sort of marginally interesting people. We get the names and a bit of vital information from your people's applications and then run the data. If you've done anything public or are connected with anyone famous, we'll know it. We also run a credit check (we get some juicy information there, as I'm sure you would know), and make up stories to get other information out of employers or whoever. In your case that would be Simmons.

"Sometimes," she went on, "actually, we're a client of yours. Mostly we use your company when we need special field muscle – like when we're trying to figure out how the FBI is staking out a prominent businessman, or why a local official has just purchased an expensive car. We do most of the computer research ourselves. Can't afford to have more than our own people know what our sources are, especially dicks. Can't trust you guys much from one day to the next, ya' know?

"A connection here between you and me, though is really coincidence. I just happened to hear of that work you did tracking down OJ's tax refund a few months ago and realized it was mailed from my address. Once I saw you and got the rundown from property management, I knew this would be a good meeting."

Harris was still thinking how she had rolled the word *dicks* around on the end of her tongue. He wasn't surprised by her paper's methods. Hers was basically the kind of investigative work he did.

She was silent for a moment. "How the hell did you crack OJ's financial records, anyway? Those were supposed to be in lockdown!"

He raised himself on an elbow and pulled her to him, thinking how perfectly her areola fit in his mouth. "Well, let me tell you," he mumbled into her warm sternum.

*

They kept up their meetings for a few weeks until the novelty wore off. Neither had any illusions. She was too bossy for him, and although the sex was good and she certainly took his mind off his growing sense of personal failure, it was more like going to the gym for a tough workout than satisfying a romantic need.

Harris found himself saying little in most of their conversations – and *feeling* little as well. It was something about her personality, he thought. She held him at a distance that was almost inhuman. It was like fucking some famous actress, he thought. He was beginning to wonder about new job possibilities, though.

"What does work for *Midnight* entail?" he asked one afternoon. They were eating a tuna and spinach salad sitting up after a long session.

"Treestat calls you up, says he wants you to look into such and such a person at such an' such a time. You go, take notes on what you see, maybe a couple pictures if you can, and then whatever you make up that's interesting you post and wait for him to approve it. Usually it's a hundred for a story that he doesn't use and a grand when he does. Two hundred and fifty for each photo, too. It's gotta be fast, though. None of this writer's block shit. He gives you a call at 2:00 a.m. more often than not, and you gotta have the copy on his desk by 6:00. Photos by 8:00. That's a.m.

"Can be serious money, though. If you're good, you can make over five thousand a week. If he likes your work, you get assignments daily and have a shot at a staff position. If you get a scoop yourself and it's something hot, you can negotiate better deals, too."

Harris was confused by how he was responding to this. It was sort of like going to bed with her. He felt nothing, but all of a sudden it seemed like the only thing he wanted to do.

"If you take a job, we probably shouldn't do this anymore, though," she concluded. "I don't want any sense of conflict with you. I'm kind of bored with our routines anyway. Maybe it's time for you to really turn it on with your wife. Hell, I'd fuck her."

He got up from the bed, put on his clothes and told her he would like to meet her boss. They kissed one last time before he left. The light in the hall was brighter than that in the bedroom, harsher. It was then that he saw it – the slight tightness in the lips, the eyes that refused to meet his, something about the way she clung to him for just that last moment. The alien attitude was a front. This woman was sad. There was more emotion here than she would let on. He could feel it. She liked him. And he kind of liked her. Little did he know that their relationship had just begun, and that each of them would be the source of some of the only warmth in the other's life for years to come.

CHAPTER 8

Coral Justine McGrey lives on her brother Buzzer's farm ten miles south of Fayette and about eight miles west of Columbia. It is actually her farm, too. McGrey Farms was run by their parents, their father's parents, and their great grandparents.

It is a small farm by modern standards at roughly 230 acres. The main house where Mother and Coral live is a white, two-story modified New England saltbox with a wraparound screened-in porch used to store tools, small machinery, old magazines, rusting metal furniture, cans of paint, sacks of cement mix, and several Gaylord boxes full of automobile, truck, and tractor parts. Coral's great grandfather originally built the house in the late 1870s. It has gone through countless repairs and renovations. The kitchen and bathroom were added in the early '50s by her dad. The porch was rebuilt in the late '70s just before his death.

The north corner of the porch is reserved for slaughtering dinner poultry and cleaning fish, with a waist-high plywood table rebuilt four times in Coral's memory and countless times before. Next to the table is a deep steel sink with exposed 5/8-inch copper pipe. A floor-to-ceiling shelf, perhaps three feet deep and eight feet across, holds every brand of brown, white, and gray paint sold at Harrisburg Supply for the past forty years. The McGreys inventoried this collection in 1996 and moved the lead-based cans to the top shelf.

Coral tried to get Buzzer to let her take them to the county hazardous waste drop, but Buzzer said he had use for them. They spread better, he felt.

The main working section of the farm consists of an eight-acre plot to the northeastern side of the white house, along with two old barns, one for cows, the other for equipment. There is also a new barn fenced in half – chickens on one side and geese on the other – plus a longhouse for ducks, and open space for parking equipment and trucks. On the southwestern side is Buzzer and his wife June's underground home with a parking area in front for his two Chevy pickups and her blue Camaro, along with the baby duck shack, and a final large, raised, roofed-in garage of sorts at the southern side for four tractors, the combine, and various pieces of equipment such as a mower, manure spreader, disker, field rakes, several hay balers, and a seeder that doubles after two hours of adjustments as a fertilizer spreader.

Fanning away from the central eight acres are four different forty-acre plots and several smaller parcels of land covered by trees, shrubs, and thickets of undergrowth. Up near the road, which runs the full western side of the property some one hundred yards from Buzzer's home, stands what the McGrey family calls the worker's cabin – a small shack constantly in a state of repair.

The view from Buzzer's kitchen window, the only exposed wall of his underground house, is of the baby duck shack, and then beyond that a tidy manmade lake stocked with catfish, blue gill, bass, sunfish, and several crappie left from when Buzzer's father first built the lake in the '50s. They'd fenced it in several years back when they expanded the poultry side of the operation. Buzzer was tired of dredging his fishing hole. It is a view Coral loves, especially in the summer when the trees are plump with succulent leaves and the cicadas trill during the day as well as the night.

Only one section of the major crop-producing portions of land is visible from the main house. Three of the four plots are off to the southeast. These are usually planted in rotation with corn, barley, wheat, or sorghum. They are separated by irrigation ditches and lines of sycamore, ash, and oak planted by the eldest McGrey when he arrived in 1873. Coral has come to love this view because he can often be seen there first – before he comes to her. Sometimes he stands on the road for as long as twenty minutes, making sure, she supposes, she is alone.

Buzzer, June, and Coral are having a hard time making things work these days. They weathered the worst times in the '80s by running a haymaking business on the side and with June taking two nursing shifts at the hospital whenever she could. They laid off all the workers except Jimmy and Dean who are two kids working for room and board so that they can learn about farming. Dean Belkin had nearly received a master's degree in agricultural economics from Cornell when he decided he wanted more hands-on contact with the land first. Jimmy Harper had planted trees in Oregon for a while after completing his MBA at the University of Illinois. He lured Dean away from Cornell after finding Buzzer and McGrey Farms.

In the '80s, Coral drove tractors and bucked hay with the men in the late afternoons. But more than two decades later things are different. Buzzer is one of the few farmers who hasn't sold out to Lucas Fancher's people. It isn't as if Buzzer doesn't know what he's doing. He has a master's degree himself in soil science from the University of Missouri and has applied most of the new organic farming concepts now in fashion. His crops are consistently high yield, especially the sorghum and wheat. He just can't compete with Fancher's investors – whoever they are. Every time land would go up for sale Fancher would outbid him for it. The McGreys are some of the only people in the area who still live on land they own. Fancher is practically the only one left to whom Buzzer can sell his haymaking services, and for reasons that are impossible for the McGreys to discern, Fancher has no need for their help.

Although she never married, Coral was raised to be a farm wife. Mother handed over her duties when Buzzer and June got married. Coral cooks breakfast and makes lunches for the men, runs the family garden, and oversees most of the livestock operations, including the marketing (though Buzzer does the slaughtering). She is also responsible for the poultry operation on the farm. Her first job when she was growing up was to collect and clean chicken and duck eggs. When she turned ten, her father bought ten geese, and she became responsible for their eggs as well. A year later, the geese had multiplied to twenty-nine, and he gave her the new job of feeding and watering all of the birds as well as collecting and cleaning the eggs.

After their father died, Buzzer decided to take the life insurance money and invest it in upgrading the poultry operation. They added a new barn, refurbished the long house where most of the ducks were kept, and built automatic feed and watering troughs in both buildings. They also bought 500 new chickens, 50 new geese, and 800 baby ducks. In all, the poultry population on the farm is now approaching 5,000.

June was the only one on the farm who felt they were being a bit hasty. As a nurse at Boone County Hospital in Columbia, she always maintained she didn't know much about farming. But the truth was she wasn't fond of the animals. It was the ducks mostly that spooked her. She didn't like the sound of them at night, and she didn't like the way they all went silent and looked at her with their faces turned so that one eye could watch when she walked into the barn. The geese were just plain mean and the chickens were stupid, but the ducks seemed to have a group consciousness that was spooky.

Coral is fourteen years younger than Buzzer, but at thirty-six this doesn't matter much anymore. Her brother respects her knowledge of poultry and knows he can count on her to hold up her end of the operation. He does worry about her, though, because she isn't interested in marriage, nor is she interested in men as far as he can tell.

She used to tell her brother that she saw different colors coming off people like fogs. She knew how they were feeling by their color. Red and orange meant they were thinking deeply; blue and purple meant they were happy; yellow was for anger; and green meant they were dangerous somehow.

Coral also told her brother that occasionally she knew something was going to happen before it actually happened. Usually, it was a vague impression that she only became fully aware of after the fact. Sometimes, though, things were more defined. The morning before their father died she begged him not to go into Columbia to a livestock auction. He went anyway, and on the way home he had a heart attack and crashed his pickup. Most of the other things she knew would happen were minor, and Buzzer figured it was just coincidence. Their parents were never really aware of most of her quirks, but her vehemence at the age of twelve about keeping her father from going to town had been very clear. After he died, Mother had grown somewhat distant from her daughter; their conversations became brief and surface level. Coral knew her mother found her odd and even a bit frightening.

Her sense of things about to happen and her ability to see colors emanating from people diminished by the time Coral was nineteen. These perceptions always seemed to be just under the surface in her adult life, and for the most part she figured she had it all under control. But she would always feel that she was different from others. It was hard for her to attract men because of this. It was hard for her to attract friends at all. She was happy on the farm, though, especially when she had graduated from high school and could work full-time helping her brother run things.

*

From the road she can look south and west across the fields to the shoulders of the bluffs rising above the Missouri River near Rocheport. She loves this view in both the winter and summer. It is the broadest vista around. In the winter she watches blizzards rolling in over the bluffs, snow and wind climbing from the bottomlands and western flats heading from Kansas City some 110 miles away. The weather comes up and over the bluffs in dancing swirls of serpentine silver carried by spinning white and gray winds, curtains of time locked and bent on covering everything in the distance. Sometimes she has hours, sometimes only minutes before a storm hits. From the bluffs it's a distance of over three miles.

She has always been intrigued when these storms come before the winds, when a shroud of freezing rain slowly takes out the distance and the horizon simply moves closer. Sometimes this will transpire over several hours and she'll become so lost in waiting that she feels the clouds are no longer moving and that she's being transported to them. On good days, she can hold this feeling until the rain strikes her face and the wind picks up and the world stretches back to its normal dimensions. But it is summer Coral loves the most. Storms scramble and howl across the distance like swirling dark animals consuming everything in their path. Claws of lightning lash at anything tall. Winds sometimes knock trees over and blow down fences and barns, even flatten young crops. She loves the violence and how the storms serve to humble the life her family leads out in the open. She loves, too, the way the clouds turn yellow and black and gray and foam up over hills and smell of ozone and earth.

Summers also bring heat ghosts with them, ripples of evaporative waves shaking and shimmering in the distance – no wind, just cicada and grasshopper sounds and humid white sunlight. She knows it's an optical illusion, but she feels a closeness to this weather effect even more profoundly than what she feels for the storms and wind that rip across the shallow valley.

In the pulsing, heat-filled days and the dense moist air, her skin crawls with sweat. She thinks often how wonderful it would be to walk around the farm naked, fully exposed to the bright sunlight, watching the heat ghosts off in the distance. She wonders what it would be like to lie against a bale of hay with her shirt under her naked back beneath the sun and the full empty pale-blue sky, a small pool of warm salty water filling her navel, while the open air humps all around her.

On this particular day she stands on the edge of a field several hundred yards from the house, gazing across the valley, feeling the long yellow grasses of the summer brush against her calves. The air is thick, and she wonders whether there is a relationship between its density and the heat ghosts. Her hair is the same color as the grasses–a burned, starchy blonde. Sweat soaked, it sticks to her cheeks and the back of her neck. Saltwater rolls in trickles down her chest. Across the valley she watches the grasses tremble beneath slight breezes. In the distance the hazy sky makes the grass liquid. She feels these lazy motions move through her mouth then roll down the back of her throat. She sticks her tongue into the air and moves slowly, wading through the tall grass up to the road and then across the hot concrete to the embankment on the other side. The heat ghosts are shining and glowing, sparkling. She wonders if she is the only one who sees these mirages this way. Trembles run through her starting with her eyes and forehead, working their way down her spine and through her tummy, between her legs, and then down to her bare feet.

She has waited a long time. Tonight is the perfect night. Everyone has gone to town. She's by herself until around 11:00 when Mother needs to be home so that she can get her sleep. Coral wonders if he will come. If he does, they will have nearly five hours together before he has to sneak away.

She moves back across the road and through the dogwood, crosses the sloping field, and heads down the path to the houses. She knows who he is, or seems to be, and knows, too, that it's a near impossibility that he would be interested in her. Sometimes she wonders if she's losing her mind or just dreaming a very heavy, realistic dream.

It has been going on for some time now – nearly two years. He is much older than she is. He usually leaves in the middle of the night after she falls asleep. This is why the idea of it all being a dream occurs to her. She also wonders how real this is because she has not yet fallen in love with him. She knows, in fact, she never will, though she finds that her desire for him can consume her if he stays away too long or if there isn't enough time for him to satisfy her. But she doesn't love him.

He says little about what he does with himself, where he lives, who he is. He knows Lucas Fancher, though. And he knew her name when he first showed up. He knew he could step out of the woods that evening two summers ago as she turned to walk back to her truck and simply smile at her and she would trust him. He asks her questions about what she thinks, what it's like for her to be lonely, tells her she is beautiful, shows her how to skip stones across the pond. They built a dam once on the tiny creek out of rocks and twigs and mud. They met there two more times in the early fall before finally making love.

After that, he would show up at the farm when she was by herself in the evening. He has a strange sense of when to appear. But then, he has to. If she isn't crazy and isn't dreaming, he is, somehow, some way, Elvis Presley.

His hair is long and gray, the sideburns are gone, he looks to be in his early sixties, but could be as young as forty or as old as eighty. He wears black jeans and flannel shirts covering pocket T-shirts. The body is a bit different than it appears on the VCR. The hands and arms are more delicate, he seems a bit shorter than she would have thought, his eyes smaller and closer together. But it *is* him. It has to be. Either that or she is consumed by something she has no control over. She thinks a great deal about insanity when he is not with her. Not that she's worried about her mental state; she is just curious. Do people know they're delusional when they're crazy, or is that why they're crazy – that they don't know they are confronting illusion and tricks?

Occasionally, he says nothing to her the whole time they are together. They walk or sit by the creek or stand in empty fields looking at the night sky. Sometimes they don't make love and he simply holds her and buries his face in her hair. Sometimes he cries. She feels his quiet sobbing, but says nothing. She wants to ask him who he is, wants him to tell her what is going on, but she's afraid that it will ruin everything. So she just waits for him and fights the idea that she is crazy.

After a little more than a year and a half of this the sightings started. She reads about them first in the *Tribune*. He has been seen at a revival meeting outside of Rocheport. The references are vague. No one has taken a photo. He sat through most of the service and left when people began to stare. Several weeks later some teenagers saw him walking on a road at sunrise just after he'd left her. Two days later, a local radio talk show spent an afternoon on Elvis sightings and more than thirty people called in saying they had seen him on and off over the past ten years, since just before the Great

Recession. One woman called in and said that her daughter claimed to have had sex with him.

He came to Coral that night but she didn't ask him what was happening. He was somewhat distracted and more quiet than usual. He told her he would be back the next Tuesday night, but he never made it.

*

The Sunday before Elvis was supposed to return to Coral, he showed up at the revival tent again, this time going up front to ask for a miracle. The crowd was already in a state of intense fervor. His presence was not surprising to anyone. He said he wanted to atone for his sins and bring the Lord back unto himself. His voice thundered through the PA. People began to go into trances and speak in tongues. He begged forgiveness. He sang the opening lines of "Amazing Grace." The tent went still with shock. The voice was *the* voice, this was *the* one, it *was* Elvis. He left in the confusion.

It is front-page news for the *Tribune* and the *Missourian.* By Wednesday afternoon it also makes some of the national tabloids. The person who gains most by this is the Reverend Montgomery Sumter. He had simply been running the Christian Witness Church, a small, semi-profitable nonprofit, when all of a sudden his membership doubles and there are TV crews from LA and New York filming him and interviewing him. With no real photo of Elvis, Sumter is the next best thing. His face is all over the front pages of *National Enquirer*, *US Watch*, and *Midnight America.* Headlines read: "Preacher Calls Elvis from Grave!" and "Elvis Chooses to Testify" and "Elvis and the Holy Ghost."

Sumter has no illusions. This is his moment. In less than twenty-four hours he comes to understand personally how rumor has become the main form of entertainment in the country. Once articles are printed about you, you only have two choices: either you add and embellish on the myths, or you deny everything and claim no comment. The easiest thing, and the most profitable, is to become part of the fiction. Fiction as truth is what people have always wanted anyway. It isn't even a moral dilemma. The truth can ruin the hopes of millions. The truth is never as exciting or fantastic as myth. It's journalism's job to put zip into life.

Yes, he tells everyone who will listen, he has been in contact with Elvis for years – has helped hide him actually. Elvis has been his inspiration, and, truth be told, helped him found the church. It was originally Elvis's idea to call it the Church of Maternal Witness. Elvis had come to Sumter for help contacting his dearest mother. No, he had not died. He simply wanted to have time for peaceful prayer and meditation on the Lord. Elvis was convinced for a while that he was the Second Coming.

Sumter was beginning to wonder if his buddy wasn't right. Elvis tells him he is sure that his mother, who visits him in spirit every afternoon, is the reincarnation of Mary herself. They spent days discussing the theological implications of breaking the news to the world. Sumter convinced him that no one would believe them and that they might also assume he was an impostor. Or worse, if people did believe them, then Elvis would have to return to public life.

This quieted him down, points out Sumter. He tells interviewers they had moved toward a mutual understanding. Sumter would protect him and provide spiritual counsel as he grappled with the metaphysics of religion. Gradually, though, Sumter helped Elvis come to terms with the fact that he wasn't the Second Coming, that he was, simply, Elvis – and a lowly sinner like the rest of mankind. This lasted for almost six years, said Sumter, until Elvis came to understand the power and importance of public testimony.

They discussed the matter endlessly. Sumter advised strongly against public exposure. After all, he was supposed to be dead. The teachings of the church were too strong, though. In short, the preacher had no idea his friend would reveal himself to the world. But now that he had, Monty Sumter can only say that he is relieved to talk about this most fantastic of confidences with the rest of mankind.

This is the story Sumter tells the tabloids, anyway.

He has just finished editing copy for a new brochure and website that will finally put initiation dues in his membership requirements.

Anyone can attend revival sessions, but only members can bear witness and be saved. It is the will of the Lord that only people with commitment be allowed to use their faith as a means of salvation - $795 annual dues and then $20 per session for members and $50 for non-members. He runs the numbers on his calculator: 300 members times $795 plus about 200 people per show, times $20 and another 100 non-members times $50 comes out to almost $700,000 a year if he does 50 shows a year. And that's with things going the way they are. He figures the $700,000 is guaranteed – it could possibly be closer to $2 million if he plays his cards right and focuses on marketing and periodic attendances by *The King.*

All he needs is an Elvis – and Branson, Missouri is a simple phone call away. It had been too easy.

CHAPTER 9

The only time Lucas Fancher is guaranteed solitude comes in the early morning just before dawn. It was hard to train himself to get up earlier than everyone else, but it was worth it. He cherishes the quiet and the time to think. Fancher has a very important job from sunup to sundown and this is the only time when he can reflect without interference on exactly what they are doing and why he is helping them.

Kennedy's assassination came just three weeks before his 21st birthday. The insanity of Oswald and his subsequent shooting by Ruby moved Fancher close to despair. But Lisa's death the day after Oswald's murder put him over the edge.

They'd met just six months before. She came from a prominent Monroe County family. Her father had been press secretary for Senator Stuart Symington and had worked on Kennedy's campaign in Missouri. Lisa was more in love with politics and more filled with a sense of mission than any girl he had ever met.

Fancher grew up with Harry Truman's picture in his mother's kitchen and had seen Truman five or six times when he took his famous trips across Missouri. As the state's favorite son, Truman made the office of President and the sense of national politics a reality to most of the people in Fancher's rural community.

I would like to receive information about:

- ☐ The Fellowship Community
- ☐ Becoming a Community Member
- ☐ Becoming a Co-Worker
- ☐ Volunteering

I would like to contribute to:

- ☐ Maintaining and Refurbishing Buildings & Grounds
- ☐ Fellowship Community Elder Fund
- ☐ RSFF Community Co-Worker Fund
- ☐ Scholarship and Otto Specht Program
- ☐ The Tulip House purchase

Please make checks payable to R.S.F.F.

Name: ______________________________

Address: ____________________________

City, State & Zip: _______________________

Phone: ________________ Email: ________________

Kennedy, though, had been *his* President. Fancher was too young to vote, but the man gave him a sense of hope and commitment to life that led him to enroll at the University of Missouri when he was nineteen with idea of becoming a state senator or even a congressman. Back then, Fancher's life was close to perfect. He saw now the naiveté and the innocent hope. Being a hick with a social conscience would probably have led him to booze or Jesus in the end. Then came November of 1963. Life would never be the same.

Lisa was on the way home to her parents for Thanksgiving when her car hit a patch of glare ice and careened out of control into an oncoming truck. Accidents of such magnitude made it easy to change the course of one's own life.

After that there didn't seem much point in turning twenty-one. The only good thing was that he could drink legally. He took advantage of this new privilege for nearly twelve years. By then his old personality had been shed completely. He possessed a masters degree in agricultural business and was just finishing the process of getting a real estate license. He suffered two bouts with venereal disease and eventually got a seventeen-year-old girl pregnant. It was 1975. He told her he would drive her to Kansas City for an abortion, but at thirty-three he would have nothing to do with her if she wanted to keep the baby.

Fancher understood now that he was testing himself – and her. How divorced from the world could he get? She was a great lover for a kid, but he didn't need love or commitment.

How simple life could be when other people made decisions for you. She opted to have the baby and went to live with her sister in Richmond, Indiana. She knew he was testing himself to see how far his disgust with life could be taken. And with a baby in her, she knew that it could be taken into eternity. Once the line was crossed, the world could always be in an infinite, directionless haze one simply had to endure. She knew this because the decision for or against an abortion was hers. She looked at Fancher, watched him, listened to him, even smelled his breath in the morning, and knew that she did not want to end up where he was. Having the baby was a way to get rid of him, but it was also a way to have something important to hang on to, something real amidst the dark clouds that Fancher brought with him.

Sitting on the porch with the soft moist morning air hovering around him, he thought back to that time in astonishment. His daughter appeared one day when she was fourteen and stayed for nearly four years until it was time for her to move on. He managed to hide the truth about the compound from her while she stayed with him, but it wasn't easy. They'd lived in one of the smaller houses on the property. He did most of his work while she was away at school. The group gave him plenty of leeway there. Strangely enough, she was as important to them as she was to him.

They'd be waking up pretty soon now. Jack was always the first. He liked to sit under the sycamore on the first hill with his clipboard and pad and make up his schedule for the day. Norma would follow soon. She would take juice out to Jack and sit with him, watching the sunrise in the distance.

It looked like they spoke to each other sometimes, but it was hard to tell because they shared a way of communicating in just a few words and they had both become so quiet and sad. Their dream just wasn't going to happen, and they didn't know what to do with themselves after more than fifty years of planning and scheming.

The Brothers would appear just after sunrise and spend the next hour going in and out of the house trying to wake Janis and coax her out for voice exercises. Croach and Whack usually stayed in their unit all morning, writing or meditating in unison. Everyone had been pretty surprised by how well they got along. Whack was opposed to bringing Croach in from the beginning, but the Brothers did it anyway. Whack's opposition provided them with a better challenge than just fooling the public; they were defying one of the residents. They knew they had Jack's support, so there wasn't much Whack could do about it.

The Brothers had come in to the compound that night whooping and shrieking that they had pulled another one off while they hauled the bag out of the back of the Willies. Their boots were covered in mud. It had been raining hard all the way back from Louisiana, and they had to get out and push the jeep several times.

Today is different though. They are each worried that they might not be able to revive this one. He is the most important so far. Everyone is hopeful, no doubt, but they know the risks. And this time it means so much to all of them.

Having his quiet spirit in their midst has become very important ever since Jack and Norma withdrew. But Jack pointed out two nights before as they waited for the headlights of The Brother's truck to come into view on the bluffs to the west, that it was a good test of their collective power. They hadn't done anything truly audacious since the summer of 1977.

It was past 4:00 a.m. when the first sparkle of headlights appeared on the horizon. Fancher was worried by the direction the truck seemed to be heading and how the lights flickered. Why weren't they coming in through the tunnels? It was as if they didn't know where they were going. The others didn't say anything, so he figured everything was okay. Sometimes it worked that way. There was only so much he could understand of what they were doing.

The group mind thing would always spook him. The silences that sometimes lasted whole days filled him with both dread and awe. He was, after all, privy to a kind of magic – even if he couldn't participate in it. Telepathy had to be magic somehow. It was, anyway, in Fancher's mind.

The strange thing was that no one talked to him about it much anymore. It was just an accepted form of communication. So it wasn't like he had any evidence that it existed. The only real proof was this kind of prolonged absence of sound throughout the compound – that and a poignant sense of loneliness he had long since come to accept. They were there, he could feel it, but they could only be with him when they weren't with each other.

*

Jack instructs Janis to go into the storm cellar and pump the power several times to let the Brothers home in on the location. Whack and Croach feel this is another example of his changed disposition but keep silent. He is still their leader. Everyone knows the whole thing is risky, but they also know that Jack has a better idea than any of them about their next steps.

The bag feels so light. Johnnie, the latest arrival and still trying to shed most of the blues licks he'd taught himself over the years, asks Janis if it might be possible that no one is inside. She just smiles conspiratorially and says, "They drained him of just about everything wet, and he wasn't too big to begin with. He can't weigh more than fifty pounds now."

Johnnie accepts this and fights his desire to peak in the opening. He knows the procedure even though he's only been there for a little over a year.

"Man, we couldn't tell where the fuck we were going," laughs the smallest of the three brothers as he slaps Johnnie on the back. His face is broad, his lips full, his nose is wide and flat. He is dark-skinned, half African, part Irish and part Native American. His eyes seem to glow in the darkness.

The stocky one and the skinny one with the full beard and wire-rimmed glasses come out of the truck and move to the back without a word. They want a look at the bag, too. By this time everyone is crowded around in the darkness.

"I hope this works," says the stocky one.

"You been saying that since we left New Orleans yesterday, Jim!" says the short one, laughing.

"Yeah, well you know what happened that one time." says Whack.

"Fellahs," says the one in the glasses, "how many times do we got to visit that? She made it, didn't she? She knows she fucked it up. But she made it and now she's fine, 'cept for that one thing."

"Yeah, well, that could have been avoided. You weren't here yet. She didn't quite have what it took, and we should have known that."

"We had no idea that she was on Quaaludes, brother. It was just one of those things. It's not like she goes back all the time. It's just when we need her to. It was a blessing in the skies."

"Yeah. So...what do you guys say? Should we get on with it?" says the short, dark one, eyes blinking like a tiger's. They call him JJ.

"Johnnie?" says JJ. "You been practicing that stuff like I showed you?"

He looks over at the kid, eyebrows raised in gentle recognition. They all had the same kind of problems before they got here: drugs, alcohol, crime, an inability to figure out if life is for the present or the future.

The tall, thin one adjusts his glasses and says, "Yeah, you know JJ's right, chaps. It's time to jam. Let's start out with something easy and see how the kid has progressed. Janis, while we warm up, can you get the tea ready? We need to be in full sync if we're going to raise the dead."

Fancher lets himself consider then that Miller had not been there waiting when he'd driven by the McGrey farm. But he knew Miller would end up there eventually – at least, that's what Jack had said. With any luck, Miller would also be in Coral's bed.

Everything was going according to the plan, then. The policewoman, Sergeant Simpson, was investigating the murder. Miller had stumbled all the way from Chicago. The reporter had the perfect balance of cynicism and curiosity, and the boys in Washington were getting antsy and on their way out here. It was perfect.

Still, something told him to be careful. But then, something was always telling him that.

CHAPTER 10

Over raspberry pancakes and ham Frank Harris reads about the homicide with mild interest. He is also thinking about how long he'll have to wait to get a drink, and is still trying to control his anger with Treestat for this inane assignment. He hears talk about the murder around him but doesn't pay much attention. This is just more proof that he has been sent to a backwater town. In Philadelphia there are sometimes three murders a day. Instead, talk of murder draws him into thoughts of King Jones's suicide.

After struggling to get an interview with the singer for nearly a year, the handlers finally gave Harris fifteen minutes during the intermission one night. They talked quickly, Jones waiting for the questions as he drank from a bottle of water. Harris thought he could do the whole thing without being personal. He prided himself on his ability to maintain distance from his subjects. But the performer had proved to be too much for him. The mixture of shy boy and intelligent, world-weary man was confusing. Jones had a quiet confidence and charisma that was disarming. Harris had planned to ask about the breakups with Lisa Ann, the supposed secret child, Jones's take on the new book out by Bertram Waters, the kid who had brought the first pedophile accusations against the star. But Jones's vulnerable quiet was far too powerful.

When Harris walked in, the singer's newly tattooed arm was exposed. It was the caricature of Jimi Hendrix from *Axis Bold As Love* with a red tear sliding out of the eye. The cobras, Hindu deities, Mitch Mitchell, and Noel Redding were missing. It was just Hendrix's head and shoulders down to the multi-faced and bearded Shiva emblazoned on Jimi's belly. The right hand was raised palm out, thumb and forefinger holding an orange guitar pick. Beneath the Shiva image the caption read, "I'm the One Who's Got to Die When It's Time for Me to Die, so...."

"What comes after the so?" asked Harris.

"Hmm. You should listen to the song." The voice was eerily calm and confident.

"Lots of people getting tattoos these days."

"Yeah. I'm following a trend." Laughter, like an inside joke.

"You like Hendrix?" Harris knew the answer, but he needed to start somewhere.

"Yeah. I saw him once, when I was nine."

This Harris didn't know. No one did. He scribbled away. He'd gone through a Hendrix phase at Penn. "A lot of sexuality in his guitar playing," Harris offered.

"Not really if you compare him to me or Madonna or McKenna Joombs. You ever see Madonna when she was younger? That was sexual."

"I never saw her." Harris had seen her many times.

"Well, if you didn't, you missed nothing. Music isn't about sex, it's about aesthetic. Somewhere in there is sex, but that's only part of something bigger. That's what Hendrix was doing. His was full chunks of sex and groove and thought and utopia and the whispers of everything that could have been but didn't become true." More informed laughter.

Jones raised the bottle of water to his lips and sucked on the small opening. He smiled slightly, aware of the effect of this statement.

"Hendrix also talked a lot about death," Harris offered.

"Not really. He talked about other lives, different worlds. This tattoo marks one of his only real references to death. I'd say it was more giving the finger to everyone who thought they knew what life was about."

"So, is that why you wear the tattoo?"

Jones covered it with his hand and reached for a robe hanging on the back of the chair. He seemed embarrassed. He put on the robe.

"I don't know why I wear it," he managed after a few seconds.

"Your music is so clean and straightforward, so little real violence or anger. More spiritual, maybe? Do you feel any affinity at all with what Hendrix was doing?"

"Hendrix was Hendrix. I'm me. I try to make my music go to the same core as Jimi's, but this is a different time. He wasn't really doing what I do, anyway. His was all just a reason to play open-ended, to express himself perfectly with the guitar. No one had ever done that before, you know. He could have been a painter or an actor or even a politician and he would have had the same effect on our lives. He just happened to find the guitar first."

"Do you think he was murdered, as people now believe?"

Jones smiled. "He said '...let me live my life the way I want to.'"

"When?"

"After what my tattoo says. After the so." Jones's face became serious here, almost angry. "I think he was fed up with everything." he continued. "All the same shit I gotta deal with. And I think that drugs gave him too clear an eye into life. So much beauty in *Little Wing*, so much frustration in *Manic Depression*, so much pure wishing in *Bold As Love*. It was sort of like he was trying to do with sound what Picasso did with paint or what Faulkner tried to do with words. But the thing is, what artists try to do, the ones on the edge, that's only possible if you're outside of time, and only a god can be outside of time, that or someone beyond the will of God. *The* God you know, anyway..."

"So, you believe in God?"

Jones took another swig of water. "There's a lot going on we don't understand," he finally said. "Sometimes I feel like I'm supposed to...." He stopped and waited. The door opened and the sounds of the concert hall floated into the room. Jones froze for a moment. A look of fear crossed his face. Terror, really. Harris followed the gaze.

In the doorway stood Astro, his bodyguard - five foot seven, maybe 280 pounds.

"King, you got five minutes." The bodyguard's gaze dropped to Harris and a slight sneer crossed his lips. Harris felt that he could smell the fear in the room. What was going on with this gorilla and Jones?

"All right, Astro."

"You okay, boss?"

Jones answered quietly and with his patented high, thin voice, "I'm fine, just tired." Harris realized he hadn't used the voice during their entire talk.

"Soon. Okay?" said the bodyguard.

"Sure."

Jones turned his attention back to Harris. He put up his hand and shook his head back and forth. "No more questions."

Harris closed his notebook. "Okay. Sorry." Jones shook his head again and let a chuckle roll from his throat. "You're going to stick around for the end, aren't you?" His voice was shaky.

"Wouldn't miss it."

"Well, why don't you stay backstage and get a close-up view. I'd like to talk more after, but I probably can't because I'm going to be very busy." With that he got up and took off his robe. As a man of nearing fifty, his physique was still remarkably young. For one moment his face was caught by the golden light in the room. Harris was startled to see a smudgy black tear suddenly slice through the singer's thick eye shadow.

In his androgynous voice, Jones said, "Thank you for your time, Mr. Harris. I hope you like the rest of the show. I've got a surprise in store for people. You didn't really need to do this interview. Whatever I say is just my thoughts. What I really am is what I do out there – on stage."

*

Journal Entry 1311: Cecil Miller

An image comes to me sometimes when I'm deep into listening to a song. A black sock and a white sock are spinning back and forth in the air, swirling around each other, locked in a battle of dominion. Whose direction will win? All in a singular universe where there is nothing else that may be seen save a background pool of bright golden light and the sound of music thumping madly, the two socks, yinning and yanging back and forth in time to the music.

Slowly, as the music washes over me and loud guitars twang away on top of syncopation and thundering bass, a shifting glissando of keyboard swinging through everything, the socks change form and shape, morphing into two tadpole-like creatures – catfish maybe, coated with primordial fluids, but still beating out time. A white catfish and a shining indigo-black catfish arguing about which of them shall have dominion over Time in my head. Back and forth, up and down, in and out. It's the struggle. Time in the rough air of the mind.

Something physical or mechanical in my brain is actually working up this set of images, even though I know I'm just sitting in my living room, eyes closed, no longer sure if I'm even breathing. An actual functioning set of cells projecting this hologram into my mind. Calories burn off as these creatures go back and forth in their dance.

None of this should be surprising. We are, first of all, obviously hooked into time through sex. And sex is as animal and pure and natural an activity as there is – save for taking a crap and letting the laws of pressure and gravity evacuate our bladders in streams of warm, golden fluid. Life happens from the inside out and so does rhythm. It is primordial – linked to all of life, not just human beings. We can't escape genetics. We can only revel in finding new meanings for the codes of our parents.

This image of the socks and the tadpole catfish may not actually be a figment of imagination at all. It may, in fact, be the discovery of a mental mechanism. I may have stumbled onto at least the representation of that part of the nervous system that joins consciousness to the physical body and the linkage which melds the body and mind as one with time. Terence McKenna thinks he found it with the ampersand sign – maybe he just didn't get it exactly right.

It's not like rhythm should be seen as some supreme, human quality that puts us in touch with the gods or makes us immortal; that it's yet more proof we have dominion over nature. It's there in all animals in one form or another. Watch cats scratch themselves, watch fish swim, humming birds hover, or dogs dig holes in the ground. It's always there. It has to be. Rhythm is one of the many overlooked survival tools that allows organisms to function and survive. It is so basic and at the root of being an animal, we don't think about it. Or when we do, we keep it on some higher plane. And so we miss how intimate it is. Simple as that. We try not to think of our commonality with other animals. We miss the most important truths, for surely those mechanisms of instinct and pure mental connection that are as much a part of birds and reptiles as humans, are the most important and well developed of all cognitive processes available to us. It is, indeed, the inexplicably simple, ignored, and even belittled elements of existence that are quite possibly the ones from which it becomes possible to link ourselves with the cosmos and to each other.

CHAPTER 11

Jill wakes up on her couch in the late morning. She needs to get her meeting at headquarters over with before she hooks up with Stoddemeier at The Pancake House. After checking her cell phone for voice mails, she takes a shower and changes into her uniform. There are two messages from Baines. One is just to confirm that they had found nothing else of interest at the crime scene. The second is to let her know that the coroner report showed no signs of obvious drugs like alcohol or cocaine in the victim's system, but that there had been trace levels of several types of chemical compounds they had no data on. Baines notes at the end of this message that he found the absence of alcohol interesting, since the body had so obviously smelled like whisky. "I was gonna say something out there, Sarge," Baines says, "but there wasn't time. It just didn't seem like that body was as dead as you'd of thought. Not sure what I mean, but.... I don't know. That's all I got, I guess."

Wearing her uniform makes her think about her final choice of profession. Becoming a cop had been a clean break from her past, that was certain, but she'd always wondered what would have become of her if she'd stayed connected to the life she'd been stuck in. Through the worst of it, there had been something she felt she was linked to ever since that night with Heimer at The Dip.

She considers Bainesie's cryptic last statement. She, too, can't shake the sense that something about the body wasn't right. Her lack of forensics training and the whole way the CPD had taken budget hits since 2008 pisses her off no end. She'd managed somehow to rise up in the organization just as it was falling apart. Ever since the country had been waylaid by anti-government groups and the weird patriotism of the Tea Party, the CPD had just kept cutting funding for professional development every year, and were forced to outsource all lab work to St. Louis or Kansas City. She'd known the day would come when her lack of homicide experience would be a problem. Now here they were with little to go on except intuition and hunches – and weird toxicology reports that made little sense.

*

Cecil gets off the bus. Under the mid-afternoon summer sun he has a broad view of sloping fields full of emerald-green crops and a few small stands of trees. A veil of lavender haze softly covers everything in the distance. Two hours before, as the bus lumbered down Interstate 70 through High Hill, he had taken 1800 milligrams of EGG-68, a dose two times as strong as he usually took. He has turned himself into a homing device.

His vision has that vibrating feel to it, like his eyes are being massaged with electricity. His fovea is taken over by the new unrestricted flow of energy in his brain cells. In the distance, through the humidity, ribbons of watery light look like Technicolor shower curtains strung one after the other into 120-degrees of rippling physical distance, overlapping ever so slightly in rainbow flashes, glistening in a sun made for teenagers and movie directors – neon orange, fluorescent lime, metallic blue, purple, aquamarine, magenta and yellow.

It seems for just a moment that through a copse of trees and wedged in between two hills several hundred yards away he can make out the faint outline of a large white barn or warehouse. It seems, too, that he is looking at the torso of a vast beast covered with white scabs, sleeping in the shade of trees. This is the part of the drug that gives its allure, but it's also the most meaningless aspect of the experience. It is eye candy and he knows it's only necessary to wait it out. It will be gone soon enough. The beast turns back into a barn.

The rippling air is now screaming with neon navy blues, pollenous oranges, and white-yellows. As usual, part of him is instinctively frightened. But another part simply watches with practiced clinical interest. The psychedelic effect of the horizon scrapes up against his thoughts. Bright colors sweat out of the sky like currents of liquid electricity. Actually, this doesn't seem to be a hallucination. It is just the way things look. It's the wet Missouri heat that makes everything shimmer this way. He thinks about the paper he completed several months earlier: "Paranoia, Fear and Social Survival: An Examination of Psychedelic Isolation in the Twenty-first Century." The flight instinct is one of the most rudimentary aspects of consciousness – from insect to lizard to human.

He stands on a bone-white cement road. Long cracks with grass growing out of them like hairy fangs snake along the edges of the rural highway. Lumbering now into the distance, the bus is like a dying cow heading into the wavering panorama. He feels that bending over and licking the road might be a simple way to start the festivities, but he can't because his back is stiff from the bus ride and he is thirsty as shit. It's also interesting to watch the road rise and fall, weaving across the near silent farmland like a flowing finger looking for a hole all the way off into the empty horizon where the groans of the bus have trailed, the road sliding its way through the vehicle's ass and out its roaring mouth into the unknown and hopeful distance of all who remain onboard.

Between the road and the distant trees is a flat, balding field halfheartedly growing tufts of what he knows somehow to be sorghum. Across a fence nearly two thirds of the way into the field it looks like better-kept alfalfa. The field doesn't ripple like the distant horizon. There seems to be firm ground there.

He loves the way EGG turns the world into allegories. But no veils drop away from reality to reveal new truths, this he is sure of. The mind simply oozes into the open air, covering things with its energy, the world becoming a mold for the infinite possibilities looming up out of the dark, hidden life of emotion.

Wanting to get to firm ground where the undulating road and the scaly, electrified trees can at least be mediated in stereo, Cecil takes a step from the shoulder onto the concrete. Heat blasts off the pavement with thick-tongued hostility, stopping him dead in his tracks.

As if to say, "Where are you going, sonny boy?" the road and trees stop rippling for a moment and listen, wondering, perhaps, at the audacity of his movement. He fixes his feet together after two more difficult steps and roots himself to the road.

In the great, still distance a wooden door slams and he understands once and for all that the white building is probably a house. But the stillness is becoming nauseating. He realizes his perception of time is faltering, and he wonders then whether the door had actually slammed or if he is hallucinating into the future. He shuffles his feet, and the rippling effect of the road and trees starts in again. His sense of time starts up, too, because a figure, a woman, radiates through the trees and into the open field. She is coming toward him.

The June temperature is as powerful as an emotion. The woman walks across the alfalfa field, her hair is either short or tied in a bun. Her form does not waver with the surroundings. She wears a red skirt and a white shirt. Although it's hard to make her out in detail, still some 120-yards away, it seems that she is young, but she moves with the assurance of a woman who understands how she fits into the world. She is clearly walking toward him. He lights a cigarette and squints into the sun-whitened sky. Where is Fancher?

The woman slows for a few paces. She tries to make out who he is, then stops. Her body language says she is embarrassed, maybe a bit shy. Then she keeps moving in his direction but with less confidence. By the time she's fifteen yards off, he can feel that she wants him to be someone else. Her face seems disappointed, but she composes herself as she draws closer.

She appears pretty, with large eyes, tanned skin, and thin brunette hair which he sees now is tied back in a ponytail. But there is also something slightly odd about her appearance. Her nose is long and her cheekbones are pushed up more into the front of her face like two peach pits under the skin. She is very tall, maybe taller than him, and extremely thin, almost gaunt. He can't help looking at her chest as she closes on him. Her breasts are small. The shirt is open to the base of her sternum, and the usual rise of smooth flesh does not exhibit itself.

"You aren't who I thought you'd be," she says. It's as if they have met before, the way she begins talking.

He doesn't know what to say. She seems not to be bothered by his silence, putting her knuckles to her hips, walking down the middle of the dry, white road.

"What bus was that?" she asks over her shoulder. Her voice has a slight rural twang which is pleasing. The "what" sounded like "wuht." He guesses she's in her early thirties. He fantasizes about going to bed with her.

"Kansas City and destinations West," he manages a bit shakily. The drug's effect on social situations will always be a drawback.

She turns to face him. Or is it just to look in the other direction, the direction the bus lumbered some fifteen minutes ago? She is wearing dirty, red, low-cut Converse tennis shoes and short black socks. Her legs are unshaven.

In the sky he sees a black speck circling slowly through the air. With the heat, looking into such distance brings tears to his eyes.

"Is that a hawk?" he asks, feeling stupid as soon as the question comes out.

She doesn't turn to look. "Buzzard."

He nods, though she still isn't looking at him. He considers saying, it's hot, or that he likes her shoes, anything, but he just keeps nodding. He wonders again where Fancher is.

"I'm waiting for the duck man," she says, finally, but more to the hot landscape than to him. He notices now that cicadas and crickets are screeching and chirping in a jerky chorus. Every once in a while a grasshopper on the embankment off the road spreads its dry wings and floats across the tops of the tall grass, the black and yellow wings cloaking it with superhero grace.

He feels the silence between them spreading out across time, and realizes that no response to her statement might be viewed as an act of hostility. The seconds expand through the air. He is about to lose the timing for any response whatsoever.

"Duck man?" he manages finally, gasping for room, feeling the security of social discourse swell gently in his stomach.

"Guy comes every Wednesday with a case of duck eggs and a box of six or eight new baby ones. I love the way they peep. We're working on building up our duck business."

She looks at him and finishes with a smile – to herself mostly. He smiles back and takes a last hard pull on his cigarette, then stamps it out on the road.

"You got a spare?" she asks.

"Sure." He reaches into his breast pocket and pulls out the Marlboros and a pack of matches.

"Darn. I thought they might be Lucky Strikes," she says, genuinely disappointed but taking one from the pack anyway.

"Sorry," he manages. He thinks to make a joke, that if he wants to get high he wouldn't smoke Lucky Strikes a joint would be better. Lucky Strikes are strong and raw, like smoking iron filings. But the time spans out between them again. It's too late to make the joke. She lights up then hands back the cigarettes and matches. He looks into the distance while the trees continue to waver like the Aurora Borealis.

"What do you do with ducks?" he asks while she smokes.

"Not much, really," she replies. "They take care of themselves, more or less. I mean, about a quarter of 'em die, but that's that. You water, feed, and hay 'em; you keep things warm in the winter, pick up their eggs, watch 'em grow and screw and make more ducks...." She gazes in the direction of the metallic click of a flying grasshopper.

"Is that your farm over there?" he asks, pointing.

"It is," she says with a hint of pride.

"I always wanted to live on a farm."

"Yeah?" she half asks, half guffaws. He hears the sarcasm

"Sorry," she says. "It's just that I've heard that quite too many times from people coming out of cities - especially students from Columbia."

"I worked on a farm for several summers once...long time ago," he replies, trying to shake the power of the drug.

"Yeah?" she asks. He can't tell if she is interested or not. The cigarette and the empty space make her responses suspect. She owes him, since he's given her the smoke and they are alone together.

She coughs like a child and holds the cigarette between her thumb and forefinger.

"So, are you waiting for someone?" she asks, turning finally to look at him.

He realizes he's beginning to lose it. The EGG is thumping into his forehead. His bowels move around below his stomach. He needs to take a shit. The only logical thing to do is to ask her if he can use her bathroom. It will sound funny, though. He doesn't know what to do. She stares at him.

It starts to happen then. He just has to let it keep happening. He realizes he can read her thoughts if he just lets the language go. He concentrates on his breathing. It is a technique he has been using for years and he has nearly mastered it.

She continues to stare at him, then asks, "Uh, did I say something wrong?"

He slips out of it.

"No. I...." He pauses because he doesn't know what she has said. "Could you repeat the question?" She probably thinks he's crazy.

"You waiting for someone?" she asks gently. He likes the warmth of her deep voice.

"Oh. Yeah. Um, guy named Fancher? Lucas Fancher?"

"Oh." She says it with finality. "What do you want with him?"

"I'm not sure, really. It's a long story. I'm just supposed to meet him."

She doesn't like the guy. He feels this.

"Well, no one's really seen Fancher in months, maybe years. I was beginning to think he was dead. Or maybe moved on. Hoping, anyway. What do you want with him?" she asks.

"It's a long story. I called him from St. Louis a while back and he said to get off here and he'd pick me up." Cecil isn't about to tell her what really happened. He realizes then that he probably is crazy – seeing himself through her eyes.

"Well, if Fancher's coming here, I gotta see this."

Cecil doesn't know what to say. He truly has no idea who Fancher is. He just knows he's supposed to meet him sometime, somewhere in the area.

"Hey, look," he says, in control of himself now. "I've got no idea who the guy is, I'm just supposed to meet him here."

"No need to apologize," she replies carefully. "I actually don't want anything to do with him."

"Why?"

"I don't even know you," she says. "On second thought, I don't want to see him. I gotta go." She steps off the hot road back onto the shoulder.

"Wait. Sorry. I don't know him!" He realizes his concern is probably a bit too amplified.

"I heard you. You're supposed to be meeting him, but you don't even know who he is. So, how'd you ever get set up to meet him?"

"You wouldn't believe me if I told you."

"Why is it that everything about Fancher is weird?" she asks.

"Well, who is he? What's the problem?" Cecil knows he's about to be hit with another EGG rush. He waits for her answer and looks around for a good hiding place to squat and take a crap. There is a fallen sycamore with large leaves still somewhat green on the other side of the road. Probably out of sight from her house. The leaves are big enough to use for wiping, though they look a bit dry.

"Fancher owns a lot of the land around here. He wants our property because it's right in between two others of his. It's understandable, I suppose. But he's done some weird stuff over the years. And no one knows where he gets his money. We did some research about fifteen years ago when he was really putting the push on with us and he owned over 12,000 acres around here. He's just slowly been buying up other farms. It's a typical farmer capitalist thing, you know? Even bought up a bunch of useless properties the government buried missiles in years ago. We figure he's buying for some big company like Ag-On or American Earth or Colorado Growth Industries. But no one can tell for sure.

"What's really weird is the things he does once he buys a property. He does his damnedest to isolate that land from everything else. He re-fences – usually with electric fences and barbed wire. He levels most of the outbuildings and houses, plants huge new sets of trees and shrubs to hide things. In a few cases he's even succeeded in getting the county to divert roads off his properties. Couple of years ago they needed to put in a new stretch of Route A heading up to Higby near the Hungry Mother Recreation Area, and people say he actually paid to send a four-mile stretch in a bow, way west of the park, off his land and through some rifle range. I mean, it's pretty clear he's trying to hide something. He seems to farm it and all, but a lot of crop never even makes it to market, as far as we know. Seems like most of his work is performed at night. We've done some jobs for him ourselves, but no one I know can tell me what's going on. Some say it's dope, but we'd see that. We'd know. It's all just really weird.

"My main problem with him, though, is that he won't stop trying to buy our farm. He's been at it for years. Goes back to the early 1970s, actually. That's when he bought the Percie's and Duff's places, and when he made his first offer to my dad.

"Now things have gotten a lot worse. Our pond was kind of poisoned by a couple leaking barrels of insecticide the sheriff says was buried years ago up on the road. Runoff carried chemicals down into the water. The state did the cleanup, even gave us money to help with damages. Must have killed four or five hundred ducks, and we had to spend nearly four thousand dollars of our own money in the end to have the others tested and their egg production watched. Most people figured it started back in the fifties when there was a test station put in by the Army at one of their missile silos, but I don't think so. It was Fancher.

"And it's not like he's been doing all of this on the phone or in letters or anything. He used to stop by a couple of times a week just to piss us off and to take advantage of Mother's good neighborliness, and also, I think, her loneliness."

The woman stops here, flinching at the sound of a car in the distance. A series of odd images passes through Cecil's' head: a face he somehow knows to be Fancher's; a naked woman looking in a mirror, her face up close to the glass and looking down as if she's peering into another room; he is the woman. His breasts are small, his thighs thin, his skin the color of winter hay. Something small is moving behind him: a child. He has little feeling, but it seems someone is stroking the insides of his thighs. He turns to see who it is and finds a huge open space in full moonlight, men and women walking slowly to tractors and trucks and several enormous combines, starting all the engines up in unison and driving as if for a long journey in single file across open fields with their lights on. He has a strong sense that he is heading home, that he knows how to play guitar. Fancher's face comes back into view, a porch at sunrise, the sense of being the only person in the world, and awareness of pure silence, not a bird, not a cicada, not even the wind stirring the leaves with sound. He realizes he isn't breathing.

"You okay?" she asks, moving closer to him and looking into his face with concern. "You better sit down. I mean, it's hot and you're sweating all over. Jeez. You're really pale."

"I'm okay." he manages. "It *is* hot though...." His voice trails off as he looks into her eyes. He feels all of her emotions then. All at once. She is very genuine with them. There is nothing there to directly mask her concern. She is strikingly beautiful now. Something in her face is quietly charismatic, something sensual and self-confident, but wary and distant, too. There is also something hidden from him, something the psychedelic cannot touch.

She also feels his emotions and knows he is interested in her. She wants to pull her shirt closer to hide her chest, feels a tingle in her legs, senses something else in her mind just for a moment. Memories of lying on Elvis' jacket and the sensation of his warm weight thumping down on her give way to the feel of his fingers softly pinching her nipples, his mouth sucking into hers. She blocks these thoughts and turns to look at the house.

"I gotta go," she says.

His disappointment shoots through her like a grass cut. She is stunned. He senses this, too. He realizes that it is the echo of her sensing him.

She turns and heads down the embankment to the edge of the trees.

"Wait!" he calls.

She stops.

"Can I use your bathroom?" He feels foolish.

Looking back up toward the road at him, she considers for a moment and finally laughs.

"Sure. I guess Fancher will just have to wait. Why don't you leave your stuff up there so he knows you're around. He'll probably honk his horn anyway. We'll hear him. Put it over there behind that fallen tree."

He places his backpack and duffel bag next to the sycamore. Relieved, he comes down the embankment. As he gets close, she heads into the trees, a slight skip in her stride, her dress billowing in the hot summer wind.

Part III
Revival

"The machine that we built,
It would never save us, that's what they say.
(That's why they've not come with us today)
They also said 'It's impossible
For a man to live and breathe under water forever,
That was their main complaint..."

-Jimi Hendrix

CHAPTER 12

As Coral leads him to the bathroom through the living room, she bends over to pick up a magazine on the floor. He looks down her shirt. Her breasts and nipples in the gray shadows of her shirt seem to him extremely familiar, as if he looks at them every day and touches them, washes them in the shower. At the same time he knows he has never seen such perfectly mysterious breasts. They are shaped like small fruit, he thinks. They are freckled and warm. He knows at this juncture that he is beyond help. No matter how sacred his quest for understanding, he wants to be with her.

In the bathroom he sits on the toilet and tries not to let loose with too much sound. His bowels evacuate quickly. As is always the case with EGG-68, the stool is loose and watery. He holds his penis by pinching the skin beneath the edge of the glans and feels the relief of muscle relaxation as he urinates quietly against the side of the bowl just above the water.

He wipes himself and stands to pull up his pants. The penis is growing, he thinks, noting that being amused by something like this is not like him. A trembling warmth in his jaw and groin make it difficult to properly reposition his jeans. Am I cold with amusement? he wonders.

He wants to taste her and suck the center of her body. He can almost feel her hardening nipples between his fingers, the fleshy roll of her freckled breasts heaving against his palms. It's too much. Only the details of his assignment are being altered, not the assignment itself.

Leaving the bathroom, he finds her in the kitchen looking out the window toward the road. He moves close behind her, a bit to her side. The look on her face is somewhat obscured by shadows roaming the kitchen. He makes out a sort of sad resignation. But it isn't directed at him. When she finally turns to face him, her eyes seem to sparkle for just a moment, then she chuckles with her deep voice and leans into him. His hand falls to her waist. A thick, warm feeling courses through his body and their lips meet. His right hand travels up from her waist and inside the opening of her shirt. He lets it roam from one breast to the other and hears her sigh. Her nipples tighten. Against his eager palm, her breasts seem larger than he'd expected. Her mouth is taut and muscular, somehow, but delicate. Her breath is fetid from a day of sweating and working. But it's good to taste. He lets her take charge with the kissing and hears her breathing speed up. She inhales big gusts of air through her nose as he pinches a nipple then palms a breast. His penis strains against his jeans. One thing he's never done is have sex in a full-blown EGG-68 session. The exercise has never occurred to him. Her skin is surprisingly soft and he thinks about the chemistry of two epidural systems meeting.

Coral pulls her head back and looks into his face. She smiles. "I've never felt like this with anyone before. Not even him…."

He leans toward her and kisses her lips softly and carefully. His fingers continue to play with her nipple. She pulls her face away again and looks down at his hand.

"I want to go to my room."

He removes his hand from her shirt, unsure of what she means, then steps aside.

"No," she smirks. "I want you to come with me." She takes his hand and leads him through the living room and down a hall, past the bathroom to the last room on the right. It's a simple room – a single bed, a dresser, small table, and a closet. Overhead is a fan turning slowly. She closes the door, locks it, then finishes unbuttoning her blouse. He senses slight embarrassment as she removes the white shirt, and they catch each other's eyes again.

"You are strangely beautiful," he says. His eyes drop to her breasts. They are firm and long, like capsules, he thinks. Her areolas are puffy, swelling possibly with her desire. Her nipples are only partially erect, but he can sense how sensitive and full of lust they can become, how hard and tight.

There is no guile to her mouth, no seduction. But there is something else. Her smile is confident and sensual, as if she knows she could be a seductress but chooses instead to simply be a woman stepping into something she's comfortable with, something where she knows she will get what she wants. She unzips her skirt. He can tell she knows what he wants her to do. He sits on the bed to watch. "Your breasts are like nothing..." he says.

She looks down at them. "Nothing?" she pouts. "You mean, not very big," she jokes as she slides the skirt down her hips.

"They are so firm, and I like the way they stick out."

She shakes her head and offers him an exaggerated sneer. She stands now before him in nothing but white panties. He sees the rise of pubic hair underneath and a slight moisture stain. He lets his hands begin unbuckling his belt, his eyes moving up her lithe torso to her long face. He ponders the extreme need to release the pressure.

"No," she says stepping forward. "I want to undress you." She kneels on the floor and slaps his hand away from his belt. She is still staring into his face, her two upper teeth sliding back and forth against her lower lip. He thinks, "Nervously?" And hears in his mind, "Not nervous. No. I want you. I want you so much, but I don't know why I'm so worked up here. I've never felt like this. I've never...."

He leans back on the bed, watching her. She unzips his fly and he understands exactly what's going on. "There's more to telepathy than just chance," he thinks. "Telepathy?" he hears, and then she has her hand inside his jeans and is making sure there is no longer any pressure holding in his penis. "Telepathy? How about your cock," he hears. "I want it!"

*

In the ending pieces of daylight they lie on her bed smoking cigarettes. The smell of sex still fills the room, but they are finished. He watches the ceiling fan spin in slow motion, chopping streams of their smoke into layers of haze. The first cooling breezes of evening dance through the window, trickling across their exposed bodies. The vivid connection of their minds has been broken. He has only altered the details of his assignment, not the assignment itself.

*

It's over, she thinks. He was so much older. It wasn't the same as this one. She likes this man next to her. He is much younger. The connection was so much more direct. Words? In their minds together? It seemed more than just on her side. But it was hard to tell.

She laughs to herself and smiles at the ceiling. Men off the road. Strangers, phantoms, ghosts, hard flesh, wet flesh, sweat-warm flesh, what did her choice of these men say about her?

"That was something," she says.

"I didn't know it would be like that."

"How could you?"

"I'm a bit different, maybe. So are you it would seem."

"I want to know everything about you," Coral says, still looking at the ceiling.

"Everything?"

"Everything. Your middle name, where you were born, everything."

"Well, that's easy enough" he smiles. "My middle name is Jasper. I don't like it much. My parents named me for the town I was born in – Jasper, Wyoming. Cecil Jasper Miller"

"Jasper is very nice."

"I think it sounds terrible," he manages. "I go by Cecil J. Miller as a professional. That sounds okay."

He isn't used to talking about himself. He tells her about growing up in Hyde Park, his parents, attending the University of Chicago. It's done in halting sentences with long silences in between.

"So, what are you doing here, really?" she ventures.

He doesn't know how to respond at first. "It's a long story. And a bit odd, I'm afraid."

She smiles again into the smoky cool of the fan as it pushes slow air onto them. "Seems like everything about you and me is odd. But somehow I like it. Tell me." She nudges closer to him and puts her head in the flat spot where his shoulder and chest meet.

"I'm studying to get my Ph.D. in parapsychology. Do you know what that is?" The sex and his confusing emotions for her have flattened the EGG into a simple interest in things – deep, warming interest. She especially interests him. There is still something strong between them.

"Not really," she replies. "Something to do with ESP and psychic energy, I think."

"Yeah, well, that's part of it. Depends on who you talk to. It's really just the study of what we call the paranormal – anything that seems like it might be real but we don't have any scientific proof for, can't really directly perceive. ESP, faith healing, Carlos Castaneda and his conversations with Don Juan, ghosts, clairvoyants, wood nymphs, even. You name it. One of the guys I've taken classes with is studying the disappearing sock phenomenon."

"Disappearing what?"

"Socks. You know, what happens to all those socks that get lost somewhere between the time you put them in the washer and the time you take them out of the dryer. Parapsychology is the study of the weird."

"Like the *Twilight Zone* or the *X Files*." She tries not to laugh.

"Yeah, like that," he says. "But it's serious stuff. What we're doing is really just a branch of psychology and anthropology, since most of the phenomena parapsych looks at can be studied using the scientific method psychologists and anthropologists use – well, at least some of them – trying to unlock the hidden parts of the mind." He picks his head up to find her staring at the ceiling with her eyes closed.

She opens her eyes and giggles at the ceiling. “I’m sorry! It’s just that I can’t stop thinking about little socks with nowhere to go.” He smiles calmly.

“This’s why I don’t talk about what I do.”

She props her head on her hand and looks down at him. “No. Go on. I’m sorry. I’m just a little giddy, is all. I’m not sure I should tell you this, but you’re the first guy I’ve ever had sex with in the room I grew up in.”

“Hmm. Maybe you should have told me….”

“You didn’t give me a chance.”

“Okay, well….”

“Please go on. I’m sorry. I do want to understand. That was different, and I kind of want to know something about the guy who can make me feel, well, you know….” She waits, letting her smile turn from mirth to a reserved, patient interest.

“The difference,” Cecil continues, “is that we parapsychologists are usually attempting to deal with stuff that is beyond our ability to perceive direct effects for, so it’s awfully hard to be scientific. There’s two basic ways people look at things in the field. Some, the ones who get most of the easy grant money, are only interested in disproving things. Others are interested in proving things. They use statistical analysis, mostly. Only, it’s often harder because there isn’t much funding to study stuff that doesn’t make sense, stuff that’s hard to prove or disprove.”

“So, which one are you?”

“It’s been hard, really, to figure out – I’d have to say the provers. But I’m not a very good scientist, and I don’t like numbers. We operate from a kind of faith or intuition, really. My friends who study ESP have had profound moments of perception impossible to understand except as moments of mystical power. They feel they know that ESP is real because they have experienced it themselves. The task is to prove feelings. As a starting point, people began working with *déjà vu* experiences and the idea of synchronicity that Jung wrote about – the idea of coincidence. What they’ve found is that it’s mostly a matter of opening up your creative mind. But their studies all come from this original basic faith that ESP is real and that it can be understood. They can't prove much."

"So what are you studying?"

"Mine's sort of embarrassing to talk about."

He gathers himself for a moment. The truth would be better to tell her. Instead, he says, "I've been trying to understand the psychedelic experience. Do you know about psychedelics?"

"I grew up near a college town, remember? I mean, I didn't hang out with those people, but they spent enough time teaching us about that stuff in high school."

"Okay, fair enough. I'm younger, I know." He pauses and looks at her. She's waiting.

"ESP, *déjà vu*, stuff like that is all built into psychedelics, but so are a whole bunch of other things. What it comes down to is that it seems, when you're impacted properly by any number of a series of psychoactive drugs, that the mind can actually sort of leave the body through mediums like music, or light or even the raw power of, say, a truck engine."

"Or through sex?" She has a smile on her face.

"Mmm hmm." She's tracing her finger around his nipple, swirling into the nib and then reversing and gently drawing a spiral in ever-wider arcs until she intersects with his sternum. And then back toward the tiny center.

Her artistry is pleasant and distracting, but he wants to talk. "You know about the psychedelic experience, then?"

"No. I know about strange thought powers, though. I've had them on and off during most of my life. Sometimes when they're particularly strong they affect sex...especially the orgasm. I'm not sure what it is, though."

"Did something like that happen a few minutes ago?"

She thinks for a moment. "No. It didn't. At least not like that. With you it was just that I could sense you. I know you could sense me. That's easy. But something like you're talking about – you know, leaving the body, going somewhere else? That has happened before...with someone else." She lifts her head to kiss him.

"And what was that?" He likes the strawberry smell of her hair and her tobacco breath. *Someone else?*

"That, too, is a long and strange story. Why don't you finish yours first?"

"Okay. But it's all got to do with the psychedelic experience, and its kind of embarrassing talking about it. Most of this just loses meaning as soon as you try to put it into words," he says. "But there is definitely something there...something like a secret to human thought. It's so big and so undefined and so utterly basic to human experience that it's really hard to express. We don't even actually know what the question is yet, let alone the answer. And that's what I've been trying to do for the past several years."

"What does that mean?"

"Well...for starters it means I've been taking a lot of designer entheogens."

"Entheo whats?"

"Entheogen is another word for hallucinogen. It's less derogatory."

"What does it mean?"

"Entheo kind of means inspired or possessed. A lot of people say filled with God. Gen is just as you'd think."

"Generating?"

"Right. Or genesis. Coming into being."

"And, so, you're taking these entheogens? Hallucinogens."

"Yes. Hallucinogens. Psychedelics, I suppose. It's all the same. People changed the name and came up with the term over thirty years ago. Better branding, I suppose." He laughs. "I've been taking them for a long time. Scheduled, regular doses."

"You mean, like right now?" She moves just slightly away from him to see his face. Her finger stops circling his nipple and remains poised softly, just dabbing the tip.

The reaction registers with him, but he chooses to ignore it. So much has worked out between them over the last few hours. "Yeah, like right now. It's sort of weird, I guess." He waits.

She moves closer. "That's why I've been feeling what I've been feeling with you then," she says with relief in her voice. "You're latched onto something in me. There's no question about that. I don't do this with just anybody, you know. Hmm, so I just made love to a drug addict."

"Well, sort of. I'm not addicted really. It's just that I'm trying to figure something out." He's relieved by her humor and that she has re-initiated the affection.

"What's been interesting," he continues, "over this past several weeks, is that I've had this urge to travel here. Something has been pointing me to the middle of Missouri. At times it's like a voice almost telling me to come here." He pauses. "The voice has been telling me that Fancher would meet me here. I know it sounds ridiculous, but it's the truth."

"The voice is that specific?"

"Yeah, it is. It's very clear."

"Well, in your state of mind you better watch yourself with Fancher. He's one tricky guy."

"I gather that."

He waits. She's thinking, but he can tell she isn't interested in elaborating.

Finally, she says, "You can reach your own conclusions. It's just that Fancher's buying up land all over the area and he won't take no for an answer. We're doing fine. We don't want to sell. And whatever he's doing with the land he buys isn't farming. It's like he's building a buffer zone or something. And he owns so much property it's getting harder and harder to find business."

"What kind of business?"

"Haymaking, mostly. Besides poultry, we make hay for people. But you gotta have fields to do that in and he's buying 'em all and business is drying up. Enough of that, though. I want to know more about your work."

"Well, there isn't much more to tell really. You'll have to read the book. Right now I'm trying to understand this whole ESP thing – or group mind, or whatever. It's hard because nothing works with everyone. You always need people who are sort of predisposed to the kind of signals I'm sending out, and there just aren't that many around. You're one, obviously. Then there's the next phase which is this odd kind of premonition or prescience that I often feel.

"What keeps me going in all of it is the implications. I mean, if there is ESP or if this EGG-68 or even another designer chemical helps unlock some new set of mental powers, even if for just a few of us, what does that say about life? What does it imply about the existence of something like God? The magic we're talking about is so much more amazing than anything science has explained so far. In fact, it all seems to throw out a good deal of the theory about the mental process that is more or less standard in psychology and anthropology. But that's enough of me, what about you? How is it that you understand what I'm talking about?"

She rolls away from him with the question. "It's pretty strange. I mean, a lot stranger than what you're telling me. Can you deal with it?"

"Probably. I've learned to deal with anything."

"Okay. So, the first thing is that I wasn't really looking for the duck man. I mean, I do meet him out there, but I really did think you were someone else."

He waits.

"You know those Elvis sightings over at Rocheport?" she continues. "You probably read about them in the paper? Well, I think they may be true." He still waits. He hadn't told her everything that he had been dealing with.

She continues, "I guess, actually, you could say I know they're true…because I've been having an affair with a guy who is clearly Elvis Presley...I think."

He doesn't know what to say to her. There are two parts to her statement. One part seems to be saying she believes that Elvis is still alive. The other says she has a lover. Well, it was said in the past tense so that meant she had had a lover. But he feels coming off of her a lingering desire for whoever it was she was sleeping with. He realizes he feels jealous and that his ears are hot and his cheeks are flushed.

"So, you're telling me Elvis is still alive?" He has to joke through it. "What does Priscilla have to say about your little tryst?"

"I don't really know what I'm saying" she responds quickly. "I want to tell you what's been happening, though, because something has definitely not been normal. It's not a joke. I've been meeting a guy who looks and acts a lot like he's really him only older. And I know that can't be true, but it feels like it is. It really does – his voice, the way he moves, the way he smells. But he's old. You know, not like the Elvis you see in the movies. More like in his early sixties, maybe more. And now that I haven't seen him for a while, he starts popping up in other places and there's all of a sudden these sightings. It's weird. I mean, other people are seeing this guy, too, and they think it's him as well. So, maybe I'm not crazy. I don't know."

Cecil thinks for a while. He is concerned about offending her with obvious questions. "Couldn't it just be one of those impersonators? I mean, the only way any of us really know him is through his music and through his movies. Someone who looks like him could probably do a number on your imagination. Or maybe it's his double? I know it sounds just as weird, but there's a theory that it's possible for replicas to be born. You're talking about more than Elvis being alive, you're talking about an older version than he could possibly be. If it really is Elvis, he would have to be back from the dead – or was never dead. And that's pretty improbable – not Elvis, maybe his housekeeper's son or his barber's ex-wife, but not Elvis. That kind of thing just doesn't happen."

"I know all of that. But what I'm telling you is that there's something more going on. I could feel it when I was with him. He had this force coming out of him." She stops. Clearly, it's too difficult to put what she feels into words.

Finally, she goes on. "Now, I've been contacted by *Midnight America* to meet one of their reporters to tell my story...well, actually I contacted them first. They're here to cover that meeting in Rocheport tomorrow morning. I don't know what to say. But this is somehow real. I know it is."

"This is what I'm talking about," he says. "It's that whole thing about faith. You have faith that you know what you know, but you can't prove it. And it's very hard to put the whole thing into words.

You need some way to prove it all. I don't know what that way is, but...."

"You can help me," she says. They are both smiling, first at the smoke as it tangles through the air, and then at each other as they contemplate the comedy of their discussion and the strangeness of their meeting and the special joy they share naked and satisfied next to each other, strangers.

"I can try to help you...I'm sure I can do something...I don't know how, or what, but it may be why I'm here," Cecil says. "Who knows, it could be some sort of hypnotic spell; it could be a lookalike; or it could be a ghost...."

With that he rolls to his side and peers down at her, feeling the cool air humming off the fan and the heat of her skin pressing against his stomach and thigh. "I need to go get my backpack from the road. Will you be here when I get back?"

"Why don't you stay just a while more and then go?" She picks her head up and smiles down at him.

Had either of them bothered to look out the window, they would have noticed someone walking away from the house, moving quickly between the outbuildings so as not to be seen. It would have been hard to determine whether it was a woman or man. Had they noticed this person, though, they would wonder whether that person had been spying on them, and, if so, how much they had seen and heard.

CHAPTER 13

"So what was the first thing you noticed?" comes a quiet male voice. Harris turns slightly to find a man and woman sitting in the booth behind him. The man's back is to him. The woman, dark-haired with large chocolate-colored eyes and a full, sensuous mouth, is broad shouldered and athletic, like a rugby player. She seems to be in her forties. He likes that she's naturally attractive but doesn't wear makeup.

"The first thing I noticed was that those two guys left their cars running and unattended again," says the woman in a commanding tone. Harris turns a bit more at this, acting as if he's searching for the waitress. They have the unmistakable look of plainclothes police officers. She is certainly attractive, with Mediterranean features and full, prominent breasts that somehow make her both more imposing and confidently erotic. Got to be Italian or Sicilian ancestry, he thinks. Still, it is an exotic look, both for a police officer and for anyone in these parts. "Well, Heimer's okay, but Hughes should know better."

"No," says the man. "I mean when you got to the site with the body."

Harris turns back to his meal but keeps his head tilted just slightly sideways, trying to eavesdrop without giving himself away.

"I know," she snorts. "The victim was in a place we used to call The Dip, where we partied when we were kids, you know, but it just didn't look right. I was just thinking more about how unlucky I am to have Hughes on this team. It's my first chance to run a real CAP and I draw him as a uniform.

"But anyway, they were following procedure for combing the area so I didn't think much about anything at first. Heimer and Baines were there, too, and I was glad to see them. I like that Baines kid. He's smart and a hard worker. Took me about 10 minutes to figure it out, but it really seems like the body was hauled into The Dip. I guess the thing that bothered me later was that the hat was gone."

"The hat?"

"Yeah, you know they always wear their hats."

"What are the Amish doing around here?"

"They're part of that sect down from Iowa. Couple families were excommunicated or shunned, or whatever, for having kind of modern beliefs. I read about it in the paper a few years back – something about them using computers and that their group in Iowa decided that was a no-no. I think I recall something about one of the kids being a drummer, too, and that he was a wizard at creating electronic rhythms. They were kicked out when he joined a rock band.

"One thing I remember in particular, though, is that the family still adheres to a lot of the traditional ways – especially that the men always wear their hats. But that kid didn't have his hat, and we didn't find it anywhere. We left Hughes out there for the rest of the shift to look all over the field, but he didn't find it – or much of anything, really.

"So that kind of tipped me off. Hughes also found footprints that don't match our boot prints. They were much deeper than anything else around there, which could mean someone was carrying something heavy, like a body, but the ground was pretty rustled up by something, so we couldn't tell much. Could have been anything. That place can be like Grand Central Station on the weekend. Anyway, definitely no hat."

"Jill? You're telling me you think this Amish kid was killed over a hat?"

"Dale, I have no idea why he was killed," she says testily. "I'm still trying to figure out if that was even a murder scene. And no hat plus those footprints leads me to thinking it wasn't. What have I got to go on? Not much. It is true, though, that a lot of people think they're great hats - high school kids up north closer to traditional Amish communities mostly, but some of the Boone County kids are into them now, too. They're well made...."

"Kid got killed for a hat. It could be, couldn't it?"

"Yeah, I guess it could. But I'd really be more inclined, now that I've had time to contemplate it, to think that he was killed somewhere else and driven to that field. If we put out an APB for a missing Amish hat we might just find the scene of the crime." She chuckled.

"Next step?"

"I'm going out with Heimer this afternoon to canvass those new townhouses along Limerick Lane. We'll see what happens there. I don't know though, Dale...." Her pause makes Harris turn slightly more. It seems like they are aware of him. Nothing is said for nearly a minute.

Then, in a quieter voice, the male officer speaks: "I don't know how to proceed on this either, Jill. The only obvious homicides in Columbia are mostly family stuff and gun accidents. You're going to have to do the best you can. But, listen, I gotta tell you something. You need to keep things to yourself more than ever right now. Be careful. Word is that the Bureau is in town and doing something meaningful. It may be linked to that whole Elvis gig out in the Rocheport area. Or it could be something to do with Central Soft and DiscManager out in the Rockbridge area. My bet is the FBI's here because of some corporate thing with those guys. But you never know. And there's all this talk of that group Bud Sumter's been organizing...."

His voice drops more after that and Harris doesn't hear anything else. But he's heard enough. He writes the names of the two companies on a napkin, pays his bill, and walks out. As he passes the police officers, he glances down at the woman. It's her big eyes that strike him the most. She holds his stare for a moment with a kind of distracted dignity. He sees strong will and deep intelligence looking back at him.

*

Harris loves entering the clean silence of rental cars. This is a late-model Lincoln. The door closes with a definitive click. When he puts the key in the ignition the seatbelt chimes give him a gentle feeling that all is well in the world and that quality can at least be rented.

He heads out toward the three shopping malls near Interstate 70 and stops at Nowell's Liquor for a couple of bottles. The quiet of the perfectly engineered Japanese-Detroit half-breed, and the slow stream of cold air from the Quick Response Cooling System make him salivate. He needs a drink.

At Nowell's Harris buys three bottles of Dewar's and a case of Hamm's. He's looking forward to cheap beer in the bathtub at the end of the day.

He takes I-70 west toward Rocheport, waiting to get beyond city commuting traffic before he pulls out the first bottle of scotch and takes a long pull. It is too warm and stings. But the spasm of nausea is what he's after, and he feels moderately satisfied for the first time in nearly eight hours. After three more hits, he twists the top back on and slides the bottle under the seat. Now he can get down to work.

CHAPTER 14

Rocheport, Missouri is a small town resting beneath meandering bluffs that overlook the Missouri River. Like many central Missouri towns, it is not so much a place to own a home as a place to say you live near. There are nineteen houses within the town limits, one church, and a rundown warehouse that used to double as a meeting hall. Down close to river here are also sixteen restaurants and taverns, two bungalow-style motels, and one large motor lodge. These were all constructed during the early '90s for the new tourist trade attracted by a regional weekend antique fair closer to the highway. The fair ballooned from a parking lot event taking place on the first weekend of June, to occupying an eleven-acre fairground with over 400 furniture and knick-knack dealers, running every Saturday and Sunday from Memorial Day weekend to Labor Day weekend.

Harris slows the car as he hits traffic and throngs of people walking. He's not surprised by the crowd. With the international attention from the Elvis sightings, Rocheport has become a Mecca for media broadcast vans, helicopters, and TV trucks. Backyards throughout the town have been converted into parking lots for the thousands of fans and media streaming in to catch a glimpse of The King. The $25 a day parking rate is the steepest Harris has seen for these kinds of phenomena, but it doesn't surprise him.

He is told he is lucky to have gotten there so early. He has his choice of yards to park in and finally finds one sophisticated enough to offer a receipt. They charge an extra $10, but the $35 in cash is worth the guarantee of reimbursement on his expense account. By the looks of it, media people fill the small backyard because of the receipt offer. There are minivans and satellite trucks from all over the country. He counts four Channel 6 vehicles and three Channel 3s, stations as far away as Kansas City, St. Louis, Little Rock, Topeka, Omaha, and Des Moines. He also sees evidence of national teams from Fox and ABC. It's likely CBS and NBC are nearby as well. It occurs to him that the appeal here may be the same as his disgust: ever since the Recession Years of the early 2000s, so much of the central Midwest was just falling away from what was going on in the big cities. His disgust came from being sent into Nowhere. But Nowhere was kind of an attraction as well, especially to TV and Internet broadcasters who could use visuals – sort of a backwoods, old-fashioned America that time had forgotten. And here in its midst were fanatics and kooks and Bible Thumping Christians frantic for a glimpse of a ghost that still represented the world they had all left behind so long ago in the past century.

He gets directions to the Mark Twain Motor Lodge from the daughter of the family whose backyard he's parked in. It's a half-mile to the river where the facility sits. Walking with a stream of photographers and reporters along with TV and radio people, he wonders what this interview will be like.

The woman meets him in the lobby of the motor lodge but leads him to a basement meeting room. She is older than he expected and very composed, not like most of the fruits he interviews. As she shuts the door he feels something distinctly sexual pulse through his mind. The silent room cooled by a window-unit, makes him think of the rental car. It also makes him feel, confusingly, that he is having an affair with this woman and that she is about to disrobe for him. The floor is covered by a multicolored carpet design of abstract paisley mingled with brown and orange daubs of leaf-shaped objects. Against the wood-paneled walls and low ceiling, the carpet lends a sort of synthetic forest floor feel to the room. The full west wall is occupied by windows looking out onto the river.

Before the woman begins to speak, another man enters. He is young with red-tinted blond hair worn in a ponytail, and large, red-rimmed green eyes that roam the room before they fall on Harris.

"Mr. Harris, this is Cecil Miller," says Coral McGrey. "A friend of mine. We just met last night, but he seems to understand what I have been going through. I felt I should bring him along."

Miller and Harris shake hands. The young man's grip is bony but strong. He holds Harris's gaze and smiles a slight acknowledgement. The eyes burn with something Harris remembers from his past...maybe twenty or thirty years ago. He tries to hold the young man's gaze but drops his eyes to the swirling carpet after a second or two. The woman catches this and smiles.

Harris asks them for permission to record their conversation. She says it's all right, so he fumbles around for a few minutes setting up the tiny tape recorder, then positions it on the table.

"Ms. McGrey, I'm here in Missouri to find out more about your claim that you have been talking with Elvis." Harris tries this with a straight face, watching the blond tabletop. He meets her eyes after the opening, waiting for an answer. The kid is sitting next to her, smiling. Coral smiles. Harris wonders if they are on drugs or just addled from too much for too long.

"I called your paper because things are getting out of hand, Mr. Harris." Her voice is deep for someone so thin. It is quiet too, and soothing. "This religion thing here today is something I know nothing about. It's hard for me to believe. I've been...sleeping with him." Harris looks at the recorder to make sure it's working. "He hasn't said anything to me about who he is or where he's from, but I know who he is."

"How do you know this?"

"I've seen the old movies. I've been down to Branson to the Elvis Festival. I know how impersonators act and how they look. He's not an impersonator. It's him. Seriously. I know it is."

"Okay," says Harris. "I'm not going to challenge that. But I'm going to need more from you. If he's really who you say he is – and what others seem to believe – we'll find a way to prove it, but I need to know what in detail you and he have talked about. Key words, patterns of interest, what he eats, what he wears, his approximate shoe size – whatever. Things like that to feed into the Web so that we can track him down or at least verify some of your descriptions. I mean, if he wears a size 10 shoe and my search shows that Elvis wore an 11, we know we've got a problem. If he likes peanut butter and banana sandwiches a lot, and we find on the web that Elvis did too, then we've got verification of at least something.

"And then I do a search on long-term purchases of peanut butter and bananas through our sources. May narrow things down to a hundred people or so. Whatever. The point is that we do this with enough variables until things start to lock in. I call it multi-input triangulation. It works." He is lying to them, but the truth isn't the point.

Cecil clears his throat and leans back from the table. "Mr. Harris, before you get started, are you so sure that this guy is a real person?"

"You mean, do I believe Ms. McGrey here? I want to, that's my job. But..." Harris doesn't want to be the one doing the talking.

"No, I mean is this real?" Cecil finally asks. "Couldn't this be something outside of real?"

"It could be a hallucination, I guess, if that's what you mean."

"No. I mean we could be talking about a ghost, or whatever you want to call it. Something paranormal." The younger man uses his eyes when he speaks, almost as if they are what is making the words. "Couldn't we?"

Harris smiles his best journalist's smile. He knows better than to argue the point, or to even move into that line of questioning. It is far too easy.

The kid persists. "You need the right receptors and the right cognitive predisposition, but it isn't unlikely, really."

"Yeah, well, lots of people think like that, kid. I don't know one way or the other, but I do know that with the proper data we can come up with a good story. I take it you're sort of predisposed to this kind of thing yourself?"

"I'm finishing a degree in parapsychology."

"Well, my orders are to get the data and do the search and see what I turn up. I don't know anything about ghosts and witches and ghouls. I can give you the name of a woman on the staff who does cover that and maybe she'd be interested. But even then, she's only going to get the assignment after I've done my work here. If you ask me, what you probably have is an Elvis impersonator taking advantage of his resemblance." He thinks about the other sightings and the revival meetings. "Someone with good voice training and a weird sense of humor, maybe. Oh, and someone on the payroll of the Christian Witness Church?"

The kid smiles at this, then yawns. Harris shrugs his shoulders and sighs, turning his attention back to the woman.

"What do you think, Ms. McGrey?"

"I honestly don't know anymore. I never saw him eat anything that I can remember, for starters. If he is a ghost, I couldn't tell. I could feel him, smell him, taste him. We...made love...." Harris is glad the recorder is on and that they haven't asked him to turn it off. He is also surprised that they haven't discussed money yet. This usually means that he is assured of an interviewee who really believes in what they are saying.

"Okay, Ms. McGrey, why don't we start with a composite? Try to speak slowly so that the recorder can pick everything up and do your best to limit voice inflections. What color hair did he have?"

She answers his questions as best she can. Her voice is calm and in the monotone he knows is used by those who believe in what they have to say. The description of the face seems close to Elvis's but older, which Harris finds interesting. So far that hasn't been verified.

In a little over ten minutes they have what she considers the best she can do. They move on to other questions: the type of clothes he wears, his age, build, etc. Every so often Harris glances over at Miller. The kid seems to be in a sort of trance, his big eyes fixed on the tabletop, his breathing slow and steady through his nose, The nostrils flaring ever so slightly on the inhale.

"Okay, that does it for the basic questions. Now, to the interview. You say you have met with this man for the past two years? That you have been lovers?"

She hesitates in answering this at first. They had been meeting for several years, but she doesn't love him. She couldn't tell if he loved her, really, but it didn't seem he did. He talked about weird things – his feelings, loneliness, disappointment, how good it felt to cry, the shape of fruit tree blossoms, how funny long shadows were in the glowing light of summer evenings, whether the Indians burned the great plains for better game land or whether it was settlers.

This guy has to be leaving tracks on the Internet somewhere, thinks Harris. He has to have a bank account, charge card, food stamps, or something. No one can survive without some sort of electronic footprint. How can he narrow the search to just five or ten people in a world with nearly 8 billion? He fishes for as much information as possible. It will take most of the night, but he will upload the recording of their conversation into *Midnight's* data banks and wait for the reply.

Then he remembers something else. It worked once in an interview when he was trying to track down Marlon Brando after his supposed failed suicide.

He asks her: "And you don't think this guy could be an Elvis impersonator?"

"I don't know. If he is, he's not trying very hard. His clothes, his hair, his whole body aren't like any of those guys you see in Branson or on TV."

"Has he ever even hinted at his identity? I mean, that he *is* Elvis? Even some vague reference? Some sense of pride? Even remotely?"

"Not really. I never asked him his name…he…well…. It was…a lot of…." She turns to Cecil here and then back to Harris. "It was a lot of intimacy and me listening to him some. After the third or fourth time I met with him it just didn't seem necessary to know who he was."

"No reference to The King, rock and roll, nothing?"

She thinks on this for a few seconds. "Well, he once talked about oak trees being the king of the trees, and corn the king of foods...but not anything relating to Elvis."

"That's okay. That might do it." He taps at the recorder. "I think that's it. I'm not sure, but I think I can narrow a search down with all of this. Then we just need to get a fix from the linkage sites. It'll take some code cracking, but we've got all week. I'll find this guy. It'll take some time. But I'll find him." He knows now that there was no point in doing the research. He will use the tape to fully verify if she believes what she's told him. If she does, then he can write whatever he wants and she will back him up. It had worked like a charm with the Brando stories he'd done.

The kid looks at him. "I don't see why you want to find him using Google. I mean, wouldn't it be better to just write the story as is? Ms. McGrey says she was having an affair with Elvis Presley?"

"It would, but that's been done a few times already by others. What we're trying to accomplish here is to find the guy who keeps appearing at these revival meetings. Regardless of whether he's an Elvis impersonator or a ghost, he's got the kind of charisma that people want to read about. I want to find him because he's Elvis to a lot of folks."

"So," says Coral, a bit dismayed, "You aren't going to tell my story? That's what I came to you for."

"I don't know what I'm going to write, Ms. McGrey. I don't know the whole story yet. I know what you just told me, but I need more – even for *Midnight*. That's why I'm here. Please be patient. I need as much of the puzzle as you can possibly give me. I'm going to go find this revival group in a few minutes and see what they can contribute as well. Now, if you'll excuse me, I must be on my way."

Standing, Harris shakes hands with them and makes his exit.

Coral and Cecil wait for him to leave before they sit down again.

"Was it what you thought it would be?" asks Cecil.

"Yes and no," she says after a moment. "I thought he would make me feel more defensive, but now I just feel like I have no control."

"That's what he was hoping for," says Miller. "The guy is paid to write things people don't know they want to read until they see the headlines in the supermarket."

CHAPTER 15

During the hour Harris is in the room interviewing Coral and Cecil, Rocheport transforms into a full-scale community traffic jam. Campers, media vans, and cars of all makes idle in the sun looking to park. Helicopters hover overhead. It isn't difficult to locate the fairgrounds and revival area because hordes of people and camera crews lumber in a straggling line, all headed in the same direction. By the time Harris sees the tent, he knows that his press pass isn't going to get him very close to the actual meeting. There seem to be more media people than civilians. He wonders if Janie will be there. This is certainly her thing.

After ten minutes of walking, he spies her on the other side of the street with her USA Network crew. One guy carries a large orange card in one hand and microphone cables in the other. Harris calls out to Janie as he slides into the street, dodging slow-moving cars, flashing on their early days after she'd gotten him his job with *Midnight.* They'd covered OJ together and the rumor of what many at the time were calling Madonna's shocking, practical-joke marriage to Kevin Costner.

As he expected, she is hesitant to be friendly but doesn't deny him information. The orange card entitles her crew to tent access and full coverage rights. Later, he will learn they had paid $40,000 for this privilege and that three other crews paid the steep fare as well.

"I knew I'd run into you here," he says as he steps up on the curb next to her.

"If you're going to ask me whether you can be on the team," she replies, "the answer is no." She is still the same little girl alien. But he also knows where her anger is coming from.

He moves in close to hug her. She smells of Ivory Soap as he kisses her cheek. Stepping back quickly from the greeting, she squints one eye while arching the brow of the other. She wears jeans and a sleeveless red blouse, partially unbuttoned to show a bit of cleavage.

"Aren't you a tad far from your wonderful office overlooking Washington Square, Frankie?"

"Hey, it's a media world now, babe."

"Just worming into people's lives with the rest of us, Frank? Sometimes I think you should all just let me report back to your offices and you can just write up your impressions of my coverage. It's such a waste that there should be several thousand of us covering the same event."

"Well, sometimes we get little angles of difference, Janes."

She waits for him to go on. But he knows the look in her eyes. Finally, she says, "Okay, Harris, what have you got that I don't got?"

"Can't say, dearie."

"You got a scoop?"

"There are many distorted worldviews out here," he says, smiling.

"Don't tell me you tracked down that sycophant claiming to have screwed The King!"

"She's got the right stuff, Janie." As usual, Janie Hawthorn has been contacted before him. Coral McGrey's story was probably turned down by a number of broadcast companies before it worked down to print.

"The right stuff for *Midnight* maybe – and Aaron Treestat," she taunts. "Really, Frank, when are you guys going to learn? Just because they think it's true doesn't mean you have to report it. Sometimes your methods are so juvenile. Treestat is so predictable. You guys learned nothing from your Cosby fiasco."

"Actually, Janie, that's why he sent me out here. I'm doing my penance. Treestat doesn't like it when he has to pay to lie. Seems I didn't fully establish several sources. They jumped ship as soon as they were subpoenaed. Sometimes I forget the simple stuff you taught me back there in the beginning."

"Don't pull that good buddy shit with me, Harris. The way you left the last time really pissed me off."

He moves in as close as she will let him. He doesn't need the crew hearing about Red Bluffs.

"You knew I was only there for the day!" he says quietly. "I got in, got the story – and I might add I helped you get an even better story – then I got out. I needed the data and the site links for Treestat. That was it. I couldn't stay. They would have gone for my head. You knew that."

"I did, but I also know that you spent nearly four hours at the airport sucking down scotch and eating peanuts after you left. You could have at least woken me up."

He uses a smile and his large blue eyes on her.

"That was over four months ago," he protests. "You don't forget, do you?" He is still close so that only she can hear.

"No, I don't forget that kind of thing. And I'm not falling for that look of yours, either, so just get out of my face, okay? You want to be in on this with us? Huh? Is that it? Okay, what are you going to do for me? You gonna owe me now? You gonna...oh, Jesus Christ, just keep your fucking mouth shut, and no, you cannot get in on any exclusive interviews. So just—"

"I'm really glad to see you, Janes. You can't stand it, can you? Owing me? Well, I'm not drinking these days, and I'm assigned a long haul here, so maybe we can pick up where we left off. What do you say? God, you're so sexy."

She glances around at her snickering crew. Harris is one of the few men who can get to her. The last time they'd been together he couldn't get it up no matter what she tried. It had been a long night, and though he'd satisfied her in other ways, somehow it just didn't seem fulfilling to either of them without giving him pleasure as well.

"I can smell it on you, Frank," she says with disgust. "I hope you're doing better these days anyway."

*

Once they enter the fairgrounds, it takes nearly half an hour to get to their seats. An area for the paying press has been roped off eight rows back on both sides of the stage. Camera-feed and lighting cables are strung in a tangle leading to the edge of the tent where portable transmitter dishes have been placed. Reporters and directors stumble over the cables with digital microphones in one hand and mobile phones in the other. As usual, Janie's team is outfitted with the best new technology. This time they all have on headsets and mini-mikes that feed into a single, palm-sized wireless satellite dish. With the crowd as big as it is, one man has to guard the dish which sits on top of a small chrome tower they are unfolding. Other than that, Janie's crew is able to concentrate on setting up for the shoot instead of erecting their system. Janie sits on a camp chair with her iPad in her lap, typing lines as the PDA green-lights the send direct to her Washington headquarters.

Harris figures there are at least 600 people under the tent and another two to three thousand surrounding it. Even in the late morning sun, the interior needs to be lit by several banks of portable high-pressure sodiums in the middle of the seating area. Harris wades through the crowd to the perimeter, where he would have been had he not met up with Janie. It is the usual chaos. People of all types wander around the edge, looking toward the stage for a glimpse of the man who brought them there – small-town reporters, underequipped TV crews, tourists in from St. Louis riverboat tours, local people, a number of Elvis fans, what appears to be a motorcycle gang, even a contingent of the recently formed King Jones Mourning Society. The bulk of the crowd, though, seem to be the members of the Christian Witness Church – men and women dressed up for a Sunday sermon. Glancing around, he sees Coral McGrey and Cecil Miller quietly edging their way to the front of the crowd in the middle of the seating as the stage lights go out and the huge tent goes somewhat dark.

A spontaneous note is hummed by the parishioners as soon as the darkness hits. It's like a Buddhist congregation chanting OM, only this group extends out a long, slow "AMEN," in almost perfect unison.

They do this three times, and on the third long phrase something clearly clicks in; Harris can feel it, and the voices blend into one, making a single rushing, focal, wave of sound wash over the whole tent. Harris's hair feels like it is alive, like it's floating in the air, charged with static electricity. And then there is silence.

He waits for his eyes to adjust to the low lighting before returning to Janie and her crew. Just as he begins to feel comfortable with his vision, the stage lights power on. In front of him is an empty stage. In the shadows near the back sit a group of thirty or so men and women dressed in purple choir robes with gold trim and tassels. As he begins to move in Janie's direction, a portly man with closely cut white hair and wearing a business suit comes out from behind the choir, walks confidently to the podium, and begins to speak:

"We are visited here today, my friends, by the world awaiting! This is our Lord's will. Done on earth. And we should be both thankful and humbled." He gestures toward the crowd with an open palm turned upward and is greeted with another drawn-out, unified *Amen*.

"Friends, I will not keep you in suspense. Nor do I wish the world that bears witness to our meek gathering to feel deprived of the truths we come to see here today.

"Over the last month we have been visited by our emissary twice. He is a man who has stepped out of the shadows to help bring us closer to our God.

"And I have known him for many years. Before that, when I was a young man, I knew his mother. Most of you do not know this. I was with his mother when she died. She was a woman filled with the pure light of the Lord. Her son, tortured and transfixed by earthly passion and sorrow, is now ready to have us bear witness to his coming into the light."

"Is this Sumter?" Harris whispers to Janie. She nods in affirmation, still watching the stage.

At the podium the speaker breathes heavily. His hands shake slightly. Harris thinks of the bottle under the seat in the car and the cigarettes in his pocket. The minister lets the silence in the room linger long enough for several coughs to be heard and for a woman to clear her throat.

"Thus, we are here today to allow a member of this congregation to come forward, regardless of his past, to ask for salvation. We are here to make ourselves one in the eyes of the world. We do not use machines to do this–as some idolatrous monstrosities do; we do not claim to own metaphysical truths, as others do; we do not seek miracles. We seek only grace. We seek unity with our Lord. We seek redemption."

He pauses again. The crowd remains quiet, waiting. The effect of the media on people is probably taking hold. Harris figures that the very idea the world is watching and waiting is probably more likely the reason for the reverence than because Sumter is saying something important. They are all performing, he realizes.

"Is there then such a person in this house of God?" asks the minister finally. "Is there a man amongst us who has been so cherished and loved as to be emptied of humility and full of himself?" He waits, looking into the crowd.

"I ask you," he continues, "if you are such a man, come forward and let us embrace you. Let us bring you into our fold and make you one with us."

He continues to wait. No one comes. People begin to glance around at their neighbors. Harris and Janie look behind at the audience and then to the front of the tent. The minister is sweating from the heat of the stage lights, and seems, to Harris, suddenly very tense. Janie catches Harris' eye and winks. Harris has to hand it to the Reverend, he has directly and succinctly managed to hit the nail on the head. It is the same basic rule of journalism these days: get in, get out; and when you're in deliver the juice.

At that moment the crowd begins to murmur and stir. Harris swivels to see a dark figure coming down the aisle some forty rows back. As the man approaches out of the shadows, Harris can see by the bearing and gait that this is who they have been waiting for. He is surprised to see the man dressed in a dark T-shirt, blue jeans, and cowboy boots. But there is no mistake: it is Elvis – at least it seems like him. The man passes on his way to the stage. He seems shorter than would be expected. What he says to them, though, will decide things once and for all. Harris and Janie exchange satisfied smiles and watch the man almost reluctantly climb the steps to the stage.

Sumter meets him with open arms as the audience sits stunned. A confused silence swims through the tent. Even outside everything has fallen quiet. Harris hears only the whir of cameras and a gentle hum reverberating from the generators nearby. Not a word, not a cough, not a cleared throat. Sumter hugs the man in the T-shirt and says a few words to him. The mike gaff moves over them, but with a sharp glance Sumter gestures it away. The two speak for a few seconds in the silence. The cadence of their voices is barely audible in the stillness of the tent. Then Sumter motions to the podium.

As Elvis moves to where Sumter has indicated, Harris sees out of the corner of his eye two people stand and leave. It is the McGrey woman and her escort. Just then, the voice of the man quietly echoes through the tent. Harris makes out a tear on his face. He glances at Sumter who stands to one side, just barely visible on the edge of shadows.

"My friends," begins the man. The smooth, slightly nasal baritone is unmistakable. "It's been a long time. It has been too long. But I am here and I am ready to testify.

"I have been lonely. Despairing. Full of pain. I ask that you take me into the fold and love me as you love all others who are brethren."

The silence is obliterated by an explosion of applause and shouts and screams. Several people in front rush forward and try to climb the stage. Sumter, attempting unsuccessfully to hide his joy, moves forward, motioning several of his bodyguards up with him. Many people stay in their seats at first, but others lose control as well and burst forward down the runway toward the stage. Harris steals a glance at the media on the other side of the room and sees the crowd is trampling equipment and has pushed the few camera people who'd stayed with their gear out of the way and even down to the floor. He hears a gust of people behind him. He stands looking for Janie as the crowd rolls forward. She is nearby, clutching her iPad and sticking close to a cameraman as people push toward the front of the tent.

Around him, people grunt and groan with what sounds like a request for something they do not understand. Others speak in a language he can't comprehend. And everyone pushes forward toward the stage. Looking over their heads, he sees that a few people have already mounted the steps and are moving toward the group of bodyguards surrounding Sumter and the man who has just spoken. The crowd has become one mass of bodies, pushing forward rhythmically. He hears the screams of people in front. He becomes aware of the sensation of the breasts of the woman behind him on his back, her hands on his waist; he smells her hair as it falls across his shoulder, feels her sharp chin in his back. He feels also the press of his pelvis into the back of the camerawoman in front of him. He senses that she is having trouble bearing his weight and the push of his body forced against her. He smells her sweating head and wonders whether she feels the dazed, edgy anxiety of utter abandon that he does.

The camerawoman's legs begin to buckle. He knows she's about to go down. He manages to spread his legs and arch his torso backwards, giving her enough room to regain her balance and shift forward. He sees her head turn and glimpses her right eye squinting in thanks.

At this point, Harris watches a huddled phalanx surrounding Elvis and Sumter moving toward the back of the stage while parishioners continue to teem forward, leaping now onto the raised platform. He sees the arms of people who have presumably been crushed, groping for help, and then several of the more rational people on stage reaching down to pull them up. Some he sees hauled into the air continuing to flail about, others are limp and possibly unconscious. One looks as if her neck has been broken.

And then Sumter and his group have disappeared. Harris doesn't see them leave, but he presumes they have slipped out the back. He notices people on the stage edging to the rear, a bit bewildered. Others understand quickly that the object of their frenzy is now gone. Things begin to calm down. The choir, in their fancy robes, disperse and mill around the stage. He hears sirens in the distance and several gunshots from the back of the tent and then feels the pressure from all sides subside. It is over. The whole thing took less than two minutes.

Part IV
Detective Work

"Once in a while you get shown the light in the strangest of places if you look at it right."

- Robert Hunter

CHAPTER 16

Only one person died during the melee. A teenage girl named Mary Shadduck had indeed broken her neck. Harris accompanies Janie to interview the parents as they are leaving the emergency room. The father feels his daughter was now a martyr. The mother is enraged. Janie can't decide which story to focus on. Harris advises her to focus on the mother. Janie chooses the father.

While they interview the girl's parents, the rest of Janie's crew is trying to figure out how much of the riot they got on disk and how much of their equipment is still functioning. There is enough footage of Elvis and the first rush to issue a good story, so after the interview Janie goes off to finish the piece with the crew, while Harris returns to his car for a quick nip and to make sure the recording of his interview with Coral McGrey is okay.

As he opens the door, the chime of the rental is still oddly soothing. But in the silence of the enclosed car the crackle of the paper bag containing the whiskey violently reminds him of what he witnessed several hours before.

The thought that he just saw Elvis shocks him. He is surprised at how easy it is to suspend reality and what he understands to be a truth. He knows it's ridiculous to think he saw the real Elvis. It's a scam, there's no question about it, but the whole scene created a strange level of communal reality that he finds hard to ignore.

He sucks down more whiskey, and as the sharp, acidic liquid hits his gut, he recalls the swagger of the man and the way he held his head – all just as he would expect The King to do. There isn't much need to track him on the Internet now anyway; he is right there in town with Sumter. Whoever he might be.

Harris eases the driver's seat back, places his laptop on his thighs, and begins to write:

(Rocheport, MO) For those who have joked about whether Elvis lives, and for those who have mourned his death over the last 40 years, 3,000 people here today were so overwhelmed with passion and the excitement at finally seeing him that a riot broke out during a Baptist service held by the Third Christian Witness Church.

Yes, indeed, Elvis lives.

Under a canopy for "members only" and the press, the Reverend Montgomery Sumter offered a brief statement to the crowd prior to Mr. Presley's entrance. At 1:15 P.M., in front of worldwide media and enthusiasts of all kinds, Elvis appeared in the crowd and made his way to the front stage. No one knows yet how he got in.

After mounting the stage and exchanging a few words with Sumter, Presley turned to face the crowd only to be surrounded by security as frenzied Christian Witness members and curious onlookers charged the stage in order to be closer to this miracle.

Broadcast worldwide, the riot that ensued lasted close to half an hour. 29 people were injured, 14 were hospitalized for internal injuries and broken bones suffered when they were trampled. One teenage girl died of a broken neck. Within minutes, Elvis and Sumter were rushed out of the back of the tent by security personnel.

To those who think this a hoax, it is only fair to say for the thousands who witnessed his presence here today, there was no mistaking that walk and that bearing. Yes, he was a bit aged, and although dressed in a T-shirt, blue jeans, and cowboy boots, there is no question that the gathering was in the presence of who could only be The King. That he was still fit and trim has caused speculation.

Nancy Fronmeier, a mother of three living in Fulton some 45 miles away, said "He's clearly the second coming of Elvis."

Jeanetta Harlon, of nearby Columbia stated, "I don't think there is any question that he's a double. It's probably a hoax, but it could just be some crazy who spent too much time in front of a mirror."

For Tru Jansen, a local painting contractor: "I don't believe in ghosts, I don't believe in second comings, I don't believe in anything. But I saw what I saw, and there's no question it was Elvis."

Whatever the truth, the spectacle today culminated weeks of strange, haphazard sightings, seemingly unverifiable claims, and wild speculation. Reports of Elvis sightings have become more and more frequent in this quiet, out-of-the-way farm region, while throughout the rest of the country they have become almost nonexistent. Several young girls in and around Columbia and Fayette have recently laid claim to having affairs with a man who looked and acted like an older Elvis Presley. And several times over the last month, a man answering this description has been identified at smaller Christian Witness revival meetings. It was even reported during the first week of June that he sang "Amazing Grace" to the congregation in that unquestionable voice.

Whether hoax or paranormal entity, visions of The King have this sleepy little town hopping. Elvis music can be heard everywhere. T-shirts and other paraphernalia abound. A bus from Branson, Missouri, arrives every day bringing tourists and the hopeful. Perhaps we can all be born again.

*

The message light is blinking on Harris's cell phone when he returns to his room.

"Mr. Harris, this is Coral McGrey. I need to speak with you. Please call me at 555-449-6787. It's important. I'll be here this evening."

He writes the number down. No time to call her until later. Janie might possibly stop by. He needed a nap. Then he needed a bath and several beers. And, finally, with time, he needed to shower and brush his teeth in order to get the alcohol smell out of his system.

CHAPTER 17

Jimmy steers the truck off the blacktop and passes through the gate into the field he knows Dean is working. The news is on all the radio stations and he is disturbed.

As he shifts the truck into low gear to climb the newly mowed pasture, he contemplates their options. His new hat sits on the seat next to him, covering three farmer's sandwiches - thick sliced bologna and homemade ketchup on Wonder Bread – a McGrey family specialty. He is drinking a warm Pepsi.

Coming to the crest of a hill, he sees Dean Belkin sitting in the shade of the only tree in the field – a fat, spreading sycamore. Glancing in the rearview mirror, the rolling farmland opens behind him – dark curtains of green trees lining roads, lighter greens representing young corn, alfalfa, and soy. He says to no one in particular, "The soft palm of God."

His friend looks up from the job of opening his lunchbox as Jimmy drives up. A thermos of iced tea rests on the ground within arm's reach. It came out of the icebox that morning frozen. Now it's nearly warm. Dean has farmer's sandwiches as well.

"I don't know what we should do," says Jimmy, moving for the shade of the sycamore that overlooks nearly 120 acres of baby clover. It has already been a long day and is just the beginning of a number of them on this tract. It will take at least another four days to mow, dry, rake, and bale this field.

"What are you talking about?" Dean has finished his second bologna sandwich and is starting on the last one. A baggie containing four Little Debbies rolls from his lap to the ground. He chews the sandwich slowly and waits for his friend to explain.

"You don't read or listen to anything, do you?"

"Current events only matter if you know about them. You know that. I don't read and I don't listen to the radio and I don't watch TV and I certainly don't play around on the Innernet, or whatever the fuck they're calling it now."

"Sometimes that's a pretty stupid philosophy, Dean. One of those boys we got our hats from was killed last night."

Dean stops chewing. "No shit?" He squints, looking off in the distance. "Which one?"

"Don't know."

Dean waits for more details, but they don't come. Then he realizes the implications of the statement.

"You think they're going to tie us to that?"

"I don't know. But I do think we ought to contact the police before they contact us." They both gaze into the distant swelling land, considering the issue. Dean has a record in Chicago for dealing marijuana and acid.

"I don't know, Jim. I mean, how can they trace us? No one knew about the thing 'cept them boys and that little kid and he...he's still alive, isn't he?"

"I think so," said Jimmy. "Paper said one Amish man in his late teens was found murdered off Limerick Lane near the Forum Shopping Center."

"In Columbia? That's almost twenty miles from here. How do you know it was one of our guys?"

"I don't. I been pondering it all morning, though. And chances are it is. The article I read said that he was found without his hat. Anyway, seems like we need to at least call the cops and talk to them."

"Man, I don't know. You know how I feel about those guys."

"Your drug days are behind you, man." Jimmy pauses. "What I really wonder about is how those sounds we heard play into the whole thing."

"Those sounds? Those were more like a UFO or something. I don't think I want to get into that with anyone."

Jimmy looks at his friend doubtfully and says, "What about the light and—"

"God damn it, Jim, it was too fuckin' weird. The cops would think we were freaks, 'specially when we're in there talking about a fucking murder to them."

"I don't think they would be fazed by anything these days, Deano. You got Elvis sightings, Sumter's group evangelizing all over the place, freaked-out revival meetings, and now a murdered Amish kid. What's weird sounds in the dark and a vanishing light in the whole mix?"

"It's us looking like a couple fruits is what it is. I don't need that, man," Dean says. "The thing is, though, that it happened so far away from where we saw those boys. I mean, if we keep quiet and they do finally come to us, we can just say, 'Oh, yeah. Hey, we never thought about the connection."

Jimmy considers this point. Dean did three weeks working for the narcotics division of the police force in Chicago's south side during 1999. He was caught dealing LSD and bromo-mescaline, plus a quarter pound of Thai stick. When they caught him he was tripping on the bromo. He had the presence of mind to keep his altered state to himself, but he'd spent the rest of the night on the streets setting up other dealers. He got off three weeks later without even having his fingerprints or his photo taken. But it had been a horrible experience. He'd set up two Dead Heads and the University of Chicago chemistry major who had given him the bromo to sell.

"Deanie, we're not criminals. We didn't do anything. We do know something, though, that might help the cops. One of the guys we met with was murdered, man! I mean, central Missouri and all of a sudden there's a fuckin' killer out there! If we don't go talk to them, they're going to figure us out sooner or later. We gotta do something." He waits for his friend to respond.

Dean picks the bag of Little Debbies off the ground, takes one out, and hands the rest up to Jimmy who takes one out then hands the bag back. They both eat the chocolate and fluff in one bite. A faint smell of gasoline and diesel cuts through the thick scent of fresh-cut clover and warm, sticky chocolate. The screech of insects is barely audible in the distance, far away from the violence Dean has just committed, mowing down their habitat.

A single, fat locust the size of a mouse head clicks blindly through the air. The two men swallow the hot, sticky cakes, looking back toward the road below and the endless patchwork view of farmland heading into haze.

Finally, Dean says, "Okay. But you do the talking. I don't feel good about this. And let's just leave the kid out of it for now. He's probably barely able to write his own name, let alone plan a murder."

"Let's just see what goes down, man," says Jimmy. "I don't want to do this any more than you. And unless we have to, we won't say anything about the lights or the stuff we heard. Okay?"

"All right," says Dean, tossing the bag of Little Debbies on the ground near Jimmy's feet. There are two left. Jimmy goes back to the truck to get his sandwiches and another warm Pepsi from under the seat. When he turns from the cab he sees Dean Belkin staring at the bag of cakes like they are infested with ants.

CHAPTER 18

Jill chides herself for letting people make assumptions. She now has proof that the murders took place somewhere other than Limerick Lane. The two farm kids haven't gotten her any closer to the killer (or killers), but they have at least reminded her to be careful about assumptions. At least she was right about the hat.

She looks at the two straw hats the farmhands left with her resting on the shelf next to her printer. Clearly, they won't lead her anywhere just this minute, but they give her some degree of confidence that the murder took place other than where the body was found.

She has no suspicions about the two men from McGrey Farms. They'd even offered to ID the body. She knows where to find them anyway. If what Dean Belkin and James Harper told her is true, then she needs to get permission to do investigative work up near Fayette – smack dab in the middle of three county borders.

She calls Hughes into her office. Handing him four samples of hair in small plastic bags, she says, "I need you to label this one as Harper and this one as Belkin, then this one as Belkin's Hat and this one as Harper's Hat and then go get a sample from the victim and label them appropriately."

Hughes takes the samples, looking at her quizzically.

She tells him, "Those two kids who were just in here said they saw three Amish youths, that same night, as much as twenty miles from where we found them."

"They telling the truth?"

"Seemed like it. And it sort of corroborates my thinking. I'm gonna go with what I got."

"What you got? Where'd they see them boys?"

"Up near Fayette. They work a farm called McGrey's. They were out partying last night with the Amish kids and traded a couple bottles of Wild Turkey for two of their hats." She taps each hat on the shelf.

Hughes's idea of sucking up to her is to summarize her investigative logic. "This hair comes from those hats, and you need me to check the samples to corroborate their story?"

"That, and we're going to need to send the samples to St. Louis."

"Why don't they get us our own forensics lab, Sarge?"

"Why should they with express mail the way it is? You pack this stuff out by noon and we'll have it back by tomorrow a.m."

She looks at Hughes for a long moment, reading his thoughts. Sending evidence away for analysis has always made her feel more secure. There is something about the department that never feels right. Finally, she cocks an eyebrow and sighs. Hughes backs out of the room without another word.

Motive is clearly the key to the case, she thinks; then the weapon; and then opportunity. Finding the site that the two McGrey hands described might get her partway to all of these. She'll have to call in the sheriffs from both Howard and Boone counties on this, too – maybe even from as far west as Saline County as well. They'll need to enact the jurisdictional privilege of M-Squad. The Major Case Squad consists of designated personnel from all law enforcement agencies in the five-county region. As one of seven sergeants in the CPD investigative branch, Jill's three-year rotational stint coordinating the Crimes Against Persons Unit also makes her the department's M-Squad liaison.

It's getting to be a big job. But as far she can tell, this is still her case. Wilson will be coming in any second for an update, and the press will be after him soon enough – even with the Elvis sightings and the riot. Who knows? Maybe Elvis did it, she chuckles to herself as Robert Wilson, on cue, walks through her door.

It is common knowledge in the office that Lieutenant Robert Wilson, known as Bobby to everyone on the force, sees himself as an unappreciated civil servant who has risen to middle-level administrative duties as his reward for over thirty years of toil in Columbia's police department. Officially, he is director of administration and deputy chief of police. Unofficially, he is considered over the hill and not suited for modern investigative work. Jill knows that he understands all too well he will never rise to the rank of captain, which had been a life-long goal. She also figures he knows Jill will – probably before he can retire.

Bobby Wilson is a victim of change, she thinks. He'd made his opinions known early on as she began to rise through the ranks that opening up recruitment to women had created too much competition for too few jobs and had effectively eliminated the system of natural progression. They'd already jumped her in the three-year rotation to head up M-Squad and CAP. If that three-year stint pans out, everyone knows she's on her way to take charge of the Special Tactics And Response Team once Stoddemeier finished putting it together. This means promotion to captain and oversight of four different teams and twenty officers, including three sergeants and a freelancer of her choice to direct the inner-perimeter strike response and negotiation team.

It takes a great deal of daily effort, but Wilson has made his peace with coordinating Public Affairs and Administrative Services. She knows he works hard to find solace in being on TV and controlling the department's budget planning. It isn't police work, but he is in charge, and that counts for something. Besides, they'd moved Jill so far up in the hierarchy, the only person she could report directly to was him.

"Well, you got yourself one now, don't you?" he says closing her door.

"Yeah, Bobby, I got one. And I don't aim to fuck it up either."

"I'm sure you won't, Jill."

She cocks her eyebrow. "You do want me out from under you, don't you?"

"You're not under me, Jill. Just need my input, is all. I want to help all I can. What have you got so far? You contacted the family yet? We need an ID on the body."

"Wait. Before we get to that, what's this I hear about the FBI hanging around?"

"The Feds? Not bloody likely, Sergeant! What would they be hanging around here for?" It is the mocking tone that she doesn't like.

"It's a rumor, Bobby. Just a rumor. But if it's true and if it has an effect on my case, I want to know about it. So what's the deal?"

He moves to take a seat. "Okay. In all seriousness, we've been informed they're here for this Elvis thing. Not because they believe any of it, but because they're watching the Sumters. Remember we smelled something fishy last Christmas? Well, the Bureau smelled something, too. They actually had their eye on things almost a year ago. It's standard these days. These cults are too fuckin' out of hand. Just protecting the public, as far as they've told us. We're cooperating. I don't think they're here to investigate the murder of an Amish man, if that's what you're worried about. I'd introduce you to Agent Gold, but he's in Fulton looking up Sumter's accountant."

It's the politics she hates most about the job. She knows Wilson doesn't deal with her the way he could, but it isn't just the petty interpersonal stuff, it is all sorts of other things that he brings to the job. She is younger than him and still moving up the ladder; she is a woman; she is smarter; she has a better education (after her stint in juvie); she has known most of the guys on the force for a longer time – grew up with many of them; and now she has a case that can give her attention, and, if all goes well, the attention will spread to the national media looking into the Elvis scam.

As far as she can tell, though, politics on the job is not played out with ruthless, cunning intelligence. Politics is manipulation of everyone else around you, all the time – just in case. And it never stops for anyone. She can't shake the feeling of confusion and doubt it causes. It's always more difficult than any of the crimes she works.

It never goes away. No one wants to play, but everyone does, in a sort of muffled, hopeful way. Just in case. It doesn't seem like anyone really wants to hurt other people, but it also doesn't seem like people have a problem talking out of both sides of their mouths - just in case.

In Wilson's situation, she knows he resents her, like many of her colleagues over fifty. She also knows that the *lingua franca* of politics is information. Wilson may know more than he's letting on or he may be completely on the level. Either way, she figures he thinks he's got one up on her. If he knows more than he's saying, then he's got her in the dark. If he's just told her the truth, then she owes him. Choosing the lesser of two evils, she looks at Wilson: "Okay, Bobby, I guess I gotta owe you one. But unless I hear different, this is my case, right? Which reminds me. I'm implementing M-Squad jurisdiction on this one."

"Sure, Jill, that's what they tell me. You're in charge of all M-Squad activities regarding crimes against persons for at least the next two years," says Wilson. "Now, did you contact the family yet?"

This is one of the things she doesn't like about her job. You can't just think of the family as aggrieved in these cases. You have to go into it wondering if they are suspects. And even if it seems clear they aren't, then you have to try to find out if they know anything without them feeling like they're being interrogated. She's done this some with what turned out to be accidental shootings and with a case several years back in a crime of passion. But those were fairly straightforward. Here, with this young man, there is a very real mystery. She has no way of knowing how his family will react. She has to be focused. She has to thread the needle.

Then there is the final curse. She has to release the name of the victim to the press, and they have the potential to make the family's life a living hell. It's possible to stall for a while, even try to keep the name confidential as a matter of policy. But word will get out anyway, and then the press will think there is a cover-up, therefore doubling their efforts to hound the family. The one thing she's counting on is the Elvis sightings. They have created such a stir, maybe the murder will get handed to some of the less experienced junior staff, maybe even to a J-School intern.

"It took Heimer a bit of time to locate the farm," she says to Wilson, "but we know where the family is. Pretty long way, actually, from Limerick Lane. Over near Hallsville on the east of town. Heimer's story is that they are practically self-sufficient and rarely leave the general vicinity of their land. They grow their own food, use groundwater, run a couple mini-hydro stations. You know, little dams for electricity? And they even have a small pickup fired by wood. We're looking in the area where the body was found for the truck, but we may find it at the property. Who knows? I'm going out this afternoon to talk to them. They don't have a phone. Probably don't get the paper, either, or have a TV, even. They know we're looking for their son, but they don't know he's been murdered."

"Jesus, it takes all kinds, don't it?" says Wilson with a slight tone of sympathy and a bit of conspirator thrown in. She knows he's done this sort of thing before.

"Just remember it's all pretty funny right now, Jill. We got Elvis, the FBI, rioting religious fanatics...." He trails off and thinks for a moment. Finally, he asks, "You gonna release the name when you're done with the family?"

"I don't know. Couple of local reporters are waiting for a statement or something from us already. The big dogs will be in here, too, before long. I don't know, you're much better than me at stuff like that, Bobby. You wanna do it?"

Wilson looks at her for a few seconds, then says, "Sure. Okay, I guess we could work that into the press release. Just give me the word once you've been out to the family. Warn 'em, too, Jill. They might be under siege for a bit."

"Thanks," she says. "Bobby, I need one other thing."

He waits.

"We got a tip that may mean things actually happened up in the Fayette area. You know that area near Routes J and EE? I need those maps."

"Sure, Jill, you go get 'em."

She decides to end the conversation. "Right. Then I'm glad we had the time to talk, Bobby." She reaches for the phone as Bobby Wilson backs out of her office.

*

"You know, Jill," Dale Stoddemeier says, "if you can't find the place where it all happened, you're going to have a hard time solving this case." They're in The Pancake House again, having an early dinner.

She's been out to the Amish family's and is still trying to figure things out. She'd decided best taste dictated bringing along a photo of the body, instead of requiring them to come in. A formal ID could happen later. The look on the mother's face was still fresh in her mind.

They hadn't seen any of their older sons since the morning after the murder. This surprised Jill. She got the names: Stephen, Marston, and Gerhart Jergensen. She described the body and the direct hit to the heart, watching the mother struggle to acknowledge it was Stephen, her third and youngest son, who was dead.

Several times, Jill asked if they had seen or heard from the other two. The father understood where she was going with her line of questioning.

"You cannot be serious, Officer Simpson. My boys loved each other. Stephen, especially, was loved by the other two. He had a gift from God. They may be in the end of their Timeout, but they are not murderers."

"Timeout?" she asked.

"It's a special period we set for young men and women before they are baptized in their early twenties. They form groups and drink and dance and socialize. It's hard for us since we have been banished, but we still need to follow the old ways. They come and go as they please. We don't have much to offer here. Sometimes they will be in the outside world for several weeks at a time. We must give them their distance so that they may choose to come back to us. We know they're doing things that they shouldn't. Drinking, smoking - and more. But we must let them do what they need to do."

"That explains the alcohol then. On his clothing and in his blood," Jill said.

"They are allowed Timeout to experiment and play with life in the world of other men. It is taking a risk. Some have chosen what we do not wish for them. Stephen will not be returning." The father was staring at the ground.

"Mr. Jergensen, I'm sorry to ask these questions, but what about the other two?"

"I don't know. You don't think...that they are also...dead?"

"I don't know, sir. We've found no other bodies and no clues of other foul play."

She wondered about the other implication – that the other two might be hiding out in fear of something – or worse, that they might actually be legitimate suspects.

The father was the only one who could speak rationally. They hadn't taken the truck. According to him, they sometimes hitchhiked into Hallsville and even Columbia.

They were all three artisans. The father showed her chairs and a large table they had been working on together. The carpentry was fairly plain, but she could tell a lot of skill had gone into the work. Stephen had been the most skilled of the three and had designed the table. He had also designed the wood-fired truck, and supervised the building of their power system. He was also the reason they had been banished. The father showed her the boy's drum kit and a wall full of electronic recording equipment and computers.

He had no idea why anyone would want to kill his son. The mother cried quietly, rocking back and forth in her chair, clutching the youngest son and their small daughter in each arm. It was painful. Simpson felt somehow that the whole tragedy was an event for which she needed to apologize. These were not worldly people. They had done no harm. In fact, their entire way of living was specifically designed to make sure that they had as little impact on other lives as possible. The only thing strange about the whole situation was how the remaining son, who must have been eleven or twelve, kept staring at her quietly with his big blue eyes, barely blinking. Something seemed to be acknowledged by those eyes. What, she couldn't tell.

As she left, she thought to say she would find the killer and bring him to justice. But something stopped her. These people were not interested in justice. They had lost at least one son and two other ones were missing – all to a world they'd sought to escape.

She glances now around the restaurant. The air is slightly scented with machine oil, burned coffee, bacon grease, and cigarette smoke. It's a slow night and few people are there eating – several truckers, a young family with four kids under seven, an older couple, and then a man in the booth behind theirs.

She wonders how much power it takes to feed the fluorescent lighting that casts its pale lavender hue on the plastic tabletops and faces. She thinks then about the heavy wooden table the boys were making and compares it to the fiberglass booth she's sitting in, bolted to the floor and wall.

"There's another complication, Dale. Two of Stephen Jergensen's brothers are missing as well. They could be dead, could be scared of something or someone, could be accomplices, or could be directly responsible."

"What are you thinking, Jill?"

"I'm thinking I need the fucking crime scene."

"Pretty tough, Officer Simpson. There's a lot of space out there."

"We're going to find the place, Dale."

"You know, that self-confidence still gets to me," he says. "We've been friends going on nearly seventeen years since before you made your choice to become a cop. You were just a confused young student at the University of Missouri full of pain and regret, but also full of untapped smarts and uncommon insight."

"Dale, you tell me this all the time."

"I know. I'm sorry."

She sighs. "Like I say, we're going to find the crime scene. I know it."

"Well, you better find it," Stoddemeier says. "And you better do it quick."

She squints at him. Stoddemeier has been back on the staff for just over six months and Jill has naturally gravitated back to him. There's talk in the office, she knows, but both of them have kept things professional. It's clear to her Stoddemeier is interested, but so far she's managed to steer them away from intimacy. He is nearly ten years her senior and although he is fit and attractive, she figures she knows, as she's always known with him, that she needs a mentor more than she needs a lover. Besides, he isn't really her type. There is something too reserved about him, too self-possessed and under control.

"You don't need to remind me about expediting things, Dale. I know how cold a trail can get. But we're doing all we can. I went out with Heimer today and did the canvassing. We got nothing. "I've got Baines and Hughes out near Hallsville doing some searching now around the area those kids lived to see what they can turn up. I've also got someone down in Rolla picking up USGS maps of the area. We're pretty sure things happened close to Fayette and then the body was transported to Columbia."

Dale chuckles. She'd asked for maps three or four times because of just this kind of thing. The mid-Missouri countryside has slowly been acquired by larger and larger conglomerates. Whereas once it was possible to look at county property maps defining the areas owned by families and small-scale farmers, over the years huge tracts of land have become open space, void of any definition. And ownership of the land is hard to trace. With a paucity of people outside the towns in the area, few had reason to travel through the back roads. Then there was the problem of the old silo installations and secret federal lands. It had been sold off – mostly to Fancher – but surveys of that land had never really been something the Columbia Police Department had data on. No law enforcement group in the region did. Besides, the CPD has a $2 million computerized geographic information system for city maps and crime reports but nothing for the surrounding counties. Whenever Jill needs topographic information, Bobby Wilson makes her get online – something she hates – to use the updated USGS database and Google. This is wonderful deskwork, but she needs the old hardcopy wall maps of the area. She's done the research. There are six for the M-Squad region, but a hardcopy of practically anything other than best sellers is hard to come by these days. The USGS in Rolla is the nearest source and the cost is $109.50. She wants three of each type of map for her field team. The total budget item sits close to $2,000.

It is an odd kind of wilderness – rolling hills, empty valleys, acres of trees surrounding circular plots planted with various high-yield crops, large holdings of alfalfa and clover, even small plots split by gravel roads that over time had nearly washed away. Wilson kept denying her requisition request for maps. It had become a departmental joke. The use of arbitrary power over her amused everyone because it meant that Bobby had reached the end of the promotion line and that he was running scared.

"At least I'll get the maps out of this," she muses.

"Where you going to put them, though?" he asks. "You put 'em on your wall and Wilson will never hear the end of it. You better keep 'em rolled up and in their tube."

It's her turn to chuckle. "I'll keep them out of sight unless they help me break this case. But if we find what we're looking for, they're going up right in the squad room next to the metro streets map and he can eat shit."

*

Frank Harris sits in the booth behind them smiling at the belligerence of the woman cop. He is beginning to like her a lot. He considers, however, sitting in a different spot next time, just in case they noticed him.

He recalls covering Jones's death again. It had made him notorious with his peers and colleagues, but it had been the lowest point in his career.

*

From backstage he could see that Jones was in a frenzy. Anger was written on everything he did. There was an abandon to each move that Harris had never seen before. He wondered if he was just perceiving things differently after meeting the singer, or if somehow Jones really was planning something. The performer went into his now famous medley of *Danger is in the Dark* songs, fingers snapping at Abe Dohrmacher, the drummer, and Cindy Black, the bass player, clearly wishing them to pick up the tempo. Sleighmaker Hayes bent over his white Les Paul, stringy silver hair obscuring his face, firing off screeching licks and glancing at the singer every so often, surprised by the hectic pace. Julie Haddonfield clutched her chrome synthezar and angled it at the laser strobes, shooting beams of rainbow light into the darkness and the crowd.

It was hot just watching the manic moves of the singer. Harris took off his corduroy blazer and placed it on the back of a speaker stand. He noticed the bodyguard watching him closely from the other wing of the stage. A few minutes later, Astro was standing next to Harris, eyeing him carefully.

They launched into Jimi Hendrix's "Fire" and "Manic Depression," each time with the same introductory chords, Dohrmacher's simple, hard techno-punk beat heavy with tom-toms and bass drum. Jones's voice was grittier than it was in the first set, his dance steps more and more repetitive during the guitar breaks, always circling the same imaginary middle of the stage in a sort of tribal stomp. His eyes looked far away, cheeks streaked with grimy black makeup, sweat, and tears.

The group slowed the pace as Jones stood frozen in the center of the area of the stage he had circled while he whispered the words of Michael Jackson's "Hold Me." The house lights were brought up a touch so that the singer could see the crowd. It was then that Harris noticed the mood. The usual fever was gone. They watched in utter silence, almost stone-faced, as the volume moved back up the decibel scale with the snared intro to "Debbie Lynn" and the deep bass line. Even with the jerky, quick moonwalk illusion, the standard roar never came. Jones had them in some kind of trance, or they had him.

Finally, he moved into the "No One to Love/Country Soul" finale. The usual tightly choreographed dance routine was left out. In fact, no dancers appeared on the stage at all. Jones bounced and whirled and pranced and stomped, exhorting his band to play faster, twirling his arm in the air, spinning in circles. And then the crescendoed end of "Country Soul": power chords flailed again and again by Haddonfield, the bass and tom-toms thumping in unison louder and louder, Sleighmaker fingering his guitar neck, gently moving his pick hand across the strings in scrabbling light speed, the guitar shrieking and roaring and crying the desperation of the moment – the crowd back in darkness, the musicians playing faster and faster and faster, looking for a way out.

And then silence and the lights, the singer alone on stage, the pearl-handled .45 in his hand, raised to his mouth, the brief moment that would stay in Harris's mind forever. Jones sucked on the barrel. Then somehow, seeming to change his mind at the last minute, taking the gun away from his lips, pausing, a sense of relief issuing from the stunned crowd (was it only part of the act?).

In the end, however, came the dazzlingly quick movement of the pistol next to his right ear and then the report of the .45 as he blew his brains out in front of 20,000 confused and panicked fans – what little innocence left in Harris's life, and theirs, now gone forever.

Three days later, after the funeral and the frenzy, after people had started to live their lives again, and the video of the final moments of the concert was no longer being played on TV every hour, Harris found a small envelope in the breast pocket of the corduroy jacket he had worn during his interview and taken off backstage. Inside was a handwritten letter. It read:

Dear Maria,

You of all people should at least partly be able to understand why I did what I did. Maybe the method was not to your liking, but my life has been hell. I know I started the whole thing with the lizards in the living room and the heat chamber, and all the surgery, but when things took off, nothing was good enough except the worst. After all we did for him, to this day I don't know why Bertrand was so intent on destroying me. I can't help thinking that somehow Joseph had something to do with it.

But, more than anything, I want you to know I love you. You never liked it, but "Angels Beware" was actually written for you, my mother.

Around the time I was writing "Danger is in the Dark" I couldn't get the idea of my own death out of my head. What I'm really asking in that song, is whether my mother's love will be in heaven when I die. I'm asking whether you will forgive me, too, for all they say I did, because I know that even when they made it up, I made it possible for them to pretend it was true. And in a very real way, I guess all of it was true on some level.

But I live on. I have to. That is what being King Jones means, if nothing else. In the music and in my dance I have made myself eternal – and in those moments on stage. I told you about them. I have felt, at times, the audience coming through the beat and into my soul, grooving to me and me grooving to them. And somehow, with all of that happening, even just for a few moments, there's too much magic going on when I'm out there for things to be otherwise, I know there is some higher power.

This is not the end. I will always look down on you, Maria, and love you and protect you. It should be easier for me from where I am now than it was up until tonight. My father could always get in the way. My brothers and sisters, too. And your religion.

So do not worry. I am eternal. You are my mother. I love you. God will understand what I have done. I'm not like other guys. You will be there. Angels beware.

Love forever,
King

Harris kept a copy of the note in a strongbox in his apartment and never showed it to anyone.

*

Sitting in his booth and thinking about death, he is suddenly reminded of the McGrey woman's message. The phone number is back in his room. He would have to remember to call her, even though she had already served her purpose.

CHAPTER 19

Two khaki-clad deputies are waiting for Jill, smoking cigarettes in the shade. She's worked with them already on a few M-Squad cases. Baines and Hughes sit in the air-conditioning of their car. She feels sympathetic today. It's becoming clear this is going to be a long case.

"You guys waiting long?" she asks the deputies. They watch her move toward them. She ignores how they watch her breasts, shakes hands and makes eye contact.

"Your bosses showing up?" The deputies say no.

Smoking on the job has even become too political for her. She pops a tab of Trident in her mouth and says, "You guys know about this homicide?" One of them nods yes.

"Okay," she begins, turning back to find Baines and Hughes still sitting in their car. "We got a tip that somewhere out here two kids from McGrey Farms met up with the victim a little before the estimated time of the murder. Seems to me it didn't happen anywhere near where we found the victim, so I'm hoping we learn something out here. I already talked to my county sheriff's office.

"In addition," she continues, "the victim's two brothers are missing. We may find bodies or clues to what happened to them as well. We don't know."

Baines gets out of the car and walks over. Hughes remains. The deputies introduce themselves to Baines as Woods and Crenshaw from Howard and Saline Counties, respectively.

She waits for the three of them to exchange comments on the heat and then continues, "I know your bosses sent you out to assist us, but we don't really need your help here. I just wanted to ask permission to do our work. We may need to interview some citizens, we'll definitely be going back and forth between counties, and I know I'm way out of jurisdiction. If we find out conclusively that the murder took place here, I'll certainly recommend to my chief of operations that we inform your bosses. Is that okay?" She doesn't like how fast she's speaking. Too uncertain.

They agree that there is no problem and seem relieved they aren't needed, then leave.

Hughes gets out of the car as soon as they drive off. They may have as much as four hours before the day is over. Jill goes back to her car and pulls a long cardboard mailing tube out of the back. She hesitates a moment, glances to see if she's being watched, then calmly unholsters her Glock and slides it under the seat. Shaking her head, she locks the vehicle and walks toward Baines and Hughes, fairly certain that they hadn't seen her stow her weapon.

"Wish they gave us RVs for this kind of work," grumbles Hughes as he moves to check the barbwire fence for an easy place to cross. She tells Hughes he will go northeast and Baines northwest while she heads due north. They agree to check in with her every half hour.

"You're looking for anything out of the ordinary. Anything. Strips of black cloth, bullet casings, a whiskey bottle, signs of dragging, footprints maybe; I have no idea what we could find." She spreads the topographic map out on the hood of her car then looks up at a ridge in the distance. "This area doesn't have a lot of roads running through it so we may have a hard time pinpointing each other's whereabouts. When you make it to the top of that ridge up there, head toward me, I'll wait in the center."

Baines makes to start off. Hughes says, "Sergeant, that's at least three miles from here. Could take all afternoon by the time we get back to our cars."

"You're right, Officer Hughes. Sorry. But look on the bright side: if you find the evidence, you get to be the hero of the day."

She shakes her head and starts walking. "Won't that be a change?" Squinting at Baines, she turns her back on Hughes.

As they fan out, Jill makes sure to reduce her gait, giving the other two officers ample time to head away from her. She needs to be alone. It's hot, but there is a slight breeze and the sounds of birds, cicadas, and grasshoppers calm her immensely. If they didn't have any luck today, then they weren't going to have any at all.

*

Several miles away, King Jones is waking up. Weak and covered with sweat, his head feels light and tense, the whole right side still aching where the gun report occurred. But the peaceful song of birds quickly soothes him. For once he has nothing to do. The only reason he even needs to get up is so that he can pee. But the luxury of lying in bed and just listening to the sounds around the house makes him worry. He is still shy. No matter what this process has done, it hasn't taken away his basic personality. Besides, he doesn't know where the bathroom is, and he doesn't want to make his debut in the group by letting them know that he has to pee.

A woman he recognizes from when they first came to him years before enters the room as he contemplates bladder control. She carries a tray with a tomato, cheese, and lettuce sandwich on it along with a tall glass of iced tea. He wonders how long he can keep his bladder under control as she glances over the tray at him and says, "Least it wasn't your whole body, was it? Just your head." She points at the bandage near the back of his skull as she smiles mischievously down at him.

"It's not bad yet" she continues. "Wait till you get up and try to function normally. It takes time to get used to your new circumstances. You can eat, though. And it feels just like the real thing...well, it is the real thing, sort of." She searches his eyes for something, then gives one of her cackles.

"You don't know what the fuck I'm talking about, do you? Really! Me? I did it all with downs, man. And booze. Well, also smack, but it was the whiskey and the ludes that did it. It all came when I didn't want it. And it took a long time, just like you, once I got here, to overcome my need to get wasted. Most of us have had to deal with that – it was our whole bodies that we put down; but for you, you just acted weird all the time and made people wonder about your cock and why you wore gloves.

"I'm here to take care of you, though, not confuse you. I'm sorry. You been away longer than any of us. Nearly four months. Had some worried, but not me. Like I say, it takes awhile.

"Worst thing is just coming out of it, getting used to a different sense of equilibrium. And there's some things that are impossible which we can talk about later, like you'll never have to pee again and all that body stuff. 'Course, music's got to be sort of relearned. But it all starts in your mind now, not in your body. Ain't that a gas? I always thought it was the body that drove the soul or the groove or the funk or whatever you want to call it. But it isn't. It's your mind. That's your soul. Everything from there out is learned. The body is nothing but an extension...at least it is for us now. Maybe it was before, too. We don't really know. There's a lot we just really can't figure out."

Jones gets a good deal of this, but he still needs to pee. "Um, I need to go to the bathroom," he finally says quietly.

"Oh sure, it's down the hall. Second door on the left." She waits as he tries to sit up.

"Sorry," she says finally, and bends toward the bed to help him. She isn't surprised at how light he feels and how easy it is to help move him. She wonders, though, how much he will need her help figuring things out. That's the main thing everyone is concerned about: he just isn't like a lot of them. His ego is practically nonexistent. They have no idea if he will make it all the way.

When he comes back, she sees the look of confusion she expected. Again, the sly grin. "Didn't have to, huh?"

He looks at the floor.

"It takes a while for your body and mind to figure each other out again. Your body doesn't have to pee, your mind does...which means that you don't really have to go. It's just learned. After awhile you'll stop feeling that pressure. It's not really there. That's the good thing. The bad thing, and none of us talk about this much, so don't tell anyone I told you, is that sex is out the window. Easiest way I can put it is that we're not really here. Even if you feel like you need to rub your eyes or yawn or scratch something, it isn't actually there. This state we're in allows a good deal of compensation for not being here, but we can't totally overcome the reality of physics. I never paid attention to stuff like that until I got this way, and now I wish I'd read more when I was in school, but I'm learning. When you talk to Jack he might be better able to help you make sense of it all, but most of us spent our lives creating, not learning how things work."

"Are there children here?" he asks.

"Kids? Nah. You gotta know what you're doing to get here. You're probably the closest thing to a child we have." She pauses to gauge his response and also to wonder if she has just offended him.

"At any rate," she continues, "I think your work is fantastic. It's a shame you can't share it with people anymore. But we're hoping to learn a lot from you. Now, eat this sandwich and try the tea. Both are very fresh and well worth the trip just in themselves. You've got a big day ahead of you. You've got a lot of people who are just dying to meet you. I think you're going to be surprised who you see and what you learn.

*

Jill has been walking for nearly an hour but has not crossed any roads. She reminds herself to ask Baines and Heimer on the next check-in if they've seen any themselves. It's odd but certainly not impossible. The topographic map she's using is dated 1997. On the map she notes that she should have crossed two small gravel or dirt roads and one paved state road. It's almost time to radio them again.

She paces herself slowly under the sun, keeping her eyes on the ground, occasionally stopping to listen to the sounds around her. She thinks about trackers from old movies she'd seen with her brother when she was a kid, how what old-timers were able to do used to seem such an impossible science to master. Now she knows better. It's really a question of paying attention and of keeping your eyes on the ground, being completely methodical and focused.

After noting tall grass peeled back into a near path, she finds the camp in a thicket of brambles and wild blackberries. The fire pit is recent. She holds her palm over the ashes, feeling the warmth greet her hand. Perhaps a fire for breakfast. The sleeping bag and gear are neatly tucked under a dense tangle of what will soon be a bush puffed up with wild roses. Examining the contents of the bundle of gear, she finds several interesting items, including a two-way radio, a box of .22-gauge ammunition (counting them quickly, she figures the box is missing some bullets), a ticket to the June 23rd revival meeting in Rocheport, a knapsack containing packages of dried soup mix and granola bars, an open carton of Marlboros, a can opener, several small pots, and a copy of *TV Guide* from the previous week with a picture of Elvis in white robes and the Reverend Sumter standing behind him.

"One Dog to Two Dogs. Over." She waits.

"Come in, One Dog." It's Baines.

She waits for Hughes now.

"Here, One Dog." Even on a walkie-talkie Hughes sounds like an asshole.

"I may have found what we're looking for. Over."

"What do you want us to do?" It is Hughes.

"What did you find, Sergeant?" asks Baines.

"A camp, complete with various and sundry odds and ends, including a box of ammunition. Box is opened and it looks like some six bullets are missing. Question is whether it all took place close by or whether we still need to do some searching. Over."

"What is your location? Over." Though soft-spoken, Baines is easily excited.

"I'm maybe two miles from the road. If you guys have been walking at my pace, you should be, too. I'm a couple hundred yards north by northwest of Troubadour Creek. Check your maps, adjust to the West and East and you should each be here in about twenty minutes. Over."

"Over and out, Chief."

"Officer Hughes? You got the kit don't you? Over." She waits perhaps thirty seconds for his response. "Hughes?"

"Negative, sir. I cached it about half an hour ago. It was getting pretty heavy. May take a bit longer than twenty minutes. Over."

"Well, go get it and then just get here as soon as you can. We can do some good detective work if it's all in one piece. And Hughes, jog to it, okay? Over and out."

She clicks off her walkie-talkie and reaches in her breast pocket for her gloves and the Baggies. It's far too hot for this kind of work as a one-person operation.

There isn't much to do, actually. Fingerprints are unlikely with no glass or other shiny surface – maybe the pots or can opener if they're lucky. But she doesn't hold much hope for them.

She pours out the bullets and counts them to make sure. There are 92, meaning that the guy is using an eight-count clip – probably a Beretta or a Walther. It also probably means that he has just bought the gun and neglected to purchase auxiliary clips. Indicating he's not a professional. The gun could have been purchased anywhere, but she will have Heimer run down recent purchases in the area just to be sure.

The biggest find is the two-way radio. She turns it on and listens. The battery is okay. She considers trying it, but decides against it. There is no need right now to tip anyone off.

A two-way means one very important thing: the guy is not alone. It may be the Feds. But since the gun is probably new and there are only eight bullets missing, it sort of makes that unlikely.

They had a number of marijuana farmers in the area before she'd come on board. She thinks about the stories she's heard of those days during the late '70s. They'd grown the stuff in out-of-the-way cornfields and had succeeded for several years until their operations had become too big. Wilson had coordinated a multicounty team in the days before M-Squad, ending with a full-scale armored assault on the largest camp. The camp had been located by intercepting radio transmissions. She remembered Wilson emphasizing how surprised he was that they had been able to find the radio frequency so easily.

Jill places most of the bullets back in the box carefully, depositing three of them in a small, plastic evidence bag. She still needs the murder weapon, of course. If they find it, the bullets would come in handy with ballistics.

The rest of the gear doesn't amount to much. The ticket for Sumter's event could just be a coincidence, but it's something she'll keep in the back of her mind. The *TV Guide* seems odd to have at a camp as well, but only about 50 million are sold every week. No matter what, though, a murder implicating Sumter is too easy.

She senses the movement before she hears the sound. A thick, cold emptiness rises from her gut to her chest. Her eyes glance to either side while she keeps her head down. She feels like an idiot for turning her back to the camp entrance.

There is no mistaking it now, she is being watched by someone not thirty yards away. Glancing down at her empty holster, she wishes she had kept her weapon. As nonchalantly as possible, she stands and turns, camouflaging her scan for the hidden figure by acting as if she is rubbing sweat from her forehead. A blur of red and blue through the scrub moves back into the high grass. From the looks of it, he's walking backwards, maybe still assuming he hasn't been seen. She can tell though that he is moving quickly to get out of the area.

Her hand goes to the holster as if the Glock is still strapped there. She moves to a crouch and takes aim with her clasped empty hands. "Police!" she shouts. "Hold it!" The figure turns and starts to run.

It has only been ten minutes or so, but she hopes Baines is at least close by. Several hundred yards away she sees a head of dark hair bobbing up and down and can hear the faint swish of grass flattened by the runner escaping.

CHAPTER 20

Dixon Hancock stares at the headline in disbelief, a slight queasiness boiling in his stomach. He looks at the photograph of the young girl, probably her high school picture – bright eyes, high cheek bones, large mouth, long, light-colored hair – the kind of girl he would have gone for when he was a teenager, the kind of girl like Stacey, his daughter. His hand goes to the back of his shaved head and rubs the flesh as he considers what has happened.

No charges have been filed yet, even by the girl's parents. It has been called an unfortunate accident, but he knows better. Glancing at his wig and sequined clothes and the bag containing the T-shirt and jeans, he figures it could be called things like reckless endangerment, inciting a riot, fraud, a bunch of other things. And to have it all culminate in the death of a young girl is far more than he bargained for.

Hancock has a bit more waiting to do, then he can get back down to Branson. He has work waiting for him. With the sighting on all the networks and the riot, people will be flocking from all over the world to Rocheport. The question now is how to lure them down to Branson to see The Elvisinators. He'd have to talk to the others about that. Right now, though, he needs to get out of town, home to his daughter and back to work.

A knock sounds at the door as he reaches to pick up the picture of the group. The National Elvisinators Review had started to fizzle before it ever got off the ground, but things are really going to turn around now. He looks at the group of men, arm in arm, each with his own special Elvis good-time sneer. It will be easy. All they have to do is schedule several nights in Rocheport, or even Columbia, and the rest will be gravy.

He peers through the security viewer and sees the round, bulbous face he had expected distorted in the viewing lens. He opens the door.

Sumter is hard to read. He is clearly disturbed, but the look in his eyes is not fully unhappy.

"I see you read the paper," starts Sumter as he comes through the door. He places the gym bag on the floor and sits on the bed. He's sweating. Taking several brown paper towels from the inside pocket of his sport coat, he wipes his forehead, looking around the tiny room.

"Yeah, and this is not good, Reverend. You didn't exactly tell me you were trying to incite a riot."

"I didn't know that was going to happen, boy! But it's not that big a deal. I mean, I'm sorry that kid got killed and all, but as far as I can tell it's not a bad way to go out. Broken neck starts with the severing of nerves to the brain, which means it's quick and probably doesn't hurt much, but on top of it all she was in a state of ecstasy as she moved toward the stage to touch you. I remember her face. I mean, what more could you want?"

Hancock glances down at the picture of the girl again. "Her being alive would help. Dead is dead, Sumter. And we caused it."

"Well, not necessarily, my friend. I mean, that's what religion is all about. If you're a true Christian, dead isn't dead, is it? She's just gone somewhere else. I don't know why people make such a big deal out of it if they really believe. But maybe they don't believe. Maybe that's the problem. What is faith anyway? Just shooting craps." Sumter says all of this in a mocking, deadpan tone. Hancock can't read what his attitude means.

"This whole thing is pretty amazing, wouldn't you say?" continues Sumter. "And all masterminded by me – with a little help from you, of course."

"I'm not sure this was such a good idea," says Hancock as he picks up the bag. "But you can believe I'm going to forget about this whole thing as soon as I can." He looks down at the bag.

"All twenties, as promised," chuckles Sumter. "Twenty thousand dollars for a few days of playing Elvis ain't bad, I'd say. You only have one more thing to do for me. Get out of town and don't come back unless you hear from me. We'll let the mystery ride its way out for the next few months, and then after it all fades into people's memories maybe we'll shake things up again."

Hancock starts to ask about The Review but thinks better of it. Sumter is too interested in giving advice. The idea of twenty thousand dollars now belonging to him is beginning to flood his mind with ideas. He can buy Stacey a laptop as a late graduation gift, maybe buy her mom a new TV, and he can use some of the money to rent a bus to get The Review up here as soon as possible.

"Don't call me again, Reverend. And don't worry, I won't go to the cops."

"I hope I don't need you, Mr. Hancock, but I may. And as far as the police are concerned, what would you tell them? That you were paid to impersonate Elvis? There's no way they can connect any of this to me. I can just deny what you say and claim that you duped me as well. No, boy, there's no smoking gun here except the fact that you are a fraud. So, if I need you, you'll show up. Got it? Besides, I imagine that you may like large quantities of cash more than you think. You get used to having a bit of pocket money, my friend, for nothing other than your presence and we'll be fine.

"And one more thing, Hancock. I read where you were spotted out Fayette way and a couple of ladies even called in to the radio and TV. Says you was diggin' in your spurs and maybe even doin' some serious plumbing with 'em. Is that true?"

"Are you kidding me?" Hancock says. "First of all, I don't have time for the kind of thing you're implying. And second, I don't take my likeness lightly. There's no way I'd be out there doing anything like what you're talking about."

"Well then, why do you think those little girls is saying you robbed 'em of their hearts and all, Mr. Elvis-Look-Alike?"

"I've had to deal with this kind of thing before, Reverend. When Elvis gets around, some people just start off into fantasy worlds. I've actually been chased off stage by a jealous husband who claimed that he couldn't stand to be compared to Presley."

"Well, I figure they could all be lying, Hancock, but I just want to be sure. You keep that old pecker in your pants when you're dressed up for me in these parts, you hear? I'm sure I can find others who'll do me fine if you all of a sudden stop showing up for work."

Hancock wants to respond but is halted by a strange, dark nausea. What had he gotten himself into?

*

Harris stays long enough to realize the waitress he is attracted to is married – or at least not interested. For the first two drinks her ring finger was empty. He had tired of waiting for Janie. In the dark hotel bar he'd worked hard at catching the waitress's eye. She was on top of things, he gave her that. When she brought him the third drink, her finger was adorned with a wedding band. Smart girl.

Walking down the hall to his room, he catches a glimpse of movement in the shadows near his door. He hesitates. Years in the business have taught him caution. He's been jumped enough times in the past.

Coral McGrey steps out of the shadows.

"Mr. Harris, why didn't you return my call?"

He lies. "I'm sorry, Ms. McGrey, I was going to my room to do just that."

"This couldn't wait," she says.

"What?"

"I was at the revival meeting yesterday after our interview."

"Yes, I know. I saw you. You left in a hurry."

"Because it wasn't him."

"Wasn't him?"

"The man that showed up as Elvis. It wasn't him."

"What do you mean?"

"That wasn't who I was talking about," she says simply. "You need to know that. That was an impostor." And with that she walks quickly down the hall.

Part V
Thicker Than Water

"His guitar playing spoke of an ecstasy that could be had."
-Bruce Springsteen speaking about Jimi Hendrix

CHAPTER 21

Jill prides herself on playing the dumb broad cop. She is positioned several hundred yards from the camp near some scrub trees on a rise in the pasture, done in such a way that anyone will be able to spot her if they're looking carefully. She wants to make it look good, though, so she angles herself just out of the open and even sets up the angle so that there will be no sun-flash off her binoculars. After Hughes and Baines leave, she pulls out the cosmetic pack which she carries for just these purposes and removes the vanity mirror. She doesn't wear makeup, except on these occasions.

A camp in the middle of farmland is just too odd. At 4:30, she sent Hughes and Baines back with the evidence. The plan is for Baines to return near dusk from the northeast and to stake out the camp with her from a more secret vantage point. There was concern for her safety after she ran into her visitor, but she quietly pointed out that she was their superior. Besides, they needed whoever it was to feel she was vulnerable. She is to radio in every hour on the half hour so that they know everything is all right. The only real problem is that the Glock is still locked in her car.

By the 7:30 check-in she is hungry. The idea of cold soup from the camp comes to her. She thinks back to her early days. She'd been hooked on crack and heroin for nearly two years and then gotten off the stuff through Jack Daniels and Gilbeys.

Dale Stoddemeier, in his first stint with the department, had pushed her through the worst of it. She'd been busted in a raid on a coke dealer's house in a trailer park outside of Columbia. As the supervising field officer, he'd used his pull to get her released on informant status. But she'd never had to follow through. He got her into a detox program instead.

Visiting every week or so, it became clear he had a crush on her, and although nothing would ever come of it their friendship grew. She was nearing twenty. He was in his thirties.

Just as in cases with young hospital patients suffering through long rehab who end up pursuing careers in medicine, Jill worked hard to please Stoddemeier. Her choice of cleaning up in order to become a cop was obvious by the time she announced it to him.

After release, she knew she still needed a daily buzz, but she worked hard at self-control while she went through basic training, attended classes at MU, and did her first few years on the street in a patrol car. She'd gotten off heroin, but it would take her several years to overcome the booze. Stoddemeier eventually left the department to join a federal agency in California and finally became a high-end security consultant. They lost touch.

As a newly minted alcoholic, Jill could function okay during the day, but after work she would usually be so wasted when she got home from bars that she had little energy to make herself a meal. Several times she had opened a can of Chunky Soup and consumed it cold while watching Letterman from the kitchen sink. Not until she had been promoted to sergeant did she climb out of the pit. It had been almost fifteen years now since she'd had a drink.

There had been men in her life throughout it all. Jeffrey had been the longest stand. They lived together on and off once she'd cleaned up. But she never could muster the emotional constitution to make it work.

She hadn't found anyone after Jeffrey, nor had she spent much time with Jonathan, but she'd meant to change that. She'd been meaning to change that for almost two decades. Now it was too late.

My son, Jonathan, she thought hollowly. She'd given him up to Jeffrey just after the boy was born. One thing she was proud of was that she'd never denied that her drug addiction was a problem, nor had she denied that she was an alcoholic later on. But by the time she'd truly recovered, her son was seventeen. They'd spent some time together, then. He'd come over for dinner on weekends and sometimes during the holidays and on her birthday. As a young teen, he showed up at her door when he was too drunk to face his dad. She loved him as best she could – like a mother with problems, she would say to herself. But he didn't really seem to see her as his mom. She was more like an older friend or a big sister. She went to some of his band's performances on campus during the '80s. She'd never known the extent of his drug use or his own alcoholism until it was too late. He had died on April Fools Day. Complications from cirrhosis of the liver. He was just twenty-five.

Jeffrey had never said a word about the link between Jonathan's addictions and hers. He himself had smoked dope around the kid since Jonathan was a baby. A quiet bond formed between the two parents after the funeral; a bond that was comforting yet painful. Both understood the other could only be a reminder of the son they'd lost. This was both good and bad.

They'd cleaned out his apartment with members of the band that spring. She burst into tears when they found two shelves in Jonathan's kitchenette stocked with Chunky Soup: Chunky Vegetable, Chunky Chicken, Chunky Beef, and Chunky Chowder. The microwave had been broken for years, the drummer told her, and Johnnie never used the stove because he was worried about falling asleep with it on.

She imagined him standing over the sink with the little portable black-and-white on the shelf to the right, watching Letterman, eating cold soup out of the can with one of the three spoons they found in the sink.

"Two Dogs to One Dog. Come in, One Dog. Over."

"One Dog here. Over."

"Sarge, I know its getting dark, but you gotta get over here on the double. I think I found our site. Over."

"Site, Baines? Over."

"Killing site, Sarge. I'm 'bout maybe four clicks due east. Down near a creek bed. Guess it's a small trib to the Hinkson. There's some blood on the ground, an Amish hat, couple bullet casings I can see now, maybe more. This is it! Over."

She had a dilemma. The stakeout would be compromised if she met up with Baines. At the same time it was the first real break they'd been given.

"Ten-four! Hold tight, Two Dogs. I'll be there in twenty minutes. Over and out."

*

Jill arrives with enough hazy light left to see most of the area well enough. There is, indeed, a good deal of blood, and the hat seems to be the same as the others. The shells are almost too easy to find. It's hard to tell whether they're dealing with planted evidence of some sort or whether they're on the trail of an idiot. Eight shells have been discharged several yards from the blood. It's like the shooter has just emptied the clip right there after the murders and fled.

The map shows they are only about a quarter mile from Route J. There is also evidence of something being dragged out of the wooded area they're investigating, but it's very faint. Baines calls Hughes and Heimer on Jill's cell phone to get them to bring the forensics kit. It's going to be a long night. The screech of insects no longer seems, very soothing to Jill. She and Baines stand in the middle of a violent murder scene. She can honestly say she feels uncomfortable and will be glad to go home.

*

"It's too good to be true!" Treestat tells him over the phone.

"What do you mean?" responds Harris.

"Have you any idea what you're onto? Philly is eating up your Elvis shit. And now you've got murder? I've never seen anything like it. It's all over the East Coast and out West, too. This is bigger than anything since OJ. Our clients are calling us and bidding up ad space, trying to kick each other out of contracts! We're running special editions for the next three days. This is really big-time shit,

Harris!" Treestat sends a barking snicker into Frank's ear. "I sent you off as a punishment and now you're in the middle of the most perfect story of the century. This is bigger than King Jones, bigger than Madonna, bigger than OJ. I mean, you've hit pay dirt. Just don't fuck it up, man."

"I still don't see what—"

"You know, your only drawback is that moral veil you cover yourself in whenever you're actually in the field. It's why you want to come back here. You know you can't do your job without some sort of distance."

"Right. You keep telling me. But I don't see how the murder of this Amish kid is at all related to the reappearance of Elvis Presley."

Treestat snickers again. "Who the fuck knows? That's the beauty of it. You may be one of the only people who understands the details of this whole thing right now. And you know that the FBI is there, too. I mean, you got it all, you son of a bitch.

"So here's what we do. You got Elvis showing up and causing a riot, plus a death. You got a religious kid blown away the night before. You got the woman saying the Elvis at the revival meeting is a fake. You got the fake Elvis disappearing right after showing up. You got the FBI hanging out incognito." Treestat pauses. "It's simple math, Frank. Death equals Death equals Elvis equals FBI equals Conspiracy. Un-fucking believable!"

"Aaron," said Harris. "I don't know. If I start writing that shit, no one will talk to me here. This is a small town."

"Oh, they'll talk to you, all right" replied his boss. "You break a story hinting at a link between Elvis and those murders and bring in the FBI, you'll have the local reporters beating the bushes for you within a day. I'll make sure of that. Even better, though, I want you to look up a friend of mine. He's a professor in the J-School, Hugh Croft. We go way back to my days at Reed College. He's got good contacts in the Columbia area without doubt. I'm going to call him right now. You contact him late in the afternoon and he'll be ready for you."

*

Journal Entry 1411: Cecil Miller

I continue to hear The Voice and am now convinced there really is something about music that I am expected to understand.

Before rock and roll, did we even really hear that primitive beat, did we understand the concept of the groove, did we feel the language of the guitar? There is something about power chords and the wailing lead singer that draws us in, that goes to the heart of our souls. Rock and roll does something to the mind-body continuum, something we really don't understand.

What are those emotions that are drawn out of us, the feeling of listening even to Boston or Deep Purple or REO Speedwagon as we drive down the Interstate doing 75 mph with the top down and our friends dancing in their seats? Why the hysteria over the Beatles and King Jones so beyond anything we ever managed before as a culture? And how do we explain the insane ubiquitous appreciation of this music, which comes mostly from the shores of Britain and the heart of America (Gary, Indiana, Liverpool, Kansas City, London, Spartanburg, Memphis, Macon, Birmingham, Cleveland, Detroit, Chicago, Minneapolis-St. Paul, Austin, Richmond? Then to NYC and LA for amplification and refinement and production and gestation. And then to the world. It is everywhere now.

I'm not just talking about the rock and roll of Chuck Berry, The Beatles, Savoy Brown, The Who, or Led Zeppelin. It's all rock. All of it. The categories don't mean shit. R&B, swing, disco, soul, rap, fusion, hip-hop, punk, New Wave, juju, blues, reggae, neo-soul, even country & western. Categories are merely marketing bullshit.

This is the heartbeat tuned and calibrated to the metronome of sexual rhythm and our root sense of time.

This music deifies time and emotion. They become Godly. It's about the motion of the pelvis and the body, driving through space, piercing the mind over and over again with streams of headphone-possessed sonic descriptions of Life – love, death, loss, magic, over in every song.

The mechanical sound of industry and cars, the virtue of machines, the wall-of-sound, the guitar. The guitar. Guitar as complicated phallus sending laser light and electronic sorcery out into the universe, telling all human secrets in sounds which no words are fit to make – our unfathomable depth, the shallow lies and tall tales of the blues, and moments when it all comes together, moments you feel in the crowd, everyone knows, it is there and you are part of what everyone knows, and the music says, "Yes," and it is pure; how can it end? How can it end? How does the musician in the polyphonic jam, improvising on the edge of the present, what he knows the world needs to hear, how can it end? What in his head and everyone else's will allow it to fade out and return to the normal and the mundane world? How can songs of pure beauty and mastery of time end? "Love Lies Bleeding in My Hand," "Stairway to Heaven," "Layla," Jimi's "Pali Gap," "Burning Down the House," "Gimme Shelter," "Everybody Here Wants You," "In Memory of Elizabeth Reed?"

I am in central Missouri as I'm supposed to be. Mission should begin to unfold shortly. I've managed to create a complication, however.

I met a woman.

She seems to have the same mental tendencies I do; is at least on my wavelength. Emotions are more complicated than I am able to handle in my present state, but there is something very powerful between her and myself.

Still need to go through with what I know to be the reason I am here.

*

As Coral tends to the ducks and has her morning conference with Buzzer, Jimmy, and Dean, she can't wipe the smile off her face. Cecil spent the night. They were up for hours. The only thing that worries her is the twelve-year age difference. She is glad that Buzzer has his own home and that he and June rarely visit Mother in the morning. She will wait to tell him about Cecil when they drive into Fayette at lunchtime.

When she'd gotten up, with only an hour of sleep, Cecil had opened one eye, smiled at her, and rolled back into dreamland. In sleep somehow he looked older. He had promised to stay put until she got back. Mother would be more than a little surprised to meet him unless she had been properly prepared. Coral knew she wasn't thinking clearly and that Mother would probably have a problem, but she didn't care. She was over forty for God's sake.

The news Jimmy and Dean gave them about the Amish was horrendous. But Buzzer had been impressed by their initiative in going into Columbia to talk with the police. There didn't seem that much they could do or say other than to explain what had happened, but their forthrightness made her proud to have them as employees.

With thoughts of a naked Cecil back in her room, the riot, the confusion about Elvis, and the possibility of her story ending up on the front page of a national tabloid, the murder didn't seem too surprising. It had been a strange three days.

When she returned to Mother's, she glanced at the paper and saw a photo of what was clearly not Elvis standing on a stage being rushed by the congregation. She and Cecil had just left the tent when the riot started. She'd seen all she needed. The guy on the stage was not Elvis. Not even close. She wondered if this had meant anything to Mr. Harris or if he now thought she was even more insane than he already did.

*

Hugh Croft was very organized. Harris had barely finished with pleasantries when the white-haired man handed him a printout of background information on the local police and several key contacts within the department. He recommended a call to Lieutenant Robert Wilson first. "Sometimes cash helps, but he knows everything going on in the department. I wouldn't take too much stock, though, in what he says. Mostly in what he doesn't say. He's an administrator, and a good one, as they go. He can't do detective work worth a damn, but that's not exactly the most important skill here in Columbia. He's got a couple good officers and they're listed to: the woman, Jill somebody, is smarter than hell and even decorated for valor. The man is a guy named Dale Stoddemeier. Don't know that much about him, but he used to be on the force years ago. Super cop kind of guy. He's back now in a consulting capacity or something to plan a special response team of some sort. If either of them is on the case, you may have some real news going on, but there are also probably some sticky wickets that people are worried about. Again, though, you won't get much out of either one of them because they're crafty – especially Stoddemeier. He knows how to stay low and subtle."

Harris thanked him. Did Croft have contacts at the *Tribune* or the *Missourian* that could tell him of anything going on? Well, that was the funny thing. He'd talked to his people at both papers and they had only a little, but it was off the record. The kid that was killed was from an Amish family that lived about fifteen miles from where the bodies were found. They had no phone and there were very few records on them. Reporters were scheduled to go out to the house to interview the parents once there was a public press release, but no one felt they would get much – some grieving parents maybe, a statement about justice, but that was all. The cops were doing a good job of keeping things close to their vests.

Harris leaves feeling that maybe Treestat had a point after all. It's obvious that he knows much more about most of the issues than even Croft. Something might actually be going on, but what? He would see. But first he needed a shower and a drink, and, if he was lucky, some time with Janie.

*

After nights like this, Jill wants a drink. There is still no weapon, but they are closer. The shells were .22s. They more or less match what she found at the camp. The gun would allow a full ballistics report, if they could find it, but she is now more interested in a clean stakeout of the camp and determining a motive. The tickets and the *TV Guide* with Sumter on the cover are no longer a coincidence to her, she just doesn't know how it all fits together.

It is just past 7:30 a.m. An hour earlier she'd left a message on Dale's tape and asked him to meet her at The Pancake House. He hasn't arrived yet, so she orders pineapple pancakes and sausages. Then she goes to the front of the restaurant and buys a copy of the *Tribune*. As she turns to head back to her booth, she looks down to find a copy of *Midnight America*. She stops, one hand full of change, the other gripping the *Tribune*. The headline reads: *"Police and FBI Link Elvis to Bizarre Ritual Amish Killing."* Her first expression is one of humor, but then the implications hit her.

Noticing Jill's expression, the cashier says, "We really hit the big time, ain't we, Sergeant Simpson?"

Jill buys a copy of the tabloid and moves back to her seat muttering under her breath.

It takes a few minutes to find the article. It is two short columns with several old pictures of Elvis and a sidebar on Amish culture. The only quote comes from the FBI Operations Chief in St. Louis who states that the allegations are preposterous. What she fears most she finds in the last paragraph – a reference to the Columbia Police Department's Sergeant Jill Simpson and Lieutenant Robert Wilson who are leading the investigation. *"Calls to both officers were not returned."* The byline for the article is one Frank Harris, Senior Correspondent on assignment in Columbia, Missouri.

"The little fucker probably isn't really here," she mutters to no one. She decides to check her voice mail when she gets back to the office. The big problem is Wilson. She's sure he will try to pin the whole thing on her as a leak. And he'll probably do it in a way that's indirect and quiet, seeking to erode her reputation just a little bit, as opposed to a direct reprimand. For all she knows, he has leaked the idea himself, and maybe he's made up the whole FBI thing altogether.

"Hey, Jill, I *thought* I'd see your name in this." Stoddemeier slaps a copy of *Midnight* on the table and sits down.

"I don't know a thing, Dale, honest. By the way, where'd you get your information on the Feds? Not that you're the hole, but someone's gotta be."

"I don't think my source is it. I got it straight from the Federal guys in St. Louis. It's their job to let me know when they're down. I've got an idea who though, but I'm not saying."

"Can you talk to Wilson before he gets to me, then? Cuz I don't need his shit. I talked to him about the FBI being here yesterday. I don't know who else he would tell, but I doubt it was many people. That leaves about three others at the top and I don't think they would...." She trails off to stick her fork into a sausage. The waitress comes to take Dale's order.

"Well, no matter what," says Stoddemeier conspiratorially, "I don't think we should be talking much about this in here. I'll talk to Bobby for you. He and I have a meeting with the Mayor this afternoon to go over the security issues that these media guys are creating. You any further with the investigation? It might help."

She tells him about the camp and the blood, the shells and third hat. They end their meal discussing policy issues that the multijurisdictional case brings up. As they're leaving the restaurant, Jill notices a tall, longhaired man getting out of his car. He's a bit haggard looking, but she likes his face. He's probably around fifty. She can tell by the way he walks that he is a drinker. Their eyes meet for a moment, then he drops his gaze to her badge, then her weapon. This is one of the things she doesn't like about the job. Only certain kinds of guys will go out with lady cops. As she opens the door of her cruiser, she notices him watching her from inside the foyer. She's seen him before. She is sure of it.

*

The article startles Harris as well. He is used to *Midnight's* ploys, though. Treestat has thrown down his glove. Harris is being given no choice. Treestat is also challenging the other tabloids. Now they would have to snoop around to figure out what *Midnight* had. And since it isn't much, they will likely spend the next week spinning their wheels trying to figure out where to concentrate their resources. It is why Treestat has been successful for so many years: by mixing three or four separate stories into one, even if they never got a break on information, their competitors have no choice but to check things out. What they'll turn up in this case is an Elvis impersonator, a murdered kid, and the FBI doing something – or not. Then they will dig. And while they're digging, he will already have interviewed the police and Sumter and Treestat will be out with the next concoction. Sometimes it all backfired. It was always possible to get sued if they weren't careful. They also occasionally linked things more or less correctly, giving fuel to something they were treating as a joke, only to be scooped by *Sun* or the *Enquirer*. Sometimes too, they fell for the same ploy by others. It wasn't exactly a room full of mirrors.

He's glad he dropped his gaze when she noticed him. But he's a bit concerned about why. He wishes he had been more careful coming in. She'd obviously checked him out. He had left three messages on her voice mail over the past few days. It was a slip, but he would dumb it through. He knew better than to count on lack of observation with police officers. And this one seemed sharper than most.

She is becoming more attractive. When he saw her just now, a sensation he hadn't felt since high school ricocheted through him: he felt oddly vulnerable and a bit unsure of himself. He is surprised that he just feels happy after seeing her for a brief moment. It is not lost on him that he had worked hard not glance at her chest.

*

"The first thing you need to do is go out and interview those two kids from that farm," Wilson says.

"Planned on it," Jill says. "But I just want to know your thoughts on this whole *Midnight* thing first and to make sure you don't think there's really a connection between the murders and the FBI. I mean..."

"Sergeant, I talked to Dale earlier. You know that, I know. I have no idea where the information on the FBI came from. I've already had them in earlier this morning raining hot, wet shit down on my head. So has the Mayor and the Chief. But you don't know the half of it...." Wilson pauses.

"What does that mean, Bobby? You said they were here because of Sumter's taxes."

"It means that I can't tell you what's going on, and you wouldn't believe me if I did, and even if you did, it doesn't have anything to do with what you're up to, so just keep doing your job. It *was* Sumter's taxes and now it's something else. That's all I can say."

"I see. But this article plus all these reporters here for a freak show may get hard to wade through."

"Well, Sergeant, you're just going to have to find a way to ford the water at another part of the river aren't you?"

Jill looks him in the eyes here. This isn't what she expected.

"Are we okay then, Bobby?"

He holds her gaze. "Yes, Jill, you're doing fine. You still don't have the gun, you don't have a motive, and you clearly don't have any suspects yet, but you're moving."

"How much longer do we have?"

"I'm going to make the announcement at lunchtime that you're working on the case, that the murder took place somewhere other than where the body was found, and that the victim is from an Amish family. So you ought to be out of the office as much as possible for the next few days, at least if you don't want to talk to anyone. That said, the Mayor told me you can talk to anyone you want on this. Just don't bring up the issue of the FBI, okay?"

"What am I supposed to say if I'm asked?"

"Just say you know nothing about the Federal Bureau of Investigation. Refer them to me. I'll feed 'em something. Okay? And always refer to them as the Federal Bureau of Investigation. I don't know why, but tabloid reporters love that. "

"Okay, but what about this clown with *Midnight*?"

"Harris? I talked to him a few minutes ago. He plays the game well. Stuck by his story; got no comment from me. He's going down the alley, but it's dark and we're going to let him stay there as long as he wants. Still, you should talk to him. Don't comment on the Federal Bureau of Investigation, though. Send him back to me if you have to. But give him whatever you think he wants about the murders. He'll be happy enough." Wilson looks at his watch. "Now I gotta prepare for this press conference, so if you don't mind, I need some privacy."

"One last thing. How come you're being so supportive?"

"Hmm. I guess I am. Guess I'm getting old. Just don't fuck this up, okay?"

Jill leaves his office without turning her back to him.

*

Wilson thinks for a minute, then picks up the phone. Five minutes later, Dale Stoddemeier is in his office.

"Thanks, Bobby, I owe you one."

"It's okay I guess, Commander, but I still don't get it. What *are* the Feds doing?"

"Just like you told her, Bobby, it's got nothing to do with any of this. Now, I'm glad you didn't give her a hard time, and you know that she isn't the leak, right? But someone is. So I need you to figure out who."

"Dale, I thought you two were friends. What's the story? You aren't putting her into any danger, are you?"

"She's fine. Don't worry, Bobby. You'll understand soon enough. But you need to work on this leak. It's somewhere. I need to know who."

"I'll do my best, Dale. But if it's like anything else in this department, it's most likely a matter of a bunch of little leaks. I mean, Jesus, we've got at least a hundred news crews in the area right now."

"Just do your best, okay?" With that, Stoddemeier leaves the office.

For his part, Wilson can't help thinking he, too, is being sent down a long, dark alley to nowhere. But he'd start like he always did: by giving just a few people some bad information and then see when it came back to him. He just wished he could shake the sense of futility this task gave him.

*

Harris is still surprised at how odd he feels. He has a 3:30 appointment with Sergeant Simpson. The press conference and following meeting with Wilson went nowhere. Even if he got nothing new out of Simpson, he would finally be meeting her and giving up his anonymity. It would be harder to kibitz at The Pancake House. There were ways, though, with enough money, maybe.

He goes with Janie back to her room after the briefing by Wilson. They spend forty minutes in the shower, then order a late lunch. He knows he hasn't told her of his scheduled meeting with a woman police officer on purpose. No need for her to get upset and jealous. But something deep inside makes him wonder whether there really is no reason. As he drives into downtown Columbia, thoughts of drinking completely escape him. He's worried about making the best appearance possible. He can't help it. He knows he is going to like her a lot.

CHAPTER 22

Coral returns to her room in the far corner of the house and finds that Cecil is gone. She had spent half an hour building Mother up to her news. His backpack is gone, too. Her disappointment surprises her. It had been easy to deal with Elvis' transience, but she felt somehow it was supposed to be different with Cecil. She had been betrayed – not by him but by God. This last realization frightens her. Had God left her, too?

Mother waits in the living room, skeptical more about the age difference than the fact that a stranger had spent the night with her daughter under her own roof. Mother is clearly trying to be happy for her daughter and suspend any judgment of Cecil until she meets him and sees her daughter with him.

The screen is still pushed up and hot winds enter the room, racing up from the bluffs of the Missouri, heated by the thick, photosynthetic warmth of crops sucking up sun, and by bands of burning black asphalt road. She leans across the bed, resting her arm on the white sill, staring out into the heat and the grasses and the long hazy view west. She knows she can find him. The only choice she needs to make is which way he's gone – Rocheport, Fayette, or Columbia? But she also knows that he left because he needed to be alone. The question of a pattern in her attraction to men is now a reality. She only half considers the point. She can let him be. He will be back.

She shuts the door to her room quietly and tells Mother he has gone into town and hopes to be back by supper. Mother seems unaffected by the whole thing.

Stepping onto the porch alone with her thoughts, Coral feels a dull self-pity trying to fill her. The shaded porch gives little relief from the muggy heat. With the breeze, a sad silence empties itself into the farm buildings standing before her. She doesn't hear the several thousand birds squawking and quacking in the barns. No, if he doesn't come back within the hour, she will go find him.

*

In the basement of the Rocky Point Baptist Church, nearly sixty people fill the low-ceilinged room adorned with deep brown polished tiling.

"All right, everybody, listen up. Smokey saw something a couple nights ago that I think he needs to tell you about." Bud Sumter moves back to his seat and watches the old man rise and move to the front of the room. A few more people straggle in as the older Sumter brother gives the floor to the farmer.

Smokey Hughes faces the group. "I heard it coupla' times before the night I saw it. Just a few days ago. You all know my land – that piece Bud got that extends along the bottom area. Fancher ain't got it yet.

"I been workin' it pretty hard last two years since them floods, and now, with spring the way it was, I been out in the evenings when it's dry. Couple a nights ago, though, I seen it."

He holds his audience with a pause. They are mostly men. There are some teenage boys with their fathers, a few older women. All have worked the land from the moment they could walk. They are descended from Italian, Polish, Ukrainian, Irish, and Scottish families, but the blood is all mixed around now. Many of the men smoke or chew tobacco and wear weathered baseball caps with John Deere, Allis-Chalmers, Chevrolet, and Ford emblems on them. They sit in folding brown chairs, arms crossed, backs straight, faces impassive, slightly straining to see the old man through the smoke-filled basement air.

They have been meeting every other Thursday night now for nearly a year to discuss the way things are going. Many lost their farms in the '80s during the Midwestern recession. Others had hung on and only given out after the flood of 1993. Then there was the Great Recession in 2008. They had made it through the first months of the meeting listening to Bud Sumter express anger and rage for them at the government and the banks and even the companies for whom they now farmed.

But for the past half a year his mood had changed to one of resignation and pain – consequently, so had theirs. As a group they know they can do something, but there is no one to direct the anger at. The extension agents are gone with federal budget cuts and the demise of centralized agricultural policy. The only representatives of government they have contact with are environmental technicians who, for the most part, are their children and younger relatives who made it off the land and into colleges or technical school. No one from the corporations that now own the land actually shows up.

The only person with any power in the group is Bud. He still owns a small piece of bottomland and lets Hughes farm it occasionally. But Sumter made his money like a few others in the area by partnering with doctors and lawyers in Columbia and buying pieces of shopping malls, savings and loans, motor lodges, and high-tech food processing operations.

Hughes continues. "It came up over the hills on the other side of the river. It was flying low and quiet. The quietness was the thing that startled me. 'Cuz it was a chopper. Big black thing. I just stared and wondered if they was coming to land on me. But it flew over, real quiet like, but not really, if you know what I mean."

He pauses again, knowing that people are beginning to fill with questions. "I got no idea what they was doing there round that early time in the morning. Still don't. Don't know much, really, 'cept they was probably government. Federals, I think. Big, glowing red thing on the bottom as it passed over me."

The faces in the audience don't change, but the old man feels the shift in the air and hears thc slight movement of arms tightening around chests, eyebrows lifting ever so slightly.

"Couldn't be anything else. The thing was huge. It came over me and it seemed, even in the darkness, that a red shadow was passing over. The insects stopped their humming, and I saw that light. Just a very pale red on its belly. I kind of ducked, thinkin' maybe something was bein' dropped out. Couldn't tell, really. But it was government. And it shouldn't of been there."

He stops, hesitates in the front of the room with people looking at him, waiting for more, then returns to his seat.

Holding the latest copy of *Midnight America* in his hands, the older Sumter brother rises and says to the group: "Thank you, Smokey."

He pauses to hold up the tabloid. "Smokey, I think, is too kind, folks. We all know there have been news accounts and talk of the FBI infiltrating the area over the last few months. It's possible that they're orchestrating this Elvis thing, too, and that my little brother is just being duped into acceptance. The question is, what are we going to do about it?"

He waits for effect and watches as people adjust their feet and shift their arms again.

"I for one am first of all going to do my darndest to keep anyone I know from buying this rag." He drops the paper to the floor with disdain and puts a foot on top of it.

"The next thing I'm going to do is contact the Mayor's office and demand an accounting, both of this hoax and of just exactly what the FBI is doing around here and who the agents are. And the final thing I'm going to do is recommend to you all that if the Mayor won't do anything, we do something ourselves." With that, the elder Sumter sits again.

No one speaks for several moments. The group has no structure, no rules. It had been formed by Bud Sumter to meet his own ends. In recruiting people, he told them that he had been asked by others to gather people of a like mind. No one thought to ask exactly who it was that had asked him to set things up. No one thought to ask why they were there, what their mission was. They had no name, no bylaws, no goals. If truth be told, they were just there to listen to Bud Sumter. They needed someone to organize their anger for them.

Finally, Smokey Hughes stands again.

"I'm with Bud, folks. We gotta take action. None of you saw what I saw, but it was big and it was real. I think for one, we oughta stake out that field and wait for this thing at night. It don't seem to come on schedule, but close enough. Something tells me we may be seeing it within the next few days. I don't know.

"But if we get some of us out there, regular-like, we can cover a lot of land and maybe we'll get lucky. And if it is FBI, or whoever, I mean, if we figure it's government, then we oughta just shoot it out of the sky. Lest we get straight and better answers out of the Mayor's office. I figure if someone's flying that low over land that ain't theirs, they got no rights. They do up in legal air space, but not over someone else's. We just shoot at 'em, let 'em know they're trespassing. Simple as that."

Edwin Carson, minister of the church, now stands. He's sweating from the lack of air-conditioning. Other than that, he's big and he gives everyone in the room a sense of comfort with his relaxed manner. He uses a soft speaking voice as opposed to his public preacher's voice.

"I agree with Smokey. I agree with Mr. Sumter here, too. But now's the time. We don't need to wait for a chat with the Mayor. We probably need ten to twelve able-bodied folks a night beginning tonight, and what I want to know is whether we should be thinking about downing them guys. I mean, because if we are, we really need volunteers who've got and can handle weapons." He looks to Sumter.

"The Reverend's got a point," says Sumter. "How many of you think we need to represent ourselves out there, raise your hands."

Raising his own hand, Bud Sumter smiles to see the majority of people in the room joining him. It not only means that they agree with him, but that they have been paying attention. He understands what is going on. They aren't going to say much. And he doesn't want them to. It's a question of commitment. They could show or not show when the time comes; they could come armed or unarmed;

they could stay if things get hot, or they could leave. The less people actually said the better.

"All right, then, everybody, it's settled. Anyone who wants to deal with this should meet out in the meadow down from Smokey's field. Smokey says they come late, so be prepared. We'll start at 11:30. It'll be till four or five – whenever it gets light. We don't have any idea whether we'll get lucky tonight or not. Smoke says they don't come on a pattern, but we need to start this out now. It'll be like a vigil. A vigil of preparedness.

"We'll put our heads together properly. If we want to send a real message, then we need a plan. I'll deal with the communications equipment, you all just come–and bring a weapon if you got one that can inflict damage on a helicopter. And of course, I don't need to remind you that this should all be kept to ourselves. I think the only people missing are Tony Gravers and Everett Chum. I'll talk to them later."

The meeting breaks up as quietly as it formed. Whispered conversation floats through the room and trails down the hallway. Sumter speaks to several people and waits for the room to clear.

From the back door fire escape he sees his brother's face.

"Thought you'd be here." He smiles.

"Hoax? You think Elvis is a hoax?" says Monty Sumter.

"I know he is Reverend. And so do you." They smile at each other and look through the smoke at the empty brown chairs.

*

Harris planned on shaking her hand, but she doesn't give him the chance. "I knew it! I saw you this morning and I knew you were the guy! God damn it! You've probably been listening to us talking at breakfast. Fuck!"

She isn't actually screaming or even raising her voice. It's more like she's just throwing her anger at him. Her voice is very throaty. He likes it, even though she's mad at him. In hindsight, disguising himself might have been a good idea. It had worked in the past under similar circumstances. But something made him want to face her straight. He is also surprised to find that she makes him slightly anxious.

"Sergeant, I want to apologize. My editors can be a little overeager. It's just business. I—"

"Just business?" Her voice is shifting now; the anger turns to what he feels is pure and simple superiority. "Lying is just business? Contaminating the facts in a murder investigation is just business? Casting aspersions on me and the Federal Bureau of Investigation is just business? Do you have any idea how many years obstruction of justice can get you?"

"Sergeant, I do. I cost my paper's insurance company over $20 million last year. That's why I was sent out here."

"So you can fuck up out here? With this Elvis shit?" She shakes her head and pauses.

"Uh, well, Sergeant Simpson," he says. "I've been doing this job for a while now. There's all sorts of things that happen to you when you're a reporter."

Simpson holds up both her palms to stop him. "Mr. Harris. I'm not sure what you're saying, but this is a very small community. I don't care about you or your paper – you can lie or print the truth, it doesn't matter. I also don't care whether Elvis is alive or dead, whether he's a ghost, a hoax, or part of a grand conspiracy we don't understand. And I can tell you right now, whatever is going on with Elvis, the Federal Bureau of Investigation has nothing to do with it, and they are not here in this town and, to my knowledge, they aren't planning on coming any time soon. I can also tell you that I am investigating a murder and you have just made it nearly impossible for me to get information out of people. Everyone thinks I'm letting you know what's going on. They won't want to say anything to me for fear that they'll read their names in the paper, or at the very least read what they said and implicate themselves. So I'm kind of pissed. Got it? Now what can I do for you?"

"Well, first of all, I didn't write that story. My editor did. They just signed my name because they had to sign someone's."

"I don't really care. Your editor isn't here and you are. You're his representative, so it doesn't make a difference."

"Okay. Fair enough," he replies. "Maybe I can figure out a way to minimize the damage in our next installment. But I would still like some information."

"Depends on what you want. I know the drill. And so do you. There's certain things I can say and certain things I can't. 'No comment,' is definitely in my vocabulary today."

"Okay, first off, I just need to get my bearings. Everything can be off the record." He raises his eyes to meet hers and is startled to realize how beautiful they are. It's the combination of dark brown and her long eyelashes. Something passes between them that opens a hole in his gut and gives him a sense he's about to fall down.

She waits for him to continue.

"Off the record, okay?" he manages.

She nods silently. He continues. "I just need background. From everything you've been saying, I have the impression that you're on this case. Is that correct?"

"Yes."

"We have also learned through a number of sources—"

"Wait a minute. What possible significance does my being on this case have?"

"Well, from what I've been told, you're one of the best this department has. If you're on it, then it's probably not, as they say, open and shut. Maybe there are political issues, too."

It's a gamble, he knows. Appealing to her ego so early on is a bit presumptuous. If she doesn't buy it, then he knows such a ploy won't work later. If she does, he will be in the driver's seat.

"I was assigned this case because I was the officer of record, Mr. Harris. I am in my seventh month of a three-year stint as head of Crimes Against Persons. There are no politics when you're trying to solve the murder of what appears to be an innocent young man."

It didn't work.

"Okay, I believe you. But what I really need to get at is the issue of this young Amish man. Now, Lieutenant Wilson indicated in his press conference that the guy was shot in one place and then moved more than twenty miles to where he was found. Seems to me that if that's all true, then right there politics play in."

"How so?"

"Mostly because either you have some sort of problem with Amish killing Amish. And we have non-Amish cops – you – having to figure out who did it. Or, you've got a dead Amish kid and someone else killed him, someone non-Amish. The second of those is more likely since the only other Amish in the area are members of his own family. But, whatever - someone killed some poor, gentle kid, and the question is not only why, but why Amish? Either way, we have politics at stake here. And if I was your boss, I'd make damn sure I had someone on the case who wasn't going to louse it up."

They sit in silence for a few seconds while he waits for her to respond.

"Mr. Harris, you sure are doing a good job of thinking out loud and letting me know where you're coming from. We have thought of everything you've said and our investigation is not ignoring any possibilities."

"Well, what is this family doing here, anyway?"

"They left their community in Iowa because they didn't agree with some of the community's principles."

"So, wouldn't it be possible to conceive of someone driving down from Ottumwa or wherever and pulling the trigger and then returning?"

"It would, and I will tell you that we're looking into that very possibility."

"That's news, Sergeant."

"Yes, it is, except first of all we're off the record here. And second of all, it's not going to bear out."

"How do you know."

"Because they're Amish, Mr. Harris. They're pacifists. I just had someone at Columbia College do some research for me. Do you know how many Amish have been indicted for a major violent crime with a gun since 1900 in the entire country? Not one. Not one, Mr. Harris."

"Could happen."

"Yes, it could, but highly unlikely. The beauty of this job is the fact that 99.99-percent of what you deal with is likely. Only criminals and psychopaths kill people like this kid was killed."

"Point blank? In the chest?"

"Yes, point blank, more or less. And then there's the whole deal with moving the body. You'd have to be insane to spend that much time and energy after committing such a heinous crime and then another hour or so moving the body. I have no idea who did it, but I've a pretty good idea who didn't do it."

Harris contemplates her self-confidence and her words. She seems very much to know what she's doing. There is possibly something big here, but he needs to be patient. This is not a woman to cross.

"All right, now I've got some questions for *you*," she says calmly, "and I'm sorry, but everything for us government employees is always on the record."

He shifts in his chair and waits.

"From what I read and from some other sources, you have made contact with a Ms. Coral McGrey regarding this Elvis thing. Am I correct?"

"A reporter never divulges his sources, Sergeant."

She sighs. "Ms. McGrey is referred to more or less in your article, Mr. Harris, and I'm just trying to get a fix on whether there's anything that might help me..."

"Whether there's a connection? Come on Sergeant Simpson. You don't really think there's a connection, do you?" He waits for the tease to register. She doesn't respond. "Tell you what. Call me Frank, Sergeant, and I'll talk about Ms. McGrey."

"All right, Frank."

"Good. Okay, yes, my main mission in coming here was to interview Ms. McGrey. In a nutshell, she thinks she's been having an affair with The King of Rock and Roll for the past year or so. She contacted us when all the public stuff happened, and she attended the revival two days ago. She's very sincere and innocent. I have no idea what she's actually been experiencing, but her interpretation is that something very real has been going on."

"She was at the revival?"

"Yes. And with a younger man who seems to be an escort or something. Cecil someone. Weird little guy. Seemed high on something. Talked a lot about ghosts and life after death, stuff like that. She left the tent before the riot, though."

"How do you know that?"

"I saw her. She was up near the front with this kid and then walked out as soon as Elvis, or whoever he was, appeared. Don't know what she was doing or why she left, really. I also don't really know how she came to be sitting so close. "

"Do you think she knew what was about to happen?"

"Maybe she was an accomplice? I hardly think she was the type of woman to be an accomplice, Sergeant. I was there. That was a spontaneous thing. People became temporarily insane. No, I think she left because she'd seen enough. Maybe she felt it wasn't the guy she knew. Maybe you need to talk to her." He'd already said too much.

*

Translating the maps he'd studied to the reality of the terrain that Cecil now found himself walking through intrigues him, makes him feel like an icon on a large screen TV. He's glad that he's straight for a change. His thoughts are moderately clear. Recent memories of Coral's lithe, naked body and her scent give him a pleasant sensation. Thick smells of hot green alfalfa and clover waft through the air. Grasshoppers and giant crickets the size of fingers spray to the side as he walks through thigh-deep fields of grass.

Leaving Coral's house through her bedroom window was a different experience for him, but not completely a new one. Fleeing the scene of anxiety was something that he had become an expert at years before. It wasn't lost on him that his fascination with mind-altering drugs and the power to escape reality was in part a manifestation of this problem. But he had been leaving people he loved and respected for many years.

He had other things on his mind, though. The most important issue at hand was to find Fancher. He would meet his contact on time as scheduled and see if there were any updates, but Fancher's compound was somewhere in the vicinity of the McGrey farmstead, and he knew he could find it, given enough sensitivity and medication.

Had Cecil seen the copy of *Midnight* on the kitchen table in Mother's house, he might not have left the way he did. Coral had been connected by the story to the FBI and Elvis. This was not something he would wish on this woman who had given him so much happiness. But he was ignorant of these reports. To his mind, the fact that he was under contract to the FBI, and that Dale Stoddemeier was waiting to brief him on developments, was a complete secret and he had little to fear.

He does his best to circumnavigate the cornfields. He's slightly concerned about making his meeting with Stoddemeier on time and although the corn looks to be nearly shoulder high and should therefore serve to hide him fairly well, it's hard to move through quickly.

Stoddemeier is not true NSA and is only working on their behalf. But Cecil doesn't want to disappoint him. He'd done enough of that with other field supervisors over the last few years. His orders from Arthur Gold are clear: work with the local representatives to their liking; bill for his time only after the project is complete; do good work and there would be other jobs. He is, strangely enough, getting used to the idea of being an intelligence agent.

He left the camp in a hurry two days ago in order to catch the bus. Stoddemeier had suggested he go back to St. Louis to catch it, but he'd cut a corner there. No harm. No one knew the difference.

Stoddemeier's dark clothes stand out against the light-shaded beige grasses and young beech trees. Cecil makes sure to create enough noise so that he will be heard well before he comes into Stoddemeier's realm.

"Jesus, Miller, you could be quieter."

"Didn't want to startle you."

"You're late."

"I figured. It took awhile to get out of the house."

"House? I thought you were staying out here."

"Well, I thought about it, but I managed to make friends with someone near Fancher's compound, and, well, one thing led to another and..."

"Coral McGrey? Oh shit, have you got any idea what you've done?"

"No."

"Here, look at this." Stoddemeier hands him the rolled-up copy of *Midnight.*

Cecil only needs to read the headline.

"Franklin W. Harris. Yeah, I met with him right before we went to the revival."

"You were there? God damn it, man, you were supposed to maintain a low profile. What the fuck have you been doing?"

Cecil is not happy that he's being treated this way.

"I figured I was doing some of your job, Commander. Gold isn't just trying to figure out what's happening at Fancher's compound, he's also trying to get a fix on this Elvis thing and—"

"Look, you've got no idea what's going on there. We know that Sumter has hired some guy to impersonate Elvis and that he's managed to play right into people's needs. We've got audio on them for god sake. But that isn't the game, man. It's been a screen to get resources out here. Gold wants you to help us figure out what Fancher's up to. This is much bigger. I—"

"I'm not so sure about your impersonator hypothesis," Cecil interrupts. "It may be a bit more complicated than you think, but do you know something more than me about Fancher? I mean, I spent nearly three days going over Gold's data on the guy and we *really* don't know what he's up to, even where he is. What do you know that's new?"

Stoddemeier studies Cecil carefully. "We think he may be the shooter on that kid."

"Murder isn't in Fancher's domain," Cecil says. "As far as I can tell, he's a do-good liberal." Cecil is struggling to keep from telling Stoddemeier about the voice in his head.

"Well, he may very well be a murderer now," says Stoddemeier. "There's a good amount of money at stake. People like him don't need much reason to kill. Believe me, I've heard some wild stories about him. Everybody's got their ticket price. For some it's millions, for some its only thousands. It usually gets all mixed up with power and control. Go through some of the transcripts of these white-collar fuckers and you realize just how sick and sordid money can make you. Go over the line once and it's all over. And the line isn't a matter of waking up and deciding one day you're going to kill somebody. It's more insidious. You slowly become more and more irrational and corrupted by your own sensibilities, and then all of a sudden murder just seems obvious – just a simple, rational business decision, no different than double parking, running a stop sign, or bouncing a check. It's all risk and it's all just the cost of doing business."

Cecil had heard variations of this before. "Man, I still can't think like that."

"You don't have to. You're going to move on someday once you finish school, spend most of your time in an office or lab. Me, I live this. I don't like it. I hate getting lost in what some people think of as cynicism, but I gotta do my job. If I gave people the benefit of the doubt, I'd be losing every day. But enough horse shit. The point is, we think we got our man."

"Then am I needed anymore?"

"Yeah. You are. There's no discernible connection between Fancher and Sumter. It's all coincidence that we lucked into. Gold's got a couple of regional agents on Sumter's ass down from St. Louis, but he's still after Fancher. There are a few things you should know, though. First off, they found the site of the murder less than two miles from here. The second is that they've been sort of staking things out close to where we are right now. I nearly got caught by the officer in charge of the investigation the other day. So, my advice is that we finish up here quickly and that we don't return."

"But we haven't done anything."

"I can't blow my cover, man. And as to that murder, real life isn't like the movies. Knowing what I know about you and that you've been hiding out here for several days, and not knowing about Sumter and Fancher, if I was running the case, I'd certainly make you a chief suspect, regardless of the fact that I couldn't figure out your motive."

"But you know I didn't do it."

"I don't see why you would do it. Plain and simple. Yeah, I know you didn't do it. But after a while, Sergeant Simpson may run out of leads."

"I thought you said you had your man."

"I do. The question is, does she? Only time will tell."

"You know," says Cecil. "You sort of half have a motive, but I haven't heard anything about method or placement of the suspect. Nothing. There really seems to be more evidence against me than Fancher."

"Could be. Things should start falling into place for Sergeant Simpson soon. As for you, it's time now to do your stuff. Don't get caught up in this murder shit. We've got real work to do."

"All right." Cecil pauses and removes a film canister from his pocket. It'll take about two hours to come on and for the first peak to wear off. It's late afternoon. You've got the map, right? How many choices have we got?"

Stoddemeier steps behind a boulder and picks up a narrow, three-foot long silver tube. He unscrews the cap, then removes a fairly new USGS topological map and spreads it on the ground. Red, orange, and yellow computer-generated photo images of buildings have been overlaid on the map.

"The latest infrared flyby gives us nine possibles out of maybe sixteen farms, depending on how you slice it. We've observed people at each one over the course of the past eight to nine months. It's hard to tell. LANSAT readings just don't give us enough detail, but it seems like it's one of the three they've circled in blue here.

"Fancher's bought up a good deal of land over the last few years and eliminated most of the access roads, but these three are the closest access quadrants. Seems like whatever human activity taking place around here happens at night, maybe underground during the day in those missile tunnels, I got no idea. We do know, though, that he's one crafty sonofabitch.

"I'm going to leave this with you, but you need to be careful with it. I don't want it falling into anyone's hands who shouldn't see it, especially personnel from the CPD. If anyone knew my association with the Feds I'd be compromised without question."

Taking the map and the cylinder, Cecil tries again to get an answer to the question he'd asked nearly a year ago in strategy sessions: "Can you tell me what we're dealing with here, Commander? I've never been in a situation where I have no idea who I'm looking for or why I'm looking for someone."

"I can't tell you any more than I know, kid. This guy has managed somehow to take over a huge amount of land; then he erases roads, puts up fences, levels whole farms overnight leaving no trace, and no one has seen him in years. For some reason Gold thinks it's something big. I have no idea what's going on. That's your job, to a certain extent. We need to know where this guy is, and then we need to know what he's up to."

"And you've got the homing device for me to wear?"

Stoddemeier regards the kid carefully. He actually had to respect him even if his methods were ridiculous. Word was the success rate in the lab had been nearly 100 percent. So what if he needed to take some weird chemical concoction? At least it was good for something. He'd tried LSD once when he was in college. It had been fun, even interesting, but his best friend had freaked out. He knew Jill had experimented a good deal with it before her smack and booze days. What he remembered most was how overpowering music had seemed, and how at times it felt like he could predict where guitar riffs were headed. They listened to Cream and Hendrix and Traffic and Santana, stuff he'd never paid any attention to. Now he knew. It didn't seem to matter, but he certainly understood.

"Yes, we've got a radio transmitter we'd like you to wear," he finally says to Cecil. "It's small and relatively easy to hide. You just tear these strips off and stick it to your calf under your jeans, or your back, or wherever, and then when you find what we're looking for, just switch it on." He hands the small device to Cecil and shows him the switch and the tape tabs.

Cecil would give him an hour before he took his EGG dose of 900 micrograms. He'd been straight for twenty-four hours now and it felt good.

Even with all his psychological capabilities, there is no way for Cecil to know that this will be the last night of his life on earth without an understanding of how things really are.

*

It's nearing six o'clock when Coral hoists her backpack to her shoulders and heads out. This one isn't getting away as easily.

During their night together they had spoken of many things. The one topic he had been the least interested in talking about was his connection to Fancher. This is clearly a guess, but it seems to her if Cecil is anywhere it will be somewhere on Fancher's land. The property is vast enough, so it may be impossible to find him, but with a little luck and some intelligence, she figures she can track him down. The two of them had been humored by the connection of their psyches. Now it's time to take it all seriously and see if it's real.

She walks under the late afternoon sun, inhaling the hot scent of green all around her. As she passes off her land and onto Fancher's property, at least three hours of light remain. The air isn't moving. She tries to walk slowly so as not to overheat and considers the terrain: rolling hills, gullies, ravines, creek beds, sparse stands of trees, and numerous sloping fields full of corn or lying fallow with weeds, clover, alfalfa and the occasional splotch of soy beans or sorghum. She watches the northwest sky for signs of a thunderstorm, but sees only haze. The world above is nearly empty of clouds. Light filtering through the haze would very soon begin to take on a golden hue. In the windless air the world feels empty and spent.

There is a slight chance, she thinks, that his energy will guide her in the right direction. Her pace is slow enough to allow her not to startle wildlife. Over the first hour or so she sees a snapping turtle, a black snake, a skunk, and a red-tailed hawk.

She stops to rest near a creek and glimpses a fox with what looks to be a dead rabbit in its mouth. In the insect hum, the rustle of the fox stepping through underbrush comes to her like the sound of a package being opened in another room. Glancing across the field she has circumambulated, she notes vultures and crows taking turns feeding on something. Stubbled gray corn stalks from the year before lie like broken bones in the dry dirt. The late sun continues to bake the earth with its slow heat.

She continues her trek, moving through fields and over old fences, and, as she moves, her body senses a slight presence. This awareness carries her into the open, across a long, narrow tract some quarter-mile long and several hundred yards wide, heading west in the general direction of the red setting sun and the river. She hurries now giving herself to the heat. She knows that a first good view of the winding silver ribbon of water will appear after several more ridges as long as she can beat the sun before it sets.

When she nears the edge of the long field, the ground becomes thicker and heavier. Walking fast is a burden and her thighs burn. She sees that the land slopes down toward a group of trees and another creek, and that a cliff rises out of the far side of the creek. The presence grows stronger. Choosing to cross the creek at its narrowest width, she edges along the cliff to a point where the ascent will be least difficult. Above the cliff, maybe twenty-five feet high, is a line of young walnut and in front of them an old rusting fence. In the shadow of the cliff, she stops to rest. The presence is very close.

It is in the cool of this place that she realizes she may be making a mistake coming after him. He is so young; maybe she scared him off. Maybe he doesn't want to be with her. Maybe chasing him down will only serve to scare him away even more. Why has she done this?

And then he is there, looking over the side of the cliff, his long, thin face in shadow, his young eyes shining in spite of the setting sun.

"I could feel you coming twenty minutes ago. Hurry around to the bend down there and you'll find there's an easy way to get up here. We don't have much time. I've got work to do, and I guess I need to fill you in on what I'm really up to."

CHAPTER 23

Erdenheim waits as the supplies are stored in the cargo bay. He's been trying to shake the feeling for the last hour, but there is no question that something is wrong. This is the first time he's arrived to find the Black Hawk unprepared. The sun is just dipping into the horizon. He still has time to stay on schedule, but it will be close.

He has no one to discuss things with. If he backs out, it's possible he will never hear from them again. The money is just too good. So, risk is risk. But why have they called him in for another drop so soon after the last one?

The technicians have finished checking the engines. The last load is being stored onboard. He sits in the cockpit waiting for them to leave. Working on deep breathing to calm down, he tells himself there is nothing out of the ordinary about all this. The boxes and crates are all marked for delivery to Moberly Trauma Center. The ones he is supposed to actually deliver there are identified with small red crosses. The rest he will wrap in the drop nets and parachute system as soon as the kid leaves.

"Hey, Mister, sorry we loused up your schedule."

"No problem. You done back there?"

"Yeah. We had a flat, is all. On the way in from St. Charles."

"It's okay, really. Look, I gotta go."

"Okay. Sorry again. Have a good flight."

"I will." Then, for effect he adds, "Best time to fly west is right as the sun sets. You feel like you're chasing daylight."

"Sure must be nice."

*

The kid backs out of the cargo space and returns quickly to the truck where his companions wait. He turns and gives Erdenheim the thumbs up sign from the window as they drive back to the hangar. Felix revs up the turbine, idles the props, and then quickly moves into the cargo hold to set up the special drop equipment. While he's doing this, the truck with the three young men stops behind a large shed.

"So that's Felix Erdenheim?"

"Seems so. It's been a long time since anyone saw him, but he matches the photo."

"What's in the boxes?"

"Well, the ones marked with crosses seemed like legitimate hospital supplies. The others, though, were full of sealed bags. White powder."

"Heroine?"

"No. Not cocaine, either. I got samples for the lab to run. I'm not sure what kind of case Gold is running here, but I don't think we're dealing with something so simple as drug smuggling. Let's hurry. We need to report to him quickly so that Stoddemeier can be ready."

*

Less than a mile from the happy reunion of Cecil and Coral, the members of Sumter's group are congregating in pickups and jeeps on a gravel road that leads to a humpbacked bluff overlooking the river and the flat, lush bottomlands that spread away from it. With the slow setting sun and the distant, flatter farmland heading west, the mood of the group milling around their vehicles, cleaning shotguns, admiring semiautomatic rifles, hefting pistols, even sharpening hunting knives, is one of quiet attention. Two of them were in

Vietnam, three had been support people in Desert Storm, one had seen duty in Afghanistan and had stood eye to eye with the Taliban. The rest of the group looks to these veterans as their leaders. They are, after all, preparing for battle.

The air thickens as night draws closer. Insect noise heightens and seems somehow to ease anxieties. Conversation turns easily to weapons, government conspiracy, and tales of fathers and grandfathers who had gone into battle or even to court to protect their rights. Talk also centers on the loss of property, bank foreclosures, and the lack of opportunity for children. Inevitably, Sumter's name comes up with fond references to helping him on projects, or long, personal talks at barbecues and picnics. Each man works hard, though quietly, to demonstrate to those listening that Sumter is a close friend who confides in him. Had Sumter been in earshot, he would have known that he had created exactly the right effect on these people. Had he heard their reverence for him, he would have known it was time to give the group a name.

*

At the edge of a bluff not too far away, Cecil and Coral sit eating baloney sandwiches and drinking iced tea under haze-filled golden twilight.

"Everything I told you was true. I've been studying parapsychology for a number of years. The thing is, I'm also under contract with agencies in the federal government to provide my mental capacities on certain projects that they deem issues of national security."

"Just what are we doing here, then?" she asks. "Is Elvis really an issue of national security?"

"Not really. And to be honest with you, I learned a while back to let them decide what is in the national interest. But there's more." He pauses. "I really am trying to find Lucas Fancher, but not because they want me to. Because *he* wants me to.

"After I was recruited through my grant, they made it clear they needed me to do some work for them. I was trained to use remote viewing techniques for tracking and reconnaissance work. Everything was going fine, then out of the blue a few days ago this voice starts talking to me. It tells me I need to find Lucas Fancher. It tells me I am needed here."

"So, you haven't actually been talking with Fancher?" she asked.

"I don't know," he replies.

She realizes she's having trouble with everything he is telling her. This was not what she thought it was. She'd gone in search of him because she thought she needed him. Not because he was on a top-secret assignment and worked for the NSA or whoever. She'd gone in search of him because she was falling in love with him; because the last man she'd been with had abandoned her and she didn't want this one to as well; because he had embarrassed her with Mother. She feels him reading her thoughts and tries to block him out.

He takes her hand. "Coral, I know you're confused by all of this. I'm truly sorry. You gotta believe me, I had no idea this was going to happen. I'm in trouble as it is with my contacts for making the connection with you. And if they ever find out that you're out here with me now...."

He looks into her eyes. They both feel the strength of each other's emotions flowing toward the other. Things are too complicated for her. She is with him now, and he's involved in something much bigger than both of them. She had two choices. She could go home, or she could stay with him. He senses the dilemma. She understands this and knows that he needs to wait for her decision. She squeezes his hand and searches his face.

"Are you doing it now?" she asks him.

"Very much so."

"I want to do it, too."

He hasn't considered this.

"I don't know. This is very powerful stuff. There are forces here that have taken me years to master and I still don't know what they're all about. You have no experience at all."

"Yes, but I'm with you."

"Coral..."

"Cecil, I want to be with you. I'm not afraid. You said yourself that I have power far beyond anything you have ever encountered. Let's see what happens if both of us are in the same mindset."

Her tone of voice leaves little room to argue.

"If that's what you want.... But it will be several hours before you catch up to me." He ponders the proposition for a moment. "I'm going to give you half a normal dose just to be on the safe side. And it's going to be dark soon so you need to be careful. Some people are susceptible to visual hallucinations that can make them very skittish. This is serious business."

*

They wait for full darkness to come on and for the drug to begin working. Little is said while they wait. They each focus on the merging of emotions between them and the sounds of the night. In the mix of insect noise, rustling underbrush, mosquitoes, frogs, and the occasional swish of bats and nighthawks, they hear a faint set of other noises. It is the muffled beat of a tom-tom drum, the thunking rhythm of bass guitar, dissonant chords of an electric organ, and the cry of electric guitar. Somewhere, too, in the mix of sounds is the pleading, youthful voice of King Jones trying out new lyrics he's just written. The Red House Gang has started its nightly jam early because everyone is so excited about King's new song.

*

It's Jack and Norma's night to collect the supplies from the chopper drop. They sit together on the hood of the Willies jeep just inside the firelight as the group tunes up their instruments. Norma sometimes danced to the music, but Jack's limitations made it hard for him to express what he was feeling with body movement. She usually chose to sit quietly by his side, watching and listening to the new sounds their friends made, letting the emotions in the air move her into the depths of their world.

This supply drop was the most important one of the year, and Jack generally took the responsibility for recovery whether it was his turn or not. Even with his back problems, he could easily handle the loads himself, but she went with him because the worrying while he was gone was excruciating.

They would stay for the first set and then head out over the valley to the edge of the bluffs to wait for the helicopter. The routine was now nearly thirty-five years old. Before the helicopter, they had tried plane drops, but that was too inexact. Before the plane, when the group was much smaller, Fancher had made monthly trips into Columbia or up to Moberly. In those days they had even had materials delivered to one of the farms, but that was usually only when the delivery was something large and when they still thought they were going to be able to build the starship.

Norma had taken it upon herself to talk Jack out of the idea after they'd brought Croach in. Jack's charisma and their obvious love for him and their awe of his intelligence had obscured the impossibility of his idea – that they would build a space vehicle and leave the planet heading out of the solar system. It would be a good way to die, they all agreed. And they agreed, too, that the life they led on Fancher's 12,000 acres was just too precarious and confining. The responsibility of hiding was distorting their mission. They knew that if they were found out the consequences would be immense. There were too many secrets that they had tapped into and too many powers they didn't understand. It was likely that no one would ever understand what they had accomplished. But it was also clear that the implications of what they had done might well call into question all the basic tenets of physics and religion that held the world together. The object, anyway, was to remove themselves from the world, a world each of them had grown to hate at one time; a world they now each secretly missed.

Jack's disappointment with their lack of faith in his starship plan was devastating for a time. Nobody played music, no one made interesting observations, and group harmony was a struggle. Jack, for his part, tried to go on with his daily routine, but as each morning arrived, he got up later and later. After several weeks he began to spend days at a time locked in his unit, talking to himself, reading, writing, ignoring them. Norma finally took it upon herself to break with her desire to maintain distance from all of the men and moved in with him. She'd expected jealousy and hostility, but everyone understood. And though he was more withdrawn and often silent and brooding, he finally returned to the group as their leader and again worked hard with Fancher and The Brothers to strategize on how they would survive and how they would make contact with others who might wish to join them.

Bringing in Jerry was what had finally pulled him completely free of his depression. Jerry was one of the first people to fully get the idea of transcendence, but he'd chosen to ignore the possibilities. Jerry's comic philosophical approach to music and creative expression had kept him from making a commitment to them for nearly thirty years. Then, finally in 1987, it became clear that he was ready. The Tetro mix was the only option left that would beat mortality. They'd tried once with an overdose in Golden Gate Park, but someone had found him right before he went under and he was pulled back. It took nearly eight more years of planning and waiting to get back to a point where his death would be both manageable and acceptable. He was found dead in early August 1995. The Brothers got him to the compound less than a week later and his revival was nearly immediate. Most of them had figured he would spend his first few months trading licks with JJ and catching up with Janis, but he spent most of his time discussing politics with Jack. They talked for several days about the starship idea, and Jerry was amazed to find out that the earliest telepathic attempts of the group had been directed at the writing and production of *Blows Against the Empire*, the first work of the Airplane after Jorma had left. After that they influenced others as well: Joe Jackson's *Night and Day*, Tracy Chapman, Jewel, Kurt Cobain and Greg Alexander were the best results.

The jeep rolls slowly now across a meadow in the dull light of the moon. Norma and Jack are quiet, their attention directed on the terrain and the sky. It was rare that they would run into people at this time of night, but it had happened before. They would park the truck and hike down the bluffs to get the packages. The drop was due within the hour.

*

Bud Sumter arrives at twelve minutes after 11:00. The silver light of the moon shows what he'd hoped for – armed citizens ready for action. Smokey tells him there are thirty-seven accounted for and at least four more on the way. Sumter steps from the Cherokee feeling the weight of the Colt strapped to his waist. He pulls the Ithaca Mag-10 Supreme off the gun rack in back, checks the safety, and walks to the front of the group.

"All right, this is serious stuff folks," he says. "We are about to break the law. Anyone who doesn't feel comfortable with that needs to leave now." He waits, knowing that there will be no move away from the group. He hefts the 10-guage shotgun as he waits.

"Okay. Then that's that. We need to break into clusters of maybe five or six. You guys decide. But I want you to spread over the property so we got most of it covered. Then I want four of you to go out to the bluffs and act as spotters. When you see the chopper, I want you to triple flash your lights down to us here and we'll be ready.

"You cluster groups gotta hold your fire unless the chopper's making a dead run pretty close to you. He's only got so much land he can fly over, so if we spread out right I think its pretty sure that at least one group will get him. Any questions?"

"You really want us to shoot that old boy down?" someone asks out of the darkness.

Sumter considers the question carefully. "I want you all to do what you think is necessary. What do you think?" He waits. No one answers. "We want an effect here, people," he says. "You want to just make a lot of noise and scare that son of a bitch? Then you do just that. You want to give him a major repair job before he heads home? You do that. Hell, from what Smokey says, he's flying so low the crash is going to be just a little thump in the ground. No, you do what you think is right. Any other questions?"

Sumter's style is pretty clear to the men. Things are being left to their own volition. He doesn't want too much organization for obvious reasons. There are no more questions.

"Wait. I got a question," Sumter says after a few moments. "Has anyone seen my brother?" he asks. There is no answer.

"Well, if he's coming, he better be here soon. I'm going to wait for him with Smokey. We'll try to set up the last cluster with the three of us. You all don't know this, but old Monty used to be a better shot than me."

The men leave in groups and head out over the land. The moon rides low on the edge of the bluffs. With the haze and clouds there will be little chance that the helicopter can pick up the flashlight signals.

*

Seventeen Elvis Presley lookalikes sit in the bar across the street from the Tiger Motor Lodge. The few other patrons attempt to act as if nothing is out of the ordinary. The Elvisinators' leader, Dixon Hancock, sent them to the bar, away from the motor lodge, so that he could negotiate with the Reverend Sumter in private. They trust him. He'd bought the bus and he claimed to know this Sumter guy and they had two days to kill before their next performance in Branson. He promised them they could make money here.

Waiting in the motel room, Hancock is becoming a bit nervous. Sumter is nearly twenty minutes late. He'd thought it through over and over again, and it always came out the same way. He had Sumter. Sumter didn't have him. So why was he late?

A knock comes ten minutes later. He sees Sumter through the peephole. As he opens the door he hears the report a split second before he feels the bullet enter his chest. A second shot catches him on the side of his throat as he falls backwards. The last thing Dixon sees before he dies is the fat, squinting face of Montgomery Sumter aiming the .357 and 8-inch silencer right between his eyes. The bullet enters his skull and blows his cranium into several hundred wet, bloody pieces, spattering flesh, bone fragments, and gray matter in a 180-degree half-sphere five feet in circumference.

Sumter lets the door to the room close softly and walks into the bathroom. He wipes off his white shirt, trousers and shoes with toilet paper, rinses his hands in the sink, being careful not to touch the faucet with his fingertips, then flushes the toilet with his knuckles. He steps over the body, extracts Dixon's wallet, opens the suitcase on the bed with the tip of the gun, takes out the envelope with nearly $5,000 in cash, and finally leaves the room. It had taken longer than he'd expected to get up his nerve to kill someone. He would be late if he didn't step on it.

*

Harris has been waiting in his car for nearly two hours when Simpson finally leaves the station. He has little confidence in his ability to tail her without being caught, but he figures it's all he can do. She takes Providence Road to the interstate and heads west. The traffic is light, but he maintains enough distance to be appropriately obscure – he hopes.

On the highway he lets her get a long lead then picks up speed. She's nearly a half mile ahead when he has the bottle of scotch open. He keeps her at that distance as he takes a long pull and feels the acids in his stomach begin to roll around. Usually the first pull is somewhat anticlimactic, but this time he feels the full rush of the alcohol high flood his system. It occurs to him that this feeling is what drinking used to be all about, this subtle, occasionally perfect high.

Cruising down the highway at 65 with the windows open and the cooling starlit night above, a warmth spreads out from his core. He can't help contemplating Simpson's face, her eyes and mouth, the firm way she set her chin when she was yelling at him. It isn't easy for him to fantasize about undressing her, but he tries anyway. After a few attempts he understands it's not going to happen. He likes her too much.

As soon as she puts on her blinker to exit on Route J he knows where she's going. The McGrey farm is about four miles up the road. Following her on an empty road without being seen will be nearly impossible. He pulls onto the shoulder, takes another swig of scotch, and closes his eyes.

For three days now, he's been trying to figure out what's going on with this Elvis hoax, investigating the murder of a young Amish man, swallowing his pride at having to do the bidding of Aaron Treestat in a feisty mood, and just generally trying to drink away self-loathing. The whiskey buzz is beginning to turn from gentle euphoria to dull sedation. He takes two more hard gulps to stave off the inevitable. He is horny for Janie but that will clearly have to wait. Wondering how he would deal with the complication of his old girlfriend were he to miraculously get something going with Jill Simpson, he tries again to mentally undress Simpson. Janie's pendulous, naked breasts, however, and her long smooth back and firm rump come too easily to his mind.

Ten minutes later he's driving north again on Route J. He finds McGrey Farms easily enough, turns right on a gravel road just past the property, continues up a small hill, flicks off his headlights, and turns the car around so that he can see the farm and the police cruiser from where he sits. The parking area in front of the house is lit by a makeshift wooden tower topped by four incandescents. What looks to be an underground home is roughly two hundred yards from him and partially blocked by trees. Trying now to pace his scotch intake and becoming mildly concerned about impairing his motor skills, Harris waits for Simpson to show. He keeps the car running so that the air-conditioning will work but rolls down the window to have a smoke.

Twenty minutes later, Simpson comes out of the underground structure with two men. She goes to the trunk, pulls out a tube, and removes what looks to be a map. She brings the map and the tube around to the front of the car. The three of them stand around the map lying on the hood and discuss what look to be directions for several long minutes. The taller of the two men points west while Simpson listens intently. She follows the sweeping arc of the tall one's hand, but also seems to glance right at Harris's car. She finally shakes hands with the two, watches them go back into the house, and then uses her radio. He kills the engine and the air-conditioner, rolls up his window, and gets out as quietly as possible. She is walking in his direction.

Crouching low in the near darkness, he edges around to the back of the car then backs, still crouching, across the road to a ravine. In the ravine, and still crouching, the sensation of the liquor coursing through his body, he moves carefully, looking for a place to stop where he might be able to see her without being spotted.

He hears her near the car, sees the bright streak of her flashlight, and then: "Mr. Harris. You can come out now."

Harris stands up and climbs out of the gully and she lets the light train on his face and chuckles.

"I saw you right after I left the station, buddy. You aren't very good. Though I must say, I was disappointed when it seemed I lost you back there right off the highway."

Maintaining his dignity as best he can, Harris smiles sheepishly and walks toward her.

"Problem is, Frank, I don't know what to do with you now. If I tell you to stay here, you'll probably follow me. If I tell you to go, either you'll write some stupid story about what you imagine I'm doing out here, or else you'll go back with your tail between your legs and tell your boss. And then he'll write something equally or even more stupid."

He waits. She flicks off the light. They're standing close to each other, a bit closer than they should. He smells the scent of her hair and the slight musk of her body odor. The night is all around them, the sounds of the heat-filled world pulsing in the darkness.

"So, I'm going to go against department policy and let a civilian accompany me."

"I see," he says. "And just where are we going?"

"I'm going out to find Coral McGrey. She seems to hold the key to at least a piece of this puzzle and maybe can answer some questions about this Elvis joker, and maybe the death of that kid, too.

Maybe she knows where the other two are as well. I don't know, but I need to find her, that's clear enough."

He takes a step back to search for her face in the dullness of the slight remaining light. "Sergeant, if you're willing to let me accompany you through this wonderful evening, I would be honored."

"You're accompanying me, Mr. Harris, because I'm left little choice. I don't have the time to arrest you, give you a ticket, drive you back to town, or just trust you to leave well enough alone. You're just going to have to come along peacefully."

"Fair enough. Just one question..."

"What?"

"Where are we going?"

"Mmm. Well that's a good question, all right. I don't exactly know. As you probably witnessed, I was talking with a couple of the guys who work McGrey's farm and have a fair idea where she went. It seems she's in search of her new boyfriend who disappeared from the farm early today. One of the guys said he saw her going across a valley onto Lucas Fancher's land about four hours ago. She was heading toward a creek near the bluffs that overlook the river – five, six miles from here. But all of this might be, as it were, a shot in the dark."

"She was driving?"

"No. She was walking, and apparently had on a backpack and was moving purposefully. Sounds to me like she knew where she was headed."

"So that means we're going on a hike? In the dark?"

"Yes, and, like I say, I don't know where, nor do I know why, or how long. There's a nice piece of moon out though. Let's get going."

He's having trouble figuring out how much of him wants to spend time with her and how much wanted to be in on a possible scoop. "Sure, Jill, I'd love to come."

"Good. Then let's get started. Only one thing...."

"What's that?"

"I'm *Sergeant* Simpson."

"All right. Sorry, Sergeant Simpson."

He smiles to himself in the darkness.

*

"God damn it, Monty, where the fuck have you been?" Bud Sumter is seething. He'd waited nearly an hour with Smokey Hughes for his younger brother.

"I was over on the east 80 near Smokey's house, Bud. Sorry. I was there nearly an hour. Wrong place. Sorry."

"Man, after all these years, you're still trying to make me look like an idiot. Why can't you just for once in your life be someplace on time?"

They head up river from the rendezvous point. Their group would be the last resort if everyone else missed the chopper.

"What you carrying, Monty?" asks his older brother.

"The usual. My Remington .742 and this little .357. Just in case, too, I got the Colt." He shows his brother the pistol fitted with the silencer.

"That huge thing you've hardly ever used? Do you really think that's got any decent range? Especially if you use the silencer?"

"It's fine, Bud. I been using it for target practice quite a bit over the last year. Anyway, I like the sound it makes."

"When we open fire you're not gonna hear shit, boy. But suit yourself. Let's just concentrate on the task at hand, shall we? We've probably got fifteen minutes to get to our site before we need to be ready. Look at the southeastern edge of the bluffs over there for someone to flash us. And be ready."

"You got radio contact with those guys, or are we just going to hope for the best, big brother?"

"Radio. But I want them to flash their lights, too, cuz it's quicker."

"Wasn't questioning you, just wondering."

Twenty minutes later, the Sumter cluster has achieved its objective and taken up positions. Bud contacts the other groups to make sure they're ready.

By 2:30 the sound of insects and the night heat are becoming unbearable. Buddy has established fifteen-minute check-ins by each group on the open channel, hoping that regular communication will keep at least the cluster leaders awake. He is also concerned that the monotony of waiting will provide an opportunity for people to consider the implications of what has been planned. Shooting at another human being is not an everyday event.

At 2:37 three lights flash from the dark humping bluffs and each cluster readies themselves. A few seconds later the deep flutter of the Black Hawk rolls down from the hills. They make out the machine as a large, dark shadow dropping toward the field. A very slight red emanation, a dingy ember glow, illuminates the center of the chopper's belly.

On the radio, the older Sumter states: "Cluster leaders give your command. Hold at your discretion."

A few moments later they see the flash of gunfire and hear the initial volley of shots as the helicopter edges over the first group. The second and third teams open fire almost simultaneously. Buddy realizes they are too close together as the chopper continues to move at the same cruising speed. The pilot doesn't appear to be aware anything is happening. Bud also understands that the chopper isn't following the line he had assumed, and that they will be nearly a hundred yards from the best vantage point. In addition, he knows that hope will not solve his problem.

"Monty! Smokey!" he yells over the growing commotion. "We need to move up the field toward the bluffs or we'll miss him. Follow me!"

Without response, they pick up their gear and follow Bud Sumter who is scrambling in an angle of pursuit. They hear the next three groups open fire as they hurry up the side of a raised gravel road. Sumter scans the darkness for cover. Just as he realizes they will have to stand their ground in the middle of the field, he sees gun flares from the last group. Several flashes of spark are visible as they score hits on the front of the chopper near the cockpit. The Black Hawk veers sharply off course, the tail kicking toward the night sky and the nose dipping twenty or thirty feet closer to the ground. The flutter of the helicopter's turbines and blades comes closer now, stirring up dust around them. It's only forty or fifty feet above the ground and seems out of control. He feels the two other men around him tense, waiting for him to open fire. His brother has dropped his rifle and stands erect with the Colt in two fists, the long silencer glinting in the moonlight. Sumter raises the Mag-10, the careening black target moving closer. The chopper is nearly on top of them. He waits as long as he can, tenses his arms and gut to prepare for the recoil, and pulls the trigger. The other men flanking him fire an instant later.

He is aware of gun flashes, dust, wind, and smoke all around him. He hears the roar of the giant machine, smells diesel and hot steel, hears the wet click of bullets striking thick glass.

He dives to his right, and as he hits the ground, catches a glimpse of the chopper's belly glowing like there's a fire inside. His little brother is still standing his ground, emptying the final rounds of the Colt into the helicopter belly as it falls madly just behind them.

Monty rolls to his left as the chopper drops its final fifteen feet, crashing to earth. Bud understands as it's crashing that the fire is really the glow from the cockpit lights. He also knows that somehow they've just downed a black helicopter and that they had better get the fuck out of there. His brother is already up and waiting for him to run when the first explosion comes.

Moving into a slow hunter's trot, Bud Sumter decides they should head up the bluffs and then circle back to the trucks parked at Smokey's. He figures they've got about four hours before full daylight - four hours until someone sees the smoke.

*

Harris and Simpson are just east of the bluffs and beginning to wonder if they're on a wild goose chase when they hear the helicopter. Simpson stops to listen and knows immediately that this is something to which she should pay attention. Besides the fact that helicopters didn't fly around in the dark at 2:30 in the morning, she can tell immediately by the sound that it's flying low to the ground.

Everything after that point happens quickly. They move in line with the sounds of the chopper as it passes over them. They can make out a slight red glow at the edge of the bluffs dropping down below them. Just as this is happening, several flashes of light bounce off trees. Covering maybe thirty yards through sparse woods as the first reports sound, Simpson keeps low to the ground, pulling Harris down as well. The hard cracks of semiautomatic rifle fire, and even shotgun reports, make their way up from the fields below in short bursts. The volleys seem to be coming from a number of locations below. Simpson scrambles to the edge of the cliff on her belly as the helicopter changes course and goes into a quick drop, out of control. She sees flares from gunfire in the open field and then watches the helicopter dip, spin, and finally crash.

A throbbing silence ensues. Shadowy figures make their way quickly through the bushes not more than twenty yards in front of them. The silence below is finally broken by confused voices near the crash site, then an explosion. She reaches for the mobile phone on her belt and turns to look at Harris. He's watching her face in the darkness.

Part VI
The Big Blue Guitar

We live together, we act on, and react to, one another but always and in all circumstances we are by ourselves.

- Aldous Huxley

CHAPTER 24

Journal Entry 176: Cecil Miller

In his book, True Hallucinations, Terence McKenna makes the first set of references that I ever came across about the implications of sound in the psychedelic experience. He and his brother developed a theory during their travels in the Amazon about the impact of a specific sonic phenomenon established after they ingested native-prepared ayahuasca and psilocybin. This sonic event, according to the McKennas, occurred through the human reproduction of a sound heard in the brain and might harmonically induce an effect on the DNA of those present, thereby linking the chemical structure of the mushroom with the biochemistry of the emitters. The McKennas went so far as to hypothesize that the introduction of this sound could actually stop electrons in their tracks and thus place cognitive chemistry in a state of Absolute Zero.

I'm also still trying to understand why images of Jerry Garcia come to me when I'm dosed with EGG-68. They are very dramatic and overwhelming. I feel like I'm supposed to get something, but I don't know what it is.

*

Cecil grapples with EGG-induced paranoia and uncertainty. As he nears the edge of the farm, he thinks he hears gunshots in the distance. Without the drug he would be exhausted. He knows his legs will ache later, but they have covered nearly nine miles in less than three hours. Coral had said little after she dropped her portion, but she didn't need to say much, anyway. They could feel each other's emotions even more explicitly than when they had been naked together.

It's too easy, he thinks, to home in on the farm. The signal for whatever he's sensing is stronger and more intense than anything he's ever experienced. He knows she feels it, too. They think together that part of the intensity of this process comes from the drug, but some of it also seems to come from the fact that they are in synch, and that they each amplify for the other the sensations they're feeling. It's like a room full of mirrors where the images keep bouncing back and forth into infinity.

As he peers through the inky light, it seems like the place is abandoned. He notes their location in the darkness and where they have to walk. They are a hundred and fifty yards down a long hill from the outbuildings and another fifty yards away from the house itself. In the darkness, the house towers over everything in its domain from the top of the hill. Only the porch light glows from the structure. He is aware of a subtle chill running through him, as if people had died there recently.

"What do we do now?" Coral whispers.

"Don't know. There's something like nine of these building clusters around. Could be they're at any one."

"Everything led us here, though. This has to be it."

He can't say anything to this. She's right. He sits down on the side of the gravel road and fishes for a cigarette in his front pants pocket. The pack is mashed from its ride in the pocket. He prepares himself for broken cigarettes. Pulling one out of the pack, he notes that it dangles from the end of the filter. It is certainly broken. The rest will be, too. He slides a disposable lighter out of his pocket as well.

Getting up, he whispers: "I say we go up and try to look in one of the windows. Can't really knock. It's a bit early." He flicks the filter portion to the ground, puts the cigarette into his mouth, and lights the broken end.

They are silent in the darkness. The biting, dry smoke hurts as it goes down. He has a pack of probably twelve cigarettes that will all be like this. On the one hand, this is acceptable – as everything on EGG is. It is just simply reality. But he also feels cheated and angered by this sudden inconvenience.

Reading his thoughts, Coral moves closer to him and whispers, "Don't do that."

"What?"

"Beat up on life like that. I've got a box pack of Lucky Strikes in my backpack here, and they're all good. Just let me know if you want one."

"Thanks." He drops the stub of the unfiltered smoke to the ground and crushes it beneath his shoe.

"Shall we go?" she says.

"Sure. Let's stay off the gravel, though. Too much noise."

They move slowly up the hill, watching the house. Cecil had come down off the EGG nearly an hour before and is in the part of the trip he thought of as the Third Bardo where the mind descends into a lower form of consciousness. He remembers reading once: "Now, as you recover, your consciousness rises up, like a trout leaping forth out of water, striving for its original form. Your former ego has started to operate again."

Coral, too, has come down – if she ever really peaked. She is different from Cecil in how she got high. He wishes they could have done the whole thing on a recreational basis. It has been so long.... He decides that the best situation would be a rented cabin in Canada on a small lake with no one else around. They would walk around naked, feel the energy of the trees through their bodies, listen to Grateful Dead, drink Moosehead beer, smoke a joint to get them off the peak, make love in the sunlight, in the cold water, on the kitchen table, and finally walk in the woods at sunset.

She is aware of these thoughts– especially the sexual ones. She reaches for his hand as they come to the open parking space in front of the house. Through dim light and with the help of the EGG, Cecil can make out what is clearly a person rocking in a chair on the porch. As Coral moves onto the white gravel of the parking area, the person on the porch shifts around to face them squarely.

"I been waiting for you quite a while, Miller. Looks like you brought a friend of mine with you, too. I'm Lucas Fancher."

*

Harris isn't accustomed to feeling useless. Within two hours Jill has the area swarming with a number of different law enforcement organizations. As the first officer on the scene, she called Wilson at home for help. He had in turn called the Howard County fire department, who contacted both the Boone and Howard County sheriffs. Wilson also reached out to the Federal Aviation Administration and the Justice Department, who contacted the State Highway Patrol since the helicopter had crashed within one hundred yards of a state-maintained road.

Remarkably, the chopper didn't burn up, and the flames were easy to put out. The pilot was dead, though. A review of the cargo quickly turned up several hefty bags of white powder and thirty smaller bags of brown powder. The bags were marked with pharmaceutical company labeling, however there was no manifest onboard to explain the contents. Jill had called Wilson on his cell phone, and told him that they probably had a drug-related operation. This prompted the ever-careful Wilson to phone a Treasury agent that he knew in Denver and a Bureau of Alcohol, Firearms and Tobacco agent on assignment in Rolla.

After the sheriffs arrive and Jill learns that law enforcement officials from all over the planet are on their way, she takes Harris aside.

"I'm sure you want to cover this, Frank, but you gotta be low key for a while."

"Jill. This is a black helicopter. How can you ask me to lay low? Drugs, militia, death! This is what I get paid for."

"Frank." He notes the level of familiarity in the voice and just a slight huskiness. "I'm not really asking you. I'm telling you. There may be as many as a hundred people around here by breakfast time.

I can have Captain Wilson assign someone to take you back to town, or I can let you stay."

"What do you want?"

"I think that as soon as we have a hundred people here and I've given my statement to whoever is in charge, I want to quietly go back up those bluffs and look for a way to track whoever was up there with those lights. We might get lucky. We might not. But it's worth a shot. And since you made it this far with me, you might as well go the rest of the way."

"Okay. I'll stay and I'll lay as low as I can. But they're going to want to talk to me, too, aren't they?"

"Just stay out of the way and let me do the talking. If they want you I'll come find you."

*

More than anything else, it was Jack's passivity that worried Norma. From their vantage point on the bluffs they had watched the entire scene in silence. First, the quick flashing signals and low hum of the Black Hawk as it came over the hills, then the ambush from the ground and the clusters of weapons blaze, then the crash of the helicopter; and, finally, the unaccountably quick response of law enforcement. She remembers that Jack has seen more than his fair share of war and assault. But, as they wait in the growing heat of the morning, she is surprised to see how matter-of-factly he takes the whole situation.

They had decided to stay put while the area was being investigated. With their full view of the valley below, they could tell whether anyone was heading up the bluffs toward them. The biggest worry is that the helicopter's shipment contained the key ingredients needed to keep them all alive. They had enough supplies for several more months back at the compound, but Fancher and Jack would need to come up with a plan for another drop soon or there would be serious consequences. The helicopter crash also meant a search. Pretty soon people would be looking for answers. The biggest question, Norma knew, would be just exactly what all the powder was onboard the Black Hawk. Jack told her they might be lucky; maybe the powder had burned up; maybe they hadn't opened the crates. But Norma knew better. They would need to go underground soon – the whole Red House. This was why Jack had thought the idea of a starship was worth trying out. It was one of only a few ideas he'd had that they couldn't make work.

*

"Come on up and set a spell," says Fancher. "You two prob'ly been walking for quite a while." Fancher's mouth does not move when he speaks these words.

Cecil and Coral look at each other. They not only hear his words but feel his whole body experience.

"I could sense you maybe three miles off," he continues carefully. "EGG-68 is really a pretty primitive thing to get caught up in if you're into mind games. You have so little control, such a lack of subtlety. It's all buzz-buzz and whiz-whiz. But there will be ample time to contemplate that. We need to let you two fully come down before you can enter our scene."

"Your scene?" thinks Cecil carefully.

"Yes. You've got some new things to learn, my boy. You may think you've been studying things objectively, but you've been wasting your time. Have we got a surprise for you!"

"We?" asked Coral.

"Yes, we. Welcome to the Red House. Care for some breakfast?"

*

The light of the new day is falling with greater and greater intensity as Frank and Jill sit inside Bobby Wilson's patrol car sipping coffee. A few technicians and AFT personnel continue to mill around the site, but for the most part the investigative work is complete. The major concern of the teams is the identity of the chopper pilot and the purpose of his late-night mission. She heard talk by several groups relieved that the pilot didn't seem to have an affiliation with any known agency.

So there had been the opportunity for competitive evidence gathering. The two county sheriffs were obviously concerned with yet another homicide, and she and Wilson were trying to establish whether there was a link to her ongoing investigation.

They found a number of shells and empty ammunition clips that would be useful were they to find suspicious weapons, but there was little hope of that. The bags of powder had been taken to St. Louis for testing by the AFT. The only discovery giving them a lead was a large, specially designed Colt .45 fitted with a silencer. The weapon had been tagged and taken to St. Louis as well for evaluation and would be run through the FBI's national weapons registry.

"They'll get something on the weapon," says Jill confidently.

"You mean they'll match it to an owner?"

"No question. Too rare."

"Could have been stolen."

"Sure," she answers, looking over the bluffs at the eastern sky. "But there'll probably be a police report on it. Even if there isn't, we can start with the owner and backtrack to the theft. We've done it successfully before."

"So, hopefully we get a good lead?"

"No question. One thing that bothers me, though, is that we didn't find any slugs or bullet casings that would fit it. Lots of 10-millimeter and 22-gauge stuff, but not something from a .45. Not even in the remains of the chopper. But the chamber was spent. It's funny."

"Can't it be a specially made gun?"

"Probably is. But it doesn't help to speculate. We got to think things through after we figure out whose gun it is."

Wilson's mobile phone chimes. Jill looks around for him. Wilson is talking with several of the remaining FBI technicians. She picks up the phone.

"Captain Wilson's line, this is Sergeant Simpson." She listens.

"No, Bobby's not here, Judy. I can get him.... Uh, huh. Right. Sure, I can take a message." She listens some more. "Are you serious?" Jill shakes her head at Harris, squinting. "No, I'll tell him." She disconnects and places the phone back in its holster on the dash, then turns to Harris: "That was one of our support people. You aren't going to believe this. There's been another murder. An Elvis impersonator in his room at Tiger Motor Lodge. They've brought the other seventeen in for questioning."

"Seventeen?"

"Seventeen other Elvis impersonators."

Laughing, he says, "Well, if they're all together they can't be part of the hoax, now, can they?"

"No. But this is serious, Frank. We have maybe two or three murders a decade around here, and now we've had three in the last few days and another person killed in a cult stampede."

"Which is technically a murder, isn't it?"

"I guess so, if we wanted to arrest one of the Elvises for inciting a riot."

"Have you looked into that?"

"We're speaking off the record, right? In fact, I think if we're going to have this kind of relationship, you better just figure we're speaking off the record all the time now."

She'd just called him Frank, and now she was talking about a relationship. "Relationship?"

"We'll see, okay?" She looks him in the eyes and then finishes her cup of coffee with a grimace. "I want to get back to town, and I've gotta tell Wilson about this. And shit, am I tired."

"Me, too." Their eyes remain locked. Something inside of him stirs for the first time in years.

"Okay," she says, "I'm going to have an officer drop you at your motel and I'll ride back in with Wilson. You get some sleep and remember what I said about things being off the record. Nothing's on the record with me anymore – at all. No way, no how. Got it?"

"I got it, Sergeant. Only, I'm going to remember it's because of our *relationship*."

She's quiet for a moment. Her eyes leave his and look outside the vehicle for Wilson. "Frank, I don't know why I like you. I don't feel comfortable getting close to people in that way. It always ends with pain, and it's usually my fault. So, for now, let's just go our separate ways and come back together later today. Okay?"

"Franklin."

"What?"

"My real name is Franklin. Franklin Arthur Harris."

She looks at him. "Thank you."

"Just wanted you to know."

"I can tell. Do I call you Franklin, then?"

He rubs his eyes. "No. Frank is fine. No one has ever called me Franklin except my parents when they were mad at me."

She smiles. "I can't imagine anyone ever getting mad at you."

He is beginning to feel uncomfortable. "I just…Never mind. I think we both need some sleep."

"Yes."

"But how about dinner at The Pancake House?"

She thinks. "Maybe. I don't know what we're dealing with here with these Elvises, but it may get in the way. If I can, though, I'd like to see you later. Call me at the office around three. If I'm not there, leave a voice mail and I'll get back to you. Now let me see if I can find you a ride."

*

Jack and Norma drive slowly down the narrow dirt track, back out to Route J, then follow the road to an unobtrusive gate. Norma gets out to open it while Jack watches her, trying not to think about the trouble they will soon have to confront. He's always surprised at how beautiful she is when she walks from the shade into buttery sunlight. Her short blonde hair and physique are still legendary, but the figure she cuts as she moves quickly to the gate is that of a little girl on an outing with her family. There is still that slight skip to her step.

He gives the Willies some gas and rolls it through. Norma closes the gate with a practiced stroke, pushing the bolt home, then snaps the lock in place. As she climbs in, he smells her scent in the moist air of the cab.

"I love you, you know," he says quietly.

"I do know," she replies, smiling at him in surprise. This is something he rarely lets on to.

"I just want you to know that...if something happens."

"Something isn't going to happen, Jack. We've got the whole place set up. Besides, you have to be guided to even see us."

"That's what we keep telling ourselves, but we've only seen that work with Lucas. There's a million ways things can go wrong."

"You aren't usually so pessimistic."

"I don't usually see our life source blown out of the air and then shipped east for analysis."

"You think that's what they're doing?"

"Of course. They're going to figure out what that helicopter was carrying before the end of the week, and then they're going to come back and try to find out more. That's when something can go wrong."

"They have to find the Red House first," she says. "And I don't think they even know how to get into the compound, let alone figure out which house we're in."

"I'm sure they can get on the compound, Norma Jean, but you're right, finding the right house isn't easy, and even if they find it, they still need to find us."

"It's a little bit different," she says. "But we've dealt with this before. Lucas can handle just about any scenario now. We've had hunters, real estate speculators, teenagers, convicts, and people who are just plain lost or curious over the years. This isn't any different except that these men are professionals."

"Norma, you're right about the first part. We've dealt with this before, but this time things could get hairy. It's why I wanted to build the ship. Eventually, we're going to either be found or we're going to have to just end—"

"I'm not going to believe that, Jack. We've been here for a long time. This is home. I love it here. It's the whole reason we did what we did. I'm not going to let this situation change things. You say yourself you don't have enough challenges. Well, this is a challenge. And we all need you to rise to it."

"I hope you're right. I just have this feeling and I can't shake it. Something is about to happen."

They drive on in silence. The tunnel entrance will be coming up soon. Norma looks at Jack. He's hiding something. She feels the pain coming from him.

*

"The two of you have the strangest powers," says Fancher out loud. They have been sitting in silence on the porch as the sun comes up. Coral and Cecil are amazed at the strength of his thoughts and his ability to reach into their minds and get them to think things they don't want to. He tells them with his thoughts that they have, like a number of people, a great deal of natural ability, but they have little, if any, skill in how to use that ability. They are completely uneducated. He admonishes Cecil in particular for trying to train himself with EGG. It just lets stuff in and then swishes it around, he says, but you can never do anything really creative with it.

Peyote and psilocybin are different, he lets them know. They create relationships with the world. Peyote is governed too much by the spirit of *Mescalito*, though, and secret strangers. These strangers always lead to rooms and ideas that end in mystery and new questions. Mushrooms, however, open doors to nature, and with that the full spectrum of reality; the universe becomes fair game. There are worlds within worlds within worlds. Everything is open and all the big questions hold, finally, answers. But there is more that psilocybin mushrooms make possible – so much more.

He also surprises them when he tells them that he had been watching them on the afternoon they met. He says that when he couldn't find Cecil on the road, he snuck down to Coral's and listened to them talking outside her window. He says he'd wanted to make sure they had the kind of powers he thought they did. He had been impressed. In fact, together they had more psychic strength than individually. He points out they didn't fully understand how important this was – and how rare. It was time for them to find out.

His first spoken words, then, are startling to both of them. The simple quiet of the morning, mixed with the momentum of Fancher's emotions rolling through them and admonishing them, leave both feeling exposed and sleepy. The sound of his voice sends swells of panic back and forth between them. They realize, as well, that he no longer seems to occupy their thinking.

"Pretty scary, eh?" says Fancher.

They look at each other, realizing how frightened he made them.

"How do you do that?" Coral finally asks.

"Years of practice, my dear."

"What, exactly are you doing?" asks Cecil.

"I can step in and out of it pretty much at will. It took me years to master, but I had a good amount of help."

"From whom?"

"With a little help from my friends, of course. But all will be revealed in due time."

"So, you got into my thoughts and brought me out here?"

"I did to a certain extent. But you were hard to get through to from so far away. This idea that you're a scientist doesn't help, either. And the existence of your ego has been a problem, too. But that should be expected, because you still have a body and that strong appetite of yours."

"Am I right, then, that Elvis really is still alive?" asks Coral.

"You might be, my dear. And others, too – although alive may not be exactly the way to put it."

"How do you put it then?" Cecil asks.

"To tell you the truth, we're still not sure. It seems that we've tapped into some kind of secret here. But it's not easy to put into words. You'll have to wait a bit before I can show you. You'll see…I hope, anyway." He laughs, rubbing his hands together.

"How long do we need to wait?" Cecil is feeling humbled but at the same time a bit put off by the older man's ambiguousness.

"Until you two fully come down so that we can get you into the proper state of consciousness with our own, um, medicine. In the meantime, please come inside, have some breakfast, and make yourselves comfortable. I need to mix up a batch of the stuff in the, um, basement, and with the sun coming up now, it'll be hot and uncomfortable out here very soon anyway. "We have other visitors who'll be along shortly, too. Probably not for a while, though. It'll give us all time to get further acquainted."

CHAPTER 25

The Sumter brothers have fucked up big time and they know it. They've been on foot all day, making it all the way downriver to McBain without being seen and are now circling back up along the edge of the bluffs heading toward their vehicles.

The moment the helicopter plummeted to the ground the rest of the group scattered in absolute panic. Initially, Bud and Monty got out of the area with Smokey, several of his nephews, and four or five others, but as soon as there was time to stop and take stock of the situation, it was clear that no one wanted anything to do with them.

"It's just a matter of time before one of them boys squawks about us, Bud," says Monty. "You know, I dropped my Colt, too?"

"Monty, I been doing this for too many years with you. Of course you dropped the Colt. You're also the asshole who shot the fuckin' thing down. Jesus Christ. And you left a weapon at the scene of the crime. Here we go again; I gotta figure out how to bail you out of something you had no business doing in the first place."

"We all shot it down, Bud."

"Well, not exactly, little brother. You're the one gets out there like Patton and socks it to that fuckin' Black Hawk. Most of them guys can't hit shit smeared all over a blue Chevy pickup. Then you leave a weapon so they can pin the whole thing on you. I think you got a death wish."

The older brother lets his words sink in, then says: "No, it was you Mont, and you gotta be proud in a lot of ways. Shooting down an army helicopter with a pea shooting pistol."

Monty smiles, enjoying his older brother's admiration.

"But you gotta realize," continues Bud, "we weren't trying to shoot that thing down, really. Just wanted to put the fear of God into them. Maybe make them come to us and cut a deal. You missed the meeting, boy. That's what we were discussing."

"Bud, why didn't you tell me? Shit. Now what are we gonna do?"

"Boy, I didn't think you'd actually bring it down with that overgrown cap gun."

They sit in silence, surrounded by hot weeds and floating grasshoppers. The Reverend is worrying whether the grasshoppers will land on his arm or his neck. The older brother is letting him sweat and thinking how interesting it is that grasshoppers rarely landed on people except his brother.

"I think we can get out of this, baby brother," Bud says finally. "But you gotta let me fashion the story and then stick with it."

"What are you going to say?"

"That we were out doing early-morning target practice and this helicopter comes along and takes several aggressive dives at us and that we were afraid for our safety and so we opened fire."

"You think that'll work?"

"Are you kidding? You have people around here think Elvis is back from the dead. It's not hard to say anything you want in this world now as long as folks need to believe it. What do these cops want with an army helicopter mysteriously shot down in the middle of a fallow cornfield? Same thing they wanted when Jack Kennedy was shot, same thing when federal buildings blow up, same thing when terrorists crash jets into skyscrapers, same thing when rock stars commit suicide. You float answers out there. The answers don't have to be true or even plausible. They just have to exist. If they come up with a competing story, well, it's a free-market world. Ideas are the same as technology. The most effective one wins. All it's gotta do is satisfy. Simple. Doesn't have to be the best, just the most prevalent. Long as the truth doesn't show, we win. So, let's get organized."

"What do you mean?"

"First, we gotta get to everyone who was there. Probably hold a short meeting this afternoon, then head into town tonight and have a talk with Bobby Wilson. He needs an answer."

"What are you going to tell him? That I did it?"

"No, little brother. You didn't do it. The pilot did it. We were just defending ourselves. You know how sometimes when you're aiming you miss? Well, sometimes when you're trying to miss you hit."

"So I didn't do it?"

"Well you did, but no one else probably knows that except me. It'll be okay, Monty."

"All right, if you say so, Bud, but I'd feel okay if we left town for good, too."

"Brother, we aren't doing nothing of the sort. Then they'd know we were guilty. No. My plan's better."

*

Jill agreed to meet Harris at The Pancake House between 8:00 and 8:30. She doesn't arrive until 9:15. He's gone through three cups of coffee and is surprised that he hasn't had a drink all day. Treestat was intrigued by the article he'd sent back, but a bit disappointed that the sources had been protected. Treestat knows where it's all coming from, of course, by the way he asks Harris about Janie.

"I hear Janie's down there, Frank. You seen her?"

"I have, Aaron, a couple times. But you know how she can be…"

"She must have been happy to see you."

Harris' long-term affair with her had always been a source of humor to the publisher. Not because of the distance, though, but because he'd never thought Janie would settle down to one man. Also because Harris is so unassuming – compared to her. He wasn't her type at all – if she had a type.

Before he begins to think about the implications of his boss's questions, Harris tells Treestat that he hasn't heard from Janie since the tent riot. This isn't true, of course. Besides their afternoon together, she'd left three messages for him to call her that day, and he was ignoring them.

He considered having a drink several times during the day while writing, but just never got around to it. After a nap, he went swimming and had an orange juice at the pool. Staring into the turquoise water, he realized he was beginning to enjoy the hazy gold of early Missouri evenings and the rising intensity of the cicadas as the day gave way to night. Even the sound of traffic on I-70 just behind him was soothing. Cars washed through the air every few seconds trailing shadow whispers behind them. He smoked three cigarettes and read the paper, the tang of the cold juice and the amber sky mixing to make the lazy early evening pleasant and lulling. He decided to read the paper until 7:15 then return to his room for a shower.

Locally, the reporting wasn't bad, but they only had sketchy details on both the helicopter shooting and the Elvis murder. The big question on the murder was whether it was the Elvis that everyone had been seeing, or just a coincidental shooting. The other question vexing reporters was the question of motive.

An editorial on gun control also proved intriguing. In that, the editor, Hank Landers, claimed that while the recent spate of murders was chilling, they were the price of becoming a true urban environment again. What was most interesting, though, was how hard the editor worked to deny that there was any connection between the three murders. To connect them would clearly not support his argument. Urban environments were partly predicated on the occurrence of *random* homicide. Besides, coming out in favor of a conspiracy theory would be too much for any legitimate reporter.

Harris's story for *Midnight*, on the other hand, insinuated as best he could without letting on what Jill had told him, that in fact the three murders were related, and that it was only a matter of time before detectives tied things together. His argument was all based on the fact that in this sleepy little college town it couldn't be anything but a conspiracy of some sort. There was no such thing as random murder here.

*

While he waits for Jill in the restaurant, sipping coffee and smoking cigarettes, he writes down what he knows:

1. *An Amish man is shot at near point-blank range by a person who strangely empties the chamber of his pistol at the scene. The bullets were .22 caliber but they hadn't found the murder weapon. Murder One.*

2. *An advanced, army-issue helicopter has been shot down by what is probably more than one person. It was carrying a strange, yet-to-be-determined cargo of powder – probably illicit drugs. A specially made pistol is found at the scene of the shooting whose owner might be identifiable. Murder Two.*

3. *One of 18 Elvis impersonators is murdered around the same time the helicopter is shot down. Murder Three.*

4. *Somehow, in all of this Lucas Fancher is implicated. His holdings on thousands of valuable acres of farmland that also happen to be pretty much unused and hidden now from prying eyes, point to a great deal more than coincidental involvement. The properties also contain remnants of Cold War-era missile silos.*

5. *Coral McGrey and Cecil Miller believe in life after death, ghosts, and clairvoyance, and both are also linked to events. Need to run checks on them. Miller in particular must be on a law enforcement database somewhere.*

Jill arrives as he's finishing a peach cobbler.

"I'm sorry I'm late. It's a bad habit of mine. I don't seem to be good at thinking about other people's needs. That's what I've been told, anyway."

"It's okay. Gave me time to think." He can't help himself. He seeks her eyes again.

"Well, I'm sorry anyway. Lots to do. I've been thinking about you today, though," She holds his gaze.

"Oh?" he manages.

"Mmm hmm," she nods, smiling carefully, finally looking away to her menu.

The waitress takes her order. Coffee is poured, more rolls and butter are placed on the table. Jill asks for a veggie burger, coleslaw, and a glass of iced tea. She lowers her voice as the waitress leaves: "I need to talk to you about some things."

"I want you to tell me what you were thinking about me, for starters." He keeps his voice down as well, almost whispering.

She smiles. "First, I just want you to understand that I know you've managed to keep things to yourself and I appreciate it. I... ."

"That goes against my nature as a reporter, Jill."

"I know. I appreciate that." Their eyes meet again over the table. He can see she's had time to think about how she feels toward him.

"Do you get off duty sometime soon?" he asks, noticing the increase in his heart rate and a lump in his throat.

"Well, sort of. What I have to tell you may keep me on duty all night, though, but I've got my beeper, so.... Why? What have you got in mind?"

"I thought, just that you might want to go for a walk after dinner?" He had asked it in more of a question than a statement. She scares him. He knows he's fumbling the whole thing spectacularly. He's forgotten the rudiments of romance.

"We'll see about that, Frank. First, you tell me everything you know about Janie Hawthorn."

This isn't the way he thought the conversation might go. He is clearly in trouble. "What do you want to know? She's an old girlfriend and...here, and we...."

"I know most of that. No, what I need to know is who she is – really."

Her tone has moved from quiet intimacy to business. Harris wonders if Janie is going to ruin this for him the way she ruined his marriage. He glances at his watch and decides that if Jill isn't going for a walk with him and then maybe coming back to his room and

Janie is the reason, at least he can start drinking again. He'd break it off with Janie as soon as possible – whatever *it* was.

"She doesn't mean much to me at all," he finally says.

"I don't care if you and she have a thing – not right now, anyway. Forget worrying about your personal life. I'm concerned with work at the moment. We can talk about your love life some other time."

The cold, businesslike tones are expressed carefully, but he can't help feeling distanced from her. He understands that she's doing this because it's her job, but he also realizes he is becoming confused. Does she like him or not? Is she afraid of him? Is he afraid of her? Why is it that the more experience you have in relationships, the more confusion you end up creating for yourself?

"Frank, I need to know about this woman. Just forget our personal issues for now. I'm trying to solve a whole bunch of murders here. Come on." She waits for his response.

"Well, when I first met her, she was sort of a special assignment reporter for *Midnight*, but she really wanted to go into TV journalism. A bit more than a year after I'd joined the company she left for USA TV. Been a reporter there ever since."

"What else?"

"You know, I don't understand where any of this is going, so I don't really know what to tell you."

"Come on, Frank. We're getting along well here. I'm not trying to bust your balls. I'm just doing my job."

He takes a sip of cold coffee and continues: "She and I had an ongoing affair for years. It was always weird to be around her, you know? And it seemed to make sense – she's attractive, and all. I never talked to her much about her personal life or anything outside of some pretty basic issues. We hardly ever went out to dinner even. We sometimes shared a meal in her room or watched a hotel movie, but neither of us had much of a social life. It's…you know…I find it hard to talk about this to you. I feel like it's spoiling any chance I have of getting you to, uh, be interested in me."

"Frank, I'm a big girl. I don't think I can judge you for having sex with a woman who's knockdown gorgeous. I just need to understand everything I can about her, and you're the best person right now to help me. Come on."

"What's up here, Sergeant Simpson?" He knows his voice sounds a bit exasperated and demanding.

"As they say, I'm not at liberty to divulge my motives." She stares him down and he can see she's very serious.

"Okay," he pauses, realizing that he doesn't know much more than what he's already told her. He also begins to wonder how he actually feels about Janie. There was a long-term familiarity that makes him feel somewhat protective of her.

"She sort of set up our meeting back there in the beginning when I did security work, I guess. She was attracted to me. And…well, one thing led to another…and, you know…. It lasted just long enough for me to realize my marriage wasn't cutting it. And then this thing with Janie just up and ended itself around the time I divorced my wife. We went our separate ways but not until I had landed a job with *Midnight.* She helped with that. It was on and off mostly after that. I owed her, I guess.

"She set her sights higher, though. She wanted to work in television, which she finally did. But news is news. Our paths cross four or five times a year. We might spend evenings together if we're not working too hard – sometimes when we are, too. We trade leads occasionally, help each other out, you know, whatever works. We swap being aloof with each other, too. Sometimes she gets mad at me when I spend time by myself; sometimes she's not interested in being with me. I don't usually ask why—wouldn't matter if I did anyway. It's sort of unwritten between us that we're both free to do whatever we want. When she's not interested in me, I feel maybe there's someone else, but I don't ask, I just leave her alone and go off and lick my wounds. I probably make her feel the same way."

He wonders through much of this whether his drinking was the reason Janie didn't want to be around him. It was certainly the reason there were times when he didn't want to see her. But this is a detail Jill doesn't need to know. He continues:

"She's a good reporter, I think, although I don't know much about TV. She's certainly a tough cookie."

Jill watches him closely, squinting.

"You're leaving something out," she says. "I can tell, but it's mostly about yourself and not about her."

"Yes," he manages with difficulty. *I'm a drunk*, he thinks, *and she never made a big deal out of it.*

"That's okay," says Jill. "I can tell it's personal."

"I want to talk about us now." he says.

She meets his eyes quickly. "Maybe later, Frank. Right now, we're on the trail of at least one killer. We've got work to do."

"At least one?" Harris is trying to mask his disappointment. He wants to go to bed with her. Is this falling in love?

"I think I'm starting to get a handle on things now," she says with a promising tone. "But there are miles to go before we sleep. I'm starved, and we both need some giant coffees to go. I'm going for another hike tonight. Wanna come along, or not?"

*

It is well past midnight when McKenna Joombs gets off the bus with her backpack and guitar. No one recognized her once she was out of St. Louis, which gave her a small feeling of freedom. She left home five years earlier with only a backpack and guitar, just like she is returning. This time, however, she's wealthy, and although the pack is the same one, the guitar is different. She gave up the Alvarez for a Taylor.

The forces of the world have drawn her back to Mid-Missouri. She had watched news accounts of Elvis's Second Coming and then read the tabloid gossip on the murder of the impersonator. It was too much. She is worried about her father. She also wonders how Dean and Jimmy are doing. That she has gone AWOL from her tour and that her band needs her is now just a fact. She needs to be home and to make sure everything is all right. She also has a strange feeling that her own well-being and spirit depend upon her return.

Standing in the dark and watching the red taillights of the bus pull back out onto the highway reminds her of the night she left. She realizes this was exactly what Dean had seen as he watched her pull away so long ago.

She can tell a storm is coming on. It had always been this way, that she could tell what would be in the air several hours into the future, here in central Missouri, and it seemed that it had to be the work of the river so close by with its changing scents blowing over the land. It gives her comfort to smell the ozone in the air now and feel the wind picking up. The lights of the farm rise to the night clouds in a silver glow.

She is carrying secrets with her. She's also carrying her father's first grandchild. She needs a place to hide out until she can have the baby. She also needs to rest. The life of a pregnant rock and roller is not all that fun.

Life on the road had been severe at first. She'd traveled to Memphis and Nashville initially and then to New York City and finally to Los Angeles, living all the while from day to day. Much of that time she was homeless and had even lived on the streets in LA when she'd first arrived. Something happened in Southern California though that she still didn't understand. Her songs got better, and she managed to hook up with the right group of guys who liked her and liked her music. Now they were all famous – at least in some circles. The Tigermen had three albums out and each CD scored two moderate hits for progressive radio.

Their style was a mix of rock and swing with a heavy dose of psychedelic guitar and long, extended jams. Harris Mobely was the genius on lead and trumpet, but McKenna was what made the group a success. She had an innocent sex appeal on stage and in the few videos they had produced. She was short, with green eyes and large breasts (which looked larger than they really were due to her stature); she had a pouting, schoolgirl mouth which she hated, but had learned to use to her advantage along with her breasts and height. Her most defining feature, though, was her hair. It fell halfway down her back, but would have fallen nearly to her butt if it weren't so curly. She had been called a Mariah, stomping and jerking her hair around onstage almost as if it were a dance partner.

Regardless of her physical appearance, it was her music that captivated people. She was known as a songwriter's songwriter. Her understanding of the relationship between rhythm and melody was unique, and her lyrics often dealt with social issues and the philosophical problems of religion and politics. Several reviewers had noted that she wrote music like a man. Several others claimed that they couldn't unravel the secret of her success, that her songs carried some odd magical property that was impossible to deconstruct.

McKenna herself also had a hard time understanding the process of creation that she went through. She usually found several chord progressions she liked and then just played them over and over until the words came. She used a great deal of tape as a result. Sometimes the words would come and she couldn't turn them off. Songs might go on for over an hour with the lyrics just tumbling out of her, formed of nothing, just continuing to flow, phrase by phrase, all perfect and true – rhyming, melodic, and endless. Meaning was not her problem. Every phrase was at once both original and open to interpretation; she could move effortlessly from simple images of lawnmowers and ice cream, to thoughts on God, to love gone bad, to mortality, and back to other images like the sound of rain on pavement and her father's face, and then back out to God again. Her signature song was an enigmatic anthem for the Midwest called "Slow Moods in Paradise:"

In Kansas I see a whitewall rolling without tread.
Against bright, hot diamond asphalt, it's spinning through my head.
In Missouri I see a child dreaming on a lawn
Her father carries sorrow from dusk to dawn.
In Oklahoma I drink water from a cold metal fountain
I count the gulps thinking of my life.

These are slow moods in paradise.
And if you don't feel them, let my friends take you there.
These are slow moods in paradise.
Cicadas know the sound, it's in the wind, it's in the air.

Driving through Indiana the wind carries with it breath.
Clouds bleed fire in the sky. Is there magic in death?
The walls of my motel are stained a yellow brown.
Ancient memories creep through the darkness of this town.
In Nebraska red mud swarms a shallow riverbank.
I find a calf skull in the sand, its hollow face draws a blank.

These are slow moods in paradise.
And if you don't feel them, let my friends take you there.
These are slow moods in paradise.
Cicadas know the sound, it's in the wind, it's in the air.

In South Dakota I cruise the fabled desert Badlands.
Where ghosts of Custer and other white men still make their stand.
In Minnesota the streets are empty and blue.
Trees rustle like insects on the hot, flat avenue.
In Illinois I'm lonely, dressed in black.
My silhouette dances with me, back to back.

These are slow moods in paradise.
And if you don't feel them, let my friends take you there.
These are slow moods in paradise.
Cicadas know the sound, it's in the wind, it's in the air.

At times she felt possessed, as if she were an object or a vessel rather than just a person who ate fast food and watched late-night TV alone in motel rooms. Words tumbled out of her with uncanny perfection at times and she simply acted as the vocalizer and the medium. She was the audience and the engineer. Against her torso she hugged and beat on the guitar, squeezing rhythm and sound from the strings, finding in herself, somewhere, a lost animal carrying passion and emotion out into the world in the form of poetry and sonic occurrence.

The end product was a stream of songs that slowly evolved into albums, a band, concerts, and even a small cult following. She wanted to name the band The Tigermen, but their agent wanted her up front and in the public's face. No matter how much she loved the musicians who accompanied her, and no matter how much they loved her, she was gradually becoming wealthy because she was McKenna Joombs. The compromise became *McKenna Joombs and the Tigermen*, but the quality of the group itself had naturally erased her name over the few years they had been touring. *The Tigermen* had a front man in the guise of McKenna Joombs, but they also had a sound that made them unique unto themselves.

She hoists her backpack to her right shoulder, picks up the guitar with her left hand, feeling the baby shift ever so slightly. If anything, it would be nice for someone like her father to ask to feel the baby move. It might take some patience, but Dean could probably be brought around, too. It would have been nice for him to be the father, but that wasn't the way things had worked out.

*

They waited nearly two hours for Cecil to come down and for the psychoactive aspects of his and Coral's minds to dissipate. A confusing sense of jealousy comes over Cecil as Fancher ushers them into the house for breakfast. Fancher seems to be lingering in Coral's mind, although he'd cut Cecil off. Vaguely, Cecil had felt Coral's warm emotions come to him, saying goodbye as she let go of the drugs. Several minutes later the final split of their minds had come. For a long time after that he'd been aware that Fancher had returned and was quietly residing just beyond his awareness. He felt something dark and menacing there as well, some idea he should understand but couldn't. Was it Fancher or something in his own mind? Or was there yet another consciousness embedded in him, secretly watching the proceedings of the morning?

"We'll have some breakfast first and then take the correct…uh, medicine after," says Fancher as he leads them through the living room toward the kitchen in the back.

The smell of fried butter and bacon comes from the kitchen. Cecil is hungry and hasn't smelled bacon in a long time.

"Mr. Miller, I know you need to use the facility," Fancher ventures. "The bathroom's down the hall. Coral, I hope you like fried duck eggs and bacon because that's what we're having."

Fancher lets Cecil pass to go to the bathroom then leads Coral into the kitchen. Cecil hears muffled voices as he closes the door. It sounds like there's another woman in the kitchen.

As he unbuttons his pants and removes his penis, he searches for the dark presence in his mind. An unbidden sense of amusement passes through him, and he feels as if something is hiding from him. The sensation of running down a darkened hall blows through him. He thinks how beautiful the brown tiling looks with only the daylight streaming in through a skylight. Briefly, he considers what they are doing here and is at a loss to explain what's going on.

Tucking his penis back inside the fly, he recalls that he's still supposed to be on a mission for Stoddemeier and Gold. He buttons up, then bends to find the transponder on his leg. He pushes down on the pressure switch hoping, it's working.

In the kitchen the smell of breakfast consumes him. "Cecil Miller, I'd like you to meet Janie Hawthorn. Janie, this is Cecil Miller, the man I've been telling you about."

Cecil steps toward the stove where the woman stands watching the eggs and bacon. He reaches out to shake her hand. She has long black hair. There is something about her that bothers him, though, which amplifies the dark presence. She turns, moving the spatula to her left hand, smiling slightly. There is a look of recognition in her smile. She focuses her eyes on his, then the presence becomes overwhelming. He feels himself sway backwards. His last memory before blacking out is of Coral moving towards him with her arms out, calling his name.

CHAPTER 26

"Bobby, I still can't tell you the whole story, but I can let you in on a little of it."

Dale Stoddemeier has changed into his night gear and is sitting in the empty break room finishing a microwaved dinner – Salisbury chili steak, mashed potatoes, and Mexican corn – and doing calculations on a yellow legal pad. He's drinking hot coffee from a grimy turquoise travel mug with a white twist top. It is approaching 10:00 p.m. The third watch would be coming in soon. He keeps Wilson waiting in silence while he finishes his calculations.

There will be four squad teams of nine men each. They will converge on the property from four different roads. Squad B and C will have the greatest distance to travel on foot - nearly three miles. They will need to start roughly twenty-five minutes before A and D. Stoddemeier, along with Arthur Gold, will coordinate the exercise a quarter of a mile away with the surveillance group at the base of the hill leading up to the farm. The request for satellite movement had gone to Washington fourteen hours ago when Miller's beacon transmission was first received. The GPS terminal commands would be functional shortly, allowing Stoddemeier and his three NSA analysts to home in on Miller's exact location and to simultaneously watch the four squads move through the night preparing for their strike. He's beginning to wonder about Gold's motives, though.

Stoddemeier finally looks up from the yellow pad and says: "I've been here awhile now, Bobby, and I know you're not stupid."

Years in police bureaucracy had taught Wilson to keep his mouth shut in situations like this.

"I want to thank you for keeping things close to the vest all these months. This job is nearly done. I just need you to keep your guys out of my way for another twenty-four hours – maybe less.

"You're good at what you do," Stoddemeier concludes after a few seconds of silence. "So I'll answer what I can."

"The object here has been to track down and bring in Lucas Fancher. There are a number of issues we need to discuss with him. I'm on loan from the Bureau to another branch of the Treasury Department for this. Those kids in that other room are NSA. I've got almost forty commandos out there who are choice SEAL, Green Beret, and Secret Service. We've detected a great deal of activity out there in Fancher's little nest for nearly ten years – nighttime chopper drops, large sums of money going into several offshore accounts, shipments of psilocybin mushroom spores up from Mexico, you name it. Problem has been to pin him down. That's a pretty vast property he's got a hold of. Close to 12,000 acres. He's moved roads, dug tunnels, hauled in a couple salvaged NASA assemblies from varying rockets and shuttles, and a host of other huge machines. We have no idea what he's up to, but it's clearly not something good. Worst of all, some of that land contains old missile silos that may not have been fully decommissioned. For all we know, Fancher could have access to a big chunk of rocket technology – which may explain the salvaged NASA equipment. We're not sure. But that's why we need to go in.

"The final piece of the puzzle went into place with that helicopter crash last night. Besides the drugs onboard, we found the outlawed substance tetrodotoxin. The chopper itself is an experimental model developed by the Army that we thought was in Israel."

"What's tetrodotoxin?" Wilson asks.

"Tetrodotoxin is one of the most poisonous naturally occurring substances known to man. It's the active ingredient in the Caribbean blowfish. When it's refined and purified, besides being highly toxic, it can dissolve in water within a few seconds. A cup of the stuff in the water supply of a large city would wipe out the inhabitants in less than twenty-four hours."

"You think this guy is some kind of mercenary villain then, Dale?"

"I have no opinion on what he is. All I know is possession of that stuff, along with everything else we think we got on him, is enough to can him for a long time."

"Where have I heard of tetrodotoxin before?"

"Probably in voodoo stories and movies. It was first discovered by an anthropologist studying Haitian zombie rituals back in the '70s. A very small amount of unrefined tetrodotoxin powder when inhaled or absorbed through the skin, with enough time, creates a state of paralysis in its victim that makes them appear dead. Their metabolic rate descends to practically nothing, and their pulse is virtually undetectable. In the most sensationalized cases, victims have been buried alive and then exhumed as much as a week later. Shamans, witch doctors, really, are responsible for the poisoning. The myth is that once exhumed, another powder is ingested, making people come back to life. As long as the powder continues to be taken, the zombie will remain alive and happy but under control of the shaman."

"So, you're after Fancher because he might be practicing voodoo?"

"No. We're after him because he's too far out there. The tetrodotoxin is just the final straw."

"Well, all of this is far beyond my purview, Dale, so I'll just keep my mouth shut and let you get on with your business. If you really don't know what he's up to, that's something no one I work for can deal with."

"I knew you'd see it that way, Bobby. Thanks. This may be a very serious situation. Is it all right if my kids use your office while they calibrate their instruments?" He waves his hand at the window to Wilson's office, behind which three young men dressed in night suits are just finishing the process of running cables to laptops and other gadgets they're using.

"Seems I've got little choice, Dale. Carry on. We'll stay out of your way."

*

As Cecil begins to regain consciousness, he finds himself lying on a cot inside a large yellow canvas tent. The space is stifling. A muggy heat beats down on the tent walls, and there seems to be no ventilation. Picking his head up at the sound of voices, he sees Coral and Fancher talking quietly next to what looks like the opening to a tunnel connected to the tent.

"What happened?" he asks. The older man and Coral turn to look at him.

"She was too much for you," replies Fancher.

It begins to come back to him: "Jesus, who was she? What happened?"

"Well, I was just getting ready to tell your friend here, so I'm glad you're up and awake."

Coral kneels on the floor. There seems to be a hint of sadness in her eyes. She strokes his cheek. He can't feel her in him any more. The EGG effect has completely worn away. How long had he been out? It can't be more than a few hours.

Raising himself carefully onto his elbow, he surveys the contents of the tent. Besides a number of folding metal chairs and a few card tables, the only other object he sees sits in the center of the room. Raised on six cast-iron legs is a glass bowl perhaps eighteen inches in diameter suspended above a small fire pit that Fancher is busy filling with kindling and several stout logs. The bowl is filled with a yellow liquid, probably oil. As far as Cecil can tell, it is an aromatherapy dispenser.

"This will only be the first stage of the journey," says Fancher. "There are a number of steps we will need to go through. Be patient and we can go all the way in. Mr. Miller, you will find that the issues you've been wondering about over the years were, in fact, relevant. You weren't completely on the money, but close enough."

Fancher lights a match to ignite the kindling. Miller watches with Coral as the older man stands and sprinkles the contents of an envelope over the oil. Flames grow as he uses a large spoon hanging from the frame to stir the oil.

"It won't be long now," Fancher says to them.

"What won't be long?" Cecil asks.

Coral reaches for his hand and leans against him.

"It's usually best just to breathe deep and say nothing," replies Fancher.

The flames barely lick the bottom of the bowl. The room gradually fills with a musky scent. The aroma is ever so gentle, but with each breath he takes the smell grows stronger. And the heavier the smell, the more the sensation begins to take hold of him.

He looks at Coral. Her eyes are closed, but the sad smile of just a moment before has changed to one of relief. He can feel her entering his mind again. Just wait, she seems to say. You won't believe this.

He can feel Fancher, too, but there are no words coming from him. Just a feeling. The feeling of being Fancher.

And then they begin to go into the opening in the tunnel. He watches as other people come to meet them, people who look vaguely familiar, milling around and waiting for something. There are scores of them streaming in. Most are men, but there are a few women. Finally, he realizes why they look familiar. They are. Three of them are unmistakable. One is the woman whose presence knocked him out; the other two are impossibly there.

Another person comes up behind them and puts his hand on Coral's shoulder. Under the other arm he carries a large object cloaked in the same material of which the tent is made. He lets the canvas fall away from the object.

The object is an over-sized, western-style acoustic guitar finished in sky blue lacquer with tiny mother-of-pearl stars embellishing the dark fret board. Cecil looks around the room at the people. He can't believe who he is seeing. Coral, too, seems disbelieving, hands covering her mouth, eyes wide open. The man holding the guitar looks quite remarkably like Elvis Presley himself.

Part VII
The Sound of Rushing Water

On his arms appeared a thousand eyes as his demon helpers emerged to search the night for enemies. The sound of rushing water filled his ears, and listening to its roar, he knew he possessed the power of Tsungi, the first shaman. Now he could see. Now he could find the truth.

- Michael J. Harner, "The Sound of Rushing Water"

CHAPTER 27

Arthur Gold has deployed three surveillance specialists to set up the necessary equipment in Bobby Wilson's office. A dish is quickly mounted on the roof of the station, and fiber-optic cable is run down the side of the building through a window into the second-floor office. Wilson's never seen anything like the control instrument they produce. It's no bigger than a fat paperback and cased in matte black metal. To open it, two of Gold's men insert their index fingers in small openings on the front of the cover. After a few seconds, green lights on the side of the machine flash, the men remove their fingers and pop the lid. The top appears to be a tiny LCD screen but the base is not a keyboard. There are two matchbook-sized touchpads, at least a dozen micro-control knobs and switches, and what looks like a small, touchpad made of black foam rubber.

"It's really just a compact satellite management system," Stoddemeier tells Wilson. "Kind of advanced, but Gold likes to work on the 'no excuses' plan."

"No excuses?"

"If you use the best people and the best technology, then you usually have no excuse if things go wrong."

"Must be nice," snorts Wilson.

"I don't know where he gets his funding, but it's been interesting working with him on this."

"No keyboard on your little box there?" asks Wilson.

"Doesn't need one. A good amount here is voice activated except for the actual controls. What I like is the touchpads – they're three-dimensional. Your fingers can move in and out as well as back and forth or up and down. It's an very eerie feeling when you start fiddling with the thing. We think we're so sophisticated, but a hundred years of flat screen viewing really limits one's sense of space."

Wilson knows he's been allowed to view these gadgets to satisfy his curiosity and that he is now expected to leave the office to Stoddemeier and his cohorts. He gives the room one last glance and moves to exit.

"Bobby, thanks again," calls Stoddemeier.

"Don't mention it, Dale," replies Wilson. "Just make sure you take care of Jill."

"I will, Bob. I will. You can count on me."

One of Gold's men is now sitting at Wilson's computer, monitoring a remote feed to both NASA and NSA; another talks on his mobile phone to engineers in Houston and Jakarta; the third, Gold's chief of staff, Gary Parks, issues occasional commands to the controller, provides questions for his comrades to ask their contacts, and keeps Stoddemeier informed about timing for repositioning, all the while watching the screen which is registering the beacon's signal. Parks is younger than the other two, perhaps in his early twenties. Stoddemeier doesn't like him at all. The kid is razor sharp but too slick and polished. It's likely that the kid hasn't had an emotional connection with another person since he was toilet trained.

As the satellite approaches the coordinates provided by the beacon, the geographic resolution improves. After nearly forty minutes, the screen has moved to one-second refresh intervals, and the graphic depiction of boundaries has transformed from showing the red flash of Cecil's beacon somewhere in the middle of North America to somewhere in the vicinity of Howard and Boone counties.

Stoddemeier sits outside the makeshift command post in an alcove office going over a checklist from Gold. He looks up when he senses Parks standing over him.

"Sir, we're down to single-second refresh," says Parks. "Probably another twenty minutes and we'll be going to real-time imaging."

"I'll be right there, Parks."

When he enters the room he is impressed with the silence. These three are clearly A-list technicians. He's also pleased to find the office still relatively uncluttered by cabling and machinery. Parks's laptop shows a 3-point line image of most of the two counties, with hairline borders depicting large towns, major highways, and the diagonal cut of the Missouri River slicing the block image in the middle. The flashing light still only provides an approximate location and blinks much larger than the scale of the map on the screen. It's somewhere just north of I-70 and east of the mid-state bow in the river. They are down to about an 800-square-mile resolution.

"How long before we get real-time LANSAT?" Stoddemeier asks.

"Maybe half an hour after the satellites are positioned. We've got to call three control systems to activate digital imaging."

"But we'll have a true fix on the coordinates in the next twenty minutes?"

"We should. The images will be a bit grainy and still in refresh mode. It'll register clear at maybe twenty miles visibility, but we can enhance down to fifty yards with the default camera onboard the control satellite. You'll get a blurry reverse image, but the beacon will be the main thing you see."

They watch as the screen gains resolution. More towns, roads, and waterways begin to show up. Stoddemeier turns his attention to the man watching Wilson's computer screen and the other man still talking quietly into his cellular. The three satellites are moving ever so slowly toward three purple stars in a small window on Wilson's monitor. The screen is spattered with tiny red spots indicating heat sources like buildings, cars, and roads. The towns and cities are pulsing blobs of orange, yellow, and red. At the bottom of the screen in light blue is a legend showing switch sequences for the three cameras they will use to monitor the efforts of the squads.

Looking carefully, he notes in what should be open country, several small specks of red, not more than a pixel or two in capacity. "What are those tiny red dots?"

The technician looks closely. "Hmm. Could be anything. Farm equipment, pumping station, remote weather lab, you name it. There's also underground walkways and tunnels on some of the properties connecting houses to outbuildings and the like."

Stoddemeier reflects on this. He doesn't like uncertainty in operations where someone else had already defined the objective. Too much risk without knowledge of the upside.

The man on the mobile phone reads a string of numbers into his phone, takes the phone away from his ear, and begins to push keys on the phone, all, presumably, a series of security access codes. Behind him he hears a sharp muttered hiss from Parks, quickly followed by flailing fingers on the laptop's controls and finally a low-volume, high-frequency tone.

"What's wrong, Mr. Parks?"

"I don't know exactly, but it appears that someone just turned off that beacon."

*

"Thank you for remembering about your little homing device, Mr. Miller."

"Sorry, Fancher. Too much excitement. I doubt they've picked up on much definition yet. It's still early for them."

"Well, even if they have, it's okay. I've sort of been counting on them coming en masse. We need to get this over with."

"What needs to be gotten over with?"

"You'll see. Jack and I have been planning this for a while. Now, I've got some things to do, so why don't you go back to your hosts and let me keep working? The last pieces of this project should be on their way soon."

Cecil is torn between wanting to find out what Fancher is up to and getting back to Coral. He heads out the back door to find the group discussing a new song one of the latest arrivals had just finished.

"Look, I know it's in a suspended seventh root chord, you all. But it's still good. You said so yourself, JJ."

"It's just been so long since we played in a suspended seventh."

"Well, how about we give it a try?"

"Can't you just transpose it?" asks Janis.

"Just a try, Janis? Please?"

"If we want a jam out of it, it's going to be hard to do in a suspended seventh for any extended period of time."

One of the non-musicians comes over to Cecil. "If you think what you've seen so far is cool, wait till you see what happens when they actually play."

Cecil waits for an explanation, but none is offered. He's counted more than a hundred of them. Several residents have told him that there is one guy who rarely shows his face except during their time to gather. It's sort of nice to know now, he smiles, without any doubts, that there is more to life than the normal.

*

"Okay, tell me where we're going," Harris says.

They're driving in Jill's pickup on a third gravel road since leaving the blacktop. Each road has gotten a little narrower. They move slowly to minimize noise and because the road is basically one lane.

"I want to come at this from a different direction, so we're going to enter Fancher's property from the east instead of the south."

"You think Fancher is the one we're after?"

"Can you take that topo out of its tube and see if you can figure out where we are? Here's a penlight."

Harris removes the map from the aluminum tube and begins to unroll it. "I'm not sure I'm going to be very good at reading a map like this."

She drives in silence, waiting for him to get his bearings.

"Okay," he says. "I think I know where we are. That last blacktop was Route VV?"

"Yup."

"The two gravels were Akeman Bridge Road, then O.B. Brown. Now...Bell?"

"Sounds right," she replies. "It's been a long time since I was out this way."

"There's going to be a turnoff soon going east. The road bends west. The turnoff seems like what we want."

"Only it won't be there."

"It won't be there?"

"No. That's what we want."

"Whatever it is comes just before Bell turns a sharp west."

"Won't be there. That's where his property goes to."

"Jesus, Jill, is this a test?"

"No. This is a murder investigation, Frank." They see the road bend hard to the left in the headlights.

Jill slows the pickup to a crawl. Their headlights illuminate tall grass and a few trees near the shoulder. She lets the truck roll off the road onto the shoulder. They drift into grass that is halfway up the side of the door. She kills the engine and flicks off the lights.

"Got a ways to walk now," she says. "Maybe two miles. You still up for this?"

"Can we wait just a minute? I want to talk about some stuff."

"Stuff?" There is a hint of playfulness in her voice. He turns in his seat to look at her. She keeps her eyes on the windshield. They sit in the truck cab silence for nearly a minute.

"Frank," she says, finally turning to him.

"Jill."

"You're going to confuse us before we get started."

"You're beautiful."

"I'm over the hill." She's smiling.

"I've never met…"

She closes her eyes and shakes her head to stop him. "Frank, can't we wait on this until tomorrow? Everything ought to be clear by the morning. Then we can talk about other stuff."

"Tomorrow morning?"

"I think so." She waits for him to consider.

"All right, then," he says. "I don't want to wait, but I will. Hopefully you'll see that as a sign that I'm serious."

"I think I got that already."

"Well, I hope we can do something about it."

They listen to the crackle and hum of night insects.

"Let's get started," she says as she opens her door. "If we can't make something happen tonight, then things are going to start getting cold."

Harris sighs, looks out his window at the sky, then gets out of the car as well. He follows her through a few trees. The pulse and scree of insects is so dense and thick it feels almost as if they are walking through stage curtains charged full of the sound of electricity.

"Are we really going to walk around in the dark again all night with this insane mind drenching insect hum?" he asks.

"Probably." They keep walking.

"Do you have a flashlight or something?" he asks.

"I've got a penlight if we need it, but we just need to let our eyes get used to the dark. We'll be fine." They continue walking. They are side by side striding through waist-high grass.

"Can you clue me in on what you know that I don't?" he asks after about ten minutes.

"I don't know anything. I'm just going on hunches."

"So we're going on an all-night hike that could end up being nothing but a big zero?"

"You could put it like that, but I'm pretty sure it'll be worth our while. There are only nine properties we need to check. Let's be optimistic. If we're lucky, maybe it'll be the first one."

"You think it's Fancher, then?"

"I really can't say yet. But I think Fancher can tell us a great deal. If not him, then maybe Miller or McGrey. I mean, why are they all out here anyway?"

"We'd better step it up, then, Jill, if we're going to find out. Me, I'm going to think about the morning as payback for tonight."

"Hold on," she says. "There's something else."

"What?"

"I've been putting this off."

"What is it? *What?*"

"I should have told you before." She takes a deep breath, then says: "We're still checking, Frank, and I don't want to shock you here but for now, at least, it seems Janie Hawthorn died in a fire back in 1991." She tries to see his face in the dim light.

Harris stops and tries to find her face in the same dim light. "What are you talking about?"

"Janie Hawthorn, *your* Janie Hawthorn, was reported dead in 1991."

"I don't think that's possible. You guys have made a mistake."

"I wish that was true." She pauses, watching him intently now. He can't tell if she's simply concerned or if she's looking for something else. "There's more," she continues. "The coroner's report found high levels of barbiturates and alcohol in her blood…in the fire victim's system…before burial."

"Jill, you're not listening to me."

"Hear me out on this, Frank. This is important. I don't make mistakes. It seems that after her death there was a bit of a scandal in Des Moines where she had lived. Some ambitious reporter up there got the strange notion that she'd been murdered over an exposé she was working on about land consolidators. He claimed she was poisoned by some obscure organic compound that's almost impossible to trace. So the reporter makes a lot of noise and finally gets an order to exhume the body to test his hypothesis. Only, when they open the grave there is no body."

"No body? How many years had it been?"

"Three by then."

"Anything could have happened, Jill."

"I know, but Janie Hawthorn is walking around. She's your girlfriend."

"She's not my girlfriend, and you're assuming it's the same Janie Hawthorn."

"Frank. She's a well-known TV journalist. I've seen her plenty myself. Look at this picture from the obituary." She hands him the folded printout and shines her penlight on it for him to see. Without doubt he's staring at a photo of a younger Janie, but blonde. The headline says, "Rookie Journalist Dies in Mysterious Hotel Fire."

"I'm not sure...look at this picture. If it was the same Janie Hawthorn, she would have to be well over fifty by now. Have you checked whether she had relatives?"

"We have. There are a few, but very distant."

"It's impossible, Jill."

"You know, I hear you on that. But that's her, Frank. Plain and simple."

"Well, yes, but what does this mean? That she faked her own death? That she's your murderer?"

"I don't know."

"Why hasn't someone come forward, then? Why not the reporter?"

"I don't know. I've got one of my guys trying to track all of them down right now, but so far it doesn't seem there's anyone to be found. If we find anything it'll be days from now and I need my answers now."

"So that's why you were asking about her?"

Jill's response is to start walking again. They continue at a faster clip in silence. Occasionally, their shoulders bump together or their arms make contact. He wonders if he can take her hand in his. The idea of such an intimate gesture sends him back to feelings from being with girls in junior high. With these new revelations about Janie, though, his amorousness is on hold.

"What you're saying is too weird, Jill."

"I know."

"The whole thing has to be either a scam or just some big mistake a reporter made."

"It's no mistake, Frank. That's her." They continue to walk.

"There is one thing I didn't really mention," he says finally, "but it probably doesn't mean a thing."

She waits.

"I never really felt like I was connecting with her. She seemed distant and sort of preoccupied. If what you say is true...."

"What do you mean, distant?"

"It's hard to explain. Like, she's from another planet almost...."

They continue on in silence.

"You think she's behind the murders, then?" he asks again.

"Frank, would you get off it already? I *really* don't know. Nor do I care right now. We need to find Fancher and hopefully Miller and McGrey and see what they know. Something tells me, though, that Janie Hawthorn has had more to do with all of this than we suspect."

"Why would she murder an Amish kid, or that Elvis impersonator?"

"Again, I don't know. I do know, though, that this has gotten quite a lot of press of late. Maybe she's trying to drum up some business."

"Well, she's done that, I must say."

It's somehow flattering to have this woman looking to pin crimes on a woman he's slept with. And nothing would surprise him about Janie, now that he thinks of it.

"We should be coming into view of the first property," whispers Jill. "We need to proceed cautiously now and be quiet. I really want to find these people before they find us."

*

"What level of resolution did we get to?" asks Stoddemeier.

The three technicians watch each other. Parks finally says: "We can pinpoint down to maybe a twenty-mile radius."

"Can't you just extrapolate?"

The other two let Parks answer: "We weren't recording, sir. Not enough disk space."

"Your headquarters has backed up the transmissions though, right?"

"I'm not sure, Mr. Stoddemeier. It's the middle of the night. There would be a skeletal crew on call at best."

"On call being?"

"Being on call, sir. That is, in beeper communication with a dispatcher. And this is supposed to be a QT mission, so it's likely the dispatcher is actively trying to ignore what we were doing."

"It's very possible, then, that no one was monitoring the orbital shifts of three of the most expensive satellite surveillance systems the NSA has to offer?"

"It's very likely."

Stoddemeier considers this information.

"I need a solution, Parks."

"We can call up the map of all the possible locations."

"We could have done that without moving those satellites."

"I know, sir. It's the best I can offer. We can move the satellites over each property one by one until we see something. Once we get a fix on the right place, we can make the final orbital adjustments and lock in for close-up."

"Too much time, Parks."

"Sir, I don't see any other way." Parks looks to his other team members for support.

"Any other suggestions?" Asks Stoddemeier.

"Would be nice, sir, if we were allowed to use drones here."

"That's not in our toolbox yet, Parks."

"I'm just pointing it out."

"Well, thank you. But I need a real and at least nominally legal solution." Stoddemeier waits for a response.

"We have a choice of nine farms within that range and over forty men," Parks finally says. "Split our guys into teams of five or six and send them out on discovery. They'll pick something up in less than two hours. We can triangulate the satellites while they deploy back to their original squads – maybe another hour, max. By 0500 hours we'll be in business with all the feed you need. It's kind of an old-fashioned way of doing things, but it will be effective. Besides, everyone on the team is outfitted with video cameras."

"We don't have much choice, do we?" Stoddemeier looks at each of them.

*

Fancher returns to the silence of the house. He knows she will be there waiting for him.

"Hello, Daddy."

In the darkened living room tears stutter in his eyes. His face grows warm. He feels goose bumps ripple up his spine, down his biceps, and onto the soft of his forearms.

"Hello, McKenna. I've been waiting for you."

"That's the one thing about you that I've never liked, Daddy. I could never surprise you."

He waits. She takes the four steps she needs to cross to him. The feel of her in his arms coaxes a few tears all the way out. The smell of her hair and bulk of her shoulders makes him tremble with memory. But he feels her belly pressing into him, too.

"You have surprised me this time, McKenna. What is this?" He steps back to look at her and pats the distended tummy.

"You're going to be a grandfather."

His response is not what she'd anticipated. He moves away from her and slumps to the sofa. She knows she must wait for him to speak.

"McKenna, remember how I used to tell you that things weren't always as they seemed, that we were living a charmed life and that one day I would need to pay for things?"

"You were always melodramatic."

"No, I always stopped there. They didn't want you to know until you had proven yourself."

"They? Proven myself? What are you talking about?"

"I'm talking about a changing of the guard, honey. I'm talking about you taking over for me."

"Daddy, I don't want to run this farm. I never have. I never will."

"I think you'll change your mind when you see what I've got to show you. It's not so much the farm as its animals. They're a bit portable. Or, maybe I should say, they're going to be if all goes according to plan."

"What are you talking about?"

"Come with me, McKenna. We don't have much time before they get here. You need to learn what I'm really all about. My friends ought to be starting in a few minutes."

*

Simpson and Harris have been to three farms and found nothing. After the third, they cross several expansive pastures and are hiking up a long rise when the noise comes to them. Jill hears it first and stops.

"Let me see the map," she whispers.

He hands it to her as he picks up the sound as well.

"What the hell is that?"

"I don't know," she says, "but it seems like it's coming from right here on the middle northern property. Maybe half a mile that way."

"You think that's where Fancher is?"

"I think we need to follow that sound and stay positive."

"What is it, though?"

"Sounds like a party," she says.

"Makes me feel weird."

"Like we're already there."

"Like we're the only people left on the planet."

"More like we're the first."

"This is weird. This is definitely weird."

"We better get moving."

*

As they approach the house, the sounds stop. So does the sensation they each felt.

"This must be the place," insists Jill.

"Maybe."

"Got to be. Now, you wait here while I move in closer."

"Aren't you supposed to call in for backup or something?"

"I want to figure out what's up first. Doesn't seem to be much going on here. Just that one light on the porch."

"What's the deal? If you go in with your gun drawn you need backup don't you?"

"I don't have a weapon, Frank," she whispers.

"You what?"

"I left it in the car. I never carry a weapon unless I'm under someone else's command."

"I thought it was standard procedure."

"It is, but I don't care much for standard procedure."

"Well, what if you need a gun?"

"Then I'm fucked. Here, take my phone. If I'm not back in fifteen minutes, punch seven, then eight, then hold the pound sign down for the count of two. It'll get you back to headquarters and you can tell them where we are."

"Where are we?"

"Tell the desk to let Baines know it's the one he thought it was."

"You're going to be back quickly, right?"

"I have no idea."

"You should have been a scientist."

"You should learn to pay attention to the truth more."

"Careful."

"I'll be fine, Frank. Just be patient."

"I'm always patient."

"Right."

"See ya."

He hears only her first step through the tall grass and weeds, then she vanishes into the half-darkness.

*

Jill notices the slow rock of the chair just as the voice comes to her quietly, "It's still a little early, but good morning, Sergeant Simpson."

She moves around from what she'd thought was a hiding place to the edge of the porch. "You must be Fancher."

"That I am. Been waiting."

"For me?"

"Yes."

"What for?"

"Your intelligence, really – and a final resolution," he says.

"Final resolution? To what? The murders?"

"That's not how I would put it, but it'll do for now."

"Mr. Fancher, I don't have time to play games."

"Ah, yes, Mr. Harris is off in the bushes, down the hill," he says. "Tell you what – go back down and tell him that we have to have a conference and that he should sit tight."

"Sit tight? For how long?"

"Depends on how long we need."

"For what?"

"Explanations, my dear."

"Explanations."

"Go tell him not to call in until you come back."

"I don't know if that's fair to him, Mr. Fancher."

"Sergeant, call me Lucas or Fancher. I haven't been Mr. Fancher since I got lost out here in silo country nearly forty years ago." He waits, but Jill doesn't reply. "Look," he continues, "I know how you feel about Mr. Harris, but this is really a bit more important than whether he has to sit in the woods until daybreak."

She has little choice.

"I'll be back in five minutes," she says finally.

"And I'll be right here waiting for you, Sergeant."

*

When she returns, Frank is seated on the ground leaning against a tree. "First of all, it's not a trap," she says calmly as she sits down next to him.

"This is too weird, Jill. Too many coincidences. Fancher knows too much. He's not going to let you leave."

"That's ridiculous. He just let me come back here to tell you he needs some time to discuss things with me. Think of it as a conference or a summit meeting, maybe. There's no doubt he's a bit off and different, but I need to do this, Frank. Fancher's fine. He seems like he's completely under control and has something he needs to talk to me about that's pretty important."

"That's so that he can buy time."

"Look, buddy boy, I'm going to do this. Don't call in until the sun is up. Maybe six-fifteen or so. Okay? And stay put."

"I don't have much choice, do I?"

"No, not really."

"Okay. I'm coming with you," he says.

She realizes she's asking a lot of him. Their faces are close. She can smell the tang of his sweat, taste his odor in the back of her throat. The sour of his breath fills her nose. She lets herself lean into the small distance left between them; her cheek rubs against his neck. She hears his breathing stop, drinks his full body odor down her throat, and feels his fingers on her chin. They search for each other in the near darkness and then their lips meet softly. She feels all of him in the kiss. His lips aren't moist, but there is an interesting strength and powerful passion returning to her. Each of them feels the other's reservations give way to desire as the sensation of teeth and tongues and the hungry emotions they'd both been dancing around come rushing forward. One of his hands is at the back of her head, the other in the small of her back. He gently presses her forward off the ground and into his chest, scooting around so that she will be sitting in his lap.

She pulls away. "Maybe that'll hold you," she says coyly.

Harris doesn't respond.

"We've got work to do, Frank."

"I'm aware of that, but now I'm honestly not sure about letting you out of my sight."

She stands and smacks at her rear to wipe off dirt and debris. "I've gotta go now," she says.

"I'm coming with you."

"No, you're not. If I'm not back by an hour or so after sunrise, phone in for backup."

Before he can respond, she fades again into the darkness. A few seconds later, he hears her feet on the gravel drive climbing back toward the house. Her scent lingers in the air around him.

*

The squads split into nine teams in less than five minutes after getting their orders. Each team is given a different property to scout and report back on. It is a thirty-minute drive to the general vicinity and a fifteen-minute hike from the road onto the extended compound. With luck, then, Stoddemeier will have his position within less than an hour and a half, and the squads can reassemble for the assault within another thirty minutes. After hearing the plan, Wilson wonders to himself why they had needed the global positioning system at all. As far as he can tell, it's so that Stoddemeier and his boss can watch from the comfort of the police station. His opinion of these cowboys is definitely going downhill.

CHAPTER 28

"Sergeant Simpson, this is my daughter, McKenna Joombs."

The petite woman stands to greet her. Jill notices the tummy immediately. She can also see that she's been crying.

"McKenna Joombs? I've heard of you. I've seen you on TV. You're a singer? You're in The Tigermen, right?"

"Sort of. Just now, I'm trying to figure out how to have a baby and keep things quiet for a while."

Fancher is pouring glasses of iced tea from what looks like a silver vase.

"Yes, it's a vase, Sergeant. Simpson. Sorry. I like it because it doesn't spill when I pour." He hands her a glass and gestures to a chair.

"Okay, what do you need to tell me that can only be told in here, Mr. Fancher?"

"Well, Sergeant Simpson, it's a long story, and it goes back many years before either of us were born. I'd like to tell it to you, if you'd like to hear it."

Jill glances at the daughter. She stands behind her father who is busy easing himself onto the sofa. The girl looks a little aghast, to say the least.

"Daddy, should you tell that story?"

"Now, now, McKenna. You've been gone quite a while to be questioning me all of a sudden. I can and will tell Sergeant Simpson what she needs to hear, because it may be the only thing to save any of them. So just sit down and let me begin."

The daughter frowns but moves obediently around from behind her father to sit next to him on the sofa. She raises her eyebrows and sighs, accepting a glass of iced tea. He allows a moment of silence, sipping his beverage quietly and then begins:

"Over a hundred years ago, a man in this part of the country learned from several old Indians about a strange powder that could create the properties of death without killing a person. The man, an outlaw of sorts, thought that if he could find the powder, he might be able to fake his own death, get himself buried, pay someone to dig him up, and then disappear into what was left of the frontier to live a new life.

"We know today that this powder was an extract from dried blowfish. It's likely that this man, in fact, had learned of this drug from Haitian slaves, and that what they were talking about were practices of the secret cult called *voudon*, or voodoo, a cult that is more than two thousand years old and one of the only cultural remnants of the original people of the Caribbean.

"So, he planned his own murder. He inhaled the proper doses of powder daily to build up a tolerance, then consumed a particularly large dose on the night he was to be murdered. He has no idea what happened to the people who told him about the powder. What he does know is that once he'd been resuscitated, he was left by himself with enough powder for a while, but that he would need to follow their instructions if he wanted to live.

"And while that doesn't by any means bring us up to the present day or to the explanation you need for the murder you have so valiantly investigated, Sergeant Simpson, it's about all the time we have right now because by your eyes Ms. Simpson I can see that you're now under the influence of that tea you're drinking. Besides, I have only been authorized to tell you this very small part of the story. It is but a precursor to something much bigger and much, shall we say, more expansive than you could ever imagine."

Indeed, Jill had been feeling queer for a few minutes, but she'd passed it off as sleep deprivation. There is little she can do as Fancher asks his daughter to help him pick her up. She wants to yell out for Harris, but finds herself incapable of moving her mouth. She seems to be floating inside herself with little ability to guide her body. The last thing she remembers is Fancher calling into the kitchen: "Janie, I think we're going to need your help as well with this one."

*

Jill hears voices first as she regains awareness – quiet voices, like she's in a hospital. There is a dull echo to the room. The voices sound oddly familiar. They are soothing and calm and there is a lot of laughing. She tries hard to open her eyes, but the lids don't work properly; they flutter. The light is strong and feels as if it will hurt if she cracks her lids even just a little.

After a time, her vision begins to return. As her eyelids flutter, she sees faces. As her sight grows more defined, what she sees seems impossible. It's a dream, she figures, or maybe she's hallucinating. Before her stands a small crowd of people, smiling, talking quietly to one another, seeming to wait for her to speak, or to recognize them.

"I don't...."

"You do, Sergeant." It is Fancher speaking. "This is them. I assure you, it's not a dream, and although you are under the influence of powerful psychotropic drugs, this is not a hallucination. Allow me to introduce you to some of the people who figured it out. They're not all here right now. Some of them are preparing for your colleague's arrival. But, here we have Jackie Kerouac, Jim Croce, John Bonham, James Dean, King Jones." Fancher smiles knowingly.

It's too fantastic. But the people he gestures to certainly aren't denying what he'd said.

He continues. "Also, these folks over here are Jayne Mansfield, John Lennon, Janis Joplin, Jim Morrison, Jimi Hendrix – we call him JJ – and then that kind of old guy over there is one of the first people to discover the secrets of the Red House – Mr. Robert Johnson."

They wait for her response, smiling expectantly. Her thoughts are still somewhat muddled; the electric feel of psychedelics in her belly brings on a rush of images and sensations from her youth. The group waits with questioning smiles on their faces.

She still feels a pressure or weight in all of her features, as if her Being itself is bursting to explode out of its body. There is the knowledge from her adolescence that hallucinations can be more real than real. The sensations and memories from so long ago come tumbling back. But there is also an awareness that this is beyond anything she's ever experienced.

You better believe it, sister.

That isn't her voice. A big quiet waiting fills with anticipation and expectation. It seems to be sitting right outside her mind. "Is someone reading my thoughts?"

Again. *You better believe it, sister.*

"Who?" More waiting, somewhere in front of her now, as if she's meant to follow someone.

"All of you?" she asks finally.

The one named Robert Johnson, who hasn't been watching her, lifts his head: "You better fucking believe it, sister." He is speaking...at least, his mouth is moving and his eyes are now watching her. The sensation of pressure grows stronger. His face is small, the left eye squints, but he's a handsome brown-skinned man, and she somehow feels drawn to him.

We're going to lose her. It's a female emotion, but not hers.

"Maybe," comes Johnson's voice again. "But she's definitely one of us. She'll be back."

In a while, I think. It's the female again. *Everybody calm down. She'll be back. You know how things can be at first.*

The pressure seems to slack off a bit. There is silence from what she understands to be other people in her head.

An echo of an echo.

A joke.

It's the real thing.

This has always been here.

There. That has to work.

Do you see? If not, go back to the beginning and start all over.

More silence. She realizes they are waiting for her to figure something out.

Their faces look worried. They glance at one another and back to her. Again, pressure seems to build. She feels a soothing pulse this time in her belly and a slight warming sensation swirling in her gut. She is growing calmer, but the pressure continues.

I told you. The woman's emotions again. *You're okay, honey, just go with it. It's a pretty tough ride when you don't know where you're going.*

The warming sensation in her belly begins to expand to the points of her body that are experiencing the most pressure. Jill senses real heat rising now through her abdomen, expanding into her chest cavity. She thinks quickly that her heart is going to stop, that this is death.

It isn't bad, really. There are few regrets that matter. She misses her son, understands he is dead, wonders if this is what he felt in his last moments. She is wrapped in heat. Squandered motherhood is the only waste she can truly see in her life. There is a faint voice, not a whisper, but the sound of someone trying to soothe her from the other side of a house or out on a street. The voice is mildly familiar, like the others she just heard.

The pulsing heat grows stronger, spinning with a rhythm that something in her knows is all right even as the energy moves now through her throat, radiates into her jaw, and then seems to swing up both sides of her face, stretching to fill her skull. She feels it slithering to her groin, too, carefully almost, as if it's aware that it might stimulate her. The scent of sex comes to her nose, the taste of salty flesh. Gentle kisses seem to touch her thighs as the warmth spreads into her legs and arms simultaneously, finally throbbing in tiny pulses into her toes and fingertips.

The heat is in motion and she is bathed by it, but there is a dull gray form clouding her vision, growing darker. It isn't something to be feared, she knows, but she wants to resist just the same.

"Don't fight it, sister. You be all right. Take the word of Bob Johnson."

His voice is calm and soothing, a bit raspy. As her vision continues to dim, she watches the half-shut left eye, knowing that he is waiting for something – something important. And then it's upon her again, and this time the pressure is accompanied by a growing knowledge that darkness is coming and that she is now alone.

She thinks: *This is death. They've poisoned me!* Then a short hallucinogenic moment, fighting to stay in the world and, finally, nothing but empty blackness.

But there has to be something outside of this. It is her last thought before she falls into empty blackness.

*

Jill understands she was out for a long time, but there is no way to know if that means an hour or a week. Her body is no longer there. The individual sensations of each part – fingers, toes, ears, tongue, elbow, gut, lungs – have fully given way to the rolling heat that she guesses is some basic underlying energy, maybe raw nervous system, maybe some weird Heavenly Host thing that's the real deal as opposed to what all the fancy religions want you to believe. Or maybe it's just some simple drug effect.

The darkness is still with her. She no longer knows where her eyes should be. She waits in the uniform warmth, feeling its pleasantness and understanding that her thoughts are slowly refocusing, no longer simply experiencing the sensations washing through her.

There is a point of light in the distance, a single white-gold light, like a perfect piece of spark, or a solitary star. There is no way to know whether the light is actually appearing across some vast expanse of space or whether it's simply a pinpoint and right in front of her. For that matter, it's likely that something is just showing up on the inside of her retina because her drugged mind is bored.

She considers her predicament. If she's still alive, Harris is outside waiting for her. Fancher has drugged her. He might be going for Harris, too.

But there is little point in speculating about Fancher's involvement with the murders. Why he would want to drug her, or kill her, is beyond understanding. Worthless thoughts.

Bringing Harris along was stupid. She'd just wanted to be with him. It had been an act of vanity on her part. The realization comes that she is inept at romance and courting. Instead of asking him over for drinks, she'd suggested they go work a job together. She laughs at herself, and the point of light begins to move.

Or is *she* moving? The light seems to bob up and down to her rhythm. With no reference point, it's impossible to tell which of them is in motion. She wants to speak, but can't find her mouth. She tries again to find her legs, but there is no contact. If she is moving, then she has to exist outside of her mind. If the light is moving, then it's either governed by an external force or at least it exists beyond her.

Is she breathing? Can't tell anymore. If it is all simply part of her thoughts, then she should be able to stop the light, extinguish it, bring it closer, change its colors – something.

*

"She's not going to turn off."

"Yes, she is. We just need to wait. It took Kerouac three weeks."

"And he knew what was going on."

"You know, I don't think I really did. How can you? It's so weird."

"You did, in some way or another. You wanted to be here. You can't get here the way you did without fully wanting it."

"You keep saying that."

"Whatever. The point is, she's having a tough time."

"Well, we don't have a choice now, do we?"

There isn't much anyone can say to that.

"Think she's going to figure it out?"

"She will."

"Might take weeks."

"Might be soon if you guys would shut up. She's got more of it than most of us. Jesus, this is serious. Can't we just be quiet for once?"

"Sorry, Janis."

"Sorry, my ass. You say too much of what you think, John Lennon. I can see why you'd made it so hard on Paul there at the end."

*

Harris is just dozing off when he hears a twig snap. Someone is about thirty feet behind him in the brush. A few moments later, he hears the crunch of boots moving quickly across gravel. He's glad he's hidden himself off the road.

The motion is all around him now, brief thuds on the ground, the tinkle of metal on metal, cloth rubbing against leaves. He can smell them. Turning as carefully as he can so as not to disturb the brush, his peripheral vision tells him they are everywhere. Glancing back at the house, he sees shades of men in the early sky-glow of sunrise advancing slowly up the hill. They are armed and wearing dark gray fatigues. This isn't any force he's ever seen before. Each man is equipped with a small headset and microphone. He can hear their faint whispers as they communicate during what appears to be an advance on the house.

In the dim twilight luminescence, the quiet movement of gray men is eerie. He realizes they are still wearing night goggles. The gray uniforms are camouflage for moving through twilight.

Harris senses the motion behind him just before the cool of the gun barrel pokes into his neck. The face he turns to see is expressionless. The mouth speaks quietly into a microphone.

"We have a citizen, sir."

Harris is not privy to the response in the headset.

"Okay mister, we're staying put."

He watches as well over two dozen gray figures slide from moving crouches to kneeling positions on the ground, surrounding the house. He wonders if Jill can see them through the window. Their weapons are across their knees. They seem ready to wait. He wonders how long that will take.

CHAPTER 29

The point of light begins to expand and the heat sensation begins to diminish. She sees inside of it and they are coming back. There is still no contact with her body, but she knows she is alive.

"Here she comes!"

She feels their excitement flood her as waves of curiosity and tenderness.

"Wonder what she's going to say."

"It'll be interesting."

And then she's back. They are still around her. She can see them smiling down at her.

"What the fuck?" she gasps.

"It's kind of an out-of-body experience," says Fancher. "Well, for you and me, anyway, since we still have bodies. These guys though," and he points to the people to whom she'd been introduced earlier, people she now sees are obviously who they are said to be, "they're really more out of their bodies now."

"Just let her get into it a little first, okay, Lucas?" It's Janis speaking.

"What the fuck is going on?" This time Jill isn't just frustrated, she's mad.

"You made it," says the one they call Janis.

"Made it?"

"To the other side," says Fancher.

"And just where is that?" Jill asks.

"Well," he looks from her to the group, "we don't actually know. We just know we're here and it's not like life as you know it." This time it's Jim Morrison. He grins and shrugs his shoulders.

"Break on through to the other side?" she says.

"You got it...."

"You're really Jim Morrison."

"Right. There ya go. You get to keep your sense of humor." Morrison turns to wink at his companions.

They are all obviously amused. She can feel their humor like a big set of hands bobbing just in front of her face.

"All right. Here goes," says Morrison, rubbing his hands together. "It's like this: you are completely in your mind. Your body is here, but it doesn't have to be. We're all here with you. We're each tripping same as you only a bit differently since we're...well, you know...we're actually dead. The energy of our bodies is still here, though. Our energy. Our vibration. We're dead, though. It's a little tricky. Each and every one of us, technically, is dead...but we're not really dead, if you know what I mean."

"Not sure anyone knows what you mean, man," says Jim Croce. "What you're trying to say is that we've proven something kind of obvious, but still...the mind and body are not one thing. They are because we don't know better, is all. The mind is a lot more complex a mystery than anyone gives it credit for. Our problem is that we use our minds to think about our minds."

They all wait for Jill to say something to all of this. She senses a feeling of victory or superiority or something coming from them.

"All right, everyone, let's get her up. Okay?" says Janis. She turns to Jill. "This is one of the more fucked-up things about what we're doing, honey. See, there's only a few of us women-folk in the group. So I've often got to be a tad more forceful than you'd think. I'm pretty mellow most of the time, aren't I guys?"

"Yeah, right," replies Kerouac. "Real mellow. Like a little sister."

"Whatever. Let's just help her up. Get her walking around. Check it all out."

Jill can feel the woman's excitement. There's pride coming off all of them.

"We've got about an hour before we start," says Lennon.

Jill feels the pressure of cool fingers on her back and neck. "Here, Sarge, I'll help you up." It's Jack Kerouac.

"Hey, man, be gentle with her, now. You know how easy it is to lose them at first." This seems to be Hendrix with his deep, throaty emotions, and his sing-song rhythm, like everything he says is lyrics. She is struck by the tenderness of his voice and his calm.

She feels herself being moved, but is still fighting off the acceptance the whole scene calls for. It's obviously a big hallucination. Isn't it?

Then she sees them. They stand at the back, watching the others quietly. There is no mistaking them. They still wear their black clothes and white shirts. It's the three Amish kids. All three turn their heads slightly to acknowledge themselves to her.

"Yup, that's them," says Janis simply. "And if you look over there in the corner you'll find the other two you're after, Cecil Miller and Coral McGrey."

"What's going on?" she blurts out.

"It's okay, honey, really. Just wait here for Lucas. Most of us need to take our medicine and get ready for the evening."

And with that they all seem to fade away, except for Miller and McGrey and someone behind them sitting in repose, holding an enormous blue guitar. She realizes she has regained a more natural sense of her body – it appears to be her body, anyway.

You better believe it, sister.

*

"You've waited long enough, Sergeant Simpson. Or do you mind if I call you Jill?" Fancher pauses, feeling for her thoughts.

"You can call me whatever you want."

"Okay, Jill, I'm going to leave the history of this up to the only person you should hear it from, but yes, you are alive, still, and no, you are *not* hallucinating—at least not in the normal sense of the word. We are here, you and I, and all of them. The Amish boys are here, too. They're all dead except for the two older boys and Mr. Miller and Ms. McGrey and that one there behind them. It takes a lot to stay in this state of being, and only a few of us can even enter it. I can, you can, *they* can because of, as far as we can tell, some fluke of nature, some trick life has played. Or maybe it's just best to think of it as a genetic trait that creative people have—the geniuses, that is. Those two brothers have been having a hard time staying on top of things, but they've got enough of the talent in them to stick it out. You need to take them with you when you go, but they are awfully attached to their younger brother. It's been hard for them to leave. They'll be ready when it's time though."

"This isn't possible," she says.

"Given the proper dose of certain mind-altering chemicals, anything is possible. Surely you know this from your drug days back in the '70s. Anyway, you should be fully recovered now. Shall we walk? I want to take you to him so we can get the explanatory stuff out of the way."

Jill has little choice. They move from the brightly lit tent area out into what seems to be daylight.

It is a fairly normal farm, she thinks. Footing is loose, the ground hard and dusty, littered with bits of straw, leaves, twigs, feathers and the occasional clump of grass. They start with a view of the front of the main house, the one she'd originally entered, but Harris is nowhere to be seen, and things don't seem to be quite right. The light falls differently, the air is far less dense, and there is no temperature at all. She sees that the house has become more than just a four-sided box dwelling. The structure as they turn to pass along the side is massive, with porches etched in on all three floors, huge vaulted windows, some of stained glass, others nearly invisible with transparency giving view to massive hallways and rooms full of books and empty desks. There is a long screened-in veranda with a lavender ceiling and ten or so tables laid out for the serving of a formal meal, wine chilling in silver ice buckets, pitchers of cold water, all illuminated by candles and torches. A brick *esplanade* opens in front of a sweeping stairway swirling up toward the veranda. She notices other staircases climbing the side of the long wall as well, some reaching to the roof, others halting at small landings that lead in turn to ornate doorways that presumably afford varying entryways into the vast building.

"We've sort of made some improvements," come Fancher's thoughts to her. "Look out across the property."

She turns her gaze to the yard and the fields beyond it. The scene is striking: rolling hills bathed in soft honey-colored sunlight and populated here and there by equally ornate and stunning farmhouses made small and toy-like by the distance. All of this gives way to what had to be a trick of sight – the river floating in the air above what can only be an ocean even farther in the distance. She sees water flowing overhead, the movement of boats, birds, even large fish nipping at food on the surface of liquid motion in the sky.

"No need for perspective as you know it. It's a bit disorienting, but quite soothing, wouldn't you say?"

Indeed, it was. The power of this pastoral view defied the laws of dimension, flowing into infinity, turning her sense of equilibrium and depth on its head, consuming her with awe and tranquility.

For some time now she had been aware that Fancher's lips weren't moving, that he was solely communicating with her through thought.

"Once you've talked with him, I think you'll feel better."

"With who?" She speaks this and feels a flood of gentle humor come from him.

"You may speak to me if you wish, but you don't have to. It's all the same…well, almost anyway. The spoken word has the added advantage of sound and can therefore be more laden with meaning and power. Here, in our heads, though, we can carry on a conversation much faster and with less effort. It's also easier to understand thoughts than words, is it not? Try it. Emotion and meaning are no longer implied, they are fully experienced." He turns to watch her as they move around one of the barns.

Okay. I'm thinking this.

Yes. I feel you and it's nice.

It's….

Embarrassing?

I feel naked somehow, like I've showed up at school without my clothes. It would be easy to think all sorts of things and almost drag you around through my mind. The ugly parts, you know? The parts I don't want you to....

That's true to a point, Jill. But, you have to contend with my mind, too. If you start going off somewhere, I can counter that with my own thoughts. Part of this requires trust. But don't worry about that. Wait until they play. Then you'll understand what this is about. And we're here already....

"Wait a minute, Fancher," she speaks. "I'm having a lot of trouble here." It's a relief to speak these words. The amount of effort required for telepathy is draining."

"I know, Jill. I felt like that, too, when they let me in on this. And I know you have a murder case to solve. But can you just wait a bit? Let things develop? They brought you here to solve your case. And for another purpose as well. So, just hold on, okay?" Fancher has spoken this. She notes mixed with her own feelings of anger and frustration a deference and almost a sympathy for her situation that can only be coming from him. This is probably where the strain of reading thoughts comes from – the requirement of translating other emotions and receiving words while one's own thoughts are at work as well.

"Do I have a choice?" she finally asks out loud.

"Not while you're under the influence of the Tetro mix. But, Jill, this is really important. Don't you see what we've got here? This is real. We're existing in another dimension. And you're lucky enough to be included in it. So, just hold on to your horses. I want to introduce you to someone who can at least begin to explain it. Then we'll get to the next step. Very important things are about to start happening."

What could she say? She was either under the influence of the drugs and hallucinating like never before, or this was real and she would have to let go of her need for simple reality.

"Believe me," Fancher says. "This is real."

"Okay. Let's get going, then. Take me to your leader."

You have no idea how correct you are.

She realizes she has no sense of wind and there are really no smells and the usual sound of insects in the summer air is gone—replaced by silence.

*

"Mr. Harris," says Dale Stoddemeier. "Can you tell us when Officer Simpson went into the house?"

They've taken him down the road to a small group that is clearly in charge. A copse of trees blocks visibility from the house. A culvert ditch runs by them. They are standing next to a large black iron grate, a drainage system opening. He recognizes Stoddemeier as the man Jill met at The Pancake House. But the other two men are obviously directing the exercise.

"It was a few hours ago."

"Was Fancher armed?"

"Not that I could see."

"How long did she say to wait? Did he say anything?"

"No, I don't...look, who are you guys? What's this all about? How many men do you need to capture one simple guy?"

"Mr. Harris, we didn't expect to find you here. This guy Fancher may not be alone, and he may not be as harmless as you and Officer Simpson think he is."

"But you've got over forty men. This is ridiculous."

"No it's not," says the man who seems to be in command. "Not if you see this as a hostage situation."

"A hostage situation? She's not a hostage. She went in on her own free will."

"Probably. But, we can't take any chances."

"Jesus." He looks to Stoddemeier, who is obviously uncomfortable with the situation.

"Harris," begins Stoddemeier. "This is a covert operation. We've had this whole region under surveillance for over a year. We can't tell you why we're here, but what I can tell you right now is that Jill's life may be in danger, and we need as much information as possible. So, can you just cooperate?"

They wait for him to come to terms with this information. This is clearly more than a murder case now. He's tired and wants a drink. It *is* possible, he thinks, that Jill is in danger. It may also be possible that these guys are idiots and that their presence is putting her in danger.

"Look," he says, "we got here a bit before dawn. I'm not wearing a watch, I don't know what time it is now. Maybe 7:30? 8:00?"

Stoddemeier looks at his watch quickly. "7:23"

"Okay. So it's probably been about two and a half hours."

"What did Fancher say to get her to come inside?" asks the man in charge.

"I didn't go up to the house where he was. I waited down this way. She came back and told me he wanted to discuss something."

"Why didn't you go, too?"

Something begins to register with Harris. Fancher isn't the murderer. Fancher wanted to talk to Jill about something completely different. He remembers her telling him that Fancher had wanted to have a conference and how strange the guy had seemed, how he'd been expecting her. When she came back to tell him she was going in, she'd talked about how in control of the situation Fancher seemed to be.

He begins to wonder why he hadn't just called in for backup when she left.

"She wouldn't let me go with her," he says finally. They look at him with slight, disbelieving smiles.

"Sounds like Jill Simpson," Stoddemeier says. "What exactly did she say?"

"She gave me her cell, told me to stay put and call in for backup if she wasn't out by sunup."

This gets their attention. "And did you?" Stoddemeier is doing the talking, but it's obvious the issue of backup is of concern to all of them.

"No," he says reluctantly.

"Why not?"

"Don't exactly know. I guess it just slipped my mind."

"Slipped your mind? She's in the middle of a murder investigation and has just gone out of sight, alone, and into a key suspect's home, and you don't call for backup?"

"No. I didn't. Something kept me from doing it. Just a hunch, I guess. Or maybe it was that she told me not to."

"You're sure?"

"What? That it didn't seem necessary, or that I didn't call?"

"You didn't call."

"No," says Harris. "No, I didn't call, and it really wasn't necessary."

He's beginning to understand. Whatever they're doing here, they don't want company. And Jill's presence inside is probably complicating things even more.

They leave him with two armed guards and move even farther down the road to talk out of earshot.

"Either of you got a cigarette?" he asks the guards.

"No, sir. No one on this team smokes. We're probably taking you back to town soon, though, so we can stop for some on the way."

That makes it clear. Getting him out of the way means they're up to more than a standoff with Fancher.

*

"I say he knows what's going on already," Stoddemeier tells the other two.

"I sincerely doubt that," says Arthur Gold. "Since we aren't really sure ourselves."

"No, I mean, that we're here to extract Fancher and anyone else in there and then search the rest of the place before we level it."

"So, what does that mean we do with him?" asks Gold's assistant, Gary Parks. Parks has gone from stuck-up techno-genius to obsequious assistant ass kisser in the course of one night, which isn't sitting well with Stoddemeier.

"If we send him back to town, he'll know something's going on," continues Stoddemeier.

"He knows something's going on anyway," says Parks. "If we keep him here and don't let him closer, maybe he'll just figure we're here to arrest a dangerous murderer and then…."

"But Fancher isn't a dangerous murderer," replies Stoddemeier, trying to hide his growing exasperation.

"We know that, but Harris doesn't."

"Okay, then what? I mean, Simpson is the complication we need to worry about here."

"Leave her to me," says Gold.

"What's that supposed to mean?" Stoddemeier asks carefully.

"Don't worry about her," says Parks quickly.

"I'm not."

"She can take care of herself, right?" says Gold.

"She can as long as nothing strange happens, sir."

"Nothing strange happens when I'm in charge, Mr. Stoddemeier. Nothing."

"I know that." Right. Nothing strange ever happens when he's in charge. That's what Stoddemeier is worried about. He needs to let Harris know what's going on.

*

"Sergeant Jill Simpson, I would like you to meet Jesse James. Jess, this is a law enforcement woman. Take it a bit easy on her, okay?"

As the man turns toward her, she is stunned for a long moment by the intensity of emotion slamming into her. Even if she hadn't been under the influence of drugs, he would have bowled her over like this. Her cop senses tell her that she is meeting someone with extreme personal power, the kind of power possessed by criminals, politicians, and actors.

"Sorry," he says finally. "Forget sometimes what I can do to people."

"You're who?"

"Uh, name's James. Jesse James."

"Mmm hmm." She sees Fancher smile and feels a gentle humor tingle through her.

"You can believe it or not," says James curtly. "But we're here right now, so I'm gonna trust you know enough to just shut out—whatever—and deal with what you're experiencing."

"I can't just opt out?"

"That's what I'm saying. You've got no choice, m'am."

"All right. So, what's the deal? I'm a bit confused."

"Deal is, we figured something out."

"*You* did Jesse," says Fancher.

"Lucas, you want to take a leave or something? I can handle this."

"Sure, Jesse. Sorry."

They watch Fancher saunter off to the front of the house. As he turns the corner, she feels a sense of awareness pass with him, and realizes his consciousness has left her alone with Jesse James. Or is she alone? There seems to be some other presence just beyond her thoughts, a threatening presence, dark and secretive, slightly confused. What was it? Who was it?

Don't worry about that right now, come Jesse James's thoughts to her. *Just let me clear some things up for you first. It's kind of a long story, woman. You want to hear it?*

Am I going to hear it or feel it? she asks, smiling at him and trying not to laugh at the thought that she is supposedly having a discussion with one of the most storied bad guys in history.

James had always interested her. She had read accounts of his great train robberies and bank heists, but the most intriguing thing about him was his pedigree. Both of his parents, Robert and Zerelda, were well-educated. Robert, who had a masters degree and was an ordained Baptist minister, was one of the founders of William Jewell College in Liberty, Missouri. Zerelda was more educated than most women of the day and married a physician after Robert died. Frank, who was the more cold-blooded of the famous brothers, had been deprived of completing his studies in classics, but was fond of quoting Shakespeare. Frank married a schoolteacher who had gone to college. One of Jesse's sons became a lawyer.

Details of some of the James gang robberies had interested her as well. The patience and extensive research and planning that went into them usually led to successful crimes with no violence. She knew it wasn't true that James robbed from the rich and gave to the poor, but she suspected that James was a compassionate and just man who understood the value of helping those in need. According to what she'd read, he only killed in self-defense. The James brothers apparently had turned to a life of crime out of anger at post-war policies limiting the rights of Confederate supporters and soldiers.

There had always been controversy over whether James had faked his own death. In 1995, an historian working with a group of forensic scientists tried to resolve the questions by locating and eventually exhuming what many believed to be James's body from a crudely marked grave near Joplin, Missouri. DNA sampling only proved that the body in the grave was related to Zerelda, since hair from her corpse had been the marking index. Whether it was actually James continued to be the subject of debate. Was this the outlaw Fancher had told her about?

"Yeah, Fancher already told you the basics. And I know you heard the stories. Some's true, some's bullshit, but that isn't what I'm here to talk to you about.

"I told this story a few hundred times now to everyone who's come in here. This is how it goes." He pauses, seeming to gather himself and she realizes he is speaking and not thinking anymore to her. "You ever wonder what the appeal of soul is?" he begins. "Why we talk about it all the time, know that there's something there, but don't really understand it? Soul, you know. Not that simplistic, little Christian thing! I'm talking about what's really in you, not what's supposed to be there, what someone else says should be there. Soul! Like the music? Like the source of you? The feeling of feeling things, so deep.... How deep no one ever thinks.

"What the old blues guys mean by *Mojo*. You ever heard of Robert Johnson before you came in here?" James feels her acknowledgement before she can speak. "Well, was Robert Johnson just a freaked-out poet who beat on a old guitar? Or did he know something other people didn't? Did he see soul for what it was? Not some mystical thing. Just more like that something we forgot was there, can't see because we're too busy living with each other, scratching out comfort. What's in to most is nothing compared to what's out. Only what's out–we all know this—is never very special and it's always changing and making us do things we don't want to do.

"What was Bob Johnson really supposed to be selling his soul to the devil for? The ability to play guitar better than anyone else? Or make up a captivating blues song? Is that a good reason to sell your soul? Just to play music? Or is there something more? Something to the music?

"What the hell is it about this music that makes it work? Why do we pay attention to it? Why does it get so much affection? Is it some weird connection to all our African roots, or does it go much deeper than that?

"And the blues, the telling of human suffering, why is that so universal and easy to pick up the very first time you hear it? Only a fool would miss the power that that music has to reach in and touch the soul, to tell us that it's real.

"See, there's something more there than what meets the ear. It's what makes this place here work! It's what we tap into. That new kid, King, and old JJ, of course, understand it better than anybody. They're closest to its source, too. Closer than me, that's for sure.

"It's *the* soul. It's *the* spirit. It's the Mojo in you. And that's why blues music was so important to the psychedelic experience." He isn't looking at her, but she knows every bit of him is concentrating inside her mind, paying attention to her reactions as he speaks in words.

"You think I don't know what psychedelics is about? I do, pretty baby. I been there for a long time. Been around for a long time, girl. A long, long time....

"All the layers of life get peeled away if you're connected up right. You're naked in the land of the spirit. Life starts whizzing around and your Being gets caught up in it. And sound becomes the medium for experience, and experience becomes the medium for things...I mean, things are no longer out there; they're in here, in with us, all of us, if we pay attention.

"But it can get out of hand so easily. If you look around you carefully, outside there's nothing but chaos going on in the world.

There's only power and energy in flux, vibration out of control, banging and bouncing around.

"When you're in the living world you've got that weird little trick which lets you fool yourself into thinking there's order and structure, but that's only because you're thinking into the past. The past is all you own. The present is never there except when it's happening, and the future is an endless dream of hope and desire...and fear, if you're so inclined.

"Music, though, is a way to harness all that power to locate the soul in a relatively controlled manner. When you're playing music, or listening to it, even, your mind becomes aligned with order. Real order. It's a vibratory alignment that is there in the present, under the chaos. You get plugged into Time. And if you pay attention to how you feel plugged in like that, everything starts to make sense. You're soothed. Chaos goes away. You're free, your ego and your soul. We can even feel that sometimes when we're focused. Here. Yup, that's what we're doing sometimes. Feeling the whole world all at once. But, I'm getting too far ahead of myself.

"It's human chaos that's the most unbearable, isn't it? I mean, out there in life. You ought to know as a cop – the unspeakable levels of suffering that people are subjected to by other people's manipulation of chaos. I know. I was there. I lived through the most horrible years this country ever faced. And I was one of those people using chaos for myself. But I was just an early version of what is everywhere now.

"The contradictions are unbelievable. Racism, lack of access to good education, shrinking healthcare benefits, the insurance industry in general, people's willingness to remain at home hooked into the Net or the Web – Hey, don't be surprised. I know about everything that's going on – whatever you call it, and so much is ignored and given up to *human nature*. But is there human nature if we choose to disregard the soul? – the real soul. Human nature is the biggest lie of all. The only human nature is what is connected to soul. But there's only a few of us has the capacity to understand this."

He stares hard at her now, his full energy forcing itself on her. She knows he is showing her his soul and that he is sharing it with her. He seems to be waiting for her to say something.

I think, somehow, she manages to think, *emotion fits into what you're saying.*

"Ah, yes. Of course. Emotion. Very astute. See, you *do* belong with us. That's really what we're talking about here, isn't it? Emotion. That's what the soul's got to be – the source of emotion. When you hear funk music, it gets down inside you, doesn't it? And when you hear Brahms it goes to the same place, just a different part of that place.

"Just emotion. It's not something words are attached to in any way. And that's really the most difficult problem with this whole thing; you can't separate people from words. Words are there. Without question. So, emotions always have to have a name, like animals we turn into pets. Sad, happy, horny, hungry, satiated, enraged.

"After awhile pets start answering to their names and they become what you need them to become. And then the soul is filtered through language and habit."

He stops and looks into her eyes. She feels all of him beaming into her – the pride, the fearlessness, his sexuality, the brashness, the crude sense of humor, the wisdom of…of what, if this is true – which is still rather hard to believe – 150 years of existence.

Nothing can go beyond him, though. He chuckles and she feels his sense of victory as he shrieks: "It's a fuckin' fountain of youth. I found it…least I think I did. And all by accident, too.

"I was just tired of running, see? And I got to thinking. I knew I was going to die soon. Either I was going to be murdered or something else would have taken me out. You can feel death, you know, when it gets a fix on you. So I started thinking about suicide. Seemed like a good thing to do. Beat that old fucker, Death.

"I carried those thoughts around with me for maybe a year and just kept on living my life the way they say I did – train robberies, bank jobs – I couldn't stop. Didn't want to, and I had a whole group of people depending on me – whole families you know – so I just kept it up. I knew I was tempting chance every day.

"Then one night we were staying with some friends. Indians. It was easy to be friends with them. They thought of us as part men and part something else. We fought the same enemy.

"So, that night during a war ceremony, one of 'em sits down with me and tells me that he smells it on me. I say, what you smell? And he says what amounts to suicide if he was speaking our language. But then he tells me I'm not ready to face death, that I need to understand there's more to death than passing out of this life.

"I don't particularly want to have the conversation, but I'm intrigued, you know? Mostly because he has managed somehow to see inside me. Then he starts talking about the powers of the sacred mushroom. He talks in hushed tones. You know, reverent and all religious. And he tells me that some of the old slaves he knows have a whole set of stories about death and how it's possible to cross over and then back. And he tells me the stories are that the great powerful men of his tribe and of the slave tribes have mixed the mushroom with this other drug they use to go back and forth between death. Some name he gave me of the drug had fish in it. But it was also possible to go crazy if you had too much of this fish stuff, and that you could beat death but that you'd be crazy forever. Mixing the two drugs, though, was different. If you did it just right, it was possible to die but for your spirit to live on.

"So this guy, No Horses Here, that was his name, he comes to me the next day and hands me a medicine bag and shows me how to sniff this brown powder using a hollow reed. Man! I mean it hit me like a clap of thunder. I was gone. I mean, I was gone. I felt my body fall to the ground, felt pain in my knees and chin where I hit. Everything went dark, and then I was back and I was floating near No Horse and he was smiling up at me and laughing and then I saw it. My body was just lying there on the ground. There was a trickle of blood on my chin. But I was floating over it. I was nothing but spirit.

"I asked No Horse if he could see me, but he just kept laughing. I wanted to know if I was dead. And then things got dark again and I went off on a trip for a while. Cruising through different worlds is about the best I can describe it. In some worlds I saw floating cities and small flying machines carrying people everywhere with shining glass sculptures and bright pulsing lights of red and gold – things I couldn't have imagined; stuff from the future, you know?

"I moved through others where there was nothing but forest and fields, vistas and horizons with brilliantly lit sunsets and the strong, pungent odor of growing plant life in the air; and through one where it was like I was underground and part of an ant colony and I felt what they were doing and understood why, and had nothing but this urge to move and this sense of total purpose that was far beyond me. *In other worlds.* And that's what they were, too, Miss Simpson, worlds – they were so overwhelming and different! In yet another I felt like I was intruding on a criminal activity, and these wolf-like beasts came at me and they seemed to perceive me but didn't attack. They just crept closer and closer, so I moved away and they followed me, I don't know, I kept moving, running, and they pursued me through darkness across a frozen lake until I shot off somewhere else.

"To this day I don't know if they were real or if those beings I saw there saw me. I don't know. I don't know about a lot of this. But it doesn't really matter.

"I can't tell you how many of these experiences I had. Some happened fast. Others seemed to be drawn out over time, days maybe, I can't be sure.

"And then I came back. No Horse was wiping my face with a cloth of some kind. His wife had my head in her lap. My men were there, too. And my brother, Frank, had a pistol to No Horse's wife's head saying if I gave the word he'd shoot her right then and there. They thought No Horses had tried to kill me. And right then I wasn't sure if he was or wasn't. But they'd made him bring me back. I had been out like that for nearly three days. I'd more or less stopped breathing, but they could hear my heart and feel a very faint pulse.

"But that's not the most interesting thing that happened, Miss Simpson. When I fell, I'd landed on my chin. Remember, I saw the blood? And No Horses Here says that he considered I'd probably broken my jaw, since it swelled up and turned black and blue.

"By the time I came to, though, there was no sign whatsoever that I'd done a thing to it. According to my brother, it had fully healed itself by the end of the second day.

"So, after maybe a night of feeling groggy and slipping into a long deep sleep, I felt stronger than I ever did in my life, both in spirit and in flesh. And all I knew was that I wanted to do it again.

"I spent time talking with No Horse about what had happened. He told me that what had happened to me was not possible for most men. He said that there were only certain men who had a spirit that could fly off. And he advised me that I should be careful about doing it again unless I talked to people who knew more than he did.

"In the days that followed, ideas and questions about that stuff started swirling up inside me as we rode around. We were maybe a hundred miles east of Joplin where Bobby Ford lived. Somehow I'd become a good deal wiser than ever before in my life. It was like I'd come back with new levels of knowledge. Things started to fit. It was somewhat frightening, I suppose, because thoughts would come to me out of nowhere, but at the same time I knew I was on to something. And so, inside me this plan just started to evolve.

"Yup, that was around the time you probably read about where Robert Ford decided to get me. He needed the money. And everything started fitting. I needed additional information to see if any of my hunches were true, but I was becoming more and more convinced that I might have discovered some kind of real magic, and that even if I was wrong, to go out like that was a good way to die…good enough, anyway."

"So, you're saying you faked your own death," says Jill.

"Not exactly."

"Then…?"

"Why don't you just be patient?"

Jill feels his presence roaming through her. Why not just listen? There is no denying that some of this is real…somehow.

"You can come to conclusions later, lady. Just let me tell you the fuckin' story."

"All right. But why are you telling *me*?"

"That's part of it, okay?"

"Okay. Go ahead then."

"Thanks." He waits for a moment, looking into the distance.

"It was a good way to die, anyway. Or else, it was a good way to follow what seemed to be there. I didn't know. After you've been on the run for nearly twenty years and you've seen what I saw then, and you get touched by the mushroom, well, there isn't much going back now is there? Can't forget shit like I saw and felt.

"So I went looking for people who could teach me how to do things proper. It took a bit of time, me being white and all and having to kind of lay low from all the folks that was chasing me. But I finally found 'em and spent a week living in a cave maybe eighty miles south of here, learning how to mix stuff and getting the proper amount. They assured me it would work if I was full of the right power. And if I wasn't? Well, let's just say that I wouldn't be leading a gang of outlaws anymore.

"It worked, though – as you can see. I mixed the two powders and sniffed 'em then, feeling pretty giddy, mind you, with hope – and with fear. Before the stuff took effect, I went right then and there to collaborate with old Robert Ford. And, yes, he did shoot me. But I was so high I didn't feel a thing. It wasn't until I was up on a chair hanging a mirror in the parlor, looking at a reflection of the room behind me, that I understood the bullet about to be shot into my back might actually kill me if I didn't properly follow the instructions I'd been given.

"The Tetro kicked in. I wasn't breathing, I couldn't feel anything. But I was still there. They buried me. I was dead. And I mean, dead. Only I was alive too – like you was feeling a while ago. And then after maybe three days - it was interminable, you know, just interminable - things started coming back to me in a way.

"I found I could leave my body. Travel up through the earth, moving through it, my spirit, intact, flowing through molecules and minerals and back out to the world. It was amazing. I was whole and I was still me, only I was out of my body.

"But this is the fantastic part: I was still here, at least to some people. You can call it what you will. I was basically a ghost and I lived like that for years. Some people could see me, some could sense me, some could read my thoughts. Some thought I was as real as you are right now.

"And, yes, I scared the shit out of some of them people. Especially those connected to what is now called voodoo cults; people who believed in the living dead. Scared them so much they figured they had to appease me. So for a long time, nearly a hundred years, they passed on from generation to generation the secret job of leaving me the powder mix. And I survived. Through time, I just ended up here. It's not so far from Joplin. I could feel a certain power coming from this place that I'd never felt anywhere else.

"Then one day, I starts feeling stuff coming out of nowhere. Just feelings, you know? Emotions. But they weren't mine.

"Turns out it's this guitarist named Bob Johnson. People say that he sold his soul to the devil. They talk about him going down to a crossroads and waiting for the devil to tap him on the shoulder.

"Didn't happen that way at all. He learned from some of my friends the same thing that I had learned, and they'd given him the drug and he was just stumbling around in the woods not far from here, high as a kite and full of that big Mojo blues power. All emotion and push, no words, no thoughts really, just full-bore feeling. It was amazing! I found him and it took a bit of persuading, but he came on in. That's why the stories about him are so confused. We didn't do a decent job of killing him off. No one was there to witness it. It took years for all the myths to settle in.

"But it sure was nice having someone to share this with. Yup. Robert Johnson. He didn't sell his soul to the devil, he gave it to old Jesse James."

She registers a tender humor in this statement. The intensity of his presence lifts for a moment.

"So, we stumbled along through things for another thirty years or so. Then another presence made itself known. Several times over the course of the '50s a clownish feeling would pass through this area. Crazed. Half emotion, half language. Crazy! We knew it was someone who had figured things out, but couldn't pinpoint it for maybe three, four years.

"Turns out it's this fucker named Jack Kerouac. And he's hurting bad, scared of what he's learned and drinking to shut if off. But we finally got him in. And then comes James Dean; he was the first we actually went after. Knew he could understand it, just needed help. And then the four of us start realizing after awhile that we got the President of United States in our heads, and he's hurtin' too, only we gotta be careful with that because he's the President. But he understands. Those stories about the White House pool after hours are true, you know.

"I went to him maybe four times over a two-year period, and in the middle of trying to convince him we got life for him...forever...and he can get away from all the pain and the shit, he talks us into taking Marilyn Monroe instead and we do it because we can sense her, too (once people got a hold of LSD we could sense just about anyone who was able to be part of this...you included).

"Don't interrupt, though. We figure if Marilyn comes, then maybe Jack will, too. And it took a major doing on Marilyn's part, but he finally did. It worked, although we were still learning how to cover our tracks, and, as you know, we didn't do the best job of creating an open-and-closed case. I mean, we knew Oswald had been set up to take those shots, and Jack was all primed with the drug and everything, and we had it timed just right, but we didn't anticipate all the rigmarole that started after Ruby shot Oswald, nor were we aware that Zabruder would be filming the whole thing. And none of us had any idea that the country would be affected the way it was. Never underestimate a nation of fools who think fun can be had watching a screen of images.

"He's okay, though. Jack, I mean. He needed out. And we showed him the way.

"That's what we all wanted, see? Out. That great sadness in life is just too much when you get to a certain point. If you're like us, you make it to where you want to be and then you realize nothing's going to stop and you can't escape. You have to keep moving forward. But no one will let you.

"Over time it all just adds up to sadness. You get to the top or to the end and you realize it's no better than where you were when you started. The problems are just bigger and more difficult to navigate. People won't leave you alone. Sadness sets in.

"That's what the drugs and the sex was for most of these people...ways of shutting off the sadness. Also, ways of keeping the discovery outside. Because once you know what this is all about, that your soul is able to glow on its own, you're in deep trouble. Everything in the world comes at you louder, faster, bigger, hairier, and hornier. It's a festival and a disaster all in one.

"It comes, too, from being a genius - for want of a better term. Not smart genius, but connected to life and to the gut all at the same time. Some in the world's got it, most don't.

"See, that's part of it. A big part. We figured out that the effect of the drugs only works on those few of us who are expressives, those of us who can project our personalities onto the world, and who in turn can absorb the world into our souls. We're here, and we're immortal if we stay plugged into a maintenance dose of the Tetro-mushroom mix. But we don't know why.

"Doesn't matter anymore, though. We keep growing. We've got Martin Luther King, Junior, Jimi Hendrix, Jim Croce, Jayne Mansfield, John Lennon, Jim Morrison, Janis Joplin, and many more who you've never heard of because they figured it out before they fully faced what brought the rest of us here.

"And, Elvis." Jill reminds him.

"Well, now that's different, you know," he says somewhat solemnly.

"What do you mean?"

"Why don't I let Lucas tell you about him," says James. It's the first time in their conversation where he lets her feel he is vulnerable. "For now, let's just say we've made some mistakes with all of this and Lucas understands more than me anyway why Elvis is so important to everybody. I also got a less-than-objective point of view here."

"What's that supposed to mean?"

"We'll talk about it later. Right now we got a hootenanny to get up. Kind of a raising of the spirits. Let's go join 'em."

"But what about my investigation? I saw those three Amish. What are they doing here?"

"All in good time, Ms. Simpson. All in good time."

He stands and begins to move toward the front of the house. As she follows him around the corner, she glances up at the wraparound porch and notices the figure of a woman crouched behind a worktable.

"Don't worry about Janie," says James. "She's got a job here that's special – sort of the bodyguard enforcer. She's worried that you're going to misinterpret what we're telling you and what you see here today. I've asked her to pay attention to you while I'm talking. Just a precaution. She's really quite harmless."

Jill can't help the sense of violation she feels, realizing that it is Janie Hawthorn whose thoughts have been intermingled with hers as she's listened to Jesse James tell his story. Understanding who has been kibitzing now, she senses an eerie, cold unapologetic anger flow through her. This ESP phenomenon was certainly a messy way to communicate. How much of it was real and how much just echoes of something much deeper, something constructed by a mind opened in on itself and the possibility that everything imaginable is real?

Somewhere inside she feels a gleeful laugh of victory welling up to the surface of her awareness. Was this someone else, or her own mind beginning to come to its own conclusions?

CHAPTER 30

Many of them stand in the circle. Some sit on the ground with percussion instruments. A number of others congregate in small groups, talking quietly. She feels her thoughts restrained, almost as if her mind has been pushed under water and held there. Jesse leads her over to Fancher, then moves to the other side of the circle where a space opens up for him. She notices Janie Hawthorn standing in the circle across from her, looking down at the ground.

"How many of you are there?" she asks Fancher quietly.

"One hundred thirty-eight, excluding a couple of us," replies Fancher.

"Excluding?"

"I'm not one of them, you gotta remember."

"Then how can you read my thoughts?"

"Some people are born that way, some develop it over time. It takes a lot of focus to keep from losing it, though. One of the things about human reality is that there are many powers and tendencies just too impractical for normal existence. Forget ESP. Think about art and creative thought in general. All young children have the gift of inventiveness and artistry. Three-year-olds are incapable of knowing how to color inside lines or of having, as they say, taste. They are the antithesis of intellectuals. There are no pretensions. And, so, they can't help creating things. Really creating things, you know? They don't pay attention to rules. Everything they do is basically for the first time. It's all 100 percent creative.

"Artistry is a power all people are born with. But it begins to disappear for many by the time they are seven. And once children reach twelve, most are more concerned with how they appear to others than presenting to others how they truly feel.

"At any given moment each of us is capable of an infinite number of acts. We are always in our lives absolutely, purely and fundamentally free to act with boundless creation – anything we want, every single moment. But we choose, for reasons that are hard to understand unless you subscribe to the notion that people are more or less just simple animals, to act and think in some 'ordered' fashion, as if there were a virtue in choosing to eschew the powers we have. Maybe we give those powers up because it takes too much courage to do otherwise; maybe, like Freud says, we need civilization for survival, to overcome the reality of chaos, the fear we have of several billion human potentials all loosed on reality at once; or maybe we've simply been heading in the wrong direction so long we just don't know any better.

"The magic of art is that it's the result of a human power we don't understand. Most people snuff out their creative talents early on so that they can get on with the business of life. The same is true of most psychic gifts. Things like ESP, psychokinesis, precognition, and faith healing are simply blotted out by children as they develop language and become integrated with the world. Such power is, in fact, impractical and unworldly. It goes beyond what it means to be human, goes into the realm of impossible magic.

"You've heard the old saying that in the land of the blind the one-eyed man is king? Well, in reality I think you would find that in the land of the blind the one-eyed man is hunted like an animal. Too much power outside the rules is the biggest danger anyone can bring to oneself. The one-eyed man may never be caught, but he will be hunted for eternity by those of the blind world.

"So that's what these people are, then. It's kind of like they're royalty who can see. It's simple. You know how you feel at a concert or even just listening to a great song, especially when the music is really loud? Well, think about how these people feel all in tune, all synched into the same groove, big bass rolling through them, sound louder on the stage than just about anywhere else, pure sound anyway. You ever think how Pat Metheny and Lyle Mays feel while jamming out their tunes? Ever see them do "The Awakening?" Or what about those hour-long versions of "Red House" Jimi did? Or how about King Jones and Sleighmaker Hayes? Even Kerouac on one of his drunken word jams? It's all the same. Those who create at that level are tapped into so much more than the rest of us are. And the farther into it they go, the more joy and lust they feel for the world they've tapped into. So—"

"So, this is that world?" she interrupts him.

"In a way. But, there's so much more. It's hard to understand. But hopefully we'll get you there. Some get it, some don't. Most here believe you're going to make it. I trust them."

Jill thinks about the strangeness of Coral McGrey and Cecil Miller and how they had seemed jokes to her just a few days ago. She notices them watching her from outside the circle. "What did you mean," she finally asks Fancher, "excluding a few of you? McGrey and Miller over there? You said two of the Amish boys. Anyone else?"

"One," he says simply, but she can tell his attention is drifting elsewhere. Her own thinking is becoming somewhat muddled. Fancher finally turns back to her and says: "It's all right. They need to keep us out for just a while so that they can get in tune."

"What are you talking about now?" she manages to ask, feeling somewhat awkward and worrying that people will hear her.

"You'll see."

*

Let's calm her down with something in A, comes a voice in her head. She knows, as if a group of people are acknowledging him together, that it's Robert Johnson who has made the call.

It starts out small and quiet. One guitarist playing the opening chords, filling the silence that has set in around them, finger-picking a slow, rhythmic, happy melody. Robert Johnson? She doesn't know and doesn't care. Something odd is happening. She can feel it.

Okay, let's go.

It is tentative at first. A few congas begin tapping quietly. Cadence. *Hunting for time,* a voice says to her. *We're searching for the beat of all of us. Takes time. Comes a time. We've been there all along, riding like loving babies on the horse of time, trying to create more than what is known on its warm back. When it's here, it is what we know comes after love.*

It's here. We're on it.

Here we go.

And she is there, too. She's with us!

The rhythm grows more complex, expands off in many directions all at once. *Time is many dips into darkness everywhere, and we can't figure out if it's in us. There are so many genetic hues, rainbow colors, and always that surprise of rushing water, so much the sound of wind and also many hands clapping.*

There may be something more here, outside us, something big and thinking and clunking along, feeling its own pain beside ours, its own joy, its own wandering ecstasy, booming in.

Here we come.

A three-note syncopated heavy bass takes over with electric guitars, *as electric as a distant city, numb, at a loss for people, gleaming in a hot night sky, sunset going from scented gold to bruised pink, pulsing blood, digestion and hair, the scent of heads the wind carries along to those who would be present, digging thunder and sound, carrying thought in primal pulses out and over these long rolling fields, ghosts of heat in the distance, gyrating now and thinning into vapor and quantum sparks, like salt-lights poured into warm water, spreading in perfect equilibrium throughout the world as instantly as smells carry across a cornfield on a summer afternoon. Time is here, now.*

The beat is there, too, and still the first cadence Jill heard, the congas. Other rhythms stream in and out of the first one. The melody flows through all of them, a big chorus of hearts letting loose pure emotion. It is more than music – so much more.

Yes, you have it, but this kind of time is carried on sound, so, it is music still. But, yes, of course, you have it.

This comes to her from more than one voice, several (a multitude?) in unison, more powerful than just one or two.

We ask ourselves, what good, though? What is the root of this, this walking through time on the back of it? Singing and taking sound into us, and then, of course, returning it to the world?

She begins to understand. She knows that somewhere in Lucas Fancher's basement or a back room, her body lies in some kind of a coma—his, too, possibly, his daughter's, Janie Hawthorn's – and yet they are all dreaming together and there are more, so many more. At least that's what it seems.

Or is she dreaming under the influence of some strong and possibly new psychotrope and none of this is real, has not happened at all? Even Harris?

But then she understands what they need her to get for herself.

They don't know! They aren't sure.

They don't know if they're real, either. They don't know what's happening. And they certainly don't know why.

"Don't think. Not now," comes Fancher's voice.

The music rolls through her, seeking to shut down her thoughts. She knows she needs to let it take her; she wants to let them take her. She wants to let it happen.

CHAPTER 31

Stoddemeier tells Arthur Gold, "We're not going to be able to bring this task to completion with him around here, sir,"

"You may be right, Dale, but we don't have much choice." Gold is sipping on coffee from a metal Thermos cup.

"Well, sir, we do. We can just escort the guy out of here."

"He's press. We take him out of here and it's surely to rile his sensibilities. Get him on us sure as shit."

"So your plan is to what? Carry the whole operation off under his nose without letting him in on the problem?"

"Seems like we don't have much choice."

"Then there's the issue of Simpson," says Stoddemeier, trying not to sound like he's pleading. "She's going to understand exactly what happens here."

"I'm not too worried about Simpson. We can take care of her."

"What are you talking about?"

"Lieutenant Stoddemeier," chuckles Arthur Gold. "You overestimate my intentions here...and my wherewithal. There are very simple ways to keep Sergeant Simpson, shall we say, out of the loop without killing her."

"I wasn't..."

"You were, but that's okay. It shows you don't know what to expect from me and that's the way I want it. No, Commander

Stoddemeier, she's in there now, and we've got to get her out no matter what before we finish what we came here to do. We've got a team set to bring her out – unconscious. It's pretty simple."

"How are you going to knock her out?"

"Let me worry about that, okay?"

*

There is something undeniably different about musicians in a circle playing music for each other. With no audience. The communal sensation of the circle, with sound traveling to the center, isn't the same as the broadcast outward in hopes of entertaining a mass group of people almost wholly unknown and unknowing; darkened, in fact, by the play of swarming, bright stage lighting, the audience experiencing the power of 100,000 watts blasting groove, melody, and the feeling of the musicians unified in their attempt to communicate what it isn't possible to express in words and never has been since music was first conceived.

*

"All right, I want everyone ready to move on my order." Arthur Gold is speaking quietly into his headset.

"What are you doing?" asks Harris.

"You stay here, Mr. Harris."

Gold speaks into his mouthpiece again. "Check that. I need two men from B-Team back here to watch the civilian."

"Just tell me what you're doing, Gold," says Harris. "You've got a police officer inside the building. You've got no idea what the situation is."

"I don't have time for this, Harris." Two men are moving quietly toward them, grim looks on their faces. "I'm going to say this once, okay? This is not a normal situation, Mr. Harris. These guys are going to stay with you because we can't afford to have you in the middle of things. We've got a job to do here."

"You've got a job to do? What job have you got to do? There's a few people in that house. That's all! Why don't you just go up and knock on the door to find out what's going on?"

"Out of the question," retorts Gold.

"Jesus Christ, man, you're insane," Harris says under his breath as Gold, speaking into his mouthpiece, begins to move up the driveway. He notices Stoddemeier watching him carefully as well.

Gold turns quickly. Too quickly, thinks Harris. "All right, you know what?" says Gold hotly. "I don't feel good about you. Commander Stoddemeier, you stay here with this fuck instead." Gold tells one of the guards to come with him and orders the other one to cuff Harris to the grate on the drain opening.

Before Stoddemeier can protest, Gold turns and continues his march back toward the house with the guard following.

*

She has no idea where the sounds are coming from. A chorus of synthesizers roams through her head, four or five different rhythms now, guitars, drums. The synthesizers give off different timbres but play the same lonely, deep, sustained harmonic, like the drone note in an Indian raga. And then there is the voice. It is male, but high and sweet, like Robert Plant's of Led Zeppelin. But the figure the sounds come from looks nothing like Plant. As he sings, a soft light pulses in modulation with the song.

Jeff Buckley, come words unbidden. *Extreme exaltation like grace.*

She recalls that Harris interviewed Buckley just before the singer mysteriously drowned in the Mississippi near Memphis.

The music seems to weave through her thoughts; it's becoming more and more difficult to separate herself from it. Lennon, Hendrix, Joplin and Morrison are singing background. "*Close your eyes forever, for time. Close your eyes in the shine. Close your eyes for time. Close your eyes in the river. Close your eyes and imagine forever.*"

She does, and sees it all, finally. They are there – still – all of them. In her mind? But they are – all of them – Garcia, Croce, Bonham on drums, everyone, along with Buckley whose voice seems to reverberate now in shrill, piercing wails which Hendrix mimics with his guitar. She sees Robert Johnson picking away calmly, head down, nodding in time to the music. *It's always been here.* Johnson's slide starts up, electric now. Lennon and Croce playing acoustic together, the rhythm driving with Bonham's signature beat: One-Two-Pound. One-Two-Pound.

This is our last goodbye. This from Buckley.

There's more here than just music, she thinks.

Yes, comes from all of them at once, only it's not a word. It is a feeling. *That's what we're trying to get to. It is called affirmation. It is called Amen. But it's in music beyond and behind and out in front.*

Anything we think can go through these sounds, she realizes. *I mean, we can transmit light with music. It's coming through the sound.*

Again, a chorus: *Yes, but energy, vibration. There is no such thing as music.*

I…

We know.

Why is this a secret? It's incredible.

Not everyone gets it the right way.

Well, no. I understand. But still…

There's more.

She thinks, *What?*

But the music is taking her somewhere else now. She senses them waiting for her to figure something new out. The word *Beauty* comes to her. Then *Time*. Then *Breath*. Then, finally, *The Sound of Rushing Water.*

The sound of rushing water takes over. She'd been hearing it on and off but thought it was just static. It was more than that, more like the sound of hard wind swirling through a winter forest of pines and naked black oak and sycamores, or the resonant applause of an appreciative crowd in a mammoth auditorium.

It is all sound mixed together, all the colors of music and noise moving in unison. It is the sound, they tell her, of hearts beating together from inside all the bodies of the world, the flush of blood flying through the body in love—or close to ecstasy, and the mumbling reverberations of thoughts spoken to the mind with the assumption that no one can hear them except the thinker.

We're home.

We're here.

She sees them. They stand on the side of an undulating road, the whole crowd of them, rose petal scent in the air, warm sun on their faces, the road moving past them like a river in the sky as they watch and continue to play their music.

On the flowing road she sees everything: first, the close world, vast clover fields dotted with puffs of amethyst flowers and orange poppies; the dark motions of Gold's men, Stoddemeier, and she knows instantly that he is not who he said he was; and Harris, talking with Stoddemeier – she is very fond of Frank Harris – Stoddemeier has removed bracelets from Frank's wrists. They are moving now. The road brings her to the city, and she sees the Sumter brothers and understands what Monty Sumter has been up to, that he has murdered Hancock, and she knows as well that Bud's ridiculous militia group shot down the helicopter out of pure ignorance. And she understands that the helicopter was delivering tetrodotoxin powder and equipment for them to continue growing mushrooms.

Buckley sings, *That was all real. That was so real.* His voice chills her. She understands that so much of what these people created in their life was leading them here from their very beginnings.

A single electric guitar plays an arpeggio of sorts, single notes of a chord repeating over and over until, finally, a defining echoed bent note from Hendrix.

Buckley's voice comes out of another momentary silence, singing of a secret chord then moves off with guitar and drums, *I'm taking you down to the holy rolling zoo, where the stars are bright and you can really let loose.*

"You're getting it," comes Morrison's voice in the pause. "It's never too late."

She wants to open her eyes, but feels a unified, *You can't. You're with us now.*

Buckley's voice continues: *Your mother's there with her long brown hair, and your father, with his deep sunken eyes. They will dance for you, and you will cry because you ain't seen them for a very long time.*

The road continues to flow past her. Farmland, forests, lakes, railroad lines, highways, families watching TV, bright-colored cars, candy stores, empty baseball parks at night, beaches in the winter, churches, vegetable gardens, street lights in the rain, trees rocking in the wind, ashtrays full of cigarette butts, public bathrooms tiled in light gray, auditoriums full of people in fur coats and down parkas, cartoon characters – Bugs Bunny, Mickey Mouse, Batman, Spiderman – cloud shadows dancing across the endless Rocky Mountains, schoolrooms at sunrise, kennels full of stray pets, cityscapes in the distance marked by their famous landmarks: St. Louis, Chicago, Minneapolis, Pittsburgh, Philadelphia, New York, Los Angeles, Seattle, Dallas, New Orleans, Cincinnati, Detroit, Phoenix, Indianapolis, Miami, Salt Lake City.

This is Life, she thinks.

Yes, and the answer's coming. First you must hold your breath. Do not breathe. Go through the pain. Come to us. Listen to the music. Let it make you forget your body. Come. There will be answers to your questions. Do not breathe. Let go of the last ribbon connecting you to the world.

She does as she is told. There is no choice. Once again there is no sense of connection to her body. The music is now mostly voices in soft choral notes. On some far-off periphery, she senses a slight discomfort. Her lungs need new oxygen. She knows this. But the awareness of pain is only subtle. She focuses on the music. The pain begins to slip away.

Buckley sings: *Well there comes a time when everything makes sense and people call you out to the back fence.* The music shifts again – strings, muted brass, and woodwinds – French horns, tubas, oboes, bassoons, and clarinets, fading into near silence. Just as it seems that the sound has fully faded, she picks up Garcia's noodling baby song melody. As always, he builds it. Time is ticked and metered out by soft cymbals. Garcia circles. She knows its coming just as it hits. He holds the note and every one of them melds into it, like they're flowing into a tunnel in unison. There is a spark flitting at the corners of her eyes. *It is the feeling you get from the word Pure.*

Far off she hears something else now. It is nothing more than a small bit of static, or like the ripping of fabric in a large room on the other side of the house. The volume increases ever so slightly, beginning to pile up in the background. And then the sound is clear. She holds her breath. The pain begins to grow.

It is an obvious sound. It is the sound of rushing water. But as she acknowledges this, she feels her body grow suddenly cold. The music is drifting away now, but the sound of flowing water fills her head, gaining strength, moving towards a roar. The sensation of cold, she understands, could become unbearable, although she also understands it has to be an illusion of some kind.

For a moment everything goes black and the roar ceases, leaving pure silence and she has a sense of sliding until there is a loud splashing sound and a pop, and she is back. Her body is with her and she is with her body. She hears applause and a kind of stuttering, jumpy cheer from all of them.

Welcome!

She knows she isn't breathing, but she is there. And she understands everything now.

"This is the place where everything begins," she tells them with her voice and feels the affirmation coming back to her, all of them loving her and proud of where they are, what they have discovered.

Buckley's voice says back to her: *This is the place where everyone creates.*

But she still feels their uncertainty, the confusion, a sense of futility. They are here but that it isn't enough. There should be more. Where are we?

She feels the nagging sense of something else, too; that there is a question she needs to ask and an answer she needs to hear that will make everything all right, that will give her knowledge about something; she isn't sure; but it is there, just out of reach – that feeling of being on the edge of awareness, on the tip of the tongue, just not quite there.

CHAPTER 32

"I wouldn't say he's really insane," Stoddemeier says to Harris.

Frank watches Gold rounding the bend in the driveway. "If he isn't insane, then what is he?"

"Committed."

"To what?"

"He won't tell me everything, but he thinks Fancher has it coming."

"Jill has nothing to do with that."

"I know. I'm not sure anymore what his intentions are, and I'm not sure we want to find out. He's got a look in his eye..."

"So, we're just going to sit here?

"I'm not sure yet."

"You've got a plan?"

"Not really, but I'm thinking."

Harris's wrist is beginning to irritate him where the handcuff is rubbing. "Look. Why don't you release me? I'm not going anywhere without Jill, and I'm certainly not going to get in the way of that crazy motherfucker."

Stoddemeier looks at him: "Give me time to think, okay? If I'm going up against Gold, I want to do something useful here."

Harris eyes the shiny metal bracelet on his wrist, thinking about how heavy it seems compared to his images from childhood games and movies. The cuffs are sturdier than the grate they are attached to.

Then, looking into the shaft covered by the grate, he feels something odd. Underground drainage systems should give off a slight cool breeze and smell of algae and mildew. Coming through this grate is warm air and the faint smell of bacon.

"Shouldn't there be cool air coming out of here?" he asks quietly.

Stoddemeier doesn't answer. He squints sidelong at the guard Gold ordered to watch them. He doesn't seem to be paying much attention.

"This air is warm here, Stoddemeier."

"What?"

"It's warm. The air coming out of this shaft. Smells like bacon and gas or something."

He has Stoddemeier's attention. He asks again: "What do you think it is?"

"I don't know," Stoddemeier replies. He moves closer to the grate and looks down. "There's a ladder of sorts," says Harris. "I say we take a look. I mean, what else are we going to do?"

*

Major Tyle Sandover watches from his seat in the operations room in Langley as twenty-two closed-circuit images blink in front of him. He has dismissed the usual operations staff so that he can speak with Arthur Gold in private. His fingers massage the console to his left; he can choose another eighteen shots for the forty video transmitters carried by the group on their helmets. He wants to believe that Gold is doing the right thing, but he knows better. Gold's history is to go overboard.

Many of the screens show the same basic image. The men are using portable hydraulic excavators to dig 45-degree angle trenches eighteen feet into the soil. They will then slide C-4 explosive packets into place and carefully install detonators with automated, radio-controlled triggers attached to them. The detonators are all calibrated to the same frequency for synchronic destruction. There will be twenty-four in all, fully encircling the compound. The plan is bureaucratically foolproof: Gold needs Sandover's direct approval to set off the charges. He knows that Sandover will require two other approvals and that those will be verbal and from near the top of the chain of command. There will be no traceable accountability in the exercise, and the farm will be almost completely imploded into the missile cavern it rests on. Ideally, all organic matter will vaporize. Save for the large crater that they will fill in with rubble and soil, nothing will remain. Whatever is actually going on with this whole phenomenon, it should be gone by sundown.

"Major, we'll be ready in a few minutes," comes Gold's voice through the room's speaker system, from more than a thousand miles away. "You have the approvals?"

"I do, Dr. Gold."

Sandover recalls their last meeting before Gold left.

"Your memo was appreciated by the subcommittee, Doctor, but they aren't sure what you were actually saying."

"Major Sandover, if I said what I really mean, they would be implicated."

"Implicated?"

"Yes, sir. We need to eliminate what is going on out there."

"Eliminate?"

"Yes, as efficiently as possible."

"Because a few people are being taken in by a hoax?"

Gold is looking at the floor and seems to hold his breath. Finally, he brings his eyes up to meet Sandover's. "That's just it, Major. I'm not sure it is a hoax."

It's Sandover's turn to remain silent. His eyes move from Gold's to his computer screen. He knows Gold has no sense of humor. Was this a conversation with a lunatic? "Let me get this straight. You're telling me that Elvis is really alive, that he's been faking his death, and has been in hiding all these years?"

"Not exactly, but that's close enough."

"And he's just decided, for some absolutely incomprehensible reason, to show himself now, after what, thirty-five years...and on global television to boot?"

"We've done a lot of analysis of as much footage as we can find of those revival meetings, Major."

"And?"

"And, my people tell me that they don't get normal image analysis for whoever or whatever that thing is that turned up at the first meeting, and then at the next one there's nothing at all out of the ordinary."

"I thought there wasn't any recorded information from that first time."

"We had someone on the ground."

"Jesus. Without my authorization?"

"My people are—"

"Your people? You don't have people. You've got—"

"I've got contractors—"

"You've got ghost busters and clairvoyants. I know. I sign the requisitions."

"Yes, and there are certain various people in key positions who have found these powers useful and even efficacious over the years, which is why you sign those requisition orders."

"So your plan is to blow the whole place up?"

"Got to."

"Because?"

"Because there's too much at stake here."

Sandover clears his throat, wondering if he himself has been in the game too long. "What exactly is at stake, Doctor Gold?"

"Major, I'm not sure you want to have this conversation."

Sandover is no longer interested in humoring the guy.

"Look, god damn it, I'm the one who's got to stick his dick out here. I want to understand what the fuck you really think is going on or I'm not even going to consider a single issue you bring up. You work for me, Gold. I want to know what you think you're up to here. Got it?"

Arthur Gold is used to this kind of response from his clients and bosses. He knows that he has a communication problem with his customers, that he enjoys withholding information. But he also understands that Sandover's response means that he has gone too far with things. It was time to let the Major in on how it all worked. He'd done it enough over the years. He'd done it so much, in fact, that it was getting a little tiring. He had to watch himself or he would come off as sounding condescending.

"Major Sandover, I've talked some about the MKULTRA experiments by the CIA. Remember?"

"Yes. I recall. All that horse shit about psycho warfare and ESP, experimenting with LSD as a weapon, lacing Castro's cigars with synthetic peyote. Dumb fucking stuff, if you ask me. Almost as dumb as some of the bullshit SI cooks up these days, and right under my nose, I might add.

"Yeah, I know MKULTRA. I was given this position partly to clean up all the idiocy that MKULTRA spawned. What about it?"

"MKULTRA has an expansive history, Major, one that most people don't know about, not even you."

"I was busy doing real work, Gold."

"Yes, you were. However, sir, there are many things about MKULTRA that were ultra-classified, things that have a particular bearing on what's going on with these Elvis sightings."

Sandover snorts. "What kind of things?"

"Well, sir, I think I'm going to have to give you a bit of background first. But I repeat, I personally don't think you want to have this conversation."

"We're going to have it, Gold, or this meeting is over and you aren't going anywhere."

"Suit yourself, Major."

Gold raises his eyebrows, inhales, and begins:

"It all started innocently enough – innocent for us, that is. Soviet KGB agencies were developing numerous psychological capabilities for espionage and even warfare. They were employing and training every kind of kook you can imagine – clairvoyants with remote viewing powers, people with extrasensory perception who could read minds and even throw their thoughts, telekineticians. They even had a couple women who they proved could see into the future.

"So, a great deal of competitive work was underway, mostly at Fort Meade in Maryland where NSA's task center is. And a great many intelligence organizations were in on it. The Special Action branch of INSCOM, CIA's Weather Group, NSA's Intelligence Research Center, the Army Security Agency, even the President's Security Council.

"I was a participant in a lot of the planning and evaluation then, but had little to do with the experiments and the full-scale operations. I've talked to some of the people who actually did the work. There is little question that this stuff happens, that certain people in the population are capable of all sorts of weird things – self-healing, precognition, remote viewing, thought transferal and reception, you name it – but it's also clear that these phenomena are practically impossible to control and that there is virtually no predictability to them.

"MKULTRA's Subproject 136 got going in the late 1970s. Right around that time other scientists and physicians completely outside the intelligence community were making huge strides in understanding consciousness through the mirror of psychedelic drug use. We had all been aware of John Lilly's work with dolphin language and sensory deprivation tanks. We were also mildly amused by the exploits of Timothy Leary and Richard Alpert, but none of them seemed able to move beyond the religious and magical thought levels of hallucinogens. Then Terence McKenna came along and changed everything.

"At first he seemed like the fruitiest of all the psychobabble drug heads we'd encountered. He was a perfect caricature of the flaky hippie: skinny, bespectacled, unkempt greasy hair, a full beard that he rarely trimmed, and that slow sort of innocent, high-pitched Boy Scout voice that spewed forth sentences full of the most insane gibberish anyone had ever heard – terms like *hyperdimensional space*, *the rose window topologies of the galacterian beehives of the di-methyltryptamine* (that's DMT), *violet psycho fluids*, *deep blue hallucinations*. He was a joke. The conclusions he espoused included notions that the source of hallucinogenic experiences was really aliens trying to communicate with us. And he would talk about taking psychedelics and having conversations with little cybernetic elfin machines representing the drug state of DMT who, according to him, said that the five-billion-year history of the galaxy was trivial.

"But we watched him anyway. No one seemed to understand what he was saying at first, but one thing was clear: Lilly and Leary and all their cohorts were listening. In fact, they weren't just listening, they were listening closely, and they seemed to be in awe of the guy. So we started listening too. And we read and analyzed his books and papers and lectures.

"McKenna was experimenting with rare organics – rare at the time, anyway. He'd actually gone into the Amazon and tracked down tribes of people who had access to very potent psilocybin mushrooms called *Stropharia cubensis* that contain a significant amount of tryptamine, which is part of the DMT molecular family. DMT in those days wasn't unheard of, but it was one of those ghost drugs that no one understood.

McKenna and his little club were also using something he termed an MAO-inhibitor. It was some weird kind of vine that enhanced the DMT effect by slowing the body's ability to process DMT on the molecular level, thereby allowing for it to have an effect on someone who has taken it orally. This mixture was what they learned the natives called *ayahuasca*. It had a dramatic effect on the whole psychedelic universe that we're still trying to contain.

DMT – and psilocybin mushrooms, too, for that matter – all pointed to what we now understand is an opening up of the serotonin chemistry of consciousness. Serotonin is many things, but neurologically it's the main pleasure receptor for the brain. Serotonin and a number of other neurochemicals are amplified dramatically by tryptamines, the result being these crazy, semi-spiritual states that excited the hell out of a lot of McKenna and his people. They thought they were having apocalyptic religious experiences.

"And that was it. He had opened something up that we couldn't ignore. He made his experiences public in books like *Food of the Gods*, *True Hallucinations*, and *The Invisible Landscape*. The little hippie fucker had taken his overeducated middleclass brain into the Amazon and stolen secret shamanistic powers from a bunch of ignorant savages. He had no idea what he was doing.

"Funny thing was that he really had discovered something, even if he didn't know what it was. We didn't know what it was, either, but we knew it was something. He'd made contact with a *Thing*. I mean, it was a real Thing. It was an extremely powerful and virtually incomprehensible Thing, but it was real nonetheless. And when we started our *psi* subjects on McKenna's concoctions, all hell broke loose.

"One of the most amazing things about DMT – at least when it's purified in a lab and then smoked – is that the effect is very overpowering but very short, usually only about fifteen minutes. However, subjects tested say that they are transported into multiple worlds and numerous dimensions of awareness, and that it feels like a lifetime. Many liken it to being locked in a vortex of insanity. It is clearly a transformative and overpowering psychic event. But when the subject's blood is drawn after the drug has lost its effect, we have found literally no trace of the substance in the system. With alcohol, nicotine, marijuana, LSD, mescaline, opiates, and virtually all the designer drugs of the last few decades, we find significant quantities of the active substances in people's blood and urine – sometimes as much as three months later. But fifteen minutes after smoking DMT – not a thing.

"There really did seem to be something going on with McKenna's findings. DMT is actually a very common substance in plant life everywhere and it can even be found naturally in the human body.

"I'm getting ahead of myself, though. Subproject 136 replicated most of McKenna's experiments – if you can call them experiments. And we realized that *psi* might be enhanced through the use of hallucinogens. Up until that point, MKULTRA had been playing with LSD for more than twenty-five years with few truly productive results.

"My job at the time was evaluating the merits of all this work. Psychedelic drugs seemed to me – and many others in the mix, I might add – nothing more than self-induced insanity. My conclusion was that we could use the stuff as another weapon to confuse enemy decision makers, but there was no way to control things. The end result would be chaos and mayhem. Things could just as easily backfire if we spiked a drinking water supply or laced Castro's scrambled eggs with LSD. MKULTRA's search for the use of psychedelics and other drugs as some sort of predictable trigger for psychological manipulation was pretty much a fruitless endeavor.

"By the early '80s we had duplicated almost everything McKenna had discovered. And he was right. There is something overtly different about the tryptamine experience; something completely different from any other drug. You really do go into another place. When we sent our top remote viewers there, we got the surprise of our lives. They didn't come back for weeks. I mean, their bodies were with us, but if we didn't rouse them, they would be connected to this world of McKenna's for huge chunks of time. We had them on modest IV drip doses of DMT. They were in this kind of cyber-trance – half here, half there – and if we hooked them up for intravenous feeding and waste collection, they were usually more there than here.

"Every one of them would report the same things: securely enclosed inside a domed cave with vibrating walls pulsing with color and images of a distinctly Egyptian motif surrounding them; little creatures - sometimes elves, sometimes robots - telling them to pay attention and do as they were doing; an overwhelming clairvoyant sense of the future; precognition; a sense of the ancient past as well, an almost poetic understanding of the history of the human soul; knowledge that they were connected by a silver thread between the two worlds and that if that thread were somehow broken they might never come back; and, when more than one of them went together, a clear understanding that they were all connected, and remarkably similar descriptions of visions and hallucinations.

"It was, according to the researchers on the project, anyway, astounding to witness. And even more so because after the first several hours of intensity, the subjects were often able to report back to us, for a while, on their experiences in fairly lucid and highly detailed descriptions without losing their grip on that other world.

"But this was the clincher for MKULTRA: given the proper adjustment period, subjects were also able to remote view, it seemed, practically any coordinate we gave them with almost perfect accuracy. For the first time after decades of study, we had proof of an odd, replicable kind of psychic power. I can't tell you how profound that moment was. It was like we realized that magic was real, or, at least, that human beings were capable of magic when given the right input.

"That was in the late '80s. We were starting to make extremely fruitful strides in using the technique, but we were also beginning to realize that we'd stumbled onto something far more important than a human LANSAT radar system. We had essentially split the atom in the world of psychology.

"Unfortunately, several of our subjects were beginning to show signs of psychosis, along with a new sense of morality that was making them far too difficult to work with. I was brought back in to devise a plan that would seek out the appropriate people, move them into the process, gauge the psychological changes, establish a cutoff point that was, as I was instructed, 'humanitarian,' and then establish a debriefing program which would ensure that they could be reinserted into the world with no detrimental effects to the work.

"Before my plans could fully take shape, our first and best subject, Pat Price, suffered a fatal heart attack. I don't know the circumstances, but the entire program was eliminated in one fell swoop. It all just ground to a halt – and the project directors and chief scientists just disappeared. Zip. I mean, they vanished.

"So when MKULTRA finally came out in the press and congress investigated, most of the work was already deep under. Key records were destroyed. Individuals had disappeared. It was classic stuff. And that's where I reentered the picture once again. They needed someone who understood the implications of the work, who could also run the gauntlet for them with the press and with the new guys sent in to clean out the old spooks. They could have chosen any number of the people who worked on the project. But they chose me for the same reason that you have to work with me: I'm dangerous, but I rarely let that side of me show. I know too much. I've been in too many meetings. More to the point, I know who made all the decisions on MKULTRA in the beginning. I mean, I *knew* them, knew who they were, where they lived, what they ate, their favorite drinks. Shit, I played softball with them and met their spouses.

"Now, you're probably asking yourself who *they* are. And you know the answer I'm going to give. I can't tell you. In fact, I'm not completely sure myself. I knew them, but I'm not sure what they really did, who they worked for – all that. You're not always supposed to know. That's another thing I do well and another reason that they picked me. I understand when it's inappropriate to ask questions.

"The people at the top who they pinned MKULTRA on, Sidney Gottlieb for one, weren't the real players. Gottlieb was like me. His job was to facilitate decision making and to take the heat. He was the guy who coordinated project funding and went up the Hill to sit in congressmen's offices. But the real guys calling the shots stayed back there in Langley and Fort Meade, or wherever they had been assigned, and got the work done."

Sandover is standing near a window as Gold finishes his story, looking off into the distance as the glow of the rising sun just barely begins to touch the edge of a McLean shopping mall roof. He enjoys the silence and solitude of the CIA's control rooms when he has the opportunity.

Gold's voice through the speaker system startles him. "It's all been pretty fun, Major, but now we have this problem here in Missouri and it's my job to make sure it doesn't get out of hand."

Sandover rouses himself. "Problem?"

"Yes, sir. This is not, and never was, intended to get out of our hands. We can't let the public know about this. Ever...."

"So, you're telling me that, what? You want authorization to go figure out if this person that people claim is Elvis has figured out what MKULTRA's been up to?"

"We know what's going on. We've made contact with them already. We just need to find where they're physically located and...."

"...destroy them?"

"Yes, more or less."

"Dr. Gold, I'm not following you. What's the connection?"

"These people are using the tryptamine in those mushrooms – probably mixed with some optimal dosage of that other drug tetrodotoxin – to travel to the same places we did. I have no idea who's out there with Fancher, but they have to be stopped. This is too far outside the norm for the public to ever know."

"And the Elvis impersonators are?"

"Sir, we don't think it's an impersonator."

"Then who is he?"

"You don't want to know."

"Yes, I do, Dr. Gold. That's exactly what I want to know."

Sandover hears a sarcastic sigh through the audio system. Gold says, "We're pretty sure he's linked to Fancher's whole enterprise."

"What do you mean? Pretty sure? Gold, you're making less sense than you were a few minutes ago."

"Major, we're just not fully certain, but whoever he is, roaming publicly like that is eventually going to draw a big crowd – much bigger than we've seen so far. And it's only a matter of time before Fancher's property is linked to him. The thing is, we just can't get a handle on any of these people. Fancher keeps disappearing for long periods of time. That's why we have that kid Miller on the job."

"Can't you use your remote viewers or your people who see into the future?"

"Sir, I've told you already. It's not that simple. You can't control this stuff. It comes and goes. A tremendous amount of static occurs along with the right signals. We've got to physically be there in order to fully establish their whereabouts. And, obviously, to put an end to this mess."

Sandover considers the implications of what Gold has been saying. It goes far beyond stupid spy games. It is clear that Gold isn't giving him the full story, but he's heard enough to know that if the public became aware the CIA had discovered psychedelic drugs actually enhance paranormal powers, every half-assed soothsayer and lottery player in the country would be growing mushrooms in their homes and tuning in to the freak show Gold had described. It was easy to see that this went far beyond the recreational exploits of sixties youth culture.

"What does Elvis Presley have to do with any of this?"

"If I told you, sir, you wouldn't believe me."

"Try me."

"I can't, sir, you don't have clearance."

"You need to let me know *something*, Gold."

"I can tell you this. It seems that what we discovered with tryptamine is only the tip of the iceberg. Lucas Fancher has a much bigger grasp on what this is all about than you can possibly imagine. He knows much more than any of us. We need to end this now. I thought we'd done our job back there in 2010 and 2011 when we twisted up all those supposed scientific studies performed by Hubert Streetman and Allison Tuttle looking at the connection between DMT trips and religious trance experiences. That was just a little PR work there. We had to deal with some kid who made a documentary on Streetman's work, too. They called the documentary "The God Detector." That was easy. This stuff affects the veracity of religion more than anything else. We just fed a little bit of information to the Vatican and the Southern Baptist Convention and let them go to work. Now we need to use our hands and get a bit dirty, is all. The idea is to protect this country from itself."

"And I've got to go along with what you're proposing, don't I? You're little hand-dirtying exercise?" Sandover says.

"This has come from higher up. You know that. We're doing our jobs. That's all."

"I know, Gold, but what about the media?"

"Leave it to us, Major. That's an easy one. Always has been. Always will be."

Sandover needs to end the discussion and move on. Gold is going to do what he's going to do. Sandover's job is to take the hit if anyone ever finds out. That's why Gold spent the time getting authorization from up top first. He had to hand it to him, Gold was good. He'd been at it for more than forty years and no one had fingered him yet.

"Proceed, then, Dr. Gold. But make sure you don't get caught. I don't want anyone outside of this office hearing what you just told me. I'm not sure I believe you myself, but I know that I don't want anyone else to try, either."

"Thank you, Major."

Sandover hears the audio click off and remains motionless, standing at the window as the first rays of orange light splay up over the roof of the mall. To the silence in the control room, he says, "If this DMT shit is real, then how does it work?"

*

Watching the exercise actually unfold on the monitors, alone in the operations room, Sandover can't shake the feeling that Gold is dealing with something that he may not be able to handle. But what was he supposed to do, proclaim Arthur Gold a kook? If he put a stop to the operation, there was no telling what might happen. Terminating it now meant he would need to document the decision and create a paper trail. He would need to acknowledge what was going on to at least two different subcommittees. There was risk all the way around, so this was a case of hoping for the best.

CHAPTER 33

They are standing in a cement-lined tunnel about thirty feet high and twenty feet across. Shining the light on the floor, Stoddemeier says: "Wet tire marks. Someone definitely came through here."

"How far do you think this tunnel goes?" asks Harris.

"No telling, but I'm going to guess there's several miles of these pathways connecting all the silos," replies Stoddemeier. "I smell diesel. There's been a vehicle through here recently." He directs his flashlight at the ceiling and walls. "Gonna guess, too, that we have access to the house through here."

"What about Gold?"

Stoddemeier grins at Harris then shakes his head. "I don't think I'm on his side anymore. Not sure what I thought I was doing from the get go. Come on, let's move. We don't have much time."

*

The only presences left with Jill are that of Cecil Miller and Coral McGrey. The others have vanished.

"We're still here for a reason," Cecil tells her.

"I can feel that, but *what* reason?"

"You're going to understand soon enough," says Coral. "But right now we need to get out of here."

Jill is beginning to feel cold again. She worries that she will become alone again. "Then let's leave."

"We can't. For the same reason they can't. Our minds are hooked into the drug. We're out of our bodies. We need to wait."

"Wait for what?"

"For someone to come."

"Where?"

"To our bodies. Take us out of the tanks."

"Tanks?"

"The reason we're here, the three of us, is because we can draw people in. They need that."

"I'm not ready to leave here yet. There's something I need to know."

"We all feel that way."

"No, I..."

"Officer Simpson?" It's Miller now. "This is a very delicate situation. Much more delicate than just a simple encounter with a bunch of free-form minds in entheogenic space. They are in the process of doing something extraordinary and they need us. What you're feeling – needing to know the answer to something profound, some big, important question – is something we all feel under the influence of heavy doses of psychedelics. It's part of the experience. I can't tell you the answer because I don't know it. But I can tell you the question." There's a slight pause. "Do you want to know?" he asks.

"Yes."

"It's just the question, really."

"I realize that."

"It's a bit complicated, but it goes something like this: Are we near the beginning or the end?" He waits.

"Of what?"

"Do we live in the world as a workout for some separated spirit-soul, maybe trying to get nearer to whatever is our source, or are we already beyond that spirit-soul because we find ourselves lodged in time and space and fully connected to our earth and each other, because we own the stark-raving present lock stock and barrel?"

"And you don't know the answer to that?"

"Are we to be this thing we call God? Or are we to serve God?" Coral asks.

"Still, you don't know the answer?"

"No, I don't," Coral says. "And these people, if that's what you can call them, don't know either. How could they? They are fully out of time and space. They have fallen over the edge of awareness. As incredible as this state may seem, there's also confusion and remorse that comes with the territory.

"Confusion and remorse?"

"Think about it. They have immortality of a kind if they continue in their tanks and if they continue to use the powers of the tetrodotoxin-tryptamine mix. I mean, they're in their tanks, but they can manifest themselves in the material world. You've seen this. You've done it yourself. It's amazing. But still, they are essentially trapped outside of time and space. They are beyond the material world. They have each other, but they don't have life. And worse, they don't have death."

"But they have so much more," Jill points out. "They've got an understanding that there's, there's…."

"More than we know? More than what we've been led to believe by science, religion, and common experience?"

"Yes, there are much bigger truths than the ones we know. It's so vast, so open."

"And that's the problem," Miller says. "It's so open that they're stuck in it."

"What do you mean they're stuck in it?" Jill asks.

"They chose this state over what they were. It came to them and they chose it. I would choose it, too, if I could stay in it. They could, so they did." The timbre of Cecil's voice changes.

"We're coming back," he tells her. "I sound different because most of the drug has worn off. They're barely able to get into your head now. They can't even create any static."

"We need to help them," Jill says almost instinctively.

"We have," he continues haltingly. "Each of these minds you have encountered needed to be free. It shouldn't be a surprise. But they also needed to be with each other. And to get here they found a little more than they bargained for. Yes, there are secrets to consciousness which most people miss, don't even have an inkling about. In taking the path they have, these great minds also stumbled into a clearer realm, a state of mind that allows them to perceive the rhythms of the universe in full and living color. When they make music, it all comes together. They are more or less one with each other and with the rules of nature.

"But there is a price. To get here they truly had to leave the world behind. This isn't exactly a hallucination, is it? They lie in their tanks, but they're able to be partially physical beings, at least in close proximity to their minds. But none of this is real, either. It's impossible for them to leave.

"For a while they thought they could overcome it all and completely eliminate their final ties to the body by believing in the building of a starship, but it didn't work. They are stuck here – wherever that is. So they're here and they can't go back. They've severed their ties to their families and friends by faking their own deaths. They get to hang out with each other and with whatever has made this all possible – surely you sensed that strange feeling, that sense that you're being watched? It's been overwhelming for me, but the others are completely cutoff. They have nowhere to go."

Jill begins to understand. "So we're part of some new plan for them?"

"Yes. And this one is going to work. It has to." His voice begins to fade, to blend into the periphery of her thoughts. It's becoming difficult to discern whether she's actually hearing him or whether her own thoughts are tricking her.

"What is it?"

"We're going to find out soon enough."

"You don't know?"

"Not completely," he says after several seconds. "But I think I've got a pretty good idea."

CHAPTER 34

"There's something up ahead," says Harris. It's a steel door, wider than the standard 30-inch entryway. He uses the flashlight to look for a latch or handle. "Open it?"

"I'm thinking we don't have much time to figure things out. Yeah, open it."

The handle is easy enough to find, but the door won't give. As Harris considers whether he should ask Stoddemeier to blow out the lock with his gun, he hears the faint click of a lock being turned. He pushes and the door swings open. They peer into a room full of what looks like futuristic coffins shimmering in different metallic colors, automobile colors: dark blue, enameled beige, deep green, cherry red, bright yellow, black. There are at least a hundred, maybe more. Each is connected to a grid of PVC pipes and tubes. The air in the room is moist and warm.

"Sarcophagi?" Harris asks.

Stoddemeier acknowledges the humor with a quick smirk but steps past Harris to stand inside the room at the top of an iron catwalk. Illuminated by large, well-spaced high-pressure sodium lamps, the room vibrates and hums. In one corner are six different industrial pumps and behind them a large sea-green contraption the size of a car.

"I don't think this is a tomb, Harris," says Stoddemeier. "Not sure what we're standing in, exactly, but that green thing's a generator and those pumps look like they're moving stuff through those tanks." He heads down the steps as Harris stands at the door behind him.

"What do you think it is, then?"

"That's what I'm going to find out," says Stoddemeier as he reaches the last step.

"You're not going to open one of those, are you?"

"I'm not going to *not* open one, that's for sure. If anything, we need to know what Gold is really up to and my money says he's got more than an inkling this stuff is down here. He's got over 400 charges of C-4 in six-pound lots up there. He's looking to destroy this place. I want to know why."

Harris casts a glance around the room. It's easily forty feet deep from floor to ceiling and circular in shape rather than rectangular. Stoddemeier approaches the nearest coffin.

"Not that one," comes a familiar voice from behind Harris. "Those blue ones over on the other side of the room."

Stoddemeier hesitates, casting around for the source of the words.

In surprise, Harris says: "Janie? What are you doing here?"

"Let's just say I've been expecting you two," replies Janie Hawthorn as she steps back from Harris's move to embrace her. "We've got a lot to do and very little time here, Frank."

Still that haunted, alien look, thinks Harris. He can't help himself as he takes in the sight of her face and body and recalls a montage of enticing moments with her: making love, the heavy dark breasts, the smell of her hair, her smooth-skinned waist and firm rear cupped in his palms, the motion of her hips riding him slowly, how she so easily took control. How good it felt to be inside her.

"No time, Frank," she says hurriedly, moving past him and down the steep stairway to follow Stoddemeier who is making his way across the room to the eight tanks in the far corner.

"We need to get them out, on their feet, and moving as fast as possible," she says to Stoddemeier as he lifts the first lid.

"Is this Fancher?" asks Stoddemeier.

"Yes. Help him out carefully. He's still somewhat drugged and may be a bit confused." She points at the other tanks in turn. "The others are Miller, McGrey, Simpson, and those two are Gerhart and Marston Jergensen. Their younger brother, Stephen, is staying. Hurry. I'll start with Simpson."

"Those two are the Amish kids?" asks Stoddemeier as he moves toward the tanks. "Meaning that they're alive?"

"Correct." She raises Jill's lid as Harris watches, realizing that the two women are about to meet, that he just recalled his attraction to Janie, that he still has no idea how she is involved in things, and that Jill has at least insinuated suspicions about Janie in her murder investigation – which is now clearly more confused than ever before.

"She's still out," comes Janie's voice from behind the lid of Jill's tank. "Frank, stop acting confused for just a second and come over here to help us. Lift her head out first, but make sure you support her by the shoulders. Get her into a sitting position, then gently pat her cheeks. If that doesn't work, pinch her hard on the biceps."

She moves away from behind the lid and looks up at Harris who is still standing on the landing. "Come on, Frank. Get down here. We've got to move. I'll explain all of this later. She needs you right now. I'm going to get Fancher, Miller, and McGrey up, too. Let's go."

Harris moves quickly now, understanding that he needs to stop wondering and just act. He hurries down the stairs to Jill's tank. Moving around the lid, he finds her naked and floating in what seems to be a bath of some kind of jelly. He hesitates.

"What is this stuff?" he calls to Janie.

"Ergonomic fluid. Not to worry, it's the best medium we know of for instantaneously adjusting to body temperature and movement. Just enhances the experience. Hurry!"

He moves his hands into the material and realizes that he can't feel a thing. Carefully, he lifts her into a sitting position, trying to focus on her face, averting his sight from her naked body. Seeming to read his mind, Janie says, "There are robes over there on that wall. Get one for her, and a towel too once she's come around."

Harris pats Jill's cheeks to no avail and then notices something else: "Hey, she's not breathing. She's not breathing. What do we do?" He checks her wrist for a moment then begins to feel the neck. "I can't get a pulse."

"My guy, too," says Stoddemeier as he pats the face of the first of one of the Amish kids.

"Hold on there, boys," says Janie, matter-of-factly. "Give them good, hard pinches and they'll come back to us."

Harris tries hard to keep his eyes off of Jill's breasts. He gives the skin of her upper arm a strong pinch.

A moment later, Jill Simpson's eyes shoot open and she gasps for air.

"Frank?" she asks between breaths.

"Hey, Sarge. You okay?"

"I...I'm not sure we're...don't know how.... What day? Where...."

"We don't have time to talk about this."

"I've got to get out of this tank, Frank," she says, struggling to lift herself. "I may need help." He can tell she's weak and still heavily dazed. She seems to be coming out of some sort of sedation. He watches her face. Then she looks from him to the rest of her naked body.

"I need something to cover up."

"Hold on," he says, moving away, searching the wall for a towel and a robe that will fit her. Coming back, he drapes the robe over the lid and reaches back into the liquid to grab her shoulders.

"My neck's so weak," she says.

Looking in Stoddemeier's direction, he sees that Fancher is sitting up, as are the two kids. Janie has already assisted Cecil Miller out of his tank and is busy helping Coral McGrey climb out of hers. Harris looks away as Coral straddles the edge of her tank, her small breasts shining with a coating of the jelly. He turns his attention back to Jill.

"I think I can get up with a little help," she says. "Can you make sure the robe's ready, though."

"It's right here."

"Okay," she says as she places her hands on the edge of the tank. Supporting the back of her head with an arm and holding both shoulders, he carefully raises her out of the jelly. "I'm okay, I think," she tells him once she's on her feet. "Hand me that towel and a robe…and don't stare."

Five minutes later, the group has toweled off. They are oddly quiet but seem to understand without being told that they are in danger.

*

Arthur Gold is listening carefully through his headset. "We're ready, sir. Whenever you give the word."

In ring formation around Fancher's home, they have created twenty-four shafts the width of a man's fist and six meters deep, packing each with explosives and radio detonation caps. On Gold's order, the men will fall back to safety at approximately fifteen hundred yards. The simultaneous eruption of all twenty-four charges will create a crater more than ninety feet deep and nearly three hundred feet in diameter, obliterating the specially-hardened walls of the silo. Anything within another one hundred yards will likely be turned to fine ash. It's overkill, but this situation calls for overkill. The only thing that bothers Gold is that it will take close to ten minutes to evacuate the area. He'd asked for several remotes that he could station for observation purposes as they withdrew, but that had been denied. It was viewed as wasteful to incinerate perfectly good video transmitters. He argued they needed to be sure that there was no escape. They'd argued back that he would need to be satisfied with the LANSAT shots he would have access to at the end of the day.

"Okay, Lieutenant," he whispers into his microphone. "Have them fall back carefully, but quickly. I want this to come off with no casualties."

"Yes, sir," comes the equally quiet voice. "And, sir, you're positive the calculations are right? Fifteen hundred feet? It'll take some time to do that."

"Seven minutes, tops Lieutenant Parks. Now get them going. I'll follow."

"Yes, sir."

*

"So, what's going on here, anyway?" Jill asks Harris as they hurry up the stairs.

"Stoddemeier thinks the feds are going to level this whole complex."

"I don't think they're going to do it," Stoddemeier calls over his shoulder as he leads the group back down the darkened tunnel. "I know it. I just wish I could remember my demolition physics. We need to be at least a thousand yards from here when this place goes – probably more. If we come up that shaft and there's no one around, we've got another quarter mile jog to get to safety. You all think you're up to it?"

"You know this?" asks Jill. "Dale, how do you know?"

"He's not who you thought he was," replies Harris. "He's working with the feds and—"

"*Was* working, Harris. Was," Stoddemeier interrupts. "Look, we don't have time to talk here. Let's move."

"Where do these tunnels lead?" Harris asks.

"The other properties."

"So, why don't we just stay underground and keep moving away from the explosion?" asks Harris.

"Not a good idea," replies Stoddemeier. "If they dug down as far as I think they did, the explosion will send a fireball through this tunnel that will vaporize us instantly. Our only chance is to get up to the surface and as far away as we can before they detonate it."

"What the fuck is going on here?" asks Jill.

"Stoddemeier's been working with a maniac as far as I can tell," says Harris.

"Why does he want to destroy Fancher?"

"We don't know."

Jill is beginning to tire, as are the others who have been in tanks. They're jogging barefoot in bathrobes after spending half a day drugged up on entheogens in a sensory depravation tank. The exertion retriggers a mild lapse of tryptamine sensation. She's slowing, but her mind is expanding again with the drug.

You should know, Officer Simpson, comes Fancher's voice back into her head. *We aren't sure what we've discovered, but it certainly isn't something you want the rest of world to know about. They need to eliminate us so that no one ever learns what we've done.*

She is surprised at how happy she is to hear him still communicating his thoughts.

You seem satisfied with this situation, she thinks back.

I am. It is what we had been hoping for.

"But what about the others?" she blurts out as she stops running and turns to Fancher.

"What are you talking about?" responds Harris who is staying close to her.

"Officer Simpson," Janie answers for Fancher, "this isn't an exercise to save the world. This is our secret and we have one more stage to pass into."

"We think there's another level." Fancher says out loud.

"Another level?" It doesn't take her long to understand. "But they're going to die! They're important! This has all been about a mass suicide for ghosts?"

"*What* are you all talking about?" asks Harris.

Ignoring him, Jill searches her mind for Fancher. She wants an assurance that all of this is real.

Yes, it's real, we are here, but they are going to the next level. There's not much I can do about it anyway. They've been through enough. They want to take the chance.

But it's real death, Fancher.

It is, but we don't know what that is, do we? If the rest of this is true, who's to say what death is?

That's ridiculous. They are everything good about our world. We need them.

I know how you feel, Jill, really I do. Why do you think I've devoted my life to them? I love them. They are more than what is good about our world, they are its magic – both before they left it and after.

"What about your daughter?" she speaks.

"She's fine," says Fancher. "She left in the Willies right after you went under. She'll be waiting at the bus station with Dean Belkin, that kid from the farm. I'm supposed to meet them there if we make it."

"Jill, we've got to move," insists Harris.

"Can't we stop this?" she asks Stoddemeier.

"No. Arthur Gold is not a normal guy, and although I don't fully understand what's going on here, it would seem that he wants to do away with whatever you and Fancher are talking about. I've been working with him for over a year now. He's definitely set on destroying this complex."

"Jill?"

"Yes, Frank?"

"We can't stay."

The drugs are affecting her now more than she'd known. She's beginning to feel slightly faint, her vision becoming blurry. She casts about for Fancher again and finds his presence, but senses something else. It is them. They are all there again. All of them. And a special one seems to come to her as well.

It's okay. We know what we're doing. This is what we planned. You don't need to worry. If there is this, then surely there is more.

Jonathan?

Yes, Mom. It's me.

How?

Mom, I'm okay. I love you. Don't hold on. Everything is fine. We're going. But it's not what you think.

Johnnie?

Mom, this is difficult, I know, but it's the way it needs to be. There's more. There's so much more. I know you feel it.

She understands this is what she was trying to figure out.

Until now, I could believe this, but now? I…can't. I'm making this up.

Mom, there's never any making things up. I'm here. I've always been here. We just don't know where that is, yet.

"Harris!" yells Stoddemeier. "The shaft is up around that bend. I say we've got five minutes at most."

"Jill," Harris says.

She knows she has little choice. A profound sadness fills her. *Goodbye*, she thinks, *I love you, my son.*

Look at the stars tonight and think of me, Mom. I'll always be there.

*

"Sir, we've got a problem."

"What is it, Parks?" replies Gold.

"Stoddemeier and that reporter are gone. We found Corporal Wills passed out where we left them. They clocked him hard."

Gold considers the situation for a moment. Stoddemeier was a loose end that he'd never liked much anyway. If they'd somehow managed to sneak into the house, then they were going to go up with the whole thing. The team would be long gone by the time people figured out where they'd been. And if they had headed for high ground or were looking to contact someone to put a stop to the demolition work, he wished them luck. In less than twenty minutes the team would be picked up by choppers and back to Fort Meade by morning.

"All right, Parks. Stoddemeier will have this on his head next week. I imagine he's got some idea of what we're doing, but it's too late. No one would believe Harris on this any more than they believe that Elvis shit, so we don't need to worry about him walking around. Stoddemeier's conscience maybe got the better of him. I'm surprised Wills let them get the drop on him. I assume he can move. Is everyone else accounted for?"

"Yes, sir. We have thirty-eight all in place and awaiting your order."

"Fine, Lieutenant. Carry on."

They are just over a quarter mile from the house and have the exact view he'd assumed in planning the operation. The explosion would mostly be underground, creating a low-decibel report that would roll, for the most part, through the silo tunnels. There would be a level of sonic shock, but Fancher's land was vast. If someone heard the noise, it was likely they would register it as a distant sonic boom or stray thunderhead.

Looking around him, the men are quiet, watching him or peering through cover at the target. It's a beautiful sight. From their vantage point, looking out over the shallow valley, the compound appears idyllic, a large red farmhouse and barn sitting at the top of a hill in the glow of summer sun.

"Ready, Parks?"

"Yes, sir."

"Let her rip, then."

"Yes, sir."

Gold turns off his headset and waits. He hears the meadow teeming with life around him and feels a drop of sweat spin down his back. The wind is to the rear, and he feels the trail of moisture begin to tingle as it cools. He hears the chant of birds and insects in the afternoon heat, smells the dense fumes of plant life in the air. Then something else passes into him. Something alien and confusing. Everything seems to stop – the smells, the sounds, the heat. He can't tell if he is breathing. His vision is filled with the beauty of the view, the image so overwhelming that he loses a sense of self – all memory, all intent, all awareness, save for the magic of the simple pastoral scene.

This lasts for just a moment, and then he sees the top of the hillside crumble in on itself, the big colorful house caving in, the shadow-flash of the explosions, smoke, and ash rising into the air. The angle of the sun lights the cloud of remains in a faint tint of blue. He watches with his men. He catches out of the corner of his eye a flash of fire shooting out of the ground some eight hundred yards, maybe more, down the road from the house.

"Sir, did you see that?"

"I did, Parks. That's a silo tunnel opening. Fireball running through there."

"Can that be where Stoddemeier..."

"It could well be, Parks, but it's a little past due for us to worry about him now. Call in the choppers and let's get out of here."

A lavender-blue haze grows all around them. They smell incinerated wood and metal and the pungent odor of burned soil and concrete. There is a bit more of a crater than Gold would have liked, but things can't be perfect. He knows that if Stoddemeier, Simpson, and Harris were in that tunnel during the blast, they have been instantly vaporized. That had been the point all along anyway – no evidence other than a pile of debris. The backhoe operators would be out by morning to cover things over – hopefully forever.

*

Helicopters rumble up from the south. No one has talked much.

"That'll be Gold's getaway," Harris says quietly to Stoddemeier.

"Yes, and I imagine he's pretty upset with me right now."

They are all silent. Cecil Miller and Coral McGrey watch quietly without speaking. They are beginning to give Harris the creeps. So are the Amish brothers.

"Jill," he says softly, "you seem to have a lot of explaining to do."

She looks at him, a faint smile on her face. "I know. But right now we need to get out of here. It's a long walk back to my vehicle at McGrey Farms."

*

They are less than two hundred feet into the air when they see the group.

"Sir, it's Stoddemeier!"

"I see that, Parks."

"Sir, he's got a lot of people with him. Looks like Fancher included."

"I see that, too, Parks. It's okay. Our mission is accomplished. Fancher has nothing left and Dale Stoddemeier knows how to keep his mouth shut."

CHAPTER 35

They choose a back booth at The Pancake House. They peruse laminated menus under the bright light of a wagon-wheel chandelier like two hikers just in from a month on the trail. Outside it's nearing dusk and rain is forecast, so the sky through the restaurant window is a dark, flowing purple. Harris orders blueberry pancakes, scrambled eggs, and hot Italian sausage. Jill asks for pineapple waffles, cottage cheese, and a side of honey-yogurt sauce. They're each working on a second cup of coffee. He hopes it means that she wants to stay up late. She knows that's what he's thinking, but just wants to talk.

"You can't write about this, Frank."

"I know."

"The whole thing. Nothing. Right? Let Dale clean it up. Then he'll get out of here and this city can get back to normal."

He understands she's talking about the murder case. The Sumters were arrested several hours before and charged with inciting the riot that killed the girl. They were also booked for the murder of the helicopter pilot and for conspiracy in organizing the vigilante group. Bud fingered Monty almost immediately for murdering the Elvis impersonator. No one is happy about the impersonation of Elvis and Monty's fraudulent meetings. Jill has let Bobby Wilson handle the media. It's a simple plot: The Sumter brothers had orchestrated the entire Elvis hoax for money. Who knew whether they'd be convicted.

The press in particular is incensed at being duped and wasting so much money on covering the Sumters's fraud. Jill has left Coral's claims out of the mess.

"I have to write something, Jill. Treestat sort of expects it."

"Oh, I know. But it's kind of obvious, isn't it?"

"What?"

"With several thousand members of the world media laying claim to the story, you don't have a story."

"I get your meaning. I'm supposed to have the outlandish point of view, and this whole thing is so freaky anyway, there isn't going to be anything left to say. But do you want to tell me what happened out there? I don't need to write about it. I just want to understand what you've been through. I mean, something did happen, didn't it?"

"I'm not sure."

"What do you mean, you aren't sure? Were you that drugged up?"

"I still am, I think. It comes and goes. Maybe if I get some sleep things will become clearer. But okay, you deserve some sort of explanation. I don't think you're going to believe me, though."

"Try me," he says, reaching for her hand.

So she tells him as best she can.

*

"Now, you've probably written a lot of stuff in your day," she concludes, "but I doubt even you would be able to make this story believable."

He watches her pick at a piece of pineapple waffle.

"So, the other tanks contained their bodies?" he asks.

"Yep. Fancher had quite a job keeping that place going."

"And the mushrooms? Where did they get those?"

"Most of the other silos were used to cultivate the mushrooms. They brought in huge shipments of Mason Jars once a year or so. But, yes, they grew their own. The best effect comes from fresh 'shrooms. We all knew that back in the day."

"And the money? How did they deal with that?"

"That one was easy. Most of them knew well in advance what they were doing. They just carefully moved a chunk here and a chunk there offshore and gave Fancher the proper codes."

"Okay. But there's still one thing I don't get. What's the significance of the letter J in all of this? I mean, every one of you who seems to have entered that world has a J in your name. Everyone except Elvis...."

She chuckles. "That wasn't Elvis."

"What do you mean? It had to be him."

"That was his twin brother, Jesse Garon. Jesse James rescued him when he was a baby and raised him. Found him buried in a shoe box just outside of Tupelo where the Presley boys were born."

"Another J?"

"Yes, another J. But Jesse Garon didn't work out the way most of them did. That's why he was roaming around and pestering people like Coral McGrey. He was in between two worlds. He's what you call an incubus, climbing out of his dreams and looking for sex all the time. No, Elvis died just the way they say he did."

"I'm awfully tired, Frank."

"But think about it. Think of all those people you met. Jesse James, JFK, Marilyn Monroe – Norma Jean - Jim Croce, John Lennon, Jack Kerouac, Jim Morrison, Jimmy James Hendrix, Jeff Buckley, John Coltrane, James Dean, King Jones, Jerry Garcia, Janis Joplin, Martin Luther King, Jr., John Bonham, your son Jonathan, even you. And Miller and McGrey have middle names that start with J - Jasper and Justine." He takes a sip of coffee, then turns to look out the window.

"What do *you* think, Mr. Franklin Harris?" she finally asks. "About the Js, I mean."

"I don't know. That's why I'm asking you."

"I don't know the answer, either. I don't know the answer to most of this. What can I say? If there's something to their names, then that definitely implies a higher order directing things. Or, it implies that if I had been named Sally Simpson, I wouldn't have been able to enter their world. Who knows? Was Jesus one of us? Does everyone with a

J in their initials have the thing you need to make that kind of magic?" She yawns.

"I'm just really tired," she says. "And my neck is still weak and kind of sore. I can't figure any more of this out. I just want a nice hot bath, maybe a massage, a little loving, and then a good, long night of sleep. Any chance you've got room in your bed for me?"

CHAPTER 36

She sits on the edge of the bed holding the phone in her hand as he comes out of the bathroom, his middle wrapped in a white towel with its thick stripe of motor lodge green running down the center of it. She watches him. He was a good lover: unselfish most of the time, patient, experimental even. She wants more of him. But he is leaving.

"That was Wilson," she says self-consciously. "There is no record of Gold on any of the federal data systems."

"Are you going to tell him about the house?"

"No. I'm going to wait for them to find it. Only Baines knows where we were. Dale said the plan was to pay contractors to backfill the hole. It'll get on people's radar screens soon enough."

"Could be a while. Where did you drop Fancher, anyway?"

"He got out at the bus station. McKenna was waiting for him with Dean Belkin." She takes a deep breath with thoughts of Johnnie whirling inside. "I don't need to know where Fancher's going," she concludes.

Harris notes something in her voice that is forced. She's said this oddly. He lets it go. "And the Amish brothers?" he asks. "You got them home?"

"We did, and their family was more than happy. Story is they were lost and distraught over their brother's death. Simple enough. Lame, I know, but almost true."

She waits for the next question. He moves to the other side of the bed and drops the towel. She sees a naked man who is softening around the middle but, after so many years of being alone, still wonderful to behold.

"And Janie?" he asks, reaching into his suitcase for a clean pair of boxers.

"She was the last one. I dropped her off at the airport. She said she was heading back to Philadelphia. I guess she'll be there when you return."

He pulls on his underwear in silence.

"Jill, you need to know there's always been something about her I didn't like. You don't have to worry."

"I'm not worried, Frank."

"Why do I not believe you?"

Harris watches her as he puts on the rest of his clothes. He isn't used to having to explain himself. Finally, he says: "Okay, look, I am not responsible for who or what she is. I'm not tied to her in any way other than years of friendship. Friendship that is questionable at best. I don't have a clue about her feelings, or her motives. She's....Why are you laughing?"

She can't help herself. "Frank, don't. After what I've been through, how can I worry about some stupid little boy-girl thing? I don't even know if I'll see you again, do I? Do whatever you want."

"Jill, I don't want to do anything with her."

"Whatever," she says with a final chuckle.

Harris sits on the bed and takes her hand. Looking her in the eyes, he says: "This is hard for me, too. I don't want to leave, but I have to."

"I know that, Frank. I'm sorry. There's just something about her that bothers me. When I was with them, she was there, too. I was talking with Jesse James and I felt her presence. There was a sense of evil about her, a dark, hidden awareness that gave me the chills. I couldn't very well arrest her for murder once we got those kids back to their family. But she was the main agent. She was their assassin. She planned and coordinated all of those deaths. That was Miller's camp we found, but she was the person that I ran into out there."

"That explains a lot," Harris replies. "Being a media person is a perfect cover."

"When I dropped her off at the airport," Jill continues, "do you know what she said? She said: *They're better off dead anyway.* And then she just walked off. It gave me the creeps. I don't know. There's still this kind of residual effect that those drugs are having on me. Has me oversensitive, maybe. But I just can't shake those words. Something about them makes me worry."

Harris kisses her neck, inhaling the scent of tobacco smoke and the sweet smell of her hair.

"We've got three-and-a-half hours before my plane leaves," he whispers in her ear. "Lie back. I don't want you to forget me."

"You just got dressed," she whispers as he kisses her neck lightly.

"I know. I guess you're just going to have to undress me."

*

They are idly inspecting ice cream bars in the freezer at the back of the airport snack bar. "Maybe someday you'll come visit me in Philly," Harris says.

"Maybe someday you'll send me a plane ticket," Jill says without looking up from the ice cream.

"Maybe."

"I don't know why I'm being so childish here," she says, turning to face him and trying to keep the emotion out of her voice. "I guess it's just been a long time since anyone…."

He watches her struggle with tears. Most of his adult life has been spent practicing being noncommittal and aloof. He recognizes the instinct to distance himself from her and from his feelings. But he fights it, surprised by how easy it is.

Jill moves her hand the ten inches it needs to go to touch his wrist. Their eyes meet.

"I'm going to leave you here. Okay?" she says. "It's just too weird for me."

She squeezes his wrist gently and feels both its warmth and its strength. Stepping back, she turns and leaves the snack area, heading for the stairs on the other side of the terminal. He watches the back of her head as she descends.

"I'm sending you a ticket, Jill," he calls once she disappears. There is no response.

*

Jill exits the terminal building into the night, greeted by the pulsing chorus of insects and the smell of ozone. The sensation of his wrist is still on her fingers. She needs to make sure the Sumters will be put away for more than just a few years. There isn't time to moon over Franklin Harris. She has work to do.

A cooling wind rolls out of the northwest and she feels the first few drops of rain. She looks up at the sky and sees stars straining to come into view through low, rolling purple clouds. The tears come then. She shakes her head and says out loud, "I am not going to feel sorry for myself. I know too much now."

You'll meet up with him again, comes Fancher's voice in her head.

I know.

She feels Cecil Miller's presence too – and Coral's and Janie Hawthorn's.

Shall we go?

It's Miller. She gets into the car and closes her eyes.

They're waiting for us, come the dark thoughts of Janie Hawthorn.

Janie, why are you always so impatient and demanding, reply the soothing thoughts of Coral McGrey.

Cecil, Jill, and Fancher hold off on their own comments. They seem to be searching for less obvious sounds. *McKenna has a lot of rebuilding to do once she's had her baby,* Jill thinks to them, *but I think she'll be better than her father at keeping Janie Hawthorn in line.*

A chuckle comes to her and she knows it is Fancher. Large drops of rain begin to spatter her windshield. They shimmer on the dark surface from the white lights illuminating the airport, like wet stars flashing out of a paradise that she knows wants to be found.

Deep in her mind, Jill senses the cadence starting up again. She also hears the faint sound of rushing water slowly growing louder.

RESOURCES & REFERENCES

While this story is pure fiction, the author invested an extensive amount of time and effort researching everything from the CIA, MKULTRA, Remote Viewing, the Columbia Police Department, and missile silo locations in central Missouri to the writings of Terence McKenna, Timothy Leary, John Lilly, Carlos Castaneda, etc.. In addition, numerous websites and articles on everyone from Elvis and Jesse James to Jimi Hendrix and Jack Kennedy were read over and over again to get a flavor of the personal lives and biographies of the residents of The Red House. If you go to my website, www.formalityoccurrence.blogspot.com, you will find references and links to many of the websites and magazine articles the universe fed me while I worked on this book.

In the end, the idea was not so much to stay true to life as to find twists of irony and identity that would spin this story beyond anything that the reader would expect.

Below is a list of most of the important stuff that made the writing of this story possible. These references are placed here somewhat randomly because that's the way the research went.

The Doors of Perception/Heaven and Hell, Aldous Huxley, Harper & Row Perennial Library, 1990

The Center of the Cyclone: An Autobiography of Inner Space, John C. Lilly, MD, Bantam Books, 1972

Remote Viewers: The Secret History of America's Psychic Spies, Jim Schnabel, Dell, 1997

Glimpses, an exquisite novel by Lewis Shiner, William Morrow and Company, 1993

The King is Dead: Tales of Elvis Postmortem, Paul M. Sammon, editor, Dell Publishing, 1994

Haunted Heartland, Beth Scott & Michael Norman, Warner Books, 1985

Psychic Phenomena: Clairvoyance, Ghosts, Precognition, Telekinesis, Telepathy, CG Bernard, Random House, 1997

Hallucinogens and Shamanism, Michael J. Harner, editor, Oxford University Press, 1973

Tomorrow Never Knows: Rock and Psychedelics in the 1960s, Nick Bromell, The University of Chicago Press, 2000

Lifehouse, Pete Townshend with Jeff Young, Pocket Books, 1999

The Teachings of Don Juan: A Yaqui Way of Knowledge, Washington Square Press, 1990

Beyond, Theodore Sturgeon, Avon Books, 1960

The Varieties of Psychedelic Experience, Robert Masters and Jean Houston, Park Street Press, 2000

Dead Elvis: A Chronicle of Cultural Obsession, Greil Marcus, Doubleday, 1991

The Complete Social History of LSD: The CIA, The Sixties, and Beyond, Martin A. Lee & Bruce Shlain, Grove Press, 1985

Food of the Gods: The Search for the Original Tree of Knowledge, Terence McKenna, Bantam Books, 1992

Synchronicity, CG Jung, Princeton University Bollingen Series, 1973

Ecstasy Club, Douglas Rushkoff, HarperCollins, 1997

The Further Inquiry, Ken Kesey, Viking 1990

True Hallucinations, Terence McKenna, HarperCollins, 1994

Encyclopedia of Death and the Afterlife, James R. Lewis, Visible Ink Press, 1999

The Kin of Ata Are Waiting for You, Dorothy Bryant, Moon Books, 1982

The Mammoth Book of Sex, Drugs & Rock 'n' Roll, Jim Driver, editor, Carroll & Graff Publishers, 2001

Altered States of Consciousness, Social Research, Volume 68, No. 3, Arien Mack, editor, New School, Fall 2001

The Crack in the Cosmic Egg: New Constructs of Mind and Reality, Joseph Chilton Pearce, Park Street Press, 2002

Synchronicity: The Bridge Between Matter and Mind, F. David Peat, Bantam New Age Books, 1987

Mind: An Essay on Human Feeling, Volume I, Susanne K. Langer, The Johns Hopkins Press, 1967

The Serpent and the Rainbow: A Harvard Scientist's Astonishing Journey Into the Secret Societies of Haitian Voodoo, Zombies, and Magic, Wade Davis, Touchstone, 1985

The Invisible Landscape: Mind, Hallucinogens, and the I Ching, Terence McKenna and Dennis McKenna, HarperCollins, 1993

The Psychedelic Experience: A Manual Based on the Tibetan Book of the Dead, Timothy Leary, Ralph Metzner, Richard Alpert, Citadel Press, 1993

Tripping: An Anthology of True-Life Psychedelic Adventures, Charles Hayes, editor, Penguin Compass, 2000

Storming Heaven: LSD and the American Dream, Jay Stevens, The Atlantic Monthly Press, 1987

On Poetry and Music, Aristotle, The Library of Liberal Arts, 1956

The Lords and the New Creatures, Jim Morrison, Fireside, 1987

Jimi: An Intimate Biography of Jimi Hendrix, Curtis Knight, Praeger Publishers, 1974

DISCOGRAPHY & PLAYLISTS

Not one word of this story was written in silence. Music and sound are the center of everything that is beyond the will of God. In the 1990s, as I wrote the first draft, there was no iTunes. I depended on albums loaded into my multi-disc CD player. Sometimes I would put these albums on "shuffle" and sometimes I would just let them play through progressively. There is something to be said for the randomness of music selection, but there is also an important magic that an entire album can wield on the mind when it seeks to be creative.

The initial albums that I listened to in writing the first 140,000 word draft of *Beyond the Will of God* include:

Nomad Soul – Baaba Maal
Kulanjan - Taj Mahal & Toumani Diabate
Where the River Rolls – KOPN Radio Project
The Falcon & The Snowman – Pat Metheny Group
Silver Dreams Golden Reality – Devadip Carlos Santana
Big Earful – Claudia Schmidt
The Seeds of Love – Tears for Fears
The Turning Point – John Mayall
Guru Fish Demos – Guru Fish
Caverna Magica – Andreas Vollenweider
Hart Beats – 1968 Grateful Dead
Blues from the Rainforest – Merl Saunders and Jerry Garcia
Symphonie Fantastique – Hector Berlioz
Apollo Atmospheres and Soundtracks – Brian Eno
Caravanserai - Santana
Breakfast in the Field – Michael Hedges
Agnus Dei – The Choir of New College, Oxford
Beyond the Missouri Sky – Charlie Haden & Pat Metheny

Twelve Dreams of Dr. Sardonicus – Spirit
Ozark Mountain Daredevils – Ozark Mountain Daredevils
Doctor Zhivago Soundtrack – Maurice Jarre
A Map of the World – Pat Metheny
Baroque Trumpet Concertos – Sergei Nakariakov
Terrapin Station – The Grateful Dead
Old and New Dreams – Don Cherry and Company
Grace – Jeff Buckley
Field of Dreams Soundtrack – James Horner
Winterreise – Franz Schubert
Blues for Allah – Grateful Dead

Music in 2012

Final edits of this Kindle edition of *Beyond the Will of God* took approximately two months of focused work seven days a week. Sometimes I listened to music for the Spotify soundtrack, below, but for the most part the only music I plugged into was Global Illage. Work is already underway to produce a "Deluxe Soundtrack Edition of Beyond the Will of God" fully incorporating Global Illage music into the reading experience. This is the music that The Red House Gang would have been playing if they were real. I highly recommend checking out "SushiLove Sessions" and the soon to be released "Complete Portland Sessions." Live music at its best!

SushiLove Sessions – Global Illage (you can find this on iTunes)

The Complete Portland Sessions – Global Illage

Spotify Playlist

The first of a number of planned soundtracks for this album is already posted at Spotify for anyone to listen to while they read this book. As a premium Spotify member you should be able to search for "Beyond the Will of God, Part I." Members reading this on an iPad can plug into the playlist and listen while they read on the iPad Kindle app. For those with Kindles or other e-readers, you will obviously need an Internet hookup. Here's the playlist and annotations so that you can follow my twisted musical logic. Keep your eyes peeled at www.formalityoccurrence.blogspot.com for information on more playlists.

Beyond the Will of God, Part I

Michael Jackson – Black Or White
MJ and Slash give us one of the greatest rock anthems of all time just a few years before Mike turns into King Jones. The lead-in to the music says it all. That's all *Beyond the Will of God* is about.

Pat Metheny Group – Psalm 121/Flight Of The Falcon
From the movie "The Falcon and the Snowman," this is God fully present moving off into the world beyond.

The Jimi Hendrix Experience – Castles Made Of Sand
Nothing is permanent. This is Jimi's song about his childhood and his family.

Jeff Buckley – Everybody Here Wants You
Let's just say R&B never sounded so good, and then let's say: Jill and Frank in Frank's motel room.

The Doors – Riders On The Storm - New Stereo Mix Advanced Resolution
This song played well over 500 times while I finished the first draft of the original manuscript. I put it on "replay" one night as I finished Part VI and the beginning of Part VII. If you "get" this book, you "get" this song (and vice versa). Remember, it is the last thing Jim Morrison ever recorded.

Elvis Presley – That's All Right
The first single ever released by Elvis (1954), the original was written and performed by "Big Boy" Crudup in 1946. Some consider this song in all its guises the first public sounds of rock 'n' roll.

The Allman Brothers Band – Hot 'Lanta
Frank hears this masterpiece in the opening scene of Chapter 1, driving on a gravel road looking for the Missouri River. What are you looking for?

Global Illage – Om Aquarium
Full-tilt improv by master musicians. Recall Cecil walking through a shopping mall listening to live music playing through the mall speakers.

Art Ensemble Of Chicago – Thème De Yoyo
This is tame for the Art Ensemble. Probably the greatest live band I have ever seen, they are beyond music.

Phil Manzanera – TNK (Tomorrow Never Knows) (Live)
This live version of The Beatles' (John's) "Tomorrow Never Knows" is masterful and speaks volumes for what The Red House Gang was attempting to activate.

Jimi Hendrix – Pali Gap
Bar none, the most beautiful electric guitar recording I have ever heard. Jimi died far too soon. I don't care if he's still out there. I want him here, now!

Janis Joplin – Kozmic Blues
Janis would kill me if I didn't give her representation on this list. Her voice was an electric instrument not to be denied.

Sun Ra – Enlightenment
Like the Art Ensemble, Sun Ra and his Arkestra were all about performance. He is the original musician abducted by aliens. He traveled to Saturn in the mid-1930s. Here, he plays the theme for the Sumter Brothers.

Michael Jackson – Thriller - Immortal Version
When "Thriller" came out, I knew that MJ needed to be part of the weird novel that was churning around in my head. That was 1982. I like this pared down version almost as much as the original.

Global Illage – Nomads Star
Jill goes through a lot. Birth, death, re-birth. She realizes questions are as important as answers. This music to me is about her movement into understanding what's going on.

John Lennon – Watching The Wheels
John Lennon always seemed to be lonely after The Beatles. His melancholy was palpable. I'm pretty sure this is him making up a song inside his Red House unit before he goes out there permanently.

The Allman Brothers Band – Mountain Jam - 1971/Live At The Fillmore East/Instrumental
Here it is. Yes, it's long, but you need to listen to the whole thing loud, and prepare yourself as the 24-minute mark hits.

Janis Joplin – Half Moon
Musicians playing in a circle. Janis seems to be in the middle. *"Half moon on night time sky. Seven stars, heaven's eyes. Seven songs on seven seas. Just to bring all your sweet love home to me."*

Pat Metheny Group – Are You Going With Me?
Here we have the supreme Missouri Music Boy, PM, playing the movie music for the Red House implosion scene.

The Jimi Hendrix Experience – 1983...(A Merman I Should Turn To Be)
If he didn't know where he was headed, there's no way Jimi could have written and produced this song. If you don't know where he's going by now, fahgetabowtit. "Right this way, smiles a mermaid, I can hear Atlantis full of cheer."

The Doors – Riders On The Storm - Alternate Version
And then they made it back home and sat down to work on more stuff like the goof balls they really are.

Jeff Buckley – Last Goodbye
As I was finishing up the first draft of the manuscript, I learned of Jeff Buckley's death. I wrote a very long introduction to the book where Frank interviews Jeff right before the singer heads off to Wolf River Harbor and ends up drowning. Couldn't bear to use it. I have never in my life heard a voice so profound, expressive, and powerful. Jeff was my final inspiration to see this book all the way through. The Red House Gang Lives.

ACKNOWLEDGEMENTS

No book as crazy as this one could come into being without the support, inspiration, and guidance of many people. The initial idea for this story came to me after a nightlong sojourn into acid music and the mind in 1974. I am grateful to Eric Rosenquist for listening to me talk about how it was possible that Jimi Hendrix could conceivably come back to talk to you through his music. I'm not sure Eric thought I was serious. I'm not sure I knew if I was serious either. I think Eric thought I was crazy.

Through the years, many people have inspired me to let my mind wander off into the geo-lyrical atmosphere of lavender blue reverie. I know many readers of this book have been there, too. My friend Jim Hamilton says it's all about metaphor and allegory. I say, yes it is, but sometimes you get to fall off a cliff and find yourself with the opportunity to fly if you know how to steer metaphors and allegories.

There are so many of you who listened to loud guitar music with me all nightlong and went out for starry walks to discuss the meaning of life, then, finally, watch the sunrise. I may forget some of you, but I can't forget my brother Jesse and sister Jennifer – at the end of every night it was always the three of us together…eating breakfast and smiling a lot. John Lysen was there, too, and he still is. It took him,

Steve Bumgarner and Mike Cheavens a bit of time to figure out The Dead, but once they did there was no turning back. Others in our little tribe include John Goodge, Reed Koch, Kevin McGinity, Johnnie Walker, Jill Lamberti, Steve Ketchie, Deborah Southern, Bart Wilson, Mary Fulweiler, Rodger Lenhardt, Bob Deering, David Fraga, and Rick Hocks. Rick, you're the one who started this for me when you brought over "Live Cream," "Electric Ladyland," "After Bathing At Baxter's," "Hot Tuna Live," "Bless Its Pointed Little Head," and "Band of Gypsys." I will never forget the first time I heard Jimi's "Pali Gap."

To my fellow travelers in college—Chuck Bell, Todd Kapner, Jeff Kelson, and Jack Roosevelt—all those nights in the O-Den, strolling around East Moreland on rainy nights, and playing electric Frisbee, informed what I did here. So did our endless talks about Hegel, Goethe, Alan Watts, and The Beatles.

I am grateful as well to many good friends here in the 21st Century who read early drafts of this story and gave me lots of feedback…much of which I ignored. Sally Spencer, Martha Nichols, Janet Jones, Joe Barbarese, Roger Raufer, and Dick Wertheimer, you all gave me the sense that what I was working on wasn't utter drivel. Martha, your opinion especially mattered so much. I know you wouldn't let me get away with anything as a writer…and, Sally, you and I go way back and we've discussed so many of these issues over the years (it's been 35). I figure if you thought this was an exercise at jousting with windmills, you'd tell me.

In much of the writing process I've gone through to make *Beyond the Will of God* truly reader-ready, I have to say I could not have succeeded without the support and inspiration of my good friend Paula Silici. Paula has read this text at least three times and edited it twice in the last 12 years. From the beginning, she has believed in this story and has done everything she could to remind me that I have a lot more stories to present to the world. I am grateful to Paula, and humbled by her friendship and guidance.

Last, but first, really, none of this could have been possible without my family's support and interest in all this nutty stuff I was thinking about. My three sons are amazing guys and each of them in his own way has inspired me to *go for it*, both with this novel, and with writing in general. Sam, Jesse, and Conor: Live your lives the way you want to, not the way people tell you to. Follow the path with a heart. If anyone tries to get you off that path, try not to spend time with them. And never forget how truly amazing music is, and that when you let yourself go into great music you will find your heart – and my heart – and all the love of the universe. It's really that simple. And don't forget to dance whenever you get the chance.

And then there is Marion. Marion who has believed in me and understood my need to write since we first became friends. To have a partner in life and a wife so intelligent, hilarious, and dedicated to the truth is daunting. I am a lucky person. That you are also so passionate, love to dance more than anything in the world, and don't take shit from anyone makes it a trip every day I'm with you. Of all the people mentioned here, you are the one who loved this story the most the first time you read it, and you're the one who has demanded that I finish what I started. I'm so grateful. Thank you. I love you.

I love you all.

And I truly hope you have not read this Acknowledgement before finishing the book. Your names may be on these last few pages, but your friendship is on every page. That twisted sense of life that drew me to you in the first place – and hopefully you to me – was what this story was all about from the beginning.

-David Biddle
Philadelphia, PA
Summer 2012

ABOUT THE AUTHOR

David Biddle has been many things in his life: a laborer on a duck farm in Missouri; a chef's assistant; a solar energy technician; an energy conservation educator; a kitchen manager at a Skid Road shelter and cafeteria; a student at Reed College; a graduate student in energy and public policy; a project manager for an engineering consulting firm; and an environmental planner specializing in recycling issues all over North America.

Through all of this he has published articles, commentary, and essays in everything from *The Harvard Business Review* and *RAIN Journal* to *BioCycle*, *The Philadelphia Inquirer*, and *Kotori Magazine*. He was a contributing editor with *In Business* magazine for over a decade. He has also published fiction in a number of online magazines including *WildViolet*, *ToastedCheese*, and *Sleep*. David currently serves as a contributing editor to Talking Writing, a unique and thought-provoking online magazine for writers and readers (TalkingWriting.com).

Beyond the Will of God is his first novel.

A Note on Indie Writers in America

This book was independently published under the banner of Flat Branch Press. The traditional publishing world has all but run its course. New digital publishing technologies make it possible for writers to publish independently, just like indie musicians and indie moviemakers. Independent efforts by artists of all kinds are not tempered by the old-guard gatekeepers with money.

The writing world is still behind the curve, but readers like you can help those of us really trying to change the tone of storytelling and non-fiction. Buy our offerings if you dare. Give us feedback. Complain. Pat us on the back. Tell us what works and what doesn't. We're listening.

Many of us indie folks work hard at our craft and know that we have an uphill battle. But we're also committed to producing high-quality, entertaining, interesting and provocative work. We're not toned down, dimmed or filtered by folks who want to make money off of us. We're beholden to no one but our readers. That's a really amazing proposition if you think about it!

Track down amazon.com/author/davidbiddle to find my work on Amazon. You can also follow all the weird stuff I'm thinking about and working on at http://formalityoccurrence.blogspot.com. Comment or drop me a line through that website. A full network of my projects will be up and running by the end of 2012 under the banner of www.davidbiddle.net.

And, please, let folks know about this novel. Your word of mouth is the only meaningful way anyone can find out about ***Beyond the Will of God.***

13881816R00202

Made in the USA
Charleston, SC
06 August 2012